D1022617

Also available from Dell

THE ILLUMINATUS! TRILOGY (*with Robert Shea*)

SCHRÖDINGER'S CAT TRILOGY

The Universe Next Door

•

The Trick Top Hat

•

The Homing Pigeons

Robert Anton Wilson

A DELL TRADE PAPERBACK

A DELL TRADE PAPERBACK
Published by
Dell Publishing
a division of
The Bantam Doubleday Dell Publishing Group, Inc.
666 Fifth Avenue
New York, New York 10103

ISBN: 0-440-50070-2

Printed in the United States of America

Published simultaneously in Canada

November 1988

10 9 8 7 6 5 4 3 2 1

FG

to the real Miss Portinari

Preface to the 1988 edition

There is a Glossary at the back of this book which explains many of the concepts of quantum mechanics employed in the text. The reader may find this helpful, and it may be consulted at any point when elucidation seems needed.

The story herein is set in a variety of parallel universes in which most of the politicians are thieves and most of the theologians are maniacs. These universes have nothing in common with our own world, of course.

Of course.

CONTENTS

Book One

The Universe Next Door

1

Book One

The Trick Top Hat

191

Book One

The Homing Pigeons

349

Glossary

540

BOOK ONE
The Universe Next Door

Not until the male become female and the female becomes male shall ye enter the Kingdom of Heaven.

—Jesus, in
The Gospel of Thomas

PART ONE
PURITY OF ESSENCE

For the Cherub Cat is a term in the Angel Tiger
—CHRISTOPHER SMART, *Jubilate Agno*

DON'T LOOK BACK

History is a nightmare from which none of us can awaken.
—STEPHEN PROMETHEUS IN CARL JUNG'S *Odysseus*

The majority of Terrans were six-legged. They had territorial squabbles and politics and wars and a caste system. They also had sufficient intelligence to survive on that barren boondocks planet for several billions of years.

We are not concerned here with the majority of Terrans. We are concerned with a tiny minority—the domesticated primates who built cities and wrote symphonies and invented things like tic-tac-toe and integral calculus. At the time of our story, these primates regarded themselves as *the* Terrans. The six-legged majority and other life-forms on that planet hardly entered into their thinking at all, most of the time.

The domesticated primates of Terra referred to the six-legged majority by an insulting name. They called them "*bugs.*"

There was one species on Terra that lived in very close symbiosis with the domesticated primates. This was a variety of domesticated canines called *dogs*.

The dogs had learned to achieve a rough simulation of *guilt* and *remorse* and *worry* and other domesticated primate characteristics.

The domesticated primates had learned how to achieve

5

simulations of *loyalty* and *dignity* and *cheerfulness* and other canine characteristics.

The primates claimed that they loved the dogs as much as the dogs loved them. Still, the primates kept the best food for themselves. The dogs noticed this, you can be sure, but they loved the primates so much that they forgave them.

One dog became famous. Actually he and she was a group of dogs, but they became renowned collectively as Pavlov's Dog.

The thing about Pavlov's Dog is that he or she or they responded mechanically to mechanically administered stimuli. Pavlov's Dog caused some of the domesticated primates, especially the scientists, to think that all dog behavior was equally mechanical. This made them wonder about other mammals, including themselves.

Most primates ignored this philosophical challenge. They went about their business assuming that they were not mechanical.

The fact that plutonium was missing originally leaked to the press in the mid-1970s. At first there was a minor wave of panic among those given to worrying about such matters, and there was even some churlish grumbling about a government so incompetent that it couldn't keep track of its own weapons of megadeath.

But then a year passed, and another, and soon five years had passed, and then nearly a decade; and the missing plutonium was still missing but nothing really drastic had happened.

Terran primates, being a simpleminded, sleepful race, simply stopped worrying about the subject. The triggering mechanism of the most destructive weapon ever devised on that backward planet was in unknown hands, true; but that was really not much more unsettling to contemplate than the fact that many of the known hands which had enjoyed access to plutonium belonged to persons who were not in all respects reasonable men. (See *Terran Archives:* Reagan, Ronald Wilson, career of.)

The primate philosophy of that epoch was summed up by one of their popular heroes, Mr. Satchel Paige, in the aphorism, "Don't look back—something might be gaining on you." It was a comfortable philosophy for sleep-loving people.

The use of atomic weapons was widely blamed on a primate named Albert Einstein. Even Einstein himself had agreed with this opinion. He was a pacifist and had suffered abominable pangs of conscience over what had been done with his scientific discoveries.

"I should have been a plumber," Einstein said just before he died.

Actually the discovery of atomic energy was the result of the work of every scientist, craftsman, engineer, technician, philosopher, and gadgeteer who had ever lived on Terra. The use of atomic energy as a *weapon* was the result of all the political decisions ever made, from the time the vertebrates first started competing for territory.

Most Terran primates did not understand the multiplex nature of causality. They tended to think everything had a *single* cause. This simple philosophic error was so widespread on that planet that the primates were all in the habit of giving themselves, and other primates, more credit than was deserved when things went well. This made them all inordinately conceited.

They also gave themselves, and one another, more blame than was deserved when things went badly. This gave them all jumbo-sized guilt complexes.

It is usually that way on primitive planets, before quantum causality is understood.

Quantum causality was not understood on Terra until physicists solved the Schrödinger's Cat riddle.

Schrödinger's Cat never became as famous among the primate masses as Pavlov's Dog, but that was because the cat was harder to understand than the dog.

Pavlov's Dog could be understood in simple mechanical metaphors. To understand Schrödinger's Cat you needed to first understand the equations of quantum probability waves. Only a few primates were smart enough to read the equations, and even they couldn't understand them.

That was because the equations seemed to say that the cat was dead and alive at the same time.

Every character in this book looks like Pavlov's Dog from a certain angle. If you look at him or her a different way, however, you'll see Schrödinger's Cat.

As early as 1976, a group of Chicago paranoids known as the Nihilist Anarchist Horde (NAH) printed up a single-page broadside on how to manufacture an atomic weapon. They sent this, in envelopes with no return address, to all the most hostile and embittered individuals and groups in the United States. NAH regarded this mailing as both a joke and a warning, and refused to face the fact that it was also an incitement.

NAH had already put out bumper stickers saying things like:

REGISTER CAPITALISTS, NOT GUNS

and:

HONK IF YOU'RE ARMED

and:

EAT THE RICH

And they even had a rubber stamp which they used to decorate subway advertisements with the Nihilistic message: ARM THE UNEMPLOYED: RIOT IN THE LOOP ON NEW YEAR'S EVE.

But they really outdid themselves with the build-your-own atomic weapon sheet, which was titled "Hobbysheet #4" and looked like this:

HOBBYSHEET #4 in a series of 30. Collect 'em all!
A SIMPLE ATOMIC BOMB FOR
THE HOME CRAFTSMAN

There is nothing complex about an Atomic (or Fission) Bomb. If enough fission material (Uranium 235 or Plutonium 237) is brought together to form a critical mass, it will explode. The trick is to put the pieces together fast enough to get a decent blast before the bomb blows itself apart. This can be done quite simply by means of ordinary explosive as shown below.

It was later estimated that the Nihilist Anarchist Horde, most of whom were living on Welfare, were able to mail out only 200,000 of these over the four-year period (1976–80) before they grew bored with the project.

Nonetheless, many of the equally paranoid and hostile persons who received this mailing had access to Xerox machines and were as desperate as the members of NAH itself. It was later determined that by 1981 there were over 10,000,000 copies of "Hobbysheet #4" in circulation. Eventually one of them reached the POE group, who were ready for an idea like that.

The planet as a whole continued to drowse.

ALTERNATIVE TEXTS

That is precisely what common sense is for, to be jarred into
uncommon sense.

—ERIC TEMPLE BELL,
Mathematics: Queen of the Sciences

GALACTIC ARCHIVES:

The original title of the greater part of what we have
collected in this book under the title *Schrödinger's Cat*
was *The Universe Next Door*. The book of that name was
begun as a sequel to *Illuminatus!*, but after several editors
in a row suffered psychotic breakdowns while reading it,
publishers defensively ordered that any ms. with that
title, from Robert Anton Wilson, should be returned
unopened.

"People generally do not want a new form of prose
fiction to replace the hackneyed 'novel,'" Wilson wrote in
a letter to his friend Malaclypse the Younger. "There
never has been a serious attempt since *Odysseus*."

Schrödinger's Cat Fair Copy #2, according to Wilson
scholars, incorporates later and still more bizarre material,
the text of which was allegedly dictated to Wilson by a
canine intelligence—"vast, cool, and unsympathetic"—
from the system of the Dog Star, Sirius. *Schrödinger's*

Cat Fair Copy #3 appeared much later, in 2031, under mysterious circumstances. Some claimed, at the time, that it had been received by a trance medium to whom Wilson had "broadcast" it after his melodramatic departure from this world in 1993. Skeptics have always insisted that the alleged medium actually found it in an old tampon box in her attic. A legend about the manuscript being recovered from the Masonic Auditorium in San Francisco, after the earthquake of 2005, and passed around among adepts of certain occult groups, is probably mythical.

Various alternative texts, generally considered forgeries, have circulated at intervals and many Wilson scholars debate heatedly whether this final ms. is, in fact, totally or even in major part Wilson's work. That two authors at least are here represented, often at cross-purposes with each other, is the emerging academic consensus at this time.

The present edition incorporates all material that is undoubtedly Wilson's, together with matter of such a Wilsonian and weird character that the present editor regards it as probably-Wilson's-within-reasonable-doubt.

It only remains to affirm that *Schrödinger's Cat*, contrary to appearances, is not a mere "routine" or "shaggy shoggoth story." Despite his sinister reputation and his well-known eccentricities, Wilson was one of the last of the scientific shamans of the primitive, terrestrial phase of the cruel, magnificent Unistat Empire. This may be hard to understand when many Establishment scholars still deny that anything like scientific shamanism existed in the twentieth century, but it is nevertheless well documented that Wilson, Leary, Lilly, Crowley, Castaneda, and many others pursued rigorous studies in scientific shamanic research even under the persecution of the "neurological police" so characteristic of that barbaric epoch.* Some have even proposed that *Schrödinger's Cat* is actually a manual of shamanism in the form of a novel, but that opinion is, almost certainly, exaggerated.

*See the Editor's "Clandestine Neurotransmitter Research Under the Holy Inquisition and the D.E.A.," *Archives of General Archaeology,* Vol. 23, No. 17.

ONE MONTH TO GO

Immature humorists borrow; mature humorists steal.

—MARK TWAIN

On December 1, 1983, Benny "Eggs" Benedict, a popular columnist for the New York* *News-Times-Post*, sat down to compose his daily essay. According to his usual procedure, he breathed deeply, relaxed every muscle, and gradually forced all verbalization in his brain to stop. When he had reached the void, he waited to see what would float up to fill the vacuum. What surfaced was:

One month to go to 1984.

Benny looked at the calendar; what happened next would be portrayed by a cartoonist as a light bulb flashing on over his head. He began pounding the typewriter, com-

---

Galactic Archives: New York was an independent city-state in the northwest of Unistat. It was noted for its malodorous stockyards, its vast motion-picture industry, and a huge phallic monument dedicated to "Washington," a fertility god who allegedly slept in nearly every part of the Unistat, usually with human women, bringing forth such semidivine progeny as the gigantic Paul Bunyan, the patriotic General Motors, the trickster-god Nixon, and the benign Mickey Mouse, who began as a totem of the city of Disneyland and eventually became the principal divinity of all Unistat.

paring the actual situation of the world with Orwell's fantasy.

His column, headed "One Month to Go," was read by nearly 10,000,000 people, the *News-Times-Post* being the only surviving daily paper available to the 20,000,000 citizens of the six boroughs of New York City. Nine million of the 10,000,000 readers were a little bit paranoid, this being the natural ecological result of crowding that many primates into such a congested space, and most of them agreed with the most pessimistic portions of Benedict's estimation of Orwell's accuracy as a prophet.

"One month to go to 1984" became a catchphrase to conclude or answer anybody's complaint about anything. "One month to go to 1984"—soon you heard it everywhere; it reached Chicago by December 10, San Francisco by December 14, was even quoted in Bad Ass, Texas, on December 16.

By December 23 the London *Economist* printed a very scholarly article on world history from 1949, when Orwell's book was published, to the present, enumerating dozens of parallels between Orwell's fiction and the planet's nightmare.

In Paris a prominent Existentialist, in an interview with *Paris Soir,* argued that living inside a book, even a book by an English masochist like Orwell, was better than living in reality. "Art has meaning but reality has none," he said cheerfully.

The six-legged majority on Terra were never consulted when the domesticated primates set about building weapons that could destroy all life-forms on that planet. This was not unusual. The fish, the birds, the reptiles, the flowers, the trees, and even the other mammals weren't allowed to vote on this issue. Even the wild primates weren't involved in the decision to produce such weapons. In fact, the majority of domesticated primates themselves never had a say in the matter.

A handful of *alpha males* among the leading predator bands among the domesticated primates had made the decision on their own. Everybody else on the planet—including the six-legged majority, who had never been involved in primate politics—just had to face the consequences.

Most of the domesticated primates of Terra did not know they were primates. They thought they were something apart from and "superior" to the rest of the planet.

Even Benny Benedict's "One Month to Go" column was based on that illusion. Benny had actually read Darwin once, in college a long time ago, and had heard of sciences like ethology and ecology, but the facts of evolution had never really registered on him. He never thought of himself as a primate. He never realized his friends and associates were primates. Above all, he never understood that the *alpha males* of Unistat were typical leaders of primate bands. As a result of this inability to see the obvious, Benny was constantly alarmed and terrified by the behavior of himself, his friends and associates and especially the alpha males of the pack. Since he didn't know it was ordinary primate behavior, it seemed *just awful* to him.

Since a great deal of primate behavior was considered just awful, most of the domesticated primates spent most of their time trying to conceal what they were doing.

Some of the primates *got caught* by other primates. All of the primates lived in dread of getting caught.

Those who got caught were called *no-good shits*.

The term no-good shit was a deep expression of primate psychology. For instance, one wild primate (a chimpanzee) taught sign language by two domesticated primates (scientists) spontaneously put together the signs for "shit" and "scientist" to describe a scientist she didn't like. She

was calling him shit-scientist. She also put together the
signs for "shit" and "chimpanzee" for another chimpanzee
she didn't like. She was calling him shit-chimpanzee.

"You no-good shit," domesticate primates often said to
each other.

This metaphor was deep in primate psychology because
primates mark their territories with excretions, and sometimes they threw excretions at each other when disputing
over territories.

One primate wrote a long book describing in vivid
detail how his political enemies should be punished. He
imagined them in an enormous *hole* in the ground, with
flames and smoke and rivers of shit. This primate was
named Dante Alighieri.

Another primate wrote that every primate infant goes
through a stage of being chiefly concerned with biosurvival,
i.e. food, i.e. Mommie's Titty. He called this the Oral
Stage. He said the infant next went on to a stage of
learning mammalian politics, i.e. recognizing the Father
(alpha male) and his Authority and territorial demands.
He called this, with an insight that few primates shared,
the Anal Stage.

This primate was named Freud. He had taken his own
nervous system apart and examined his component circuits by periodically altering its structure with neuro-
chemicals.

Among the anal insults exchanged by domesticated primates when fighting for their space were: "Up your ass,"
"Go shit in your hat," "You're full of shit," "Take it and
stick it where the moon doesn't shine," and many others.

One of the most admired alpha males in the Kingdom
of the Franks was General Canbronne. General Canbronne
won this adulation for the answer he once gave when
asked to surrender at Waterloo.

"*Merde*," was the answer General Canbronne gave.

When primates went to war or got violent in other ways, they always said they were about *to knock the shit* out of the enemy.

They also spoke of *dumping* on each other.

The primates who had mined Unistat with nuclear bombs intended to dump on the other primates real hard.

Benny Benedict's entire philosophy of life had been shaped by an obscene novel, a murder, and a Boston Cream Pie.

The novel was called *Odysseus* and the most shocking thing about it, aside from the searing indecency of its language, was that it had been written by a famous theologian, Rev. Carl Gustav Jung of Zurich, Switzerland. Nobody had known what to make of the book when it was first published, except to fulminate against it. The story, in fourteen chapters, recounted fourteen hours in a very ordinary day as some staggeringly ordinary characters wandered about Zurich on extraordinarily ordinary business. When Jung revealed that the fourteen chapters corresponded to the fourteen Stations of the Cross, conservative critics added blasphemy to their charges against him. Later—much later—academic exegetes adopted *Odysseus* as the very model of a modern novel and wrote endless studies proving that it was an allegory on everything from the evolution of consciousness to the rise and fall of civilizations.

Benny couldn't understand much of what these academic critics wrote, but he knew that *Odysseus* was, to him, the only book that really succeeded in making the daily seem profound. That was enough of an achievement to convince him that Jung was a genius. It also encouraged him to look at everything that happened as being marvelous in one way or another. If Jung's characters, or some of them, happened to defecate, urinate, masturbate, and fornicate during the fourteen hours, that was not because the theologian was trying to write pornography, but because the miracle of daily life could not be shown without all of its daily details. Benny didn't give a flying Philadelphia fuck about the novel's parallels with the *Odyssey* and the Stations of the Cross, which Jung admitted, or the other correspondences with body organs, colors, Tarot cards, *I Ching* hexagrams, and the romantic triangle in *Krazy Kat*, which his admirers claimed to have found. The important thing about *Odysseus* was that it demonstrated, almost scientifically, that no day was a dull day.

Jung, who regarded himself as a better psychologist than the psychologists—this was a conceit typical of theologians—claimed to have found three more circuits in the nervous system beyond Freud's oral biosurvival circuit and anal emotional-territorial circuit. Jung said that *Odysseus* demonstrated also a semantic-hominid circuit which created a veil of words between domesticated primates and their experience, thereby differentiating them from the wild primates. He also claimed a specific sociosexual circuit created by the process of domestication. And he added a fifth, neurosomatic circuit typical of mysticism and music, which causes primates to feel High and spaced-out.

But Benny didn't care about all that. *Odysseus*, in his mind, was simply the book that described life the way it really is, without sentiment and emotions.

The murder changed all that. It showed Benny that every day is also a terrible day, for somebody.

On July 23, 1981, Benny's mother, a white-haired old lady of eighty-four, left the Brooklyn Senior Citizen's Home where she lived to walk one block to the supermarket. On the way she had her purse snatched and, according to witnesses, struggled with the thief. She was stabbed sev-

enteen times with a Boy Scout knife. When Benny arrived
at the hospital emergency room, she was already dead,
but he got a look—a long look—at her crimson, mutilated
body before the doctor on duty hustled him out into the
hall and shot him full of tranquilizers.

Benny was crippled psychologically in a way that he
could not perfectly understand. After all, having reached
the fifth decade of his life, he was well acquainted with
grief: in the past ten years he had experienced the deaths
of his father, his older brother, and three close friends.
But murder is not just another form of grief: it is a
metaphysical message like Fate knocking on the door at
the beginning of Beethoven's *Fifth*. Benny found that the
whole world had turned to very fragile glass. Every police
siren, every newscast, every angry voice on the street
reminded him that he belonged to a dangerously violent
species. Benny Benedict realized that each minute, somewhere in the world, somebody was being bashed, beaten,
stabbed, shot, slashed, gassed, poisoned, robbed of life.

He could not bear to be alone at night anymore.

The Grinning Sadist began to haunt him.

This horrifying image had been imprinted upon his
neurons by various movies and TV melodramas of the
sixties and seventies. The Grinning Sadist invaded your
home, sometimes alone and sometimes with a horde of
equally moronic and vicious cohorts. You were particularly susceptible if you were blind or a woman or all alone
at night, but sometimes—as in *The Dangerous Hours*—he
would come with his brutal crew in the bright daytime.
His business was never simply burglary, although that was
part of it; his real interest was in humiliation, terror,
degradation, torture of the body and spirit. And he always
grinned.

Benny's doctor prescribed Valium, 5 mg. before bedtime. It helped Benny sleep; but when he was awake,

every noise still sounded like the Grinning Sadist furtively trying the door.

Benny bought a police lock. Every noise now sounded like the Grinning Sadist trying to force a window.

Then, one day looking through the old files in the newspaper morgue, Benny found an interview with Senator Charles Percy given in 1970, two years after the murder of his daughter. "For the first year after the murder," Senator Percy said, "my whole family lived in terror."

Benny felt a sudden sense of relief. This must be normal, he thought; it happens to everybody who's had a murder close to them. And it lasts only a year. . . .

But as July 23, 1982, approached, Benny was not emerging from the terror; it was growing worse. Well, he had been reading up on grief and bereavement, and he knew the first anniversary is always a terrible time. He found the knowledge helpful; it gave him a small purchase on detachment. Also, without his doctor's consultation, he had raised his Valium dosage at bedtime from 5 mg. to 15 mg. and sometimes 25.

Then on July 23 itself—the anniversary of the murder—the Grinning Sadist appeared.

Benny had been invited to give a talk at the Press Club on "Lousewart and Lowered Expectations." The luncheon was excellent, but Benny ate little, knowing that a belch in the middle of the speech could destroy all communication for several minutes after. When Fred "Figs" Newton began to introduce him (. . . "New York's most beloved daily columnist . . . an institution for over thirty years . . ."), Benny felt the usual twinges of stage fright, began rehearsing again his first three jokes, gave up on that and concentrated instead on his mantra (*Om mani padme hum Om mani padme hum* . . .) and was finally in the ideal state of mixed apprehension and urgency out of which the most relaxed-sounding public speeches always come.

As the applause died down, he rose to speak.

And he saw the Grinning Sadist coming right at him.

He saw the deranged eyes, the cruel mouth, the deliberately ugly clothing (like a very poor cowboy or a 1960s college student), and the *knife* in the maniac's hand.

Om mani padme hum . . .

And then he got the Boston Cream Pie right in the face.

It hadn't been a knife at all: he had imagined a knife when the pie plate was turned and raised as it was thrown.

Benny stood there, very conscious that he was overweight and past fifty, Boston Cream Pie dripping from his face, trying to remind himself that heart palpitations were not a symptom of heart attack, aware suddenly that the daily life of humankind was not only marvelous, as Jung had taught him, and terrible, as the murder had taught him, but totally absurd as well, as the Existentialists might have taught him.*

Galactic Archives: Pie throwing was common in Unistat at the time of this Romance. It derived, of course, from the territorial feces-hurling rituals of other primates. See "Expressions of Violence in Wild and Domesticated Primates," *Encyclopedia of Primate Psychology*, Sirius Press, 2775. Domesticated primates defend ideological territories (mental constructs) as well as the physical turf. Pie throwers were expressing mammalian territorial rage in a traditional primate manner by throwing guck in the faces of those who threatened their ideological "space."

AUFGEHOBEN

2 NEW PLANETS DISCOVERED
—NEWS HEADLINE, 1983

The only one in New York who didn't react emotionally to Benny Benedict's "One Month to Go" column was Justin Case, an embittered, fortyish man who wrote beautifully meaningless film criticism. Case had not liked the film of *1984* and never read books, which he regarded as too old-fashioned to be worthy of serious attention.

"Books were invented by Gutenberg in the fifteenth century and are, like all other inventions five centuries old, hopelessly archaic," Case often said.

He also liked to categorize books as "linear," "Aristotelian," and, when he was especially rhetorical, "paleolithic"; he justified this last adjective on the grounds that books consisted of *words,* an Old Stone Age invention.

Case had a Ph.D. from Yale and a D.D. (Dishonorable Discharge) from the U.S. Army. He had earned the former for a thesis on "Metaphor and Myth in the Films of the Three Stooges" and the latter for trying to organize a mutiny during the Vietnam War. His film criticism appeared in a journal called *Confrontation*. His essays usually began with the same three words as his Ph.D. thesis—*e.g.,* "Metaphor and Myth in Hitchcock's *39 Steps*," "Metaphor and Myth in *Beach Blanket Bingo*"—that sort of thing.

22

There was not much of an audience for such writing and Justin barely made a living. His dream was to become an editor at *Pussycat* magazine, where the big money was.

The FBI had been tapping his phone ever since Vietnam and had reels and reels of his conversation, which concerned almost nothing but films. Nevertheless, they kept listening, hoping something incriminating would slip eventually. A man with both a Ph.D. and a D.D. was obviously worth attention, even if most of what he said was totally incomprehensible to them.

Special Agent Tobias Knight, playing Case's tapes one evening, actually heard a long rap about Curly being the id or first circuit, Larry the ego or second circuit, and Moe the superego or Jung's fourth circuit. Things got even more confusing when Case went on to talk about the "cinematic continuity in the S-M dimension between Moe and Polanski." It got even weirder when Case said, "Polanski himself went to Chinatown three times—when his parents were murdered by the Nazis, when his wife was murdered by the Manson Family, and when he got convicted of statutory rape. We all go to Chinatown, one way or another, sooner or later." Still, the Bureau did not give up. Case was sure to say something incriminating, or at least intelligible to them, sooner or later.

Tobias Knight had listened to 42,000 hours of "private" conversations since joining the FBI. Among other things, this had clearly shown him that all the standard primate sexual behaviors were prevalent throughout Unistat. Since Knight, like Benny Benedict and most other two-legged Terrans, did not know he belonged to a mammal species, this primate behavior was profoundly shocking to him. He felt much like a Methodist who runs a drugstore in Little Rock—anguished that the Sins of his fellows were exceeded only by their Hypocrisy. This made him Cynical.

The same Cynicism was widespread in the Bureau.

Older hands who had listened to 80,000 or even 100,000 hours of "private" conversations were beyond Cynicism. They had become paranoid about their fellow primates.

Tobias Knight himself would be classified as a no-good shit by most of the primates if they knew what he was up to. He was the first pentuple agent in the history of espionage—that is, he had connections with four other Intelligence Agencies besides the FBI and was double-crossing all of them.

He also had a walrus mustache and a jovial eye. He could have been an excellent character actor in movies or TV. Everybody liked him and trusted him on sight.

That was why he was so successful in the cloak-and-dagger business.

Justin Case suspected that the FBI was tapping his phone. However, 9,000,000 out of 20,000,000 primates in New York also suspected the FBI of tapping their phones. Case just happened to be one of the 8,000,000 who were correct in this suspicion.

Case was certainly not a mutineer by temperament; his visual cortex—the most energized part of him—was neurogenetically imprinted with a dry, detached, analytical, almost passive, temperament. His world was made up of forms in space, edited into amusing montages by the passing of time; if he ever read books, he might have found that Einstein's Relativity was the mathematical analog of his own mind.

Even paintings barely won his tolerance; only film and TV, basically montage, turned him on. He was inclined to feel that anything which did not flicker, shimmer, and change rapidly was probably dead and should be decently and quickly buried.

In short, he was an electronic Taoist.

The Vietnam War had been punishing in various ways to all Unistaters, but Case, embroiled in the center of it, experienced it as very bad TV. It was like the film had stuck and Moe kept jabbing his finger in Curly's eye, over and over, in an infinite regress, until the myth and metaphor had both turned meaningless through redundance. If the war wasn't that, it was sloppy editing or just plain *bad taste*. The mutiny was the only equivalent he could find to the simple act of turning the dial to another channel.

He had tried to explain this to the lieutenant appointed to defend him at the court-martial, a sly, cat-faced young man named Lionel Eacher. Lieutenant Eacher, before entering the service, had been an expert at Contract Law, the rules by which the primates determined and marked their territories. Remember: other mammals do this by leaving excretions which geometrically define the size and shape of the claimed turf, but domesticated primates do it by excreting ink on paper. Eacher was a lawyer, an expert at proving either that the ink excretions meant what they said (if he were being paid to prove that) or that the ink excretions didn't *exactly* mean what they said (if he were being paid to prove that).

Lionel Eacher listened to Case's story with growing incredulity. At the end of the narrative he frowned very thoughtfully and said, "Would you just run that by me again?"

So Case had explained, this time in more detail, the aesthetics of proper utilization of sadomasochist material in the total structure of Significant Form.

"I see," Eacher said thoughtfully. "I think we've got a winner." He relaxed and lit a cigarette. "The usual defense is that you were reading the Bible and saw a white light and Jesus told you to give up war. But this, well, this is beautiful. You sound like a real fruitcake. I might even get you a medical discharge."

Case realized that he was talking to a barbarian, but that was normal in the military. He had an intuitive sense

that twenty years in the joint, which was what the Judge
Adjutant General's office was asking, would be even more
redundant, in the S-M dimension, than the war itself.
Very well: If a man of esthetic sensibility seemed like a
fruitcake to these primitives, so be it. He wanted to go
home.

Case explained his position to the court-martial with
great eloquence (part of what he said he even used later in
a critique of *The Rocky Horror Show*) and they did,
indeed, decide he was a fruitcake. They gave him a D.D.,
but two members of the board, he learned later, had
argued vigorously for a medical.

The Vietnam War, like most primate squabbles, was
about territory. Chinese primates, Unistat primates, the
primates of the Bear Totem from the steppes and various
local Southeast Asian primates were trying to expand their
collective-totem egos (territories) by taking over the turf
in Southeast Asia. If they had been wild primates, they
would have all excreted in the disputed area and maybe
thrown excretions at each other; being domesticated primates, they made ink excretions on paper and threw
metal and chemicals at each other. It was one of a series of
rumbles over Southeast Asia which had at one time or
another involved Dutch primates, French primates, primates of the Rising Sun totem, and various other predator
bands.

Since the Unistat primates, like other domesticated hominids, did not know they were primates, all this was
explained by a ferocious amount of ink excretions invoking
Morality and Ideology, the twin gods of domesticated
primatedom. Basically, the primates who wanted to claim
Southeast Asia said it was "good" to go in shooting and
grab whatever was grabable; the primates who didn't give
a fuck about Southeast Asia said it was "evil."

Justin Case was not verbally oriented; he thought in pictures, as a good film critic should. He never asked whether the war was "good" or "evil." It was unaesthetic.

The people who had mined Unistat with nuclear bombs had not regarded the Vietnam War as unaesthetic. They thought it was downright evil.

They thought just about everything the Unistat alpha males—in corporations and governments—did was evil.

They thought most of their fellow primates were *no-good shits*.

Justin Case had been born blissfully by a joyous mother schooled in the Grantly Dick-Read method of natural childbirth.

By the time Justin was thirty-six years old, in 1983, the Dick-Read method was as obsolete as the horse and buggy. Things were moving fast on Terra in that age.

Nonetheless, the Dick-Read natural childbirth yoga was good for its time, and Case had a permanent security imprint on the oral biosurvival circuitry of his brain. That was one reason he never worried about ethical issues.

When Justin began to crawl about the house and then rose up to walk up and down in it, his father, a former alpha male with a large corporation now on the skids due to booze, found him a pest and a nuisance. Father disappeared rapidly, pursued by lawsuits and child maintenance liens, which harassed him so much that he drank even more, earned less, and was first chronically and then permanently incapable of paying a blessed penny to Justin and Justin's Mommy.

Justin was not genetically programmed to be an alpha male, but under the circumstances he learned to do a good imitation of one.

"Mommy's Great Big Man," Mommy called him.

The anal-territorial (old primate) section of Justin's brain took an imprint of Pretend-Authority.

Then Justin discovered the *semantic* environment. He learned to read and watch TV. The books seemed clumsy and sententious compared to the immediacy of the tube. He took a visual-electronic imprint on the semantic circuit, like most of his generation.

Case's sociosexual circuit was imprinted by *Playboy,* Sexual Revolution, weed, Rock, yippies, protest, the Generation Gap, Women's Lib, and General Confusion. He was a bachelor who had heterosexual couplings as often as he felt the need, with the minimum possible human involvement.

If you're interested in superficialities, he looked like a gay intellectual or a college professor or a little bit of both. He already had a bald spot. He dressed in conservative good taste. And every four years he went to a polling booth and carefully printed with a heavy felt-tip pen, "NONE OF THE ABOVE."

This was his one flicker of Social Consciousness.

Case had one Weird Experience in his whole life. It happened in 1973 when he went to see the famous mentalist, psychic, escape artist, and comedian Cagliostro the Great, at a nightclub called Von Neumann's Catastrophe.

Cagliostro began his act with a few traditional tricks— being locked in one box and then reappearing out of another at the opposite side of the room, that kind of routine. This was followed by one of his bitingly sarcastic monologues about the tricksters in other professions, such as the clergy and the government. This was all as Case had expected from the Most Controversial Magician in Show Biz history. Then came the psychic stunts, which were sometimes frighteningly impressive.

"B.W.," Cagliostro called out. "Will you please stand up?" Case saw the unbearable bore, Blake Williams, standing at a ringside table.

"B.W.," Cagliostro repeated, "you will never finish

your twelve-volume study of quantum psychology. Not ever, in this universe. The twitches in your leg from the polio can be cured by Valerian Root tea. The incident at the Vandivoort Street incinerator is still haunting you. Your investments are all wrong—there's no future in space industry. And as for Project Pan, Doctor—Project *Pan*— naughty, naughty, naughty!"

Case could see that Williams had turned pale.

"J.C.," Cagliostro called out suddenly, "don't stand. This is private." Justin Case squirmed, half-afraid, half-skeptical, totally vulnerable. "J.C.," Cagliostro repeated, "you have created this movie that you call reality. Stay out of Chinatown. . . .

"S.M.," the magician went on, "S.M., about the Beast, now . . . that's in your future. . . ."

POE

Quoth the Raven, "Nevermore."
—POE

In July 1968, immediately after the Democratic Convention, held behind barbed wire to prevent the people from interfering in their own affairs, a letter appeared in *The Seed*, a Chicago radical newspaper. The letter said:

Brothers and Sisters:
The final struggle is upon us. The big racist-imperialist forces that control Amerika have taken off their fake

"liberal" mask and shown their true fascist nature. Look at the record: the assassinations of John and Bobby and Martin Luther King. The unending war against the people of Vietnam. The brutalities of the local police, right on television with the whole world watching, during the recent Demokratic Convention. Is it not obvious that the multinational corporations no longer even care to pretend that democracy still exists and are ready to kill us to the last man and woman if we continue to resist?

Weather Underground has chosen the wrong path, romantically allowing themselves to be known and defying the authorities to catch them.

We of POE have organized quietly. Our numbers are not for publication, nor our identities. We will not take "credit" for our actions, unlike the Weather romantics. We will not recruit new members. We will send no further communiqués to the press. We will work and study to strike the most crippling blows possible against the fascist monster.

If you agree with us, do not seek to find us and join us. Do as we have done.

Peace On Earth.

John Brown

Some readers of *The Seed* thought this was a put-on. Others claimed it was the work of an FBI *agent provocateur*. A few wondered if POE actually existed, and what it would do.

Everybody, of course, assumed that the initials POE stood for the slogan in the last line of the letter—"Peace On Earth." They were wrong. POE stood for "purity of essence." The group had deliberately taken as their model

General Jack D. Ripper in the film *Dr. Strangelove,* who launches a nuclear war to protect "the purity of essence of our precious bodily fluids" against fluorides. POE honestly felt that sanity had failed to save the world and that only insanity remained as a viable alternative.

Nor were they alone in this attitude. The same year POE was formed, the American people elected Richard Milhous Nixon to the White House, guided by a similar gut-level feeling that somebody like Jack D. Ripper was needed to confront the growing chaos of the planet with some strong counterchaos.*

The real name of the founder of POE was not "John Brown" of course. That was a pseudonym.

The original John Brown had been a fervent Idealist, which was why POE admired him. They were all fervent Idealists too.

John Brown, motivated by Idealism, had set out to abolish slavery in Unistat in the nineteenth century. On one of his first raids he murdered a whole family of slave owners. An associate, who was less Idealistic, had suggested sparing the children, but John Brown refused.

"Nits grow up to be lice," he said.

Idealists were like that. You were much safer falling into the hands of the Cynics. The Cynics regarded everybody as equally corrupt. That was the attitude for instance, of Tobias Knight and the other old hands at the FBI.

The Idealists regarded everybody as equally corrupt, *except themselves.*

Galactic Archives: At the time of this story the Unistat government had 1,700 atomic bombs for every man, woman, and child on the planet. Since a person can die only once, historians have been at a loss to explain what the Unistaters expected to do with the surplus 1,699 bombs for each human being. Galactical primatologists inform us that similar irrational behavior has been observed among domesticated apes on several thousand planets.

The six-legged majority on Terra had never developed
Idealism or Cynicism, nor had they ever thought of sin or
corruption. They had a simple, pragmatic outlook. People
could be recognized because they all had six legs. Good
people smelled right and were part of the same hive or
colony. Bad people smelled wrong and were not part of
the hive; they should be eaten at once, or driven off.

Two-legged and four-legged critters weren't people at
all and to hell with them.

The four-legged residents of Terra were, for the most
part, equally simpleminded. People had four legs. Six-
legged critters were *food*, or else they were not worth
noticing. Two-legged critters were dangerous, and should
be avoided.

Only the dogs, among all the four-legged Terrans, recognized the two-legged primates as being people.

Some of the primates also recognized the dogs as being
people.

One-tenth of one percent of the domesticated primates
recognized all the life-forms on their planet as people.

The one-tenth of one percent of the primates who recognized non-primates as people were in violent disagreement with each other about everything else. About
one-third of them were Mystics and suffered from Permanent Brain Damage brought on by fasting, yoga, or other
masochistic practices. They had attained understanding of
the *Intelligence* of all living beings through an ecstatic-
agonizing experience of ego loss brought on by their masochistic excesses. They went around talking about this
genetic *Intelligence* and calling it "God" and telling everybody it was too smart to make mistakes and incidentally
talking a lot of nonsense, also brought on by their excesses.

Another third of the primates who recognized consciousness wherever it existed were specially trained scientists,

in fields like ethology, ecology, biophysics, and Neurologic. They all talked in specialized jargons and hardly anybody could understand them. Most of them couldn't even understand one another.

The last third of the primates who had a sense of the genetic program behind evolution were folk who had eaten some strange chemicals or vegetables. They were like the blind Denebian shell cats who suddenly encounter water for the first time by falling into an ocean. They knew *something* was happening to them, but they weren't sure what it was.

POE theoretically had no leader. It was an anarcho-Marxist collective.

The real leader was, of course, an alpha male. His name was Franklin Delano Roosevelt Stuart, and he was one of the smartest men in Unistat at that time. Unfortunately, his reptile biosurvival circuit was imprinted with chronic anxiety, his mammalian emotional-territorial circuit was imprinted with defensive aggression, his hominid semantic circuit was imprinted with an explosive blend of Black street cynicism and New Left ideology, and his domesticated sociosexual circuit was from Kinksville.

F.D.R. Stuart claimed that the purpose of POE was to accelerate the dialectical process of evolution toward the classless society where all would live in peace, prosperity, and socialist solidarity, and there would be no cops.

The real purpose of Stuart's activities was to *get even*. The other primates in Unistat had raped his mother and jailed his father and driven his brothers and sisters into street crime and junk and generally maltreated him all his life. In addition they called him by an insulting name, which was *nigger*.

Second in command in POE was Sylvia Goldfarb, a refugee from God's Lightning, NOW, the Radical Lesbians, and Weather Underground. She was even smarter than F.D.R. Stuart, but she deferred to him, despite her feminist orientation, because he was a true alpha male who was a Mean Motherfucker When Crossed and had even more rage in him than she did.

To Sylvia, the purpose of POE, she said, was to create a world where all men and women, all races and all classes, all humanity, lived in loving harmony and ate uncooked fruits and vegetables.

Her real motive was also to *get even*. The other primates discriminated against her for being female, for being Jewish, for being highly verbal and a Teacher's Pet, for wearing glasses, for being an atheist, and for several dozen other reasons at least. They also called her by an insulting name, which was *dyke*.

The third founding member was Mountbatten Babbit, who was a cyclical schizophrenic. He wigged out once a year, on the average, and had learned how to medicate himself with phenothyazines to keep those periods of Bizarresville down to a few weeks each, but during those dilations of ego he was likely to be anybody from Napoleon to a Vietnamese Buddhist. The rest of the year he was a brilliant research chemist and computer expert, but it was hard for him to get a good job because of his several incarcerations in mental hospitals.

Babbit said he was in POE to create a rational world guided by sound scientific and libertarian-socialist principles. Yeah, he wanted to *get even* too. The other primates called him a *nut* or a *fruitcake*.

The other members of POE were equally brilliant and equally desperate.

THE HIDDEN VARIABLE

Markoff Chaney was a prime candidate for POE but, due to quantum wave probabilities, his orbit never intersected theirs.

Chaney detested the majority of primates because they called him *Shorty* or even more insulting names.

Mr. Chaney, you see, was a midget, but he was no relative of the famous Chaneys of Hollywood. People *did* keep making jokes about that. It was bad enough to be, by the standards of the gigantic and stupid majority, a freak; how much worse to be so named as to remind those big oversized clods of cinema's two most famous portrayers of monstro-freaks. By the time the midget was fifteen, he had built up a detestation for ordinary mankind that dwarfed (he hated that word) the relative misanthropies of Paul of Tarsus, Clement of Alexandria, Swift of Dublin, or anybody in POE. Revenge, for sure, he would have. He would have revenge.

It was in college (U.C.-Berkeley, 1962) that Markoff Chaney discovered another hidden joke in his name. It was in a math class and, since this was Berkeley, the two students directly behind the midget were ignoring the professor and discussing their own intellectual interests— which were, of course, five years ahead of intellectual fads elsewhere.

"So we keep the same instincts as our primate and

pre-primate ancestors," one student was saying. (He was
from Chicago, his name was Mounty Babbit, and he was
crazy even for Berkeley.) "But we superimpose culture
and law on top of this. So we get split in two, dig? You
might say"—Babbit's voice betrayed pride in the aphorism he was about to unleash—"mankind is the statutory
ape."

". . and," the professor, Percy "Prime" Time, said at
just that moment, "when such a related series appeared in
a random process, we have what is known as a Markoff
Chain. I hope Mr. Chaney won't be tormented by jokes
about this for the rest of the semester, even if the related
series of his appearances in class does seem part of a
notably random process." The class roared; another tone
of bile was entered on the midget's shit ledger, the list of
people who were going to eat turd before he died.

In fact, his cuts were numerous, both in math and in
other classes. There were times when he could not bear to
be with the giants, but hid in his room. *Pussycat* center-
fold open, masturbating and dreaming of millions and
millions of nubile young women all built like Pussyettes,
all throwing themselves passionately upon him. Today,
however, *Pussycat* would avail him not; he needed something raunchier. Ignoring his next class, he hurried across
Bancroft Way and slammed into his room, chain-bolting
the door behind him.

Damn "Prime" Time and damn the science of mathematics itself, the line, the square, the average, the mea-
surable world that pronounced him subnormal. Once and
for all, beyond fantasy, in the depth of his soul, he declared war on the statutory ape, on law and order, on
predictability. He would be the random factor in every
equation; from this day forward, unto death, it would be
civil war: the midget versus the digits.

He took out his pornographic Tarot deck, which he

used when he wanted a really far-out fantasy for his orgasm, and shuffled it thoroughly. Let's have a Markoff Chain orgasm, just to start with, he thought savagely.

His first overt act—his Fort Sumter, as it were—began in San Francisco the following Saturday. He was in Norton's Emporium, a glorified five-and-dime store, when he saw the sign:

NO SALESPERSON MAY LEAVE THE FLOOR
WITHOUT THE AUTHORIZATION OF A SUPERIOR.

THE MGT.

What, he thought, are the poor girls supposed to pee in their panties if they can't find the superior? Years of school came back to him ("Please, sir, may I leave the room, sir?"). Hah! Not for nothing had he spent a semester in Professor "Sheets" Kelly's intensive course on textual analysis of modern poetry. The following Wednesday, the midget was back at Norton's and hiding in a coffee urn when the staff left and locked up. A few moments later the sign was down and an improved version hung in its place:

NO SALESPERSON MAY LEAVE THE FLOOR
OR LOOK OUT THE DOOR
WITHOUT THE AUTHORIZATION OF A SUPERIOR.

THE MGT.

Markoff Chaney launched what he considered a reign of terror against the oversized idiots of the statistical majority. An electronics whiz since his first junior Edison set, he found it easy to reverse relays in street intersections, so that the WALK sign flashed on red and the DON'T

WALK signs on green. This proved to be bereft of amusement, except in small towns; denizens of New York, Chicago, and similar elephantine burgs, accustomed to nothing working properly, ignored the signs anyway. The midget branched out and soon incomprehensible memos signed "THE MGT." were raining upon employees everywhere.

His father, crusty old Indole Chaney, had been a stockholder in Blue Sky Inc., a very dubious corporation manufacturing devices for use in low gravity; when John F. Kennedy announced that the U.S. would place a man on the moon before 1970, Blue Sky suddenly began to haul in the long green. Markoff inherited a fund that delivered $300 per month. For his purposes, it was enough. Living in Spartan fashion, constantly crisscrossing the country by Greyhound (he soon knew every graffito in every White Tower men's room by heart), dining often on a tin of sardines and a container of milk, Markoff left a train of anarchy in his wake.

EMPLOYEES MAY NOT EXCHANGE VACATION DAYS. —THE MGT.

EMPLOYEES MAY NOT PUNCH OTHER EMPLOYEES' TIME CARDS. ANY DEVIATION WILL RESULT IN TERMINATION. —THE MGT.

FILL OUT IN TRIPLICATE. KEEP ONE COPY, MAIL ONE COPY TO THE OFFICE AND SEND THE THIRD TO THE TRANSYLVANIA CONSULATE. —THE MGT.
(THIS WAS USED AT A BLOOD BANK, OF COURSE.)

On January 18, 1984, the midget was in Chicago, hiding in a coffee urn in the tenth-floor editorial offices of *Pussycat* magazine. He had a Vacation Schedule Form with him, to be run off on Xerox and distributed to each editor's desk.

This form was his masterpiece; it was sure to provoke a nervous breakdown in anyone who tried to decipher and comply with all its directions, yet it was not much different, on the surface, from the hundreds of similar forms handed out in offices daily. Chaney was quite happy and quite impatient for the staff to leave so he could set about his cheerful task for the night.

Two editors passed the coffee urn, talking.

"Who's the *Pussycat* interview for next month?" one asked.

"Dr. Dashwood. You know, from Orgasm Research."

"Oh."

The midget had heard of Orgasm Research and it was, of course, on his shit list. More statistics and averages, more of the modern search for the norm that he could never be. And now the bastard who headed it, Dr. Dashwood, would be interviewed by *Pussycat*—and probably would get to fuck all the gorgeous Pussyettes at the local Pussycat Club. Chaney fumed. Orgasm Research moved from the middle of his shit list to the top, replacing his archenemy, Bell Telephone.

The thought of Dr. Dashwood remained with him all night, as he ground out his surrealist vacation memo on the office Xerox. He was still fuming when he returned to his pantry-sized room at the YMCA and slipped the bolt (to keep out the wandering and prehensile deviates who infest YMCAs everywhere). Dr. Francis Dashwood, supervisor of orgasms, and now ready to dive headfirst into a barrel of Pussyettes: the midget suffered at the thought.

But it was nearly 4 A.M. and he was tired. Tomorrow morning would be time to do something about Orgasm Research.

Chaney dreamed of Dashwood measuring orgasms with an n-dimensional ruler in Frankenstein's laboratory while men in trench coats went slinking about in the shadows asking unintelligible questions about 132 missing gorillas.

In the morning he shuffled through his bogus letterhead file, looking for something appropriate for correspondence with Orgasm Research.

THUGGEE SOCIETY, DIVISION OF HASH IMPORT AND AFROGENEALOGY, said the handsomest letterhead; this was illustrated with a three-headed Kali. But that one he reserved for correspondence with prominent white racists, informing them that the Afrogenealogy Division (Alex Haley, researcher-in-chief) had discovered that their great-great-grandmother was black. Chaney always invited the recipients to come to the next Thuggee meeting and bring their wives and sisters.

FRIENDS OF THE VANISHING MALARIA MOSQUITO (COMMITTEE TO BAN D.D.T.) was a good one, but not good enough for Dr. Dashwood. Chaney reserved it for correspondence with President Lousewart.

Finally, the midget selected CHRISTIANS AND ATHEISTS UNITED AGAINST CREEPING AGNOSTICISM, a Nonprophet Organization, Reverend Billy Graham, President; Madalyn Murray O'Hair, Chairperson of the Board.

In a few moments Chaney produced a letter calculated to short a few circuits in Dr. Dashwood's computeroid cortex:

Dear Dr. Dashwood:
When you are up to your ass in alligators, it's hard to remember that you started out to drain the swamp.

Cordially,

Ezra Pound,
Council of Armed Rabbis

P.S. *Entropy requires no maintenance.*

That should make the bastard wonder a bit, he thought with satisfaction, stuffing the enigmatic epistle in an envelope and addressing it.

Markoff Chaney loathed math because it contained the concept of the *average*.

Chaney not only loathed, but hated, despised, abominated, detested, and couldn't stand the thought of Dr. Dashwood, not just because Dashwood's work involved statistics and averages, but because is was concerned with orgasms.

That was a tender subject to Chaney. He was a virgin.

He was never attracted to women of his own stature—that was almost incestuous, and, besides, they simply did not turn him on. He adored the giantesses of the hateful oversized majority. He adored them, lusted after them, and was also terrified of them. He knew from sad experience, oft-repeated, that they regarded him as *cute* and even *cuddly*, and one of them had gone so far as to say *adorable* but absolutely *ridiculous* as a sex partner, damn and blast them all to hell.

He had tried building his courage with booze. They thought he was *disgusting* and *chauvinistic* and not even *cute* anymore.

He tried weed. They thought he was *cute* again, and even hilarious, but even more absurd as a possible lover.

He tried est. The trainers spent the first day tearing him down—telling him he was a no-good shit and everybody knew he was a no-good shit and things like that, which he had always suspected. The second day they built him up and convinced him he could control his space as well as any other mammal. He was flying when he came out.

He went at once to a singles bar and sidled up to the most attractive blonde in the place.

"Hi," he said boldly, swaggering a bit. "What would you say to a friendly little fuck?"

She gazed down at him from what suddenly seemed an enormous height. "Hello, friendly little fuck," she drawled with magnificent boredom.

When Chaney slunk back to his YMCA room and his pornographic Tarot, he vowed more vehemently than ever that he would be the meanest fuck on the planet. *Nobody* would ever call him a friendly little fuck again.

He still adored the giantesses and feared them, but now he hated them too; in short, he was really stuck on them.

Their *cunts*—those hairy, moist, hot, adorable, inaccessible, rejecting, terrible, divine, frightening Schwartzchild Radiuses of the dimension of Manhood—were the Holy Grail to him.

He knew their cunts were hairy and hot and moist, etc., despite his virginity, because he had read a lot of pornographic novels.*

Galactic Archives: Pornographic novels were novels about the things primates enjoy most, namely sexual acrobatics. They were taught to feel ashamed of these natural primate impulses so that they would be guilty-furtive-submissive types and easy for the alpha males to manipulate. Those caught reading such novels were called no-good shits, of course.

PEP

Muss es sein? Es muss sein.
—LUDWIG VAN BEETHOVEN

PEP—the People's Ecology Party—had been founded by Furbish Lousewart V following the success of his monumental best-seller, *Unsafe Wherever You Go*.

Lousewart V was a man born into the right time; his book perfectly reflected all the foreboding of the late 1970s. Its thesis was simply that everything science does is wrong, that scientists are very nasty people, and that we need to go back to a simpler, more natural way of life. The message was perfect for the time; it was simply Hitler's National Socialism redone, with only a few minor changes.

Where Hitler wrote "Jew," for instance, Lousewart wrote "scientist." Nobody but the most backward denizens of Bad Ass, Texas, or Chicago, Illinois, was capable of really getting riled up by the anti-Semitic ploy anymore, and Lousewart had, with intuitive brilliance, picked the one scapegoat capable of mobilizing real fear, rage, and hatred among the general population.

And Hitler's Wagnerian primitivism was altogether too Teutonic for young America in the 1970s, so Lousewart replaced it with a chic blend of Taoist and Amerindian primitivism.

It didn't matter that scholars pointed out that all of

Lousewart's arguments were illogical and incoherent (his followers despised logic and coherence on principle), and it didn't even matter that he had brazenly lifted most of his notions right out of Roszak's *Where the Wasteland Ends* and Von Daniken's *Gold of the Gods*. It was a package that had a built-in market. With the collapse of the Republican Party after Nixon and Ford, there was a void in national politics; somebody had to organize a force to challenge the Democrats, and the People's Ecology Party moved quickly to capture the turf.

Furbish Lousewart was an expert in Morality and Ideology; he understood that seeking out and denouncing no-good shits was the path by which one could become leader of a movement of the anxious and angry. In short, he had the instincts of a politician.

The Lousewart philosophy of asceticism, medievalism, and despair was officially called the Revolution of Lowered Expectations.

The Revolution of Lowered Expectations had not been invented by Furbish Lousewart. The whole neurosociology of the twentieth century could be understood as a function of two variables—the upward-rising curve of the Revolution of Rising Expectations and the downward-plunging trajectory of the Revolution of Lowered Expectations.

The Revolution of Rising Expectations, which had drawn more and more people into its Up-thrust during the first half of the century, had led many to believe that poverty and starvation and disease were all gradually being phased out by advances in pure and applied science, growing stockpiles of surplus food in the advanced nations, accelerated medical progress, the spread of literacy and electronics, and the mounting sense that people had a right to demand a decent life for themselves and their children.

The Revolution of Lowered Expectations was based on the idea that there wasn't enough energy to provide for the rising expectations of the masses. Year after year the message was broadcast: There Isn't Enough. The masses were taught that Terra was a closed system, that entropy was increasing, that life was a losing proposition all around, and that the majority were doomed to poverty, starvation, disease, misery, and stupidity.

Most of the people who still had rising expectations were scientists. When Furbish Lousewart realized the political capital to be made from the Revolution of Lowered Expectations, he also realized—thus demonstrating his political savvy—that having an opposition meant having a scapegoat group.

The scientists were an ideal scapegoat group because they all spoke in specialized languages and hardly anybody could understand them.

The Jews had served this function in earlier ages because they spoke *Yiddish*.

The scientists spoke *Mathematics*.

LOUSES IN THE SKIDROW DIMEHAUNTS

It is impossible now to suppose that organic life exists only on this planet.

—FURBISH LOUSEWART V, *Unsafe Wherever You Go*

Justin Case heard about the louses in the skidrow dimehaunts at one of Epicene Wildeblood's wild, wild parties, on December 23, 1983. Simon Moon, a creature with almost as much hair as Bigfoot, planted the louses in Case's semantic preconscious. The whole evening was rather confusing—too many martinis, too much weed, too many people—and Moon was regarded as somewhat sinister by everybody because he worked for the Beast (or *with* the Beast, or *on* the Beast). To make matters even more surrealistic, that intolerable bore Blake Williams was lecturing on the Birth of Cosmic Humanity to anyone who would listen, and several other conversations were going on simultaneously. Nonetheless, Moon had a manuscript with him, and a few listeners, and Case couldn't help absorbing part of what the mad Beastman was reading.

"Thee gauls simper at his tyrant power," Moon was chanting when Case first became conscious of him. What the hell was that? "He is ghoon with this seven-week booths and his mickeyed mausers into mistory. His eyes did seem auld glowery."

46

"FUCK THEM ALL!" a drunken writer from California said, cymbal-like, in Case's other ear.

"I beg your pardon?" Epicene Wildeblood, gay as three chimps in a circus, seemed to think the drunk was addressing him.

"I said, FUCK THE BLOODY CAPITALISTS!!!" the writer explained, weaving a bit to windward. "The goddamn motherfucking moneygrubbing Philistine lot of them . . ."

"I see," Wildeblood said dryly. He did not like people throwing scenes at his parties. "I think maybe you've had too much to drink. . . ."

"*Yeah???* Well," the drunk decided majestically, "fuck *you* too. And the horse you rode in on, as they say in Texas."

But that lard-assed bore Blake Williams was droning, "The whole problem, of course, is that we haven't been born yet. In fact, only now, at this point in history, is humanity about to be born." Williams was full of rubbish like that.

"About to be born?" asked Carol Christmas, the most delicious piece of blond femininity in the galaxy. Case thought at once that it would be a splendidly wonderful idea to deposit at least some of his sperm within her—*any* orifice would do. He thought this was a brilliant decision on his part, and wondered how to begin implementing it. He had no idea that every male hominid, and many other male primates, immediately had that idea when looking at Carol.

"Elverun, past Nova's atoms," the hairy Moon read on to his small circle of admirers, "from mayan baldurs to monads of goo, brings us by a divinely karmic Tao-Jones leverage back past tallchief tactics and aztlantean tooltechs to Louses in the Skidrow Dimehaunts. This way the Humpytheatre."

"I still say fuck 'em all." The drunk was a solitary bassoon against Moon's keening violin. "Capitalism is a rich man's heaven and a poor man's hell."

"Ahm yes," that windy old baritone sax, Blake Williams, bleated to the adorable Carol. "You see terrestrial life is embryonic in the evolutionary sense. In perspective to the cosmos." Old chryselephantine pedant, Case thought.

The shrill fife of Josephine Malik, Case's editor, was heard: "Moon. They say he works for the Beast." She wore jeans, combat boots and a button saying in psychedelic colors, BRING BACK THE SIXTIES. Walking nostalgia.

"Floating you see," the tuba of Williams oompah-oompah-ed onward, "in the amniotic atmosphere at the bottom of a 4,000-mile gravity well. And taking the Euclidean parameters of that gestation as the norm. Totally fetal, if you follow me, and in a very real sense blind because unborn, knowing um the dimensions of the wombplanet but not knowing what lies beyond the gravitational vagina—the whole universe *outside*."

"A 4,000-mile *cunt?*" Carol was awed by the concept. Her blond head leaned forward in doubtful inquiry. "That's a *very* funny metaphor, Professor."

"The only difference between my publishers and the James gang," the drunk went on, monotonous as a bass drum, "is that the James boys had horses."

". . . which explains the various rebirth experiences reported by astronauts like Aldrin and Mitchell and the others," Williams trumpeted (gassy old windbag). "Earth is our womb. Leaving Earth is literally rebirth. There's nothing metaphoric about it."

"The James boys hell, my last publisher was more like Attila the Hun," plonkty-plonked Frank Hemeroid in pianissimo.

Case began to feel that he had had perhaps too much hash.

"Right Wingers?" astronomer Bertha Van Ation was trilling. "We've got *real* Right Wingers out in Orange County. Let me tell you about the Committee to Nuke the Whales. . . ."

But that impossible Williams person was murmuring privately now to Carol the Golden Goddess, and Case tried desperately to catch the words, dreading the thought that a sexual liaison was being formed.

"The mnemonic," Williams was crooning, "is quite easy. Just say, 'Mother Very Easily Made a Jam Sandwich Using No Peanuts, Mayonnaise, or Glue.' See?"

Mnemonic for what, in God's name? But Moon was shrilling like a banshee now:

"Wet with garrison statements, oswilde shores, daily blazers, tochus culbook depositories, middlesexed villains and fumes. Fict! The most unkennedest carp of all. Fogt. Veiny? V.D.? Wacky? His bruttus gypper."

"I was walking on Lexington Avenue one morning around three A.M.," the drunk maundered on, "and I heard this URRRRRP, this horrible *eldritch laughter* just like in an H. P. Lovecraft story, and do you want to know what I think it was? A publisher and his lawyer had just figured out a new way to screw one of their writers."

"This the lewdest comedy nominator," Moon keened high on the G-string. "This de visions of spirals fur de lewdest comedy nominator. Eerie cries from the scalped nations! This the oval orefice sends the plumbers fur de spills. Lust of the walkregans. Think! White harse devoted. Thank! Wit ars devoided. Dunk!"

"I wish Moon would stop reading that drivel," Fred "Figs" Newton was clearly heard in solo. "I'd like to ask him how much the Beast really knows."

"Oh," the mournful oboe of Benny Benedict sang ominously, "the Beast knows *everything*. . . ."

". . . by Loop Shore and Dellingersgangers," Moon

keened over them, oblivious, "where yippies yip and doves duz nothing, to the hawkfullest convention ever."

At this point Case had to beat a hasty retreat to the john (one martini too many) and he never did get all the conversations sorted out in his memory, but the louses in the skidrow dimehaunts were firmly lodged in the Ambiguous Imagery files of his Myth-and-Metaphor Detector, right next to the Three Stooges and Chinatown.

And Cagliostro the Great.

TO HAVE LOCKS ON THESE DOORS

One of the causes of cancer is the harmfulness of cooked foods.
—FURBISH LOUSEWART V, *Unsafe Wherever You Go*

Blake Williams had the great good fortune to suffer a bout of polio in infancy. Of course he did not realize it was good fortune at the time—nor did his parents or his doctors. Nonetheless, he was among the lucky few who were treated by the Sister Kenny method at a time (the early 1930s) when the American Medical Association was denouncing that method as quackery and forbidding experiment thereon by its members. He was walking again, with only a slight limp, when he entered grade school in 1938. The real luck occurred twelve years later, in 1950, when he was eighteen; the limp and the dead muscles in his lower calves disqualified him for military service. The next man drafted, in his place, had both testicles bloodily blown off in Korea.

Williams, of course, never knew about this patriotic gelding, but he was well aware that various boys his age were having various portions of their anatomy blown off in Korea; being somewhat philosophical, he often reflected on the paradox that the polio (which had been, when it occurred, a physical agony to him and a psychological agony to his parents) had preserved him from such mutilations. Considering that the only continuing effect of the polio was the slight limp, he had to admit that Nature or God or something-or-other had sneakily done him great good while appearing to do him great evil. This was a decided encouragement toward an optimistic attitude toward the seemingly evil and made him wonder if the universe were not benevolent after all. The guy who lost his balls in Williams's place, on the other hand, became a pronounced pessimist and cynic.

Between Korea and Vietnam, while Blake was acquiring first an M.S. and then a Ph.D. in paleoanthropology, another great good fortune, in the form of another seeming evil, came before his eyes. He was walking in lower Manhattan; he had started from Washington Square, where he and his current girl friend—they were both NYU students—had just had a particularly nasty quarrel right after a biology class. He had wandered far to the west in a mood of suicidal gloom, such as young male primates often think they should experience after losing a sexual partner. Somehow, he wandered onto Vandivoort Street and found himself at the Vandivoort Street incinerator. There he saw a most peculiar sight: a rather stout man, looking like he was about to cry, was watching while two younger, thinner men were pouring books out of a truck into the incinerator.

"What the hell?" Blake Williams asked nobody in particular. It was like an old movie of Nazi Germany. Nobody had told him that bookburning was now an American institution.

He approached the stout man, who was the only one of the three who seemed unhappy, and repeated his question. "What the hell?" he asked. "I mean, are you people burning *books?*"

"*They* are," the stout man said. He went on to explain that he was an executive of something called the Orgone Institute Press and that a court had ordered all their books destroyed. Williams was curious and looked at some of the titles: *Character Analysis* and *The Mass Psychology of Fascism* and *The Cancer Biopathy* and *Contact with Space*.

"I didn't know that book burning was legal in this country," he said.

"Neither did I," the stout man said bitterly.

Blake Williams walked on, dazed. He couldn't have been more astonished if he'd seen Storm Troopers rounding up Jews. He wondered if he'd fallen into a time warp.

Later, of course, he learned that the Orgone Institute, headed by Dr. Wilhelm Reich, had been investigating human sexuality and had come to some highly unorthodox conclusions. Dr. Reich himself died in prison, Dr. Silvert (Reich's co-investigator) committed suicide, the books were burned, and the heresy was buried. But Williams had an entirely new attitude toward the country in which he lived, the scientific community which had looked on and made not a single gesture to support Dr. Reich and Dr. Silvert, and the omnipresent rhetoric which insisted that the Dark Ages had ended many centuries ago.

He remembered that Sister Kenny, at the time he and thousands of others were cured by her polio therapy, had been denounced as a quack by the same entrenched medical bureaucrats who imprisoned the Orgone researchers. How convenient, he thought, aghast, to assume that all the injustices happen in other countries and other ages: that Dreyfus may have been innocent, but the Rosenbergs never; that Pasteur may have been right, but not the researcher ostracized from the American Association for the Advancement of Science—not the professor denied tenure at *our* university, not the man in *our* prison. Blake Williams came to the Great Doubt without bitterness but with increased awareness that society is everywhere in conspiracy against intelligence. On his own, and at some expense, he repeated all of Dr. Reich's experiments and drew his own conclusions.

"There were only eighteen," he used to say, deliberately cryptic, sucking his pipe, deadpan, whenever anybody enthused about scientific freedom in his presence. If the victim inquired, "Only eighteen what?" Blake would reply, with the same deadpan, "Only eighteen physicians who signed the petition against the burning of Reich's books in 1957." He was not disappointed in his expectation that nine out of every ten researchers would angrily reply, "But Reich really *was* a quack." The tenth was the only one who would ever hear Williams's real thoughts on any subject.

The turning point, however, didn't come until 1977. It was then that Williams read a book entitled *Cosmic Trigger*. The author, a rather too clever fellow named Robert Anton Wilson, who wrote in a style as opulent as a Moslem palace, claimed to be in communication with a Higher Intelligence from the system of the dog star, Sirius. He also provided evidence, of a sort, that Aleister Crowley, G. I. Gurdjieff, Dr. John Lilly, Dr. Timothy Leary, a Flying Saucer contactee named George Hunt Williamson, and the priesthood of ancient Egypt, among others, had also been contacted by ESP transmitters from Sirius. Williams found that he actually believed this preposterous yarn. The discovery thrilled him, since it didn't really matter whether the pretentious Wilson's pompous claims were true or not. What mattered was that he, Blake Williams was free at last. (Remembering: "Free at last, free at last, thank God Almighty, I'm free at last," the tombstone which had so moved him in 1968.) Despite B.S. and M.S. and Ph.D., Blake Williams was free. He did not have to think what other academics thought. He had somehow liberated himself from conditioned consciousness.

Project Pan, in a sense, began at that moment. Blake Williams knew that he was going to do something great and terrible with his newfound freedom, and he was resolved that, unlike Reich (and Leary and Semmelweiss and Galileo and the long, sad list of martyrs to scientific freedom), he would not be punished for it. "Screw the Earthlings," he said bitterly and with *mucho cojones*, "I'm wise to their game. The trick is to be independent but not to let *them* know about it."

That night he wrote in his diary, *"Challenge a remaining taboo."* It was that simple. He had always wanted to understand genius, and now he had the formula. Freud, living in an age that prized its own seeming rationality, had found one of the remaining taboos and dared to think beyond it: he discovered infant sexuality and the unconscious, among other things. Galileo had gone beyond the taboo "Thou shalt not question Aristotle." Every great discovery had been the breaking of a taboo.

Blake Williams began looking around for a remaining taboo to violate.

This was by no means easy in Unistat at that time.

LIVING IN A NOVEL

Let there be a form distinct from the form.
                    —G. SPENCER BROWN, *Laws of Form*

Jo Malik once thought she was a transsexual. She had even gone to Dr. John Money, the pioneer of transsexual therapy and surgery, at Johns Hopkins, back in the mid-sixties.

"I think I'm a man living in a woman's body," she said.

Dr. Money nodded; that was normal in his business. He began asking her questions—the standard ones—and in only a half hour she was convinced that she was not a transsexual; she was just a confused woman. Dr. Money kindly gave her the name of a good psychiatrist in New York, where she lived, for a more conventional form of therapy.

After three months the psychiatrist announced that Jo's problem was not Penis Envy. That was hardly exciting; she had never thought her problem was quite that simple.

The therapy ground along. She learned a great deal about her Father Complex, her Mother Complex, her Sibling Rivalries, and her habit of hiding resentments. It was enlightening, in a painful way, but she was still confused.

Then the Women's Liberation Movement began, and Jo dropped out of therapy to enter politics.

She no longer defined herself as a man trapped in a woman's body, but as a human being trapped in male definitions of femininity.

It was a very satisfactory resolution of her problems. She no longer had to take responsibility for anything; everything was the fault of the men. There was no need to stifle resentments—the correct political stance was to express them, in a strident voice and with a maximum of emotional-territorial rage. She had finally learned the ABC's of primate politics. She even learned to swell her muscles and howl.

It was all so much relief after years of self-doubt that Jo remained in 1968 while the rest of the world moved into 1970 and 1974 and 1980 and 1983. That was why she was wearing a BRING BACK THE SIXTIES button at Epicene Wildeblood's party.

Jo still had one problem left over from pre-Women's Lib days. Sometimes just before sleep, she heard a voice saying, "No wife, no horse, no mustache."

Of course she knew that everybody occasionally heard such voices in the hypnagogic reverie before true sleep. You were wigging out only if you heard them all day long. Still, she wondered where it came from and why it had such a cryptic message.

Jo Malik hadn't had a sexual relationship with a man since 1968, and looked it.

She was also sixty-four years old, and looked it.

Nevertheless, there was an Unidentified Man at the Wildeblood party, and Jo suspected him of having designs on her bod. That was because he kept trying to get into every conversation group that she intercepted. He was following her, she was convinced.

"Mother very easily made a jam sandwich using no peanuts, mayonnaise, or glue," Blake Williams said.

"Of course, Skull Island was Cooper's Chinatown," Justin Case said at the same moment.

"Wham! That arbral with his showers sooty? The fugs come in on tinny-cut foets," Moon droned along.

Jo decided that she had taken perhaps a little too much of the Afghan hash that was going around. It seemed that everybody in the room—the *crème de la crème* of Manhattan intelligentsia—were all talking gibberish. She eased out onto the balcony for some fresh air and restful silence.

Eight stories below a marquee blinked up at her: DEEP THROAT, it said.

Male chauvinism.

She breathed deeply, mingling oxygen with the cannabis molecules in her blood.

And the Unidentified Man appeared.

"Hello," he said casually. "I thought I'd find you out here."

"Who the hell are you, buster?" Jo barked—the first warning.

"My *name* doesn't matter," he said. He was tall, and handsome, and very gentle in his eyes. The worst kind of Male Chauvinist Pig. The Seducer.

"*You* don't matter, either," Jo said snappily. "I'd like to be alone, to enjoy the view, *if you don't mind.*"

She showed more teeth, emphasizing the second primate warning.

"I'm Hugh Crane," the handsome stranger said quickly. "I have been sent by the Author of Our Being with an important message for you. Please listen; it's vital to your future. We are all . . *living in a novel.*"

"Take it and stick it," Jo said, leaving the balcony.

Another male chauvinist squashed, or at least squelched.

Unfortunately, back in the Wildeblood *soirée*, the first voice she heard was Benny Benedict complaining. "Women's Lib? Christ, what we need now is Men's Lib. Do you know how much alimony I'm paying? . . ."

STARHAWK'S LIFE STUDY

In capitalism, man exploits man. In socialism, it's exactly the opposite.

—BEN TUCKER, FAMOUS VAUDEVILLE COMEDIAN

While "Eggs" Benedict was complaining about his alimony in New York, a telephone was ringing in Marlene Murphy's apartment in San Francisco.

Starhawk, a bronze young man with an arrogant face, had picked Marlene up in a singles bar on Powell Street just three hours before and still didn't know her last name. He came out of the bathroom stark naked to answer the phone. Very carefully, he said, "Yes?"

"Who is this?" the voice on the other end asked sharply.

Starhawk breathed deeply. "Who you trying to call?" he asked in return, calmly, starting to smile.

"Isn't this 555-9470?"

Starhawk began to feel that he knew this voice from somewhere. "No," he said. "This is 9479. Try again, Mac." He hung up quickly.

Marlene Murphy came out of the bathroom, also naked, toweling her hair. Starhawk looked at her thoughtfully.

"You got a husband you sort of forgot to mention?" he asked.

"Me, a husband?" Marlene lit a cigarette. "Thanks for the laugh. I'd rather be in jail. A husband, Jesus, no, thanks."

"Well, somebody didn't like a man to be answering your phone," Starhawk said. "Somebody with a voice like a cop. Or a bill collector."

"My father," she said. "Oh, crap. Here I am twenty-four years old and working for a Master's in Social Psych and he thinks I shouldn't have a man in my apartment when he calls. That's the Irish for you."

The phone rang again.

Marlene answered it this time. Starhawk started to cross the room but she grabbed his leg and as he turned she took his penis in her hand.

"Daddy?" Marlene sounded genuinely surprised. "A man? No, I'm alone, studying for the exams." She was running her fingers around the crown of the penis and Starhawk was reacting with a notable swelling. "What? Look, I just told you. It was a wrong number. What am I, a suspect you got in the back room? You must have made a mistake, even if it was the first time in your whole life."

Marlene leaned forward and kissed Starhawk's cock quickly and shifted back to the phone at once. "No. I said no, Daddy, *no*, and I meant it. The Church says I'm supposed to go to Confession to a priest once a year. It doesn't say I'm supposed to go to Confession to my own father every time he calls me on the phone."

Her hand was moving rapidly now, trying to make Starhawk ejaculate. He smiled, recognizing her game, and pulled away, to kneel before her and began licking her inner thighs.

"No. I haven't seen Aunt Irene in two years. She's involved in *what?* Greenpeace? That's just to protect the whales. There's nothing communistic about it and half the people in Mendocino are in it. What? Sure, but they just *like* whales up there. What do you mean my voice is getting funny? It must be a cold coming on. Yes. Yes. Oh, God, it's the door. Yes. I love you, too, Daddy. The door." She hung up quickly, her pelvis heaving. "God, God, *God*. Oh, sweet fucking *Jesus* God."

Starhawk stood up and said, "You like that kind of game? Why don't you call the Archbishop and I'll do it to you again while you talk to him."

"You are a prize," Marlene said. "You really are a prize. Have you spent your whole life learning how to please women?"

"It's my life study," Starhawk said. "Everything else is just a hobby."

Starhawk, like most of the characters in this Romance, was a liar.

Most primates lied constantly, because they were afraid of *getting caught* and being pronounced no-good shits.

Starhawk was always afraid of getting caught, because his life study was really burglary.

Starhawk thought he had a right to steal anything and everything he could get away with from the white people.

The white people had stolen all the land in Unistat from his ancestors.

Starhawk, like the grim moralists in POE, was determined to *get even*.

Getting even was the basis of many primate semantic confusions, such as "expropriating the expropriators," "an absolute crime demands an absolute penalty," "they did it to me so I can do it to them," and, in general, the emotional mathematics of "one plus one equals zero" $(1 + 1 = 0)$.

The primates were so dumb they didn't realize that one plus one equals two $(1 + 1 = 2)$ and one murder plus one murder equals two murders, one crime plus one crime equals two crimes, etc.

They did not understand *causality* at all.

The few primates who did understand causality slightly called it *karma*. They said all sorts of foolish things about it.

They didn't even know enough mathematics to describe quantum probability waves. They said, in crude hominid metaphor, that bad karma led to *"bad vibes."*

LANDSLIDE

Bryce S. DeWitt states: "The Copenhagen view promotes the impression that the collapse of the state vector, and even the state vector itself, is all in the mind." . . . One fact which seems to emerge from the present discussions of the nature of consciousness is that it is nonlocal (*i.e.*, not confined to a certain region of space-time). . . .

—LAWRENCE BEYNAM, *Future Science*

Furbish Lousewart V was elected President of the United States in 1980 with the greatest landslide since Roosevelt II buried poor Alf Landon alive in 1936. The People's Ecology Party also gained control of both the House and the Senate and twenty-three governorships out of the fifty-one.

The PEP platform, a weird mixture of tangled religiosity and New Left antirationalism, became official policy.

The New Order began mildly—at least by comparison with what was to follow—and the major changes of the first administration consisted only of cutting the NASA budget to zilch; banning McDonald's hamburger shops (which resulted in underground "Steakeasies," where you gave the right password and got a Big Mac for $7); outlawing tobacco (a "lid" of Chesterfields was soon selling for $50 to $75 coast to coast); appointing three antitechnology fanatics to the first three vacancies in the Supreme Court; forbidding the teaching of Logical Positivism in colleges; throwing everybody off welfare (the streets were soon full of crippled and schizophrenic beggars, some of whom also slept there or even starved there on occasion, creating that Third World look which PEP regulars regarded as "spiritual"); cutting the use of electricity by 50 percent, gas by 70 percent, and atomic energy by 97 percent, thereby causing millions to freeze to death and millions more to join the army of unemployed beggars on the streets; beginning all Cabinet meetings with hatha yoga sessions and Krishna chanting; serializing the collected works of Ralph Nader in the official Party newspaper, *Doom;* encouraging Party members to beat up mathematicians, geologists, science-fiction fans, and other "non-ec" types ("non-ec" types were those either known to be disloyal to the Party or suspected of such disloyalty); encouraging the reemergence of cottage industry by rigidly repressing every more advanced kind of industry; introducing Zen meditation to grammar schools; and most important of all, blaming the host of new and tragic problems that resulted from government policies on an alleged conspiracy of "scientists" and instituting a nationwide witch-hunt to round up the members of this conspiracy for incarceration in reeducation centers.

The Revolution of Lowered Expectations had triumphed. By 1984 nobody in the country had any higher expectations than a feudal serf.

Actually, the apotheosis of Furbish Lousewart V had been engineered by the same group of alpha males who had been promoting the Revolution of Lowered Expectations all along.

These were very cunning old primates in several of the most skillful predator bands on Terra. Because of the stealth and skill of these bands—made up of successful predator families that had been intermarrying for several generations—they collectively owned 99.4 percent of all the territory and resources of Unistat.

They only owned about 40 percent of the rest of Terra, and that seriously annoyed them.

The Revolution of Rising Expectations annoyed them even more, because it led many primates to argue that the reason poverty and starvation still continued in an advanced technological society was that *Somebody Was Getting More Than Their Share*. Whenever anybody asked who that *Somebody* might be, all eyes turned on these royal old primate males who owned so much. The eyes were not friendly. Sometimes, in far-off lands where these royal primates did not completely control the governments, some of their boodle was actually seized and redistributed to the people they had stolen it from. As Rising Expectations had mounted in the first half of the century, this regrettable pattern of expropriation also escalated.

The alpha males of these tough old predator families did not like this at all. They therefore invested a prudent sum in promoting the careers of everybody who preached Lowered Expectations, from Ralph Nader and the Club of

Rome to Oriental gurus and the neo-Stoics of the post-Marxist Left.

When Furbish Lousewart came along, they invested in him, too—enough to buy the election for him.

THE QUANTUM CONNECTION IS UNMITIGATED

When Justin Case returned from the john the mad Simon Moon was still reading his nightmare version of the American Dream.

"Upper guns thou wilt, marxafactors," Moon intoned, half-chanting. "A gnew gnu cries nixnix on your loin ardors [O my am I?] as the great Jehoover fouls his files [Seminole cowhand] with marching looter congs. What a loop in the evening, bloody-fouled loop! Lawn ordures for Crookbacked Dick, pig-bastchard of the world. See, it's the stinking onion coop. Say, it's the slimey deepsea doodler. By the wampum of caponey. O turnig on, Duke Daleyswine, lardmayor of burning-town! They'll chip away yore homo hawks."

"Hughes Rockefeller Exxon," the drunken writer was muttering into his martini glass. "Thieving motherfucking . . ."

Justin decided the party was degenerating and left. In the foyer he had to pass Marvin Gardens and Josephine Malik and heard:

"Male chauvinist paranoid!" (Josephine to Marvin.)

"Extraterrestrial brainwasher!" (Marvin to Josephine.)

Justin decided morosely that the literary world had never been the same since the drug revolution of the 1960s and 1970s. "Pretty little boidies picking in the toidies," he said gruffly to both of them and walked out.

Justin had no idea where he had gotten the words about the pretty little boidies from. He assumed it was the Afghan hash going around at the party.

"I know all *about* your *plansss*," Marvin Gardens was snarling at Jo Malik, in his coked-up Peter Lorre voice. "I know why you picked Hemingway to discredit and *defame*. I know what you and your *extraterrestrial friends* are planning to do to humanity, you cold-blooded *fiendsss*."

"You know," Jo said, suddenly tired of her own anger, "you really ought to lay off that coke, buster."

"Yess, *yess*, claim that I'm paranoid, that's the *usual tactic—*"

"I say you two," Epicene Wildeblood drawled, "did either of you see Cagliostro?"

"The magician?" Jo asked.

"Well," Wildeblood asked with infinite patience, "is there another Cagliostro?"

Marvin and Jo exchanged equally puzzled glances.

"I guess he hasn't arrived yet," Jo offered finally.

"What?" Wildeblood frowned. "Why, he's been here all night."

Marvin and Jo exchanged glances again.

"I guess we missed him," Marvin said gently, with the ghastly smile of one who humors a deranged mind.

Wildeblood glared at him and stalked off.

That was really heavy hash, Jo decided. Wildeblood had been hallucinating a guest who wasn't even there.

DEMATERIALIZING GORILLAS

Knee-jerk liberals and all the certified saints of sanctified humanism are quick to condemn this great and much-maligned Transylvanian statesman.
> —WILLIAM F. BUCKLEY, JR.,
> *The Wit and Wisdom of Vlad the Impaler*

The Warren Belch Society held its annual meeting on January 2, 1984, while POE was busy mining downtown Washington with homemade atom bombs. The Society knew nothing of this and was more concerned with disappearing gorillas in Chicago.

Their tiny office was dominated by a huge oil painting of Schrödinger's Cat, executed in weird orgone-blue hues by their founder and presiding officer, the eccentric millionaire, W. Clement Cotex. All active members of the Society—eight of them, to be exact—were present.

The Warren Belch Society had been founded after Cotex had been kicked out of the Fortean Society for having bizarre notions. The purpose of "the Belchers" (as Cotex jovially called them) was to investigate those aspects of scientific theory and those alleged occult events which were regarded as "too far out" by the unimaginative Forteans, who are willing to investigate UFOs, rains of crabs and fish, girls who might have turned into swans, and similar matters, but, like their founder, the late Charles Fort, drew the line at the dogs that said "Good morning" and then vanished in a puff of green smoke.

Cotex, admittedly, was an intellectual surrealist. The name of the Society, for instance, was deliberately taken from the most obscure of all the lawmen of the Old West, Marshall Warren Belch of Dodge City, who had unfortunately been shot to death when his pistol jammed during his very first gunfight. It was Clem Cotex's claim that the Everett-Wheeler-Graham-DeWitt interpretation of the Schrödinger's Cat paradox was literally true. *Everything that could happen did happen.* There were infinitely many universes, each one the result of a collapse of the state vector in a possible way. Thus, somewhere in superspace, there must be a universe in which Marshall Belch's pistol didn't jam and he lived on to become famous. There were probably TV shows and movies about him by now, over there in that universe. Or so Cotex argued.

In general, as good empiricists, the Belch Society was more interested in odd facts than in odd theories. A UFO Contactee who could jam zippers by looking at them. A man found dead in St. Louis with his throat torn as though by the fangs of an enormous beast, with no animal missing from the local zoos (the famous Stimson Case of 1968). Documented instances of a fat bearded man with jolly eyes seen near chimneys on Christmas Eve, with a bag of toys over his shoulder. Bleeding Catholic statues. Flying Hindus. Dematerializing Buddhists. Kahuna fire-walkers. Why the signs always say WALK when the streetlight is on red and DON'T WALK when it is on green. Books in which the permutations of the phrase "heaven and hell" appeared at random intervals, forming a Markoff Chain.

"Take anybody in the world—anybody in this novel," Cotex once explained his theory to a group of skeptical fellow characters. "Like you, Dr. Williams," he added,

picking out the most erudite and wiggy in the crowd,
Blake Williams. "In one of the parallel universes, you're
probably not an anthropologist, but maybe a chemist or
something. In another universe, you might even be a
female musician instead of a male scientist. And so on. In
another universe," Cotex concluded, "*I* might be a small
businessman from Little Rock who believes the universe is
five-cornered."

The disappearing gorillas, they were all convinced, were:
(a) a major breakthrough to another universe; (b) not yet
known to those stuffy old Forteans; and (c) really hot stuff.

"If gorillas can teleport," Professor Fred "Fidgets" Digits was saying, "that may be the whole key to the Mad
Fishmonger."

"We needn't assume that the gorillas actually teleport,"
Dr. Horace Naismith objected. "It may be that there is a
Schwartzchild Radius in Lincoln Park Zoo and they sort of
fall into it and pass the Event Horizon."

This led to some lively debate on whether teleportation
was or was not more likely than a Black Hole in the
Lincoln Park Zoo, but Blake Williams suddenly derailed
the conversation with a thoughtful and uncompleted "I
wonder if this goes all the way back to the Democratic
Convention of 1968. . . ."

"Say," Cortex cried, eyes wide. "What was all that
fighting and fussing about, anyway? The way I remember
it, the radicals wanted to sleep in the park and the police
beat the shit out of them and chased them out of the park.
That seems an awfully silly issue to lead to a whole week
of rioting and tear-gassing. And why were so many
journalists—*and especially cameramen*—attacked by the
cops. . . ?"

"You think maybe the city authorities knew about it,
even back then. . . ?" Naismith asked eagerly.

"People may resist new ideas, as we all know to our

sorrow," Williams said, "but a fact this size—*over two hundred* gorillas purchased by the zoo over a ten-year period and *only two* accounted for—must have been noticed by somebody on the finance committee at least. You can bet your sweet ass the city authorities know about it. And, of course, they're imposing a cover-up, just like the air force with the UFOs. The same old government reflex. Pavlov's Dog meets Schrödinger's Cat again."

"This is a time for action, not theory," said Cotex. "Gentlemen, I am flying to Chicago tonight to begin a personal investigation. A case like this is a surrealist's heaven and a logician's hell," he added with a chuckle. He was totally nonlinear.

THE MAD FISHMONGER

There is no such thing as water. It is merely melted ice.
        —FURBISH LOUSEWART V, *Unsafe Wherever You Go*

The Mad Fishmonger was the patron saint of the Warren Belch Society. He, or she, had originally appeared, or had been alleged to have appeared, in Cromer Gardens, Worcester, England, on May 28, 1881. He, or she, along with perhaps a dozen assistants, had rushed through Cromer Gardens at high noon, throwing crabs and periwinkles all over the streets. They also threw crabs and periwinkles into the fields beside the road. They climbed high walls to dump some of the fish into gardens and onto the roofs of houses.

It was thorough, painstaking work, and since the Mad Fishmonger and his, or her, associates accomplished it all at noon on a busy day *without being seen,* the citizens of Cromer Gardens claimed that the crabs and periwinkles had fallen out of the sky.

This notion was not acceptable to the scientists of the day, who held it as axiomatic that crabs and periwinkles do not fall out of the sky. A scientist from *Nature* magazine therefore offered the Mad Fishmonger an explanation, although he failed to explain how the Fishmonger and his co-conspirators had accomplished their feat without being noticed by any of the citizenry.

Charles Fort, founder of the Fortean Society, rejected the Mad Fishmonger indignantly and claimed that crabs and periwinkles *did* fall from the sky. After Clem Cotex was thrown out of the Fortean Society for his heresies, he reconsidered the whole puzzling case of the mysterious event in Cromer Gardens on May 28, 1881. Cotex decided to believe in the Mad Fishmonger. It was the fundamental hypothesis of his system of philosophy, and the guiding light of the Warren Belch Society, that the craziest-sounding theory is the most likely one. All things considered, the motives and methodology of the Mad Fishmonger were much more mysterious than shellfish falling from the sky; *ergo,* the Mad Fishmonger probably did exist.

Among the things the science of that time could not explain, which Clem Cotex attributed to the Mad Fishmonger, were other Damned Things that fell out of the sky, such as iron balls with inscriptions on them or chunks of ice as big as elephants. There were also Damned Things on the ground, including jumping furniture, "haunts," and the Gentry. There were animals that shouldn't be and animals that couldn't be and trans-time and trans-space perceptions and religious "miracles."

The first clue to correct understanding of these things came when quantum causality was finally formulated correctly in Gilhooley's Demonstration of 1994, and nobody understood Gilhooley.

At the time of our story everybody was as confused as Clem Cotex. Most of them just expressed their confusion, or rather concealed it, in more conservative ways.

ANOTHER CIA PLOT

The spirit of decision consists simply in not hesitating when an inner voice commands you to act.
—FURBISH LOUSEWART V, *Unsafe Wherever Your Go*

Just before coming to Wildeblood's party, Blake Williams wrote one of the most heretical passages in his jealously guarded *Secret Diaries*. He wrote:

I am an anthropologist, *ergo* a professional liar. An anthropologist is a scientist trained to observe that every society is a little bit mad, including his own. He holds his job by never mentioning this fact explicitly.

Perhaps 1983 as a whole had been too much for him. In January one of the biggest breakthroughs had occurred at Project Pan, and Williams and Dashwood had to reach new heights of eloquence to persuade the other scientists involved that any premature disclosure could be lethal. At that very time, they pointed out, the John Birch Society was staging massive sit-ins and protests against the introduction of anthropology texts to high schools in Orange County.

In February the Government Accounting Office announced that all the gold in Fort Knox had disappeared sometime in the past decade.

In March three new life-extension pills were placed on the market during the controversy over FOREVER, the first life-extension pill, which was widely suspected of creating disastrous side effects. All the data on FOREVER thus far had shown one consistency: scientists not employed by Blue Sky Inc., the manufacturer of FOREVER, continually found evidence of these tragic side effects, and all scientists employed by Blue Sky continually found no evidence of such problems. (That month Blake Williams wrote in his *Diaries*, quoting Lord Macaulay, "The law of gravity would be thrown into dispute were there a commercial interest involved.")

In April average rent for a one-room apartment reached $1,500 per month and many families were renting broom closets at $600 to $700 per month or just sleeping in parks. Landlords were hanged in Berkeley, California, and Carbondale, Michigan.*

Galactic Archives: Rent was a form of tribute paid by non-"owning" users of land to nonusing "owners." The "owners," known as *lords-of-the-land,* or *landlords* for short, were originally relatives of the alpha male or king (see Nomis of Noom, "From the Baboon Food-Gathering Band to Consciousness"), but among the higher barbarians, such as in Unistat at the time of this epic, anyone with enough "money" could buy land and become a "landlord."

In May the missing gold from Fort Knox was found buried at San Clemente. Nixon still denied *everything*.

The new *World Almanac* listed the first UFO cult to reach 20,000,000 members among the major world religions.

In June the first human embryo transplant was accomplished and the U.S. troops in Tierra del Fuego mutinied.

In July FEMFREE, a drug which allegedly removed mothering impulses, was banned by the FDA, and UFO cultists and Christians clashed in Belfast.

In August astronomer Bertha Van Ation discovered two new planets in the solar system, and bootleg FEMFREE at ten times the free market price began to circulate through Women's Lib groups coast to coast.

In September UFO cultists and Moslems clashed in Cairo.

In October landlords were lynched in three more American cities, the first human brain transplant was accomplished, and UFO cultists clashed with Maoists in Peking.

In November, Mae Brussell on KPFA-Berkeley charged that Jesus had been killed by a CIA plot.

A HIT ON THE HEAD

Every society encourages some behaviors and punitively forbids others. Thus, although cultures were not scientifically designed, they act much like computers programmed for specific results. One can look at their cultural structure and predict: this one will have a high murder rate, this one will have many schizo-phrenics, this one will remain Stone Age unless interfered with, this one is going to the stars.

—MARILYN CHAMBERS, *Neuro-Anthropology*

Benny "Eggs" Benedict never got home from Epicene Wildeblood's party that night. On the corner of Lexington and Twenty-third, Benny was hit by a heavy lead pipe, which smashed his skull and killed him. The pipe did not fall by accident; it was wielded deliberately by a man named Francesco "Pablo" Gomez. Pablo did not hate Benny or have any personal feelings toward him at all and he did not grin sadistically. Pablo hit Benny with the pipe because Benny was well dressed and probably had money in his pockets. When Benny was comatose but not yet dead, Pablo dragged him into an alley and went through his pockets, finding to his delight that his surmise had been correct and Benny was actually carrying more than $50; he had $52, to be exact. Benny died while Pablo was rifling the wallet.

To Pablo, $52 was a lot of money. He went home humming happily.

That's the way things were in Unistat at the height of the Revolution of Lowered Expectations.

CLUES

Every string which has one end also has another end.
—FINAGLE'S FIRST FUNDAMENTAL FINDING

Clem Cotex had been nosing about the Lincoln Park Zoo for several days and was more puzzled than ever. The facts were undeniable: The zoo had, indeed, purchased over 200 gorillas in the past decade and only two of them were on exhibit; 198 were missing. Any sort of casual questioning of the primate house attendants brought instantly vague answers in a well-rehearsed manner. They were all in on the cover-up. The public was being protected against all knowledge of the inexplicable, the weird, the surrealistic. All part of the usual governmental pretense that human affairs were rationally administered by experts who knew what was really going on. They feared that if people ever discovered that those in power were as confused by this inexplicable universe as those out of power, then the whole charade might collapse.

There was no Black Hole in the zoo; Cotex was sure of that. All gravity conditions were normal. The gorillas were not falling through a Schwartzchild radius into the universe next door or anything really spooky like that. They were simply teleporting somewhere . . . maybe back to their homelands in Africa. Although, considering the unpredicta-

75

bility of teleportive currents as documented by Charles Fort—who had recorded cases of snakes landing in Memphis, Tennessee, and coconuts being deposited in Worcester, England—the gorillas might actually be reappearing *anywhere*.

Since anything might be a clue in such occult enigmas, Clem had carefully copied all the graffiti in the men's room at the primate house. It was the usual jumble of disparate and ambiguous signals: "Black P. Stone Run It," "For a good blow job call 555-1717 and ask for Father James Flanagan," "Help Prevent Von Neumann's Catastrophe!," "Arm the Unemployed," "Free our four-legged brothers and sisters. A zoo is a child's heaven and an animal's hell," "Save the Whales—Harpoon a Honda," "Off the Landlords," "Stamp Out Sizeism."

Probably, Cotex thought morosely, there is an important signal in there and I'm just not imaginative enough to see it.

THE ALTRUIST

God bless America.

—LAST WORDS OF G. I. GURDJIEFF

Everybody who had been at Wildeblood's party felt compelled to attend Benedict's funeral, even though none of them enjoyed it. Benny had been one of the funniest writers of his time, at least in the daily press, and it would have been appropriate to send him off with a showing of old Laurel and Hardy films or something equally in his own métier. Primate decorum forbade this. They packed him in with a dull and depressing "religious" ceremony.

"I am the Resurrection and the Life," intoned a primate with his collar on backward. Nobody knew what the hell that meant, if anything, but they tried to feel better when they heard it.

At the time Benny was buried a window washer was at work on the seventeenth floor of the Morgan Guaranty Trust at 23 Wall Street. He was an expert lip-reader and knew more of the secrets of Wall Street than anybody outside the Illuminati. In fact, the second reason he had become a window washer was to get work in the Wall Street district and pick up useful information.

The main reason he had taken the job would have been even more unnerving to Morgan Guaranty had they known about it. The window washer was a member of Purity of Essence and had already managed to place 333 homemade nuclear weapons on ledges so high nobody but a pigeon was ever likely to see them.

All of the weapons were set to go off at a signal from the POE computer—another homemade contraption but awesomely efficient. POE was full of science grads who had dropped out of the career game in horror and revulsion at the uses to which science was being put in their universe.

At this point POE had twenty-eight American cities mined. The window washer hoped that, when push came to shove, POE wouldn't have to detonate more than one of those cities. He was an altruist, like everybody else in Purity of Essence.

TAKE WHAT THOU HAST

Take what thou hast and give it to the poor.
—ATTRIBUTED TO SOME LONGHAIR COMMIE FREAK

The letter was sent out May 1, 1984, to the New York *Times-News-Post*, the Chicago *Sun*, the Los Angeles *Times-Free Press*, NBC News, CBS News, the White House, Mae Brussel, the Berkeley *Barb*, KPFA, ABC News, the London *Times*, Zodiac News Service, *The Christian Science Monitor*, the Archdioceses of New York, Chicago, San Francisco, and St. Louis, the Church of Scientology, Mark Lane, Paul Krassner, Dick Gregory, Chase Manhattan Bank, the Bad Ass *Bugle*, the Nihilist Anarchist Horde, Norman Mailer, and 237 miscellaneous other institutions and celebrities. POE wanted to be sure that their message would get out to the general public with the minimum of distortion by the Establishment.

The letter said:

May God forgive us. May history judge as charitably.

We have placed tactical nuclear bombs in over 1,700 locations throughout the United States. The targets are all enemies of the people: large banks, multinational corporations, government facilities. We will trigger one of these bombs at noon tomorrow, somewhere in the

78

eastern United States, to demonstrate that we are not bluffing.

All of the other nuclear bombs will be triggered in succession until our demands are met. If any attempt is made to apprehend and arrest us—any attempt at all—all the remaining bombs will be detonated at once.

We demand:

That President Furbish Lousewart immediately confiscate all fortunes above one million dollars;

That this money, which we calculate makes a sum of approximately three trillion dollars, be distributed at once to the forty million families, who are, according to the government's own standards, living below the poverty line, so that each poor family receives $75,000;

That all government money presently invested in weapons of war and preparations for war be immediately redirected to improving schools, homes, and hospitals in poor neighborhoods, so as to make them fit for human beings;

That George Washington be removed from the dollar bill and replaced by Walt Disney's Mickey Mouse to remind people forever of the idiocy of worshiping money.

A final word of warning: We have been working on this project for sixteen years and have the full capacity to do all that we say. The Revolution of Lowered Expectations has been a monopolist's heaven and a poor people's hell. We intend to change that.

POE

COLLAPSE OF THE STATE VECTOR

Records can be destroyed if they do not suit the prejudices of ruling cliques, lost if they become incomprehensible, distorted if a copyist wishes to impose a new meaning upon them, misunderstood if we lack the information to interpret them. The past is like a huge library, mostly fiction.

—HENRY FORD, *Neuro-History*

The doorbell rang.

Josephine Malik said "Shit" quietly but fervently. She was correcting the galleys of the second printing of her *Clitoral Politics* and interruptions were not welcome.

Jo approached the door warily. The regular lock, the bolt lock, and the police lock were all in place; the intruder would need an ax to get in if he were one of the 2,000,000 violent criminals among the 20,000,000 citizens of New York in 1984.

"Who is it?" she shouted through the door.

"Ukraine."

"Who???" she screamed.

"Hugh Crane," came the voice, louder. "We met at a Wildeblood party last December. . . ."

"Go away. I don't know you and I'm busy."

"This is important. The novel we're in is coming to a horrible conclusion. . . ."

80

"You're nuts. Go away." Jo turned away from the door and went to the closet for her Saturday Night Special, in case this maniac did have an ax.

"Listen to me, please, we've only got a few minutes," the voice shouted through the door. "Maybe you can almost remember the name Hagbard Celine. That's the name I had in the last quantum *eigen*state, the last novel, when we worked together. . . ."

Jo went to the phone. "Give me the police!" she shouted, forgetting that she wasn't yelling through a door anymore.

It was the last sentence she ever spoke.

At that moment Manhattan Island became a nuclear furnace.

President Lousewart, guided by Intelligence Agencies that had collectively listened to enough "private" conversations to be stone-paranoid, had acted within minutes after the POE letter arrived in the White House. The Unistat government would not be blackmailed. Even before TV could broadcast the story of the threat, over 10,000,000 "radicals" and possible "radicals" had been placed under arrest coast to coast. One of them, more or less accidentally, had been Sylvia Goldfarb of POE.

All 1,700 POE bombs detonated at once. Unistat as an entity ceased to exist. Nihilist Anarchist Hordes roamed what was left of the landscape.

Twenty-three hundred nuclear missiles, computer-guided to fire if Unistat were nuked, took off at the first blast and decimated Russia. The Beast had been programmed by Intelligence Agencies who were all convinced that any nuclear attack would come from there.

Twenty-three hundred Russian missiles took off the moment the first Unistat missile entered Russian airspace. They all went to China. The Russian computer had also been programmed by very dogmatic, very inflexible primates; it "knew" that any nuclear attack would come from China.

Starhawk was coming out of a bar on Geary when Frisco went. He was incinerated before his brain could register that anything was happening.

Lionel Eacher, long since returned to Contract Law, out-lived the blast. He had been on vacation in Upper Michigan and was well armed, since he had been hunting. He sur-vived by hunting and eating other mammals, including formerly domesticated primates, for nearly twenty years.

Then another formerly domesticated primate, even quicker and slicker, hunted and ate Lionel.

Markoff Chaney also survived. He was on a Greyhound in Florida, between Miami and Hollywood, when the bombs went off. He took to the Everglades and eventually even found a mate—a Seminole woman who didn't think he was absurd at all.

Their tribe increased.

The tribal stage endured 100,000 years, as it had before.

Then, suddenly, when environmental conditions were right, genetic programs reasserted themselves. The hive instinct reappeared in the primates. Cities appeared, sin and guilt were reinvented, technology advanced.

Nuclear energy was rediscovered, and misused again.

The tribal age endured 12,000,000 years the next time.

Then, suddenly, when environmental conditions were right, genetic programs reasserted themselves. The hive instinct reappeared in the primates. Cities appeared, sin and guilt were reinvented, technology advanced. . . .

The six-legged majority knew little and cared less about all this primate activity. They had solved all their social problems three billion years earlier, and saw no need to change. They followed their own DNA cycles, just as monotonously as the primates followed primate cycles.

PART ONE
THE UNIVERSE NEXT DOOR

We doctors know
a hopeless case when—listen; there's a hell
of a good universe next door; let's go
—E. E. CUMMINGS, "pity this
busy monster, manunkind"

TO CROSS AGAIN

The influence of the senses have in men overpowered the thought to the degree that the walls of time and space have come to look solid; real and insurmountable. . . . Yet time and space are but inverse measures of the power of the mind. Man is capable of abolishing them both.

—RALPH WALDO EMERSON

Mary Margaret Wildeblood had been born or reborn in November 1983 in Johns Hopkins Hospital. The very first sound she heard was a radio in the next ward playing:

God rest ye merry gentlemen
Let nothing you dismay

Localization was gradually determined: this universe, this galaxy, this solar system, this planet, this hospital. They were sawing off his penis.

Yes indisputably no doubt about it they were sawing off his penis. Seven dwarfs with evil grins were doing it. Then coming all the way out of the ether, this hospital, this bed, this morning in November 1983, Epicene Wildeblood knew at last who SHe really was. The radio sang cheerfully:

85

Remember Christ our Savior
Was born upon this day

SHe was still giddy from the ether, but that would pass; meanwhile the Voice of Dream was still talking, a fussy old professor lecturing: "One quantum jump away the ideal pretence is Real Presence. An S-T transformation. The English language limerick is restricted so that a cross carried up a hill is anisogamous but the essence remains the Body and Blood of the first amoeba. Consider the following example which some consider Donne and others describe as overdone:

> *Quoth a merrie old judge named Magoo*
> *'Perversions? Yea, I've tried a few*
> *But the best I e'er balled*
> *Were Lee Harvey Oswald*
> *Seven dwarfs and a pink cockatoo!'*

"It doesn't scan," Wildeblood protested feebly.

A gay swish of starched cloth moved queerly and a nurse's bland blond face appeared looking down at hir. "Anything the matter, dearie?" in a Brooklyn accent.

"What day is it?"

"Wednesday. Still Wednesday." The nurse spoke, as they always do after surgery, as if talking to an idiot.

The doctor recrossed on his peg leg (but that was slipping back into the dream again).

"Circumcision is a Jewish conspiracy. He bit it off, one great CHOMP! ! !—and off it came," Dr. Ahab was ranting. "I am the feet's lieutenant. Sprechen Sie Joysbrick?"

A dangling "e" fell past from another book.

They were opening the curtains to let in sunlight. The

white wall was a hospital wall. A hand at his wrist told hir
that now her pulse was being taken.

Epicene Wildeblood awakened again. "I'm Mary Margaret," he gasped happily, beached on the shore of reality, cast up from the ocean of dream.

"Yes," said the real doctor's voice (his name was
Glopberger, not Ahab), "the operation was um 100 percent successful. You are most certainly Mary Margaret
now." He beamed, an artist proud of his work, yet tentative, waiting for the Work's first live movement.

Mary Margaret Wildeblood looked about her at the
New World. This is Johns Hopkins Hospital. This is 1983.
Everything that went before was just a nightmare. I am
alive. I am me. I am free.

"How soon do I get the Curse?" she cried. "When do I
become a *real* woman?" Thinking: the Blood of the Lamb.

Glopberger's pink face, agape, was yet another Disney
caricature, the waters of unconsciousness calling hir home.
Home: back to the stars. And SHe went, she went, into
the great ether drift, into the cosmic void again, from
dina shaur to turban bay in a michaelsonmorley regurgita-
tion to the Hawkfouledest Convention in Elveron. Yes a
forty-four-year-old male rising like Venus on fours out of
the waves but aglow gleaming as in Botticelli: hir Self
surprised at this astonishingly female body a really successful crossing and one hand crept as she slept toward the
crypt rested there happy yes: it was true. A female body.
She snored hoarsely.

And Dr. Glopberger, like Baron Frankenstein, looked
on his work and saw that it was very good. So far.

MURPHY'S RELIGIOUS

I still recall vividly the shock I experienced on first encountering this multiworld concept. The idea of $10^{100}+$ slightly imperfect copies of oneself all constantly splitting into further copies . . . is not easy to reconcile with comon sense.

—BRYCE S. DEWITT "QUANTUM MECHANICS AND REALITY." *Physics Today* September, 1970

They were sitting in a VW Rabbit on Market Street in San Francisco. The marquee across the street still said DEEP THROAT after twelve years. "They never going to change that?" Starhawk asked. "Everybody and his brother been there to see that Linda Lovelace swallow peckers by now. Hell, everybody and his brother been there twice by now."

"She could swallow my pecker anytime," Mendoza said. Mendoza was a cop.

"I seen a funny one the other day," Starhawk said, starting to laugh. "In the men's crapper in the archaeology building. 'Linda Lovelace for President,' it said. 'Let's have a *good-looking* cocksucker in the White House.' College kids."

"They're all a bunch of fags these days," Mendoza told him seriously. "Fags and dopers. And they call us pigs. Anyway, what were you doing in the archaeology building?"

"I like to study my people's history," Starhawk said. "There a law against that?"

"The fuck," Mendoza said, "I don't care what you do on your spare time. You make out with those college girls? Don't tell me, I know. You make out like a bandit. You're the greatest thing come down the pike since Burt Reynolds, you are."

Starhawk started to clean his nails with an attachment on his key ring.

"Tell me about the coke."

"Murph owns more guns than the army got, up in Presidio. He's a real nut on guns. I mean, it's your ass he catches you. He won't think twice about it. A police officer catching a burglar in his own house, it's your ass. You got to understand that."

"*Dig*," Starhawk said. "It's always my ass. You think there's a crib worth knocking over they don't have guns these days? Christ, there's never been a better-armed country since we had the Revolution, is what it is. Even little old ladies. Even in Berkeley for Christ's sake. This is no business for anybody got shaky nerves, these days. College professors, their houses are stacked with enough munitions for Black Panther headquarters. What I don't understand is how come everybody in the fucking country hasn't been at least wounded by now. Everybody's even more crazy-mad than they are shit-scared. It's like *High Noon*. You don't have to tell me, be careful. I wasn't careful, I'd be one dead Indian."

"Son of a bitch," Mendoza said suddenly, sitting up.

Starhawk was almost startled. "Huh?"

"That dog," Mendoza said. "You see that son of a bitch shit right on the sidewalk? They do that all over the city, the ordinance doesn't mean a fucking thing. Dirty, filthy animals, I'd ban them from the fucking city entirely, I was mayor."

"Yeah," Starhawk said. "That's our chief problem here, dogs shitting on the street."

"It ain't funny," Mendoza said. "Filthy bastards spread all kinds of diseases. And you take your kid out for a walk and there's two of them humping and the kid says, 'Daddy, what are the doggies doing?' What are you gonna tell her, is what I wanna know. Dirty, filthy animals."

"Yeah, but about Murphy and this job."

"Okay, okay," Mendoza said. "I'm just telling you dirty filthy animals should be banned. With Murph you got to be in and out as slick and sneaky as a preacher's prick in a cow's ass. I mean, he likes guns, more than most cops. And he'd love an excuse to shoot you."

"Murphy?" Starhawk turned in his seat. "Murph and I, we never had any bad feelings."

"Well, okay, he loves the ground you walk on. Like all the hookers on Powell Street, and the housewives up in Marin, and the college girls now too. But he hates what you are. He hates all minorities—Indians, niggers, it don't matter to him, he's democratic about it. The fuck, he doesn't like me much, and we been partners going on ten years this May. And he hates burglars especially. An Indian burglar, that's almost as good to him as a nigger burglar. You got to realize that when you go in there."

"That's a hot one," Starhawk said, not laughing. "That really is a hot one. All the stuff he's fenced for me, and he hates burglars. That really is good. Next thing you'll tell me is the Vice Squad hates hookers."

"Murphy's religious," Mendoza said. "He'd love to make holes in you. That's what you got to understand."

"Support your local police," Starhawk said, "for a more efficient police state."

"Look, you on this caper or you just going to sit here and crack wise? I can get Marty Malloy, you know."

"You're religious too," Starhawk said. "I went and made fun of the department and now you're going to get Malloy. Who'll fuck up the whole job and you'll both be up in Q for the next twenty years. But at least he won't crack wise about the department. He'll leave fingerprints all over the joint, and drop the snow in the bushes on his way out, and crash into an Oakland P.D. car going home, and then lead them right to your front door, but he's got proper respect for the police, Malloy. Yeah, you get Malloy."

"Look, no need to be touchy." Mendoza was ingratiating. "I want you, I don't want Malloy. Just lay off the department, is all."

"Okay, okay. No need for either of us to get antsy." Starhawk smiled like an actor. "How much coke you think?"

"Like I say, who knows? But it's got to be around 500 Gs. That's what Amato says and he's good at making estimates like that. Say Amato is wrong for once in his life, say it's only 300 Gs, still you don't get half of 300 Gs every night you go out and knock over a house."

"It's beautiful," Starhawk said. "It's so beautiful it stinks. A cop with a couple hundred thou in hot cocaine, all I got to do is walk in and walk out, he'll never report it to anyone. That's just what bothers me. Murphy comes home and finds it gone, he's going to do something. Okay, he can't call the captain and say, 'Some thief just stole the cocaine I took from Freddy Fuckerfaster when I busted him, before I could sell it to Maldonado. Send over a squad car real quick.' That's what he don't do. So, okay, what does he do? You know him better than I do."

"He gets mad for a week, and anybody we bust better watch his ass or Murph will turn him over to wrecking crew. That's all. What the fuck can he do, you see? There's just nothing you can do when somebody snatches something you shouldn't have in the first place. Especially when you're a cop."

"There's me and Malloy," Starhawk said. "And five others Murph knows as well as me. And two I can think of that Murph doesn't know about yet. And maybe two that I

don't even know, let's say. That's let's see, about ten or
eleven guys who might have done it, afterwards. Ten or
eleven really good cat burglars in the Bay Area that Murphy will come looking for, one way or another."

"So? You had a day in the last five years somebody on
the force wasn't trying to put you away?" Mendoza grinned.
"Or you worried that Maldonado will think the coke's
already his and put the whole Cosa Nostra onto getting it
back? Balls. There's ten guys around here could do it, like
you say. And ten more might have come up from L.A.
and another ten from Vegas or Chicago or Christ knows
where. You go in as slick as you usually do, nobody'll ever
have a lead. Murphy'll have a purple hard-on for a week
or so, and I wouldn't want to be anybody he busts then,
but that's all that'll happen, all. You in or you out?"

"Wait. When's Murph's next day off?"

"Tomorrow. Why?"

"Some people," Starhawk said, "they had this kind of
merchandise, they'd hide it so you practically got to take
the walls down one by one before you find it. You know?
Case like that, you want to save yourself some time, you
watch until they show you where it is."

"Hey, Murph's no dumbbell. You think you're the Invisible Man or something?"

"It's got to be tomorrow. Believe me, he'll never see
me, but I'll see him. You was to ask me, going in today
bare-ass, before I can case the house, would be the best
way to get my balls in a sling. For all I know, he's got a
friend staked out there for when he's at work. And I wait
till the day after tomorrow, when he's at work again, he
may have already sold it to Maldonado. Am I right or am I
right?"

"Jeez." Mendoza turned to look straight at Starhawk.
"You going in there, with Murph at home, I don't like
that at all. What I don't want is somebody gets dead, him

or you. That happens, my ass is grass and the whole department is the lawn mower."

"Anybody in the department ever link me to a killing? Even suspect me? You know better than that, Mendy. I don't go in bare-ass, you know. Already, I got three plans."

"Then you're really in."

"Oh, I'm in." Starhawk stopped cleaning his nails and returned the key to the ignition. "I wouldn't miss it for the world. The only thing I like better than stealing from a cop is fucking a cop."

"Funny," Mendoza said. "Remind me to laugh on my day off. That attitude is going to get you in a lot of trouble some fine day, my friend."

THE FIRST FURBISH LOUSEWART

You must take the bull by the tail and look the facts in the face.
—W. C. FIELDS

The first Furbish Lousewart was a retainer on the Greystoke estate in England in the thirteenth century. He was a foundling, the bastard offspring of the local curate and a nun who, oddly enough, later told Chaucer a story he considered good enough to retell in verse. The nun was also the model for the Prioress in the earliest Tarot deck and her basic features remained even after that card became the Female Pope and, later, the High Priestess.

Lord Greystoke named the infant Furbish Lousewart because he looked so dainty when they found him in the manger. Furbish Lousewart was as dainty a name as you could have in Merrie England in those days, being the vernacular term for *herba pedicularis,* a most lovely flower of the snapdragon species.

Furbish Lousewart grew to manhood, married, fathered three legitimate children and died in the Third Crusade. One of his illegitimate children, by Lady Greystoke, was the only Greystoke to survive that Crusade and carried on the Greystoke line, unknown to his brothers and sisters, who continued the plebeian line of Lousewarts.

NOTHING

Everyone who is a lawyer must either be mentally defective by nature or be bound to become so in time.

    —FURBISH LOUSEWART V, *Unsafe Wherever You Go*

And Dr. Glopberger, like Frankenstein, looked on his work and saw that it was very good. So far.

But the nurse, Ms. Ida Pingala, returning along the long white hall permeated with Lysol to the snug white cubicle of the nurses' lounge, seated herself smoothing the starched white hem of her skirt over her pale white knees and punched numbers quick and neat on the phone console, white keys on white plastic the colorless allcolor of antiseptic sterility.

"Ubu, here," came the Voice in her ear.

"Roy. It's Ida." Ms. Pingala was equally crisp.

Sounds of canine panting; Roy was always a cut-up.

Ms. Pingala laughed merrily. "Tonight?" she asked.

Sounds of louder, more passionate panting.

She giggled again. "Your place or mine?"

"Yours. You know how the Bureau is. . . ."

"Eightish?"

"Nineish, to be on the safe side. All hell is breaking loose again."

"Nineish, then. You devil."

More panting.

"Oh you devil you wild man you animal."

"Nineish gotto go now love you bye."

Roy Ubu, in Washington,* hangs up and glances at his wristwatch. Time for the meeting with Babbit.

A listless Santa Claus dingdonging his bell with empty junkie eyes as light snow fell in sparse crystals, not sticking to the sidewalk, but a biting Washington wind stings Ubu's eyes as he leaves the FBI office, turning up his collar to slouch hands deep in pocket to his car. Shifting from first gear into second turning up Pennsylvania Avenue the snowflakes growing thicker and heavier as he drives, snaps on the car radio.

and so the second black uprising in Miami has ended in flame and tragedy. In Washington, President Lousewart

---

Terran Archives 2803: Washington was the capital city of Unistat. It was governed ostensibly by a baseball team called the Senators, but by the time of our story real control had fallen into the hands of the FBI and the Beast.

*is meeting this morning with the Stentorian Ambassa-
dor to discuss balance of payments amid a mood of
cautious optimism. Parents in Bad Ass, Texas, continue
to keep their children out of school in the bitter dispute
over biofeedback training. School Superintendent B. S.
Curve, still hospitalized from the bomb blast which
destroyed*

Ubu parks carefully with neat precision flashing his ID
at the Secret Service man to be passed quickly into the
White House over thick carpets under brilliant chande-
liers to the office of Mountbatten Babbit, scientific advisor
to the President: a bald and ovoid head with impatiently
piercing eyes that scanned for the exact measurement and
the precisely calibrated number.

"This ah is a very delicate matter," Babbit began at
once. "We give it an Urgent rating but at the same time
we do not wish to alarm the public you understand the
whole investigation must be carried on with kid gloves as
they say The President Himself has instructed me to make
it clear to you, to make it *absolutely clear,* that no leaks
will be tolerated no leaks *whatsoever* or a very big ax will
fall on the whole Bureau a *very* big ax have I made myself
clear?"

"Yes sir absolutely sir."

"Good. Now, have you noticed a certain ah a certain
decline in American science and technology in recent
years a withering away of talent and originality so to
speak?"

"Well sir law is my background you know sir I wouldn't
know a test tube from a bevatron sir. . . ."

"The decline has been accelerating and is becoming
critical in some respects, *critical.*"

"Yes sir but so what sir a lot of science is classified as
non-ec and not very popular with the Administration."

Babbit's eyes were scanning Ubu without warmth. "You think it is possible to draw a hard line a sharp boundary between ec science and non-ec science?"

"Well of course sir President Lousewart himself is always saying . . ."

"I'm not talking about Administration rhetoric Mr. Ubu I am talking about reality. Could you draw such a line and say this is ec research and this is non-ec?"

"Well sir I don't get involved in politics I investigate and find out the facts and that's my job sir administrative decisions are not our business at the Bureau."

"There is no difference between ec and non-ec science," Babbit said with icy deliberation. "I will never say that in public as long as I am part of the Administration you understand the President has a right to expect loyalty from Members of the Team of course but I tell you in private ec and non-ec are terms in theology in metaphysics in value judgment, *they have nothing to do with science.* It's all as absurd as saying some research is chocolate and some is vanilla and the chocolate is better than the vanilla."

"Yes sir I understand you sir you have my word I'll never repeat any of this sir."

"Good now officially the Administration only wishes to discourage non-ec science but in fact we are suffering a drastic a dangerous possibly a *lethal* decline in all science right across the board . . ."

"But sir isn't that what President Lousewart stands for? Tightening our belts, the simple rugged life of our pioneer ancestors, lowered expectations . . ."

"You damned fool we're not talking about political speeches we're talking about the realities of *survival*."

"Uh yes sir yes."

"Survival dammit *survival*."

But quantumly inseparable from Ubu nurse Ida Pingala peeks into the Wildeblood room to see if the patient is sleeping comfortably (*always got to be careful with these rich bitches especially the types we get here in Transsexuality Surgery rather be back in obs so helpless and adorable they are even if some of the mothers shouldn't be raising kittens much less humans*) and leans fixing the hem on her skirt as the figure in the bed gurgles a half-snore mutter "Master . . . escape . . ."

Another quantum jump:

"One hundred thirty-two?" Ubu repeated.

"Those are the figures that came out of the Beast," Babbit said evenly. "One hundred thirty-two of the top scientific minds who've left government since the ec programs were implemented are not working for private industry, teaching at universities, or anywhere else to be found."

SEX, STATUS, SUCCESS

It may have been coincidence or synchronicity or the quantum inseparability principle (QUIP), but the very same day that Epicene Wildeblood became Mary Margaret Wildeblood in Baltimore and Babbit briefed Roy Ubu on the Brain Drain mystery in Washington, Blake Williams was teaching a class at Columbia and Hugo de Naranja was a student in it. Since Hugo was the first human being who ever saw the Cat, he should have been paying close attention to Williams, but in fact he was a poet and felt it his duty to be bored by all the sciences. Hugo would settle for a gentleman's C in "The Anthropology of Quantum Physics." Hugo was a *Santaria* initiate, the third ex-husband of Carol Christmas, and (although he didn't know it) he worked for Hassan i Sabbah X.

"It wasn't Einstein," Williams was droning along, "and it wasn't even Heisenberg or dear old Schrödinger who drove the last nail in the coffin of common sense. It was John S. Bell, who published his memorable Theorem in 1964, nearly twenty years ago," and blah blah blah. Hugo was more interested in the ass of the girl in the row ahead of him. He wanted both his hands on that ass. He wanted her thighs around his waist. He wanted his cock way up inside her hot White Protestant pussy. Screwing Latino girls rated 0 in his book (that was only sex), screwing Jewish girls was 5 (that was Status), but screwing a White Protestant girl was 10 points and a gold star (that was SUCCESS).

Williams continues to transmit to blank bored faces:

"Bell's Theorem basically deals with nonlocality. That is, it shows that no local explanation can account for the known facts of quantum mechanics. Um perhaps I should clarify that. A local explanation is one that assumes that things seemingly separate in space and time are really separate. Um? Yes. It assumes, that is to say, that space and time are independent of our primate nervous systems. Do I have your attention, class?

"But Bell is even more revolutionary. He offers us two choices if we try to keep locality, and if there are any students in this class who are seriously interested in the subject this would be a good time to take a few notes. Um. First choice: we can abandon quantum mechanics itself. That of course means inescapably that we abandon atomic physics and about three-quarters of everything we call science. Um. Now we really don't want to give up quantum mechanics so let's look at choice two. We give up objectivity. Well, that's not too great a sacrifice for those of us who have already given up sweets and male superiority and ha ha faith in the integrity of government or even cigarettes. We can give up objectivity. Ahhh yes but the trouble is . . . Yes Mr. Naranja?"

"Ees this goan be on the examination sir?"

"No you needn't worry about that Mr. Naranja we wouldn't dream of asking anything hard on the examination I believe the last examination with a hard question given at this university was in a survey of mathematics course in 1953 yes Mr. Lee?"

"Is possibre that quantum connection is not immediate and unmitigated? Then perhaps we take choice one and give up not quantum mechanics itself but merely modify the quantum connection in a sense that it is some way sir mediate or mitigated, does that seem possibre sir?"

"Ah Mr. Lee how did you ever land at this university there are times I suspect you of actually seeking an education but I'm afraid in this case your canny intellect has run aground. Recent experiments by Clauser and Aspect shut that door forever. The quantum connection is immediate, unmitigated, and I might say omnipresent as the Thomist God."

"So. You tell us, Professor Williams, how many times Crauser's experiment has been verified?"

> *Jingle bells, jingle bells,*
> *Jingle all the way*

Rebirth, Wildeblood was deciding, is messier than first birth, despite old Augustine and his *media feces et urine* trip . . . how much he had wanted to be Annette Haven in the clusterfuck scene in *China Girl:* one cock in Her mouth, one in Her snatch, one in each hand: ah, Wildeblood, 'twere paradise enow. But the reality of it, the adjustments to be made:

Sit down when you want to pee
Sit down when you want to pee
Sit down when you want to pee

SHe was writing it out a hundred times, to avoid making *that* mistake again. Ego is much more a body image than she had known. Psychologically, she was androgynous WoMan, the Baphomet idol; physically, she had to sit down to pee.

Oh what fun it is to ride

But Roy Ubu, back at FBI headquarters, was already briefing a five-man team on the brain drain mystery.

"You mean," Special Agent Tobias Knight asked, "we're supposed to find 132 missing scientists without letting anybody know that there are 132 missing scientists we're looking for? Is that it?"

"The President Himself," Ubu pronounced in Babbit's frigid tones, "gives this project Top Priority."

"In other words, it's impossible but you want us to do it, anyway," Knight translated.

"Now that's enough defeatism, Toby, let's get to work and believe in ourselves and by Christ a busted flush can win when the guys behind it have the balls for it. . . . Now, here's the names in alphabetical order. One: Dr. George Washington Carver Bridge, sounds like a spade, graduate Miskatonic University; it says last worked for the government on Project Cyclops in the late seventies. Two: Dr. Charles Chance, nickname Fat, graduate Miskatonic, also last worked for the government on Cyclops. Three . . ."

THE SECOND FURBISH LOUSEWART

A man with one watch knows what time it is.
A man with two watches is never sure.

—SEGAL'S LAW

Percy Lousewart was born in the Ohio River Valley in 1866 and by then Lousewart was no longer considered a euphonious name. His Christian name didn't help, even though his mother had picked it due to her fervent, almost erotic, admiration for Shelley. She might as well have named the poor lad Cissy. Every time he introduced himself as Percy Lousewart, some bully or other felt compelled to make a witty remark, and a fight usually followed. Eventually poor Percy decided to change his name and went to see an educated man, a lawyer, about having the job done legally; he also wanted some advice on choosing a better, more popular title. The lawyer, alas, was more than erudite; he was a bibliomaniac, an alcoholic scholar, and the kind of crank who delights in writing letters to the *Britannica* correcting their errors. He told Percy all about the Furbish Lousewart plant and even showed him a picture of one. He was eloquent on the subject, and his passion was contagious. Percy Lousewart had his name changed only to Furbish Lousewart and took his lumps as they came. His first son was named Furbish Lousewart II and a tradition was begun.

MALLOY DON'T SING

The variables vary too much and the constants aren't as constant
as they seem.
—FINAGLE'S FIFTH FUNDAMENTAL FINDING

"The fuck," Malloy said. "Where you get an idea like
that? I don't sing, I never sing. Who's been handing you
that shit?"

It was a small furnished room on Taylor Street in the
San Francisco tenderloin. A sign outside the window advertised an establishment on the ground floor, *Les Nuits
de Paris Massage*.

Starhawk said, "Marty, I know three guys up in Folsom
because of you. They're not sure. Each one of them, he
says it might of been you, it might of been two other guys.
I'm sure. I make it a point of honor to be sure about
things like that. You pick up $20 here from Mendoza, $15
there from Murphy, and you tell them what you think
they want to hear, mostly crap. To keep them interested,
you give them a live one now and then, somebody you
don't like. You and twenty other guys in this town. Don't
crap me, Marty. I'm here to make money for you, not to
give you a hard time about it."

Malloy said, "You're crazy. You should go see a psychiatrist. You must of been back on the reservation eating peyote
again. I don't know what the fuck you're talking about."

103

"Okay," Starhawk said. "You're smart, Marty. You're so damned smart you don't admit anything, even when the other guy knows more about it than you do. My ass. You're so damned smart you're stupid, is what you are."

Malloy started to get up.

"Sit down," Starhawk said. "I keep telling you, I'm not here to give you a hard time. Listen to me, Marty, just a minute. I've got a century that's not doing anything, and it's yours." He opened his wallet and laid a $100 bill on the table. "Now, do we talk about its four brothers, and what you do to get them, or do you go on shitting me until I go out the door and find another guy that talks to cops?"

The massage sign below the window flickered on-off, on-off.

"Suppose I do it," Malloy said. "I mean, I'm not admitting anything, but suppose just this once I go talk to The Murph. What I got to know is, whose ass is in the sling, who goes up? You understand, I don't want somebody comes looking for me from the Syndicate."

"Nobody goes up, that's the beauty of it," Starhawk said. "You're just going to tell Murph about a guy got in today from L.A. He's here to do a job for Maldonado, see, and he got drunk and started shooting off his mouth about how funny it was, the guy he came to do the job on is a cop."

"Jesus," Malloy said. The massage sign flickered off and on again. "Don't tell me, let me guess. Starhawk, the man of bronze, two balls of cast iron and no more brains than a hamster. You got it in your head it's cop-hunting season and you're going to shoot one of them. And they trust good old Marty Malloy so much they'll spend all their time looking for an imaginary hit man from L.A., just because good old Marty tells them so. I take it all back. You don't need a psychiatrist, you need a new brain."

"Don't get your bowels in an uproar," Starhawk said. "It's not that kind of job. It's just a heist."

"What's this cop got, somebody comes all the way from L.A. to heist it? The crown jewels?"

Starhawk raised his fingers to his nose and made a sniffing motion.

"Jesus, Mary, and Joseph," Malloy said. "This cop, what he's got is a bag of snow, so he won't be talking to anybody else in the department when it turns up missing. I got to hand it to you, kid. Nobody could have set this up for you but another cop. The fuck, it would have to be his partner. Who's pissed because he didn't get his half, right?"

"Don't think about that, you might get so excited you'll talk about it in your sleep. The thing is, you just got to tell Murph about this Syndicate gun from L.A. and how funny he thinks it is, that this crooked cop is trying to sell some hot snow to Maldonado's boys and they just went and brought up this gorilla to take it from him, no down payment, no monthly installments, for free."

Malloy was grinning broadly. "Murph'll shit," he said. "He'll absolutely shit a brick."

"Yeah," Starhawk said. "I kind of think he will. You like it?"

"Kiddo," Malloy said, "if I wasn't so broke this week, I'd do it free. Just to watch him trying not to look like the cop I'm telling him about. The fat prick."

"I sort of figured you'd like it," Starhawk said. "Me, the only thing I regret is I can't be there to see his face myself."

"Yeah," Malloy said. "The fat prick."

IS VLAD A SYMBOL?

A class made up solely of intellectuals will always have a guilty conscience.

—FURBISH LOUSEWART V, *Unsafe Wherever You Go*

"Defection?" Ubu suggested at the second conference on the Brain Drain. "Russia or China . . ."

"The CIA was the first agency into this," Babbit said, "and they say it's impossible. They know what color drawers every commissar wears these days with the latest surveillance techniques. One hundred thirty-two top American scientists are not working over there unknown to the CIA. Take that as axiomatic." Babbit was firm.

"Well there are only twelve people in HOME. . . ."

"They haven't left the planet," Babbit said briefly. "People of that caliber do not travel about without somebody noticing—Intelligence, newspapers, TV, other scientists, *somebody*. It is as if they have crawled into a hole and dragged the ground in after them." His chair creaked screeee as he leaned forward for emphasis.

"Hell, they're not loose *inside* the country sir," Ubu said firmly. "Americans can't just disappear these days. Why to cash a check any kind of check you've got to write *both* your Social Security number and your GWB number and have them both scanned by the Beast. Sir there's never been a people better watched and protected than the

106

American people of November 1983. And we expect to do
even better sir when the new circuits are put in the Beast
next month."

He's gonna find out who's naughty or nice

But the snow falls thicker, making a blanket of foam
against the window of Babbit's office and piles against the
door of The Upstart Crow bookstore off Dupont Circle
across town, where Marvin Gardens is autographing copies of *Vlad Victorious*.

"I never got a real live autograph from a real live author
Mr. Gardens tell me why did you write two books about a
man like Vlad?"

"To make money," Marvin said in his Peter Lorre
cokehead voice. He had prepared for the ordeal of the
seventeenth autograph party in twenty-three days by snort-
ing more than his usual morning quantity of the snow and
was in no mood to conceal his divinity from the blind
uncoked Earthlings. "I have always been possessed by a
mad, passionate, almost *erotic* desire for a very large bank
account. In fact, I love the *feel* of money the crisp *crinkle*
of bills the metal *solidity* of coin the visual impact of a
large check with *seven figures*."

"Is it true John Wayne will play Vlad again in the
sequel?"

"That's just in the talking stage now and frankly I don't
care if they cast Raquel Welch the important thing is *cash
on the barrelhead* my agent is asking a million for the
screen rights and we won't settle for a penny less . . .
Yes?"

"Is Vlad really a symbol?"

O come let us adore Him
O come let us adore Him

The twelve people in HOME—High Orbital Mini-Earth—were construction engineers, six male and six female. They had originally been sent there to build, with materials shipped from Lunar Mining, HOME II, a space village for 10,000 occupants. This program had been canceled as "non-ec" by President Lousewart and the twelve colonists restricted to "ec" research, mostly astronomical, which President Lousewart turned over to his astrologers for a mystical interpretation.

HOME was located in the area called Libration Point 5, where the gravitational fields of Luna and Terra were equally balanced. This null-gravity area had been mathematically discovered by the astronomer Lagrange and was therefore sometimes called the Lagrange Area. The name for the space town, HOME, had been coined by psychologist Timothy Leary in 1977.

A friend of Leary's named Robert Anton Wilson, who wrote overly complicated novels, had suggested a team song for the colonists, "HOME on Lagrange." To popularize this idea, he had written letters about it to many space research groups and included it in a novel called *The Trick Top Hat*. Still, by 1984, the song hadn't caught on with the twelve colonists. They were not at home on Lagrange because they feared that the whole project would soon be classified as "non-ec" and they would be dragged back to the womb-planet.

ULYSSES AT HOME

My dog understands perfectly everything I say to him.
I am the one who does not understand.
            —FURBISH LOUSEWART V, *Unsafe Wherever You Go*

Mary Margaret Wildeblood's parties were the place to go
that winter because of the penile adornment above the
mantelpiece. Some even began to suspect that Wildeblood
had undergone the transsex operation only to engage in
the most flagrant excess of exhibitionism in world history.

This was an uncharitable oversimplification. Wildeblood's
mind was vast, not simple, and had more kinks than a
Pollack painting; SHe was not deep, but wide and complex. SHe actually intended to become a nun. When SHe
quoted from the gospel of hir youth, "Humility is endless," SHe really meant it. Submission was salvation; and
who is more submissive than a nun? Above all, SHe
longed to embrace the Lamb, all woolly and fleecy and
pure, but very definitely horned and Ram-signed with
Pentecostal fire. SHe had the hots for Divine intercourse.
Where Natalie Drest was merely cock-mad, Mary Margaret Wildeblood was possessed by the god Priapus.

The idea of mounting and, so to speak, enshrining
Ulysses occurred to Mary Margaret at her very first reception after returning from Johns Hopkins.

Benny "Eggs" Benedict started it by suggesting, "Norman Mailer might try to get revenge for some of your reviews by raping you."

"Let the male chauvinist pig try it,' Mary Margaret said demurely. "I've been studying kung fu."

"Oh, are you planning to join Women's Lib?" Justin Case inquired.

"I have given it some thought," Mary Margaret replied, practicing her new simpery-Marilyn-Monroe smile and positively reveling in the feel of the nylons on his, no dammit her, thighs.

"JUST A GODDAM MINUTE," a booming masculine voice cut in. This was Josephine Malik, chairperson of God's Lightning—an outfit long suspected of terrorist fire-bombings against porny movie houses, adult bookstores, and other sexist enterprises. Jo was an ideological descendant of those who thought copulation was bad for the crops. "I don't know about lib-lab wishy-washy groups like NOW," she went on, "but God's Lightning certainly isn't accepting any members who weren't *born* female."

"Oh, now," a fluty feminine voice intervened—"Figs" Newton, spokesperson for the Necrophile Liberation Front, sporting a lapel button that said, OUT OF THE MAUSOLEUMS, INTO THE STREETS. "That's hardly fair," he pronounced—like most Terrestrials, he regarded himself as an expert on morality. "People are what they make themselves," he said, good Existentialist that he was. "To hold the accidents of birth against them is practically *racism*, isn't it?"

This led to some lively debate, and it was finally decided that to hold the accident of genitalia-at-birth against somebody was definitely not *racism*, but might be *sexism*, or possibly *genderism*. Josephine Malik, meanwhile, smoldered.

"Well," she said finally, "God's Lightning is not influenced by all this *baroque* civil rights and civil liberties horseshit out of the eighteenth century. According to semantics, people don't *have* rights; they just make demands and call them their rights. It's purely a pragmatic problem. If we let this—*person*—in, what's to prevent other men from hacking off their prongs, infiltrating our ranks, and subverting our whole organization?"

This was a poser, admittedly; and while the assembled company grappled with it, Josephine delivered her crusher: "Besides, there's a lot of doubt about how complete these operations are. How do we know Ms. Wildeblood is in all respects a true woman and not just a truncated man?"

Mary Margaret Wildeblood, who had a mind somewhat bizarre even for the twentieth century, had been waiting for such an opportunity. "I can certainly prove I'm not a man," she smiled sweetly, and drew Ulysses out of her purse. Although two men fainted on the spot, the women merely blinked, at least at first. Then some of them began to titter.

Thus began the great Wildeblood *scandale* of that winter. She had maliciously saved the relic of her previous masculinity with the thought that it might provoke some sort of spontaneous Group Encounter sessions, and now she knew she had the potential for some truly memorable Freak-outs. The relic was placed in the hands of a skilled taxidermist and soon emerged, in a natural-looking erect state, handsomely mounted on a redwood plaque. This hung over the mantelpiece of her posh Sutton Place apartment, and there she began to hold parties to which were invited (along with the usual New York VIPs) precisely those persons most likely to be neurologically galvanized by the sight of a penis without a man, which is considerably more memorable than mathematician Dodgson's grin without a cat, although perhaps not as memorable as physicist Schrödinger's cat, who was dead and alive at the same time.

Blake Williams became a regular at these *soirées*, and often retired sneakily to the kitchen to make notes, which later resulted in a scholarly article, "Priapism Recrudescent: Hellenic Religion in a Secular Context." The "ithyphallic eidolon," as he insisted on calling Ms. Wildeblood's obscene joke, seemed to produce markedly different effects on various personality types. One football player, for instance, had to be removed in a straitjacket. Strangely enough, certain shy, timid, and stoop-shouldered men took it all in their stride, quite as if Wildeblood's brutally explicit rejection of masculinity reinforced their own loose grip upon that (after all) somewhat mystical estate. The Gay set developed a superstition, almost a *mystique*, and the tradition of "kissing it for good luck" was even joked about, obscurely, in certain newspaper columns. ("A new religion, of which Linda Lovelace might almost be the prophet, is now sweeping the Way-Out People, all the way from Fifty-seventh Street to St. Mark's Place.")

WHY?

Why me, O Lord?

—ANCIENT PRIMATE QUESTION

"I said FUCK THE BLOODY CAPITALISTS," the California writer was howling amid the group at the mantelpiece, below the ithyphallic eidolon.

"Mother very easily made a jam sandwich using no

peanuts, mayonnaise, or glue," Blake Williams was reciting patiently to Natalie Drest.

"TV, publishing, movies, everywhere—the extraterrestrials have *taken over*," Marvin Gardens was warning in his passionate Peter Lorre intonation.

Benny Benedict suddenly had enough of the Wildeblood high-IQ set. He wandered out on the balcony, to look at the stars and wonder, half-drunkenly, why he was so depressed.

After three years the question still came to him when he had too much booze aboard: *Why me?*

Which was selfish and maudlin. The real question should be: *Why my mother?*

Or, more to the point: *Why anybody?*

The world must be mad, that we go on living like this, and tolerate it. The primordial jungles were probably less dangerous than the streets of any city in Unistat. Was this the resultant of the long struggle upward from the caves—a world more frightening, more full of hatred and violence, more bloody than the days of the saber-tooth?

Every time I look at the TV news at seven, he thought miserably, I end up feeling this way before midnight. It's almost as if they're afraid somebody might have a flicker of hope or a good opinion of humanity (at least in potential) or a brief moment of delusory security. Every night, to prevent such unrealistic moods, they have to remind us that the violence and brutality is still continuing.

With a shock, Benny discovered that he was weeping again, silently, guiltily, privately. He had thought he was past that.

So much for booze as a tranquilizer.

He fought against it. It was self-indulgence, disguised self-pity actually. He dabbed his eyes and tried to think of something else. *Om mani padme hum, Om mani padme hum . . .*

"Nice night." An Unidentified Man had walked out onto the balcony.

"You don't feel the smog up here," Benny said, embarrassed, wondering if he had gotten rid of the last tear before this stranger had seen him.

The Unidentified Man looked up at the stars, smiling slightly. He was good-looking enough to be an actor, Benny thought, and at second glance he did look remotely familiar, as if his face had been in the newspapers sometime. "The stars," he said, "don't they get to you?"

Benny looked up. "I used to think I'd live to see people go there," he confessed, suddenly sure he had met this man somewhere before, a long time ago. "Not likely with Lousewart leading us back to the Stone Age."

"You're non-ec," the man said, in mock accusation.

"Guilty," Benny replied, realizing that this man was remarkably easy to talk to. "I think that if we used more of our brains, we'd be able to create a world where people would have a right to High Expectations."

"Hopelessly reactionary," the man said, grinning. "You probably still read science fiction."

"Guilty again," Benny said.

"Suppose I were an extraterrestrial," the man said quietly. "Suppose I were several million years ahead of this planet. What one question would you ask me?"

"Why is there so much violence and hatred among us?" Benny asked at once.

"It's always that way on primitive planets," the man said. "The early stages of evolution are never pretty."

"Do planets grow up?" Benny asked.

"Some of them," the man said simply.

"How?"

"Through suffering enough, they learn wisdom."

Benny turned and looked at his odd companion. He *is*

an actor, he thought. "Through suffering," he repeated. "There's no other way?"

"Not in the primitive stages," the man said. "Primitives are too self-centered to ask the important questions, until suffering forces them to ask."

Benny felt the grief pass through him again, and leave. He grinned. "You play this game very well."

"Anybody can do it," the man said. "It's a gimmick, to get outside your usual mind-set. You can do it too. Just try for a minute—you be the advanced intelligence, and I'll be the primitive Terran. Okay?"

"Sure," Benny said, enjoying this.

"*Why me?*" The stranger's tone was intense. "Why have I been singled out for so much injustice and pain?"

"There is no known answer to that," Benny said at once. "Some say it's just chance—hazard—statistics. Some say there is a Plan, and that you were chosen to learn an important lesson. Nobody knows, really. The important thing is to ask the next question."

"And what is the next question?"

Benny felt as if this was easy. "The next question is, What do I do about it? How ever many minutes or hours or years or decades I have left, what do I do to make sense out of it all?"

"Hey, that's good," the stranger said. "You play Higher Intelligence very well."

"It's just a gimmick," Benny said, feeling as if a great weight had been taken off him.

They laughed.

"Where did you ever learn that?" Benny asked.

"From a book on Cabala," the man said. "It's a way of contacting the Holy Guardian Angel. But people don't relate to that metaphor these days, so I changed it to an extraterrestrial from an advanced civilization."

"Who are you? I keep feeling I've seen your face. . . ."

The man laughed. "I'm a stage magician," he said. "Cagliostro the Great."

"Are you sure you're not a real magician?" Benny asked.

SCHRÖDINGER THE MAN

Your theory is crazy, but it's not crazy enough to be true.
—NEILS BOHR, QUOTED BY BEYNAM,
Future Science

Erwin Schrödinger did a lot more than just make up mathematical riddles about fictitious cats. His equations describing subatomic wave mechanics, which earned him a Nobel Prize, were among the most important contributions to particle theory in our century. Later, he turned his attention to biophysics and in a small book called *What Is Life?* he offered the first mathematical definition of the difference between living and dead systems, throwing off as a side reflection the idea that life is negative entropy. This insight was to trigger quite a few new ideas in many of his readers, including Norbert Wiener of MIT and Claud Shannon of Bell Labs, who got so deep into negative entropy, due to Schrödinger, that they created mathematical information theory and laid the foundations of the science of cybernetics, resulting ultimately in the Beast.

Schrödinger didn't even believe in his own Cat riddle;

he had propounded it only to show that there must be
something wrong with quantum theory if it leads to conclusions like that. Schrödinger didn't like quantum theory
because it pictures an anarchist universe and he was a
determinist, like his good friend Albert Einstein. Thus,
even though he had helped to create quantum theory and
used it every day, Schrödinger kept hoping to find something seriously wrong with it.

The Cat problem presupposes a Cat, a device of lethal
nature, such as a gun or a poison-gas pellet, and a quantum process which will, eventually, trigger the weapon
and kill the Cat. Very simple. An experimenter, if he
wanted to find out when the device had fired and killed
the Cat, would look into the laboratory where all this was
transpiring and note what actually happened. But—Schrödinger points out with some glee—modern physics, if it's
all it's cracked up to be, should allow us to find out what is
happening without our actually going into the laboratory
to look. All we have to do is write down the equations of
the quantum process and calculate when the phase change
leading to detonation will occur. The trouble is that the
equations yield, at minimum, two solutions. At any given
time—say one half hour—the equations give us two quantum *eigen*values, one of which means that the Cat is now
definitely dead, *kaput, spurlos versenkt,* finished, and the
other which tells us that the Cat is still alive as you and
me.

> *I never died, said he;*
> *I never die, said he.*

Most physicists preferred to ignore Schrödinger's damned
Cat; quantum mechanics *worked*, after all, and why make
a big thing about something a little funny in the mathematics?
Einstein loved Schrödinger's Cat because it mathemati-

cally demonstrated his own conviction that subatomic events couldn't be as anarchistic as wave mechanics seemed to imply. Einstein was a Hidden Variable man. He claimed there *must* be a Hidden Variable—an Invisible Hand, as Adam Smith might have said—controlling the seemingly indeterminate quantum anarchy. Einstein was sure that the Hidden Variable was something quite deterministic and mechanical, which would be discovered eventually. "God does not play dice with the world," he liked to say.

Decade followed decade and the Hidden Variable remained elusive.

In the 1970s, Dr. Evan Harris Walker solved the Cat paradox (to his own satisfaction) and defined the Hidden Variable (to his own satisfaction). The Hidden Variable, he said, was consciousness. There was muttering in some quarters that Walker was smuggling pantheism into physics disguised as quantum psychology, but many younger physicists—especially the acid-heads—accepted the Walker solution.

Professor John Archibald Wheeler of Princeton found another way of dealing with the Cat; he took it literally. Every quantum indeterminacy, he proposed, creates *two* universes; thus, the equations are literally true and in one universe the Cat lives and in another universe the cat dies. We can only experience one universe at a time, of course, but if the math says the other universe is there, then by God it *is* there. Furthermore, since .5 probabilities occur continually—every time you toss a coin, for instance—there are many, many such universes, perhaps an infinite number of them. With two graduate students named Everett and Graham, Wheeler even worked up a model of where the other universes were. They were on all sides of us, in superspace.

Some were heard to suggest that old Wheeler had been reading too much science fiction.

TO CROSS AGAIN

If I offer a child the choice between a pear and a piece of meat, he'll immediately take the pear. That's his instinct speaking.
—FURBISH LOUSEWART V, *Unsafe Wherever You Go*

Mountbatten Babbit, being methodical in all things including his madness, could pinpoint exactly the date on which he had started sliding over the porous membrane separating the sane from the insane. It had been long, long ago—back in 1941, actually, in July, the twenty-third of the month, a Thursday.

Or perhaps it had actually started the night before, on the twenty-second. It was hard to say, actually, even though Babbit was a man who detested imprecision of any sort. Say it was the twenty-second, then, even though the overt symptom did not manifest until the twenty-third. We do want to be as accurate as possible when we're lost out here.

So say the twenty-second: Mountbatten was a freshman at Antioch College then and the Carter Brothers Carnival was playing in nearby Xenia. Mounty and some friends went over to have a look-see. Since Mounty personally didn't wait around for the post-midnight private exhibition of the lustful mulatto lady and the randy pony, advertised

119

by shills in the crowd, the high point of the show for him
had been the Mentalist, Cagliostro the Great.

A girl assistant, in as brief a costume as the carnival
could get away with back in nearly antediluvian 1941 and
barbaric Ohio, circulated through the audience, while
Cagliostro, youngish and handsome for this racket, sat
blindfolded on the stage.

"Now what am I holding?" she would ask when somebody handed her a watch.

"I get the image of a timepiece . . . yes, a wristwatch,"
the magician intoned.

"What do I have in my hand this time?" The answer was
a locket.

"Can you tell me what this object is?"

A wallet photo.

Driving back to Yellow Springs, the students fell into a
debate. One guy from the psychology department gave a
long spiel on Rhine and parapsychology and scientific data
for ESP, which convinced almost everyone. Babbit was
the exception. He was not only a chemistry major but a
leading firebrand for the Atheist Club on campus and he
knew damned well that ESP was pseudo-scientific balderdash and hocus-pocus.

He spent the next day, the twenty-third, in the library,
researching stage magic and, in a biography of Houdini,
he found the answer. A simple substitution code. *Now
what* = watch. *What do I have* = locket. *Can you tell* =
photo. And so forth. Fraud, pure and simple, like everything that goes under the name of religion or magic.

Sirius shone very bright that night in the southern sky
and Mounty Babbit was back at the carnival, loaded for
bear. When the girl approached his part of the audience,
he handed her a prized and illegal possession: a dragon-
headed Japanese condom.

"Tell me what I have been given by this person."

That wasn't in the Houdini code but neither was a condom, with or without a dragon head.

"It's against the law in this state," Cagliostro intoned somberly, causing heads to turn. "And I would advise the young gentleman from Antioch to restrain his sense of humor in the future."

And don't marry Suzie from Red Lion

The second voice was-and-yet-wasn't Cagliostro's.

Mounty took quite a riding from the other students on their way back to Yellow Springs that night. "How did he know you were young?" "How did he know you were from Antioch—where was that in the code?" "Christ, a condom—you coulda got us all arrested." But nobody said anything about Suzie from Red Lion, Pennsylvania. Mounty finally forced the issue. "What was that business about the lion?" he asked with maximum indirection.

It was as he had feared: nobody else had heard anything about a lion, or about Suzie.

It was simple logic, then. ESP is fraud. Hearing voices in your head is insanity. Mountbatten Babbit, he told himself, you are in need of psychiatric help.

But a psychiatric record would be a handicap in the career he already had mapped out for himself.

Self-control, then, was the answer. Nobody really goes bananas, after all, except weaklings.

A man like Mountbatten Babbit simply would not go mad.

But Mountbatten Babbit never did marry Suzie from Red Lion; there was a rather nasty war concluded with the exclamation point of a rather nasty bomb and then there was a marriage to a more suitably upward-mobile partner and eventually there was a title of Chief Engineer at Weishaupt Chemicals in Chicago. It was 1967 and he was no longer a brash young atheist-scientist but a middle-aged scientist-businessman who knew enough to keep his mouth shut about controversial issues and steadily feed a growing six-figure savings account. He had it made. If Cagliostro didn't keep getting in the newspapers for one shocking incident or another, Babbit might even have been able to forget the whole episode in which he had thought he might be going mad.

Then he crossed the boundary again.

A juvenile delinquent named Franklin Delano Roosevelt Stuart, from the black ghetto on the South Side, stole Mounty's car from in front of the Babbit residence in Rogers Park at precisely a moment when Mounty was looking out the window. In his trained and methodical way Mounty memorized fifteen details about the boy as he ran out the front door only to catch the briefest glimpse of the car zooming away (at least six feet, blue sweater with turtleneck, Afro hairstyle, very black skin, nose more Caucasian than Negroid, drives well, face more narrow than norm, high forehead, no beard, slim build to judge from shoulders, ring on left hand with green stone, clenched-fist button on sweater, earring in right ear, get more, damn there he goes around the corner. . .).

At the trial Mounty pronounced his positive identification in the same tones he used specifying materiel orders at Weishaupt Chemicals. The jury brought in a guilty verdict in five minutes.

That was the second time Mounty went mad.

For as the boy was led away Mounty glanced at him one more time and saw a blue halo form around his head just like in Catholic art.

Two weeks later he was promoted to Vice President of Weishaupt and began to see halos around random individuals in the street.

LED, LED, LED

If every case of aging can be corrected, we might all be Methuselahs, living 1,000 years or more.

—DR. ROBERT PREHODA, 1969

A Chinese named Wing Lee Chee was Cagliostro's closest friend in those early carnival days. Wing was the world's great master of karate, kung fu, aikido, and Comprehensive Advanced Machismo, but a gentle soul when not pushed too hard. In Bad Ass, Texas, he got pushed too hard by local cops, who objected to his use of the white toilet facilities at a gas station. They told him "A chink is just a yellowed-out nigger," roughed him up, and accidentally knocked his right eye out in their enthusiasm. At that point Wing lost his temper and was subsequently apprehended and quickly tried and convicted for the murder of four police officers.

Judge Draconic V. Wasp pronounced sentence in this wise: "Young feller, you've been tried and convicted and every man in this courtroom knows your guilt is as black as hell. I have no regret in passing sentence in such a case. Soon, you little bastard, it will be spring and the robin will sing again, the flowers will bud, little children will laugh on their way to school—and you will hear and know nothing of that, for you will be dead, dead, dead.

You chink bastard. Sheriff, take the yellow son-of-a-bitch out and hang him."

Wing Lee Chee received this with no show of emotion, but then he arose and addressed the court in a steady and terrible voice. "As I rook upon the whiskey-fogged faces of judge and july in the tlavesty of a civirized coult," he said, "I know furr werr that I was foorish to ever expect justice from such degenelates. You, Judge Wasp, speak of the sweet singing of lobins in the spling and the brooming of the prants, but what can you know of the gleat Tao that moves arr of us, you four-mouthed, cunt-ricking, donkey-fucking led-neck? You desclibe the gentre voices of chirden, you glafting, thieving, monkey-faced, frat-nosed idiot off-spring of a feebre-minded goat by pulple-plicked baboon! What do you know of the innocence of rittle chirden? What do you know of anything but colluption and highway lobbery, you syph-spocked, clap-lidden, amoeba-blained white lacist? You say that Wing Lee Chee sharr be hanged by the neck until he is dead, dead, dead, but Wing Lee Chee says"—he paused dramatically, swept the courtroom with a withering glance and concluded—"you can kiss my ass until it is led, led, *led!*"

It is said that nineteen peace officers were torn limb from limb in the course of the hanging of Wing Lee Chee.

FRANK: But he was hanged anyway.

ERNEST: But they knew they had hanged a *man*.

FRANK: Like hell. They thought they'd just hanged a crazy gook.

THE VALUE OF THE CONTENT

When a people begin to cut down their trees without making any provision for reforestation, you may be sure it is a sign of the beginning of their cultural degeneration.

—FURBISH LOUSEWART V, *Unsafe Wherever You Go*

In the weeks following the car theft in 1968, Mounty Babbit's luck at poker became so pronounced that he had to start losing by deliberation on occasion to avoid the suspicion of cheating. Halos were everywhere on earth; UFOs everywhere above.

I am a genuine mad scientist, Mounty Babbit thought. Well, nobody is ever going to know about it.

Then, a month later, it all passed. He didn't know what cards the other poker players had, and he wasn't seeing halos. He moved his family to Evanston, settled into his new job as Vice President at Weishaupt Chemicals, worked actively for the Nixon-Agnew campaign, and finally quit smoking.

The pickets outside the walls of Weishaupt Chemicals (which was now the nation's second-largest producer of napalm) were the only harassment in an otherwise perfectly satisfactory life.

The Invasion (as he came to call it) began in early 1969. He was driving home from work, came off Lake Shore Drive onto Sheridan, crossed the Howard Street border into Evanston, and noted a large billboard with an eye atop a pyramid. A teaser campaign, he thought. The reverse side of the dollar bill. After a month or so of making people wonder, the advertisers would add their slogan. Probably another Friendly Loan Company.

The next morning he awoke in total horror. He recalled the symptoms from some of the psychology books he had read back when he had feared for his sanity. The Activation Syndrome: thirst, rapid heartbeat, dizzy wobbles— the body preparing for emergency. What emergency? He couldn't remember anything from the previous evening.

Beside him, Mary Lou snuggled closer. "My, you were passionate last night," she murmured affectionately.

I drove home. I must have had dinner. And I made love—better than usual, it sounds like. And I can't remember any of it.

Micro-amnesia.

Babbit kept a very close watch on himself in the following days. Not close enough, evidently. At the end of the month he found among the canceled checks returned by his bank one in the sum of $100 to the Chicago Peace Action Committee. This was the sentimental old ladies who often appeared with the raggedy students picketing Weishaupt Chemicals. "EAT WHAT YOU KILL." "NO MORE WAR." "DRACULA LIVES ON BLOOD TOO." "BLESSED ARE THE PEACEMAKERS." All those silly sentimental signs.

He had not written this check. And yet the signature was his.

Alone in his study with the bank book and checks, Mountbatten Babbit wept. He knew horror.

Some alien entity had taken over his mind and written that check.

My God, he thought, I am *possessed*.

POLITICS OF THE IMPOSSIBLE

The robot whose passport said "Frank Sullivan" landed at Kennedy International on December 26, 1983, and brought $500,000 worth of hashish through customs without any trouble, since the customs officials had orders from the CIA never to interfere with him.

"Sullivan" affixed his gas mask and hailed a cab, which took him to the Hotel Claridge on Forty-fourth Street.

In rapid succession, following a genetic script, he took a quick shower, shaved, changed into his best suit, went out for a slow stroll on Forty-second Street, and picked up a boy lounging outside the Fascination pinball arcade.

They returned to "Sullivan's" room and the boy there received a slurpingly hedonic blow job, for which he was paid $25.

The lad was then covered with rapturous kisses and compelled (out of politeness) to listen to an interminable monologue on the world's injustices to Ireland, the villainy of England, and the perfidy of the Masonic Jews. More kisses followed, the boy told a lugubrious story of poverty and legal problems, "Sullivan" coughed up $5 more, and the transaction was ended. "Sullivan" lounged on the bed for a while after the boy left, discovered that another $15 had disappeared from his wallet, cursed mildly, showered again, and set out on his night's business.

Another taxi delivered him to the Signifyin' Monkey, a

nightclub on Lenox Avenue in Harlem. He checked his Luger before getting out of the cab and darting across the sidewalk; he knew what was likely to happen to melanin-deficient persons on that street at that hour.

The maître d' recognized "Sullivan" and made an almost imperceptible movement with his head. "Sullivan" ascended the stairs in the back, knocked quickly three times, then five times, then three times more, and was admitted to the private office of Hassan i Sabbah X.

"Ah," said Hassan, "the goodies from Afghanistan have arrived."

A sordid commercial transaction followed, distasteful to both parties—Hassan and "Sullivan" each regarded himself as fundamentally a philosopher unwillingly forced to grub and hustle in the jungle of commerce. Nonetheless, each bargained professionally and they were both quite happy by the time they came to the ritual of sharing one sample of the merchandise to seal their friendship anew.

"You know," Hassan said when they were both floating, "I don't really believe you're IRA."

"That's funny," said "Sullivan" with a hash giggle, "I don't believe you're really CIA, either."

They both chortled happily, having their keys.

"Complicated world," said Hassan.

"Getting more complicated every day," pseudo-Sullivan agreed benignly.

"Could you place a Klee with a European collector?"

"A Paul Klee?" Sullivan had heard "clay" originally and wondered if he were being asked to peddle pottery.

"An honest-to-Jesus Klee original. From his mescaline period, I would say."

"Hold on to it a day or two," Sullivan said grandly. "I'll have to make a few phone calls first." He was thinking that Hassan i Sabbah X wore the most brilliantly maroon ties he had ever seen. For that matter, the rug danced with hues worthy of a sultan's harem. Definitely superior-grade hash, he decided.

A door opened in the back of the office and another man stuck his head into the room. He was a black man, white-haired, gold spectacles, rather conservative blue suit and vest: "Sullivan" automatically memorized his features and sent them through his computer to recorders-and-identification.

"Oh, pardon me," the man said, backing out.

But Sullivan—who was not IRA at all, as Hassan surmised, but was CIA, at least part-time—had already come up with a "make." The man was George Washington Carver Bridge, one of the top scientists on Project Cyclops in the seventies. Now what was a man of that caliber doing skulking about the den of so large and carnivorous a mammal as Hassan i Sabbah X?

"Who was that?" he asked idly.

"One of the boys," Hassan replied carelessly. "Just one of the boys."

But Sullivan went back to his hotel mulling over the perversities and paradoxes of the hashish state, and the ever-maddening question "What is Reality?" for his memory kept insisting that just before the door closed he had noted that the esteemed Dr. Bridge was carrying in his hand the amputated penis of a white man.

WE MIGHT WAKE UP

We mustn't sleep a wink all night, or we might wake up—
changed.

—*Invasion of the Body Snatchers*

After the day in 1968 when he found that he had written a
check to the Chicago Peace Action Committee while in an
altered state of consciousness, Mountbatten Babbit decided, once and for all, that he would see a psychiatrist.

But not right away. He would fight for self-control first.

He realized that his mental condition was highly illegal.
ESP in 1941. Halos and ESP together, after that black kid
stole his car. Now he was having blackouts in which he
performed abominable acts that might threaten his security clearance and even his bank account. That was absolutely terrifying. Anything that endangered the bank account
must be a symptom of the most aggravated psychosis. Yes:
He would definitely absolutely irrevocably commit himself to psychiatric counseling.

But not right away. He would fight for self-control first.

One night the Babbits had the Moons from across the
street as guests for dinner. Molly Moon, as usual, got
Mary Lou into a discussion of the occult. All the usual
hocus-pocus and rubbish. She was especially keen on
some Neon Bal Loon, a Tibetan monk who had allegedly

130

transferred his consciousness into the mind of an Englishman and was now writing books through the Englishman's mediumship.

"It's just the beginning," Molly enthused. "Our materialism has become a threat to the whole world. Sure, more and more of the great Masters will be taking over Occidental bodies, to bring us their wisdom directly."

Mounty Babbit concentrated on discussing the financing of an antidrug pamphlet with Joe Moon, detective lieutenant on the Evanston police. Even that was disconcerting. "It probably won't do any good," Joe said once, rather bitterly. "The kids don't believe anything *we* tell them."

The next step into psychosis was unexpected and oddly pleasurable. It occurred in the lunchroom at Weishaupt a few days later. Babbit was pouring sugar into his coffee when he suddenly *looked at* the sugar dispenser. The simplicity of the design, the one small flap that opened to let the sugar pour, abruptly delighted him. It was as if he had never seen it before.

After that he was noticing more and more things in that heightened vision. One day in the Loop he saw a mother whirl suddenly and slap a whining child. His heart leapt with shock—and then he remembered that this was an everyday occurrence in America. It was as if he had seen it from the perspective of some culture where whining and hitting were not normal communication between parents and children.

He wanted less and less meat in his diet; meat now appeared heavy and hard to digest.

The strangest and most disturbing thing of all was the way Weishaupt Chemicals itself began to change. But everything was the same; he was just seeing with different eyes. The contrast between the executive offices and the workshops was an overwhelming experience. Architec-

ture, coloring, decoration, upkeep—every kind of communication except words themselves said with total clarity
"The Masters" and "The Serfs." The typical primate pack
hierarchy, unnoticed and taken for granted before.

Strange visions came to him whenever his mind relaxed
from financial or scientific problems. He would be in a
burning jungle, running from helicopters that caused the
burning. Or he would be in a temple with the eye-on-the-
pyramid design practicing strange breathing exercises. Once
he even had a name—*Ped Xing*—and he watched as one
of his teachers burned himself to death in protest against
the war. He was Ped Xing seeing through the eyes of
Mountbatten Babbit.

His monogamy, which he usually succeeded in maintaining fifty-one weeks of the year, was falling apart on
him. He worried that Mary Lou would be growing suspicious. Women turned him on constantly, incessantly, tor-
mentingly, as in early adolescence. Not all women—just
white women. Ped Xing couldn't get enough of them. He
couldn't even get enough of any one of them. Even after
an orgasm, I would want to start again, rubbing and
caressing their moist pussies until they came a second
time. This excited me so much that I would often go down
and suck them into a third orgasm. Then Ped Xing would
ask them to suck him and drift off into aeons of tension
and pleasure, glimpsing the temple of the eye-on-the-
pyramid, occasionally even coming a second time himself,
which hadn't happened since he was in his early twenties.

The homosexual phase almost drove me to suicide. But
my ESP (I accepted it now, knowing it was all hallucination of course, but following it blindly, being dragged
along by it) was both infallible and specific. Ped Xing
picked only men of Babbit's own status and importance;
and he was never wrong. Evidently, there were more
closet cases in the world than even Kinsey had estimated.

I always took the male role, coming in their mouths, and would reciprocate by no more than masturbating them. Once, when the partner was not merely an executive but a Pentagon official, I started laughing at his moment of ejaculation, losing all control, laughing louder and louder, revealing the psychosis and not caring.

That night I looked at the tree in his yard and knew it was an intelligent being. Not with human intellect, not with the mind of a dog or a rat or a fish even, but with its own life and indwelling consciousness. There was even a scientist in New York measuring the emotional reactions of plants with polygraph equipment. And there it stood, a blue spruce, stranger in structure and more alien in intelligence than any creature in science fiction.

How can we live among so many wonders and not be overwhelmed by the sheer mystery of existence? Mounty Babbit, former atheist, asked himself. Our knowledge is so small, and our conceit is so great. . . .

Then he realized in horror that that was Ped Xing, the Buddhist, thinking.

PARTNERS

Man will never be contented until he conquers death.

—Dr. Bernard Strehler, 1977

When Murphy got into the car Mendoza asked, "Bad news?"

Murphy pulled out into the traffic, carefully.

"It must be bad," Mendoza said, looking at Murphy's face.

They drove. Murphy stared straight ahead.

"Man's your partner," Mendoza said. "He shouldn't hide things from you."

"Malloy," Murphy said, "I got to go see Marty Malloy. Only he's got a new bug up his ass; he only talks to one cop at a time."

"Shit on one at a time. You let him pull that, the next thing happens is he thinks he runs the police force. Marty, a cheap hood like Marty, you never give him an edge. On anything. You know that, Tom. Let them get out of line and all of a sudden you got another Jack Ruby. Guy like that gets an edge, he can't keep his mouth shut, going around telling everybody about his friends the cops. Dropping in to see you at home, you know? When he takes his fall, half the force falls with him."

"Your principal problem," Murphy said, "is that you're a dumb spic with a loud mouth. Me, I don't take shit from

134

any of them, least of all from a Marty Malloy. But this is different."

"It sure is," Mendoza said. "I didn't know you so well, I'd think you got a guilty conscience about something. Some hood off the street, you can call him a spic anytime, but not me. Just who the fuck you think you are?"

"All right, that just slipped out. You don't have to eat my ass about it."

"All right, *shit*. First you're keeping secrets, then I'm a spic, now *I'm* the one who's being unreasonable. This is being partners? After ten years?"

Murphy turned onto Van Ness. "Nobody's keeping secrets," he said. "It's just one of those, what they call intangibles. Malloy doesn't have as much balls as a cockroach anymore. I mean I *know* Malloy. Pushing fifty, getting shaky, scared shitless of me for years now. He doesn't fancy-pants, not with me, he doesn't. He says he won't talk to anybody but me, that's the way I play it this time around. I keep telling you, I know Malloy."

They turned down Geary. "Okay," Mendoza said. "You know Malloy. He's got the whole solution to the Kennedy assassination, or something. But, I don't know what it is, something's come over you this last week, Tom. Clam up all you want. A man can't be partners ten years without knowing."

"Joe," Murphy said, "it's just I didn't want to talk about it. Some things a man just keeps a tight mouth about. It's my sister."

"Your sister?"

"The doctor thinks she's got cancer. You know a man like me, the wife dead, family means a lot. I been lighting candles for her at church."

"Tom," Mendoza said. "Jesus, Tom. I'm sorry. Your sister. Christ, what can I say?"

"It's okay, Joe. Partners, it's like being married in a

way. I should have known you'd realize something was up. A man like me, something in the family, he don't like to talk about it."

"Christ. Yeah. Which sister is that, the one in L.A. or the one up in Mendocino?"

"Oh . . . the one in Mendocino. Irene."

"Look, she needs more money and you can't raise it . . ."

"Thanks, Joe. It's not money, her husband is loaded, but thanks. I'm glad I talked about it."

"That's what a partner is for."

Murphy parked near the corner of Taylor. "You go down to Gulliver's, have a cup of coffee," he said. "I'll join you after I get whatever it is Malloy is selling."

"Partners," Mendoza said.

"Partners," Murphy replied warmly. They shook hands.

INSIDE OUT

America is a white man's heaven and a black man's hell.

—HASSAN I SABBAH X

Hassan i Sabbah X gave up on hashish. He went to the safe and got out the LSD. Remembering . . .

Using the transitional concept that the lock is a hole in the door through which one can exert an effort for a topological transformation, one could turn the room into another topological form other than a closed box. The room in effect was turned inside out through the hole.

Remembering a lad of twelve having *Ivanhoe* rammed down his gullet by the Chicago public school system and walking out the door at 3:05 P.M. to mingle with the junkies, whores, pimps, thieves, and assorted varieties of revolutionaries (Black Panthers, Black P. Stone Rangers, acid-electrified Weatherpeople) who provided the real education in the Hyde Park neighborhood of the late 1960s. Remembering the assassinations of Malcolm and of Martin Luther King. Remembering the endless epic of Stackerlee and the famous couplet:

I got a tombstone disposition and a graveyard mind.
I'm a black motherfucker and I don't mind dyin'.

Call this the first metaprogram. It led Hassan (then called F.D.R. Stuart) far outside the ghetto into an entirely new and different world. It was easy. By acting out the imperatives of the Stackerlee "black motherfucker" script, the boy earned a term in the Audy Home, an institution for the further training of apprentice outlaws who slash tires on police cars, heave bricks through school windows, peddle merchandise from stores without first purchasing them, and answer policemen's questions with "Fuck you, ya honky motherfuck'n cocksucker." F.D.R. Stuart received the standard Audy Home training, which consists of sophisticated expert coaching in: (a) sodomy; (b) sado-masochism; and (c) assorted crimes more lucrative than selling shoplifted merchandise.

He was, after graduation, ready for postgraduate work at Springfield, once he passed the admissions test, which consists of being captured by the police while in the possession of something hot. He was in possession of a Ford Mustang registered to a Mountbatten Babbit of Evanston. Postgraduate work at Springfield included a refresher course in sodomy and S-M, together with advanced study in grand larceny; but by this time F.D.R. Stuart had begun to doubt that the Stackerlee metaprogram contained the whole answer to life's problems. A former Black Muslim, now a Sufi, was his cell mate, and taught him various things about the less-publicized qualities of the human nervous system.

F.D.R. Stuart spent many hours staring at one wall of his cell, gradually creating a hole through which he could pass into another world. There was a different kind of time over there, and eventually he discovered that angels and fairies and elves and witches and Bodhisattvas and conjurs and all sorts of superhuman folk could be contacted and persuaded to become allies.

The Sufi cell mate, a heavy cat in more ways than F.D.R. Stuart ever understood, pretended to be unimpressed with this achievement and laid down some stern raps about the perils of "Opening the Gate" without first "clarifying the soul." The upshot of it was that young Stuart spent an hour a day memorizing a page in the dictionary until he had a vocabulary that would grace a Harvard graduate. Alas, the Sufi was paroled around then and Stuart continued his explorations unguided.

In 1983, in Harlem, New York, Hassan i Sabbah X was the Horsethief of a group known as the Cult of the Black Mother. This was ostensibly devoted to the worship of Kali, goddess of destruction (and rebirth); the police suspected, but couldn't prove, that it was also a kingpin in international hashish smuggling. The FBI, meanwhile, had their own suspicions; they believed it was a Black Revolutionary Army disguised as a church. An Army Intelligence agent of appropriate Negritude and duplicity managed to gain admission to one of the lower ranks but learned only that: (a) Horsethief was a term for head honcho or boss man borrowed from the gypsies; (b) the rituals were fairly close to those of orthodox Hindu Kali worship, except for certain Masonic elements; and (c) every time a black FBI agent managed to infiltrate the Cult of the Black Mother, he died very soon of a heart attack.

The last fact was well known, and often discussed, at the Bureau. The word *witchcraft* popped up at least once in each of these conversations, and was quickly laughed down, but each agent went away harboring his own very private opinions. Some of them even began attending the church of their choice even more often than was expected by the rather Puritan standards of the Bureau.

The CIA which actually employed Hassan i Sabbah X as a spy on ghetto affairs, was well aware that he planned to double-cross them at the first opportunity, but that didn't worry them. They had their own plans for him, which were expressed in their usual jolly euphemism, "termination with maximum prejudice," a remark illustrated by a finger drawn across the throat to make the meaning clear to neophytes. But that was only for the future, when he began to show signs of shifting allegiance.

Now (it is the night of December 23, 1983, again) while a miniature sled with eight tiny reindeer was allegedly dodging past commercial airliners, communications satellites, flying saucers, and other technocraft in the skyways, two human beings of reprehensible character drove up to the Sutton Place digs of Mary Margaret (Epicene) Wildeblood in a truck hired from U-Haul only a few hours earlier. These were Edward J. Smith and Samuel R. Hall, and they had been purged from the Black Panther Party a few months earlier because of their fondness for the null-circuit neurological program induced by injecting diacetylmorphine $(C_{21}H_{23}NO_5)$ directly into their veins. This compound was known as *heroin* to white people and *caballo* to Ed and Sam's Puerto Rican neighbors. Ed and Sam called it *horse* and mainlined it as often as they possibly could—"riding the horse over the rainbow" was their expression for the null program, and it meant as much to them as Samadhi to a Hindu or the Eucharist to a Catholic. In fact, it allowed them to forget for a while that, to 90 percent of their fellow citizens, they were unmistakably identifiable as *niggers*, a species generally regarded as twice as ugly and ten times as dangerous as wild gorillas. It didn't matter, to Sam and Ed, that the people who believed this also believed in the existence of a gaseous vertebrate of astronomical heft named God, in the Virgin Birth of U.S. Senators, in the accuracy of TV news, and in premarital chastity for women.

Sam and Ed also believed in the existence of the gaseous vertebrate, the immaculate generation of senators, the pictures on the tube, and premarital chastity for at least *some* women (their own sisters, wives, and daughters). They also believed that they *were* twice as ugly and ten times as dangerous as wild gorillas, but that they had a right to be that way. They called it Black Pride.

Once inside the Wildeblood apartment, Ed and Sam were as efficient as a pair of vacuum cleaners. To say they took everything that wasn't nailed down is to underestimate their rapacity. If something that looked valuable *was* nailed down, they employed pliers and other tools. When they finally drove away the U-Haul truck was as stuffed with goodies as the miniature sled allegedly circling the skies at that moment. When Mary Margaret Wildeblood returned from her month in Vermont, she was heard to compare her condition to that of the Chinese farmer in *The Good Earth* after the locusts had passed.

Ed and Sam drove directly to the Sugar Hill apartment

of Hassan i Sabbah X, which is not listed on the mailboxes and can only be reached through another apartment with the name LESTER MADDOX on it. Ed, who knew this scene better than Sam, knocked.

"White," said a muffled voice from inside.

"Man," Ed replied.

"Native," came the voice again.

"Born," Ed completed the formula.

The door opened, and they were ushered into the home of a very respectable Afro-Methodist clergyman who had never been publicly connected in any way with Hassan i Sabbah X.

"What was that jive?" Sam demanded.

"Password," Ed explained briefly.

"Borrowed from the Ku Klux Klan," the clergyman added with some glee. "He got himself one weird sense of humor, Brother Hassan." He ushered them into the kitchen, slid the refrigerator around easily on specially built ball rollers, and they passed through to an apartment that did not exist in anybody's records anywhere.

The air was heavy with the smell of Indian hemp; an enormous statue of Kali, the Black Mother, dominated the room. A group of black men sat in a circle and Sam recognized two small cigarettes circulating in opposite directions, which he called clockwise and counterclockwise, not knowing the technical magical terms deosil and widdershins.

"You will now ascend to the sixth plane, without my guidance," said Hassan i Sabbah X to the circle. "I am returning to the earth plane briefly. Aummmm . . ."

"Aummmm . . ." came the blissful reply from the students.

Hassan led Sam and Ed to another room.

"What's all that sixth-plane shit?" Sam whispered to Ed.

"Astral projection," was the brief reply.

Hassan seated himself at his desk and smiled genially. "Been out celebrating the Lord's birthday?" he asked pleasantly. "Expropriating the expropriators?"

"We got a fuckin' *truck*load downstairs," Ed replied.

"Mmmm-*mm!*" Hassan said. "A merry Yuletide indeed. Class merchandise from Honkyville, or were you ripping off our brothers and sisters again?"

"Class," Sam said emphatically.

"And a truckload." Hassan smiled dreamily. "Why, brothers, if I'm as generous as my reputation, you likely to end up owning more horse than the Kentucky Derby!" He pressed a button and another black man entered the room. This was Robert Pearson by birth, Robert Pearson, Ph.D., according to the anthropology department at U.C.-Berkeley, El Hajj Stackerlee Mohammed during a militant period in the sixties, Clark Kent (with his Supermen) during his commercial rock music years, and now Robert Pearson again. "Accompany these cats to our warehouse and *e*-valuate the cash value of their merchandise," Hassan instructed.

Another trip brought Ed and Sam, with Pearson, to a building on Canal Street bearing the legend BHAVANI IMPORTS. Here the truck was unloaded, cataloged and priced.

"A genuine Klee or I'm a brass monkey," Pearson said once. "Your uh client has bread as well as taste."

"Now, what's this shit?" he said later, scrutinizing a saccharine rendition of two naked boys preparing to dive into a swimming hole, framed by a gingerbread copper-plated oval. "Oh, well, we can sell it as camp."

His sharpest reaction came when he confronted the redwood plaque bearing the ithyphallic eidolon.

"Jesus H. Christ on a unicycle," he breathed.

Sam and Ed exchanged glances. "We can't figure that

one out, either," Sam ventured. "Beats the hell out of our ass."

"Looks like some bozo's joint," Ed suggested helpfully.

Pearson put out an exploratory hand. *"Feels* like some bozo's joint," he amended. "Sure as shit ain't plastic." He shook his head wearily. "What I want to know is *what kind of bozo would do this to his joint?"*

Sam and Ed shrugged. "He was a white bozo," Sam contributed finally.

"I can see that," Pearson said. "A *crazy* white bozo," He rolled his eyes heavenward. "Lawd, Lawd," he said in down-home accents, "the things that white folks do, it's just too much for this simple cullud boy."

"Skin!" cried Sam.

"Skin," Pearson agreed. They slapped palms. And there the mystery rested until Hassan i Sabbah X arrived personally to inspect the new imports a few days later.

"Namu Amida Butsu," he said, peering closely. "Shee-it."

"Where do you think we can sell it?" Pearson asked dubiously.

"That I do not know," Hassan i Sabbah X pronounced slowly. "But when we do find a buyer, the price will make your head swim. This is a one-of-a-kind item."

Things were coming to a head. The key was no key.

Hassan had other things on his mind that weekend; he was well aware that "Frank Sullivan" (probably, in his estimation, a double agent for both Washington and Peking) had recognized "Washy" Bridge and *that* opened a very wiggly can of worms, indeed. Ever since Washy had told him about Project Pan, in fact, Hassan had felt increasingly like the Sorcerer's Apprentice in the legend. A line from an H. P. Lovecraft story came back to his consciousness over and over again: *"Do not, I beseech you, call up any that you cannot put down."* Like many another occultist before him, Hassan i Sabbah X now wished he had taken that warning a bit more seriously a bit sooner. . . .

Even before he left Bhavani Imports he was startled by an incident that seemed a definite *Santaria* synchromesh. "Hey, listen, man," an art appraiser cried, catching his sleeve, "I've just heard the greatest limerick. Listen, just listen: 'A habit obscene and unsavory—' " He broke down, laughing, caught himself, and repeated urgently, "Listen." He tried again:

> "A habit obscene and unsavory
> Holds the Bishop of Boston in slavery.
> 'Midst hootings and howls—"

He broke down again, then went on:

> " 'Midst hootings and howls
> He deflowers young owls,
> Which he keeps in an underground aviary!"

Hassan looked at him with paranoid suspicion. "Very funny," he said, unsmiling, and hastened out to his limousine.

"Back uptown?" the chauffeur asked.

"Broad Street," Hassan said, giving an address. He was in mild first-circuit anxiety all the way to his destination.

He remembered his first conversation with Washy Bridge. "How many?" he had asked, not in shock or in outrage but in simple unbelief, inability to believe. *They are our creation: we are their creation.*

"Fifty-seven of us." The scientist was perspiring with anxiety, now that the secret was finally out, the reason he had fled Project Pan.

"Fifty-seven," Hassan said hollowly. *Heinz 57 Varieties,* he remembered absently from the advertisements. "And all of them with Ph.D.'s and M.D.'s and more diplomas than a dog has fleas . . ."

"You've got to realize it works," Washy said then. "You just can't understand if you don't keep that in mind. It works."

"And two hundred to three hundred years in jail for each of you if it ever gets out," Hassan added harshly. "You just better keep that in mind too."

"That's why I'm here," the scientist said.

Hassan had paced the room briefly. "Wheels within wheels," he said once. "Wheels within wheels *within* wheels." Once he grinned. "At least I know why the Cincinnati cocaine market is thriving," he said with a lewd chuckle. "Cincinnati," he repeated, shaking his head. "What do they call it again?"

"Knights of Christianity United in Faith."

A *habit obscene and unsavory*, Hassan remembered suddenly, jostled back into present time. He had arrived at his destination.

The man to whom he spoke then was a stockbroker according to public knowledge but pursued certain other careers in a private and clandestine manner.

" 'Frank Sullivan,' " Hassan said. "I want to know *everything* about him. Everything."

The part-time stockbroker turned ashy-white. He got up, glared suspiciously at a window washer outside his office, and walked over to check that the window was closed all the way.

"Impossible," he said then, in a near whisper. "If I told you the one most amusing and interesting fact about him, I'd be dead tomorrow."

"That hot?" Hassan asked.

The man leaned back in his chair and gazed absently toward the ceiling. He recited some names, beginning with Jack Ruby of Dallas and ending with a senator whose private plane had crashed just the week before, on Christmas Eve. "Those are just a few," he ended, "who happened to find out too much about Frank Sullivan."

Hassan spoke only once during the drive back to Harlem. *"Secrecy!"* he said with a profound grimace.

The chauffeur looked back nervously. He had never heard so much obscene emphasis in a single word.

GWB-666

He knows when you are sleeping
He knows when you're awake

Within three days the storm had become a blizzard in most of the Northeast and Roy Ubu was feeling snowed under in every sense of the phrase, driving with extreme caution, thinking that the new Head of Programming for the Beast, whatzisname, Moon, really seemed to take some kind of fiendish pleasure in producing reams and reams of records to prove that the records were all defective. . . .

The snow whipped Ubu again as he parked and skittered into GWB to find Moon once again cheerfully perusing printouts that demonstrated, for the thirty-third time, that every single one of the missing scientists had simply stopped leaving ink or magnetic tape traces sometime between summer '81 and spring '82. Which was impossible in the age of bureaucracy: It was like an animal not leaving footprints on a wet beach.

"But the Beast is *supposed* to know," Ubu had protested once.

"GWB-666 knows *everything* that has been recorded," Moon said patiently. "It does not know what has never been recorded. You can't see behind your head; GWB-666 can't scan what was never recorded anywhere."

"But dammit nobody can do anything in this country dammit without making a record."

"Nobody but these 132 very elusive men and women," Moon replied placidly. "If you'll notice, I marked the bios where it deals with experience in programming. Seventy-eight out of the 132 have such experience. They obviously learned a great deal about Erase and Cancel codes. . . ."

Roy Ubu made a despairing gesture. "How many bits can this thing access?" he asked wearily.

"Over one hundred twenty billion bytes," Simon said. "Nearly a trillion bits. There's never been an information system like this in all history," he added with some pride.

"But it has amnesia where these scientists are concerned," Ubu said bitterly.

The robot whose passport said "Frank Sullivan" was in Washington that weekend and reported to a high official in Naval Intelligence, who suspected him of being a double agent infiltrating them for Air Force Intelligence.

After the usual sordid business was disposed of, "Sullivan" asked casually if N.I. had any interest in Hassan i Sabbah X.

"Good Lord and Aunt Agnes, no!" said the official emphatically. "Congress will have our ass if we get into anything domestic." Then he asked, elaborately disinterested, "What did you happen to pick up?"

"Well, if there's no real interest . . ." Pseudo-Sullivan gazed off into space absently.

There was a short silence.

"If it's something big . . ." the official said finally.

"Sullivan" held out his hand. Another commercial transaction took place.

"It's about a government scientist named George Washington Bridge . . ." pseudo-Sullivan began. . . .

"Miska-*what?*" Roy Ubu demanded.

"Miskatonic," Special Agent Tobias Knight repeated. "Here's their catalog." He held up a booklet blazoned with a Gothic sketch of book, candle, inverse pentagram, and the motto:

MISKATONIC UNIVERSITY
founded 1692
EX IGNORANTIA AD SAPIENTAM
EX LUCE AD TENEBRAS

"Where the hell is that?" Ubu asked.

"New England, somewhere in Massachusetts . . . ah, here it is, Arkham, Massachusetts."

"And how many of the 132 were students there?" Ubu was hot on the scent.

"Sixty-seven of them," Knight said triumphantly. "All in the classes of '66 through '69. . . ."

"By God, it's a *live* one," Ubu cried. "Two or three might be happenstance, even ten might be coincidence, but Jumpin' Jesus sixtyfuckin*seven* means something. Let's look into this Miskatonic U. and find out what was going on back there in '66 to '69, besides dope."

*'cause Santa Claus is coming
to tooooooown!*

GORILLA THEATER

Mounty Babbit took a walk in Lincoln Park one day in 1969, trying to relax and calm his mind. Every tree spoke to him; the lions looked at him as a brother; the nervous armadillo pacing its cage stopped to stare at him, and he received clearly the message, "How did we get trapped in these ridiculous bodies?"

"We need bodies," Ped Xing replied, "just as we need minds, to function in this three-dimensional continuum. Surely you remember that we are actually n-dimensional?"

"Oh, yes," the armadillo signaled, "how could I have forgotten?"

Socrates had his *daemon*, Mounty thought in despair; Jesus had the Father in Heaven; Elwood P. Dowd had his giant white rabbit, Harvey; but why do I have to have a crazy Vietnamese Buddhist?

"You make the napalm," Ped Xing told him.

Thoroughly agitated, Babbit wandered into the primate house, not noticing the sign which said "CLOSED TO-DAY." There he saw two grim-faced men, in green uniforms, and a gorilla, in a blue uniform, going through a most remarkable pantomime. One of the men would raise a sign saying "WE DEMAND JUSTICE" and the gorilla would then spray him with a can of shaving cream; the other man would then feed the gorilla.

Operant conditioning. But what the hell . . .

Even Ped Xing was confused by that one.

WHERE THE FUCK?

The night watchman at Bhavani Imports, a Puerto Rican poet and *Santaria* initiate named Hugo de Naranja, was reading a novel called *Illuminatus!* when the mysterious incident occurred. Hugo was so absorbed in the book, which he considered the greatest novel since *Don Quixote,* that he didn't notice the strange sound at first. Gradually the sound's persistence invaded his consciousness, dragged him out of the most aesthetically exquisite blow job in all modern fiction, jerked him into an alert awareness that out there in the darkness there was something odd going on.

Rats, he thought.

No, the quick trot of rat paws was different.

A thief with soft slippers, or in his stockings . . .

Not that, either.

Hugo put down his book and picked up flashlight in left hand groping right-handedly and then finding pistol in holster. Something was going on in the vast darkness of the warehouse and he had to go and look for it and do something about it. He wished he hadn't read so many Women's Lib diatribes against *machismo* and Papa Hemingway. He wished he could still believe in the *macho* values. He wished he had more *cojones* or another job.

Then he walked out of his cubbyhole office, flashing the light ahead of him, and quoted to himself from his favorite philosopher. "The ordinary man has problems. The warrior only has challenges." Then he saw the intruder.

A *cat*. It was only a cat, held for one moment in his lightbeam, then skittering away into deeper darkness as the light raced after it. Then it was caught again, higher up, standing for Christ's sake on the ghastly amputated penis plaque, its golden eyes glittering half-whitely in the flashed lightray. A cat standing on a penis, something right out of Surrealism or Dada.

"Scat!" Hugo shouted, really amused now. "Rrrow! Scat! Beat it!"

Then the cat leapt and Hugo's flash leapt after it jumping to the floor, where it would, should, must, *didn't* land. The light moved back quickly, swept several arcs, while Hugo was beginning to think: *Christ, it didn't make any sound when it landed, not even a muffled cat thud*. And his beam swept back and forth again in searching arcs, as the words formed "it disappeared in midair," were rejected (*it couldn't*) and the beam rested for a minute on the challengingly erect Penis Without a Man (what *hijo de puta* would do a thing like that?) and the question burst from his lips, aloud, the nightwatchman's vice of talking to himself, which he had always resisted before:

"Where did it the fuck jump to? Where the fuck?"

THE DISPOSSESSED

Mounty Babbit never did learn to live with Ped Xing. In fact, he eventually had a full-scale psychotic breakdown. Of course, because of his wealth, the doctors always referred to it as a catathymic crisis.

The breakdown occurred at a dinner party, worse luck.

The Moons were guests again, and this time they had their nephew, Simon—a bearded young mathematician whose father had been the black sheep of the Moon family, a Wobbly agitator. Simon himself had been arrested during the Democratic Convention riots the previous year but got off on probation.

Everything went pleasantly enough until Molly Moon got on her obsession about Oriental Masters invading Western bodies to pass on their transcendental mysticism.

Joe Moon must have noticed the look on Mounty's face because he said, "Molly, remember our host is a scientist."

"And a Taurus," Molly said quickly. "I know how hard it is for him to accept spiritual truths."

"He doesn't bore you with the latest chemical shoptalk," Joe said gently. "I'm sure you don't have to bore him with all this astrology or whatever it is."

"It's not astrology. It's astral projection."

"It sounds half-astral to me," Joe said, laughing as loud as he could, trying to get them all laughing and turn the topic into a joke.

Young Simon, however, had ideas of his own. "Aunt Molly might be right," he said thoughtfully. "The Einstein-Rosen-Podolsky paradox does lead to some freaky possibilities. But why assume only the high adepts are coming? Every primitive group in the world has some kind of magical tradition. And they've tried everything else to get out from under white domination."

"Now don't start with your radicalism . . ." Joe warned.

"I'm not talking politics," Simon said innocently. "Everywhere in the world there are people who'd like to change places with us. Live in our rich homes. Eat our extravagant diet. Drive our cars. We know a lot about the space-time-matter continuum, but we're more ignorant than Asia or Africa about space-time-mind continuum. How about the Native Americans, for that matter? Wouldn't their magicians love to take over some white bodies for a while? Is that why so many young people are wearing Indian headbands, taking Indian drugs like peyote, moving out of the cities into the woods. . . ? Ever have your car stolen by a black kid from Chicago's ghetto? Wouldn't they like to steal your body too?"

"That's nonsense," Molly Moon said angrily. "All those backward people you're talking about couldn't learn the higher spiritual arts. . . ."

"Mounty, you're a scientist," Joe Moon said imploringly. "Tell Simon what's wrong with his theory."

"Anybody can spin theories," Babbit said carefully. "Science is a matter of proof. You can make up a million and one theories, Simon, but if you go to work for a corporation you'll have to produce theories that engineers can use. The one theory out of a million that can be proven. Everything else is just idle speculation."

"Exactly." Joe Moon beamed, delighted. "Let the coons earn the right to live in Evanston, I say."

"Well, this theory *could* be checked out," Simon went

on guilelessly; but Babbit knew he was baiting everybody. "If such an uh invasion were occurring, it would be aimed at people with important positions. Business executives. Government officials. The people who control the media. Check them out and see if they're all growing a little bit weird lately. . . ."

The helicopter descended and the earth turned to flame. My daughter ran toward me, burning, screaming. Why was it an American flag on the helicopter instead of a swastika? Was it Calley or Eichmann who was looking at me with imploring eyes begging my understanding and forgiveness?

Day after day the napalm fell from the skies. Day after day children died screaming at 1,000° Centigrade. Month after month, year after year, the fire continued to consume the world, Ped Xing's world. He sat in the lotus, his *shakti* mounted on his penis, their eyes locked, until the neurological synergy occurred: They were One. And then the Others were there, too, all the minds of space-time who turned on the neuroatomic circuit, the beetle intellects of Betelgeuse, Nicholas and Perenella Flamel, Bruno and Elizabeth, Cagliostro, and, as the time warp opened, galaxy after galaxy joined in, the Starmaker appeared dimly, and the first jump was possible.

He was a flower on a rose bush in England and a poet was staring at him as he stared back at the poet: "The roses have the look of flowers that are looked at" emerged from that moment.

SHe was a microbe flailing tentatively in a soupy ocean.

He was a Terran archivist looking back at the decline and fall of the American Empire.

SHe was Mountbatten Babbit in Evanston, Illinois—a good one, grab quick, this was one of the murderers, hold on—

Mountbatten Babbit, Ph.D., became aware that everybody at the table was staring at him. Then he realized that he was sobbing. "Oh, God," he said, a mind at the end of its tether. "Oh, God, God, God . . ."

It was explained as a breakdown due to overwork. There was no psychiatrist; ambition forbade the risk, so a clinical psychologist of Behaviorist orientation was found, on the faculty of Northwestern University, and the visits were listed as consultation in social psychology for business management.

Mounty and the psychologist defined Ped Xing as a hallucination caused by the negative conditioning of the pacifist pickets surrounding Weishaupt Chemicals. A method of deconditioning was worked out, using hypnosis and aversion therapy against all manifestations of the Ped Xing persona. The aversive stimulus was apomorphine, a nonaddicting morphine derivative that provokes vomiting and sensations of death. At first Ped Xing would speak directly at these moments, begging and pleading, "Don't send me back to the flames. . . ." Later he became defiant. "We'll be back, millions of us, from all over the Third World. Living in your fat white bodies. Running your corporations and bureaucracies. All through the seventies and eighties. We'll be back." As the theory of aversion therapy predicts, Ped Xing was finally extinguished.

Safely established beyond freedom and dignity, Mounty Babbit became the ideal conditioned subject. In 1982 he resigned his position as President of Weishaupt Chemicals to become Special Scientific Advisor to the White House.

ANOTHER *EIGEN*STATE

That which is forbidden is not allowed.
                    —JOHN LILLY, *The Center of the Cyclone*

O how money makes me hum O how money makes me
hum O how money makes me hum

Benny Benedict was working on his mantra, and didn't
realize that he had wandered quite a bit from the Sanskrit
original.

O how money makes me hum O how money makes me
hum O how money makes me hum the purpose of suffering is to make us ask the important questions what a guy a
stage magician he said O how money makes me hum O
how money makes me hum

He had reached the corner of Lexington and Twenty-
third Street.

Pablo Gomez stepped out of a doorway and hit Benny
from behind, hard, with a lead pipe.

Oh mommie take me home Oh mommie take me home
. . . Benny exploded into the white light.

Fortunately the last remaining citizen of Manhattan
with a sense of civic duty, one James Mortimer, came
around the corner at just that moment. James Mortimer
carried a police whistle at all times, since he knew he was

living in a still-violent society. He blew several blasts, loud and shrill. Pablo Gomez fled without getting any money, and an ambulance arrived in time to rush Benny to the hospital and save his life.

THE ROOMS WERE TURNED INSIDE OUT

The "nervous breakdown" (as it was called) of Hassan i Sabbah X did not attract much attention; the Cult of the Black Mother had never been as well publicized as the Nation of Islam or the Black Panthers. The New York *News-Times-Post* actually referred to Hassan as a "well-known nightclub owner in Harlem," in their very brief story, and their reporter hadn't even investigated far enough to learn that Hassan was also the head of a cult with more members than the Missouri Synod Lutherans. But, then, the Cult of the Black Mother had never been publicity-minded; even *The Amsterdam News*, unaware of its membership, described it as "a small church."

Hassan had been delivered to Bellevue in a state of raving mania, under physical restraint by two of his former aides. The psychiatrists quickly pronounced him "paranoid schizophrenic" and prescribed the heaviest tranquilizer then available, which in fact kept him fairly drowsy even when he wasn't comatose. Nonetheless, when able to summon the energy to rise out of his lethargy and talk again, he would monotonously repeat to any other inmate or orderly who came near, "Look, I don't belong here.

Something terrible has happened. I'm really the President of this fucking country . . ." and so on, with endless elaborations and details.

"A deeply defended psychosis," the psychiatrists decided, and began a course of electroshock treatments.

Whenever the flipped-out black came out of his daze, however, he would begin the same schizzy ranting all over: "Hey, listen, I'm the President of this fucking country. . . ."

The electroshock was stepped up. Hassan retreated into a permanent daze and ceased to annoy anybody. By this time his brain had been fried to the consistency of a White Tower scrambled egg and his impressions of the external world were mostly olfactory and aural, like those of a subnormal toy poodle; he no longer argued about anything, since he no longer understood such abstract concepts as ego persistence or identity. The psychiatrists were satisfied: "If you can't cure a nut," their tacit motto was, "at least you can keep him from running around the ward annoying people."

Two FBI agents later discussed the matter privately.

"You think CIA did it?" asked the first, Tobias Knight.

"You figure he'd been working for them?" the other, Roy Ubu, asked in return. "I always had that notion myself. But why would they fuck his head like that, when God only knows what he might spill to somebody who'd get released from the nuthouse and repeat it to a reporter? Nah, CIA doesn't work that way. They'd just—" He drew a finger across his throat.

"I don't believe in coincidences," Knight said stubbornly. "Somebody got to him."

"Some*thing*," Ubu corrected with a sinister intonation. "You know as well as I do what he was. A witch."

"Voodooist," Knight corrected.

"Whatever. Everybody we ever sent in died of a heart

attack, right?" Ubu looked over his shoulder. "Officially, the Bureau doesn't believe in witches. But I'll tell you what happened to Mr. Hassan i Sabbah X in *my* opinion. He called up something that he couldn't put down."

THE LOCK IS A HOLE

Dr. Francis Dashwood—neat, clean, rich, and not yet forty—drove into the grounds of the Orgasm Research Foundation on Van Ness in San Francisco at precisely 8:57 in the morning. He checked his wristwatch again after he parked his sleek M.G. in the executive parking lot. It was 8:58. Excellent. A quick trot and he was at his desk before the office clock reached nine. Once again he had demonstrated the punctuality (anal-retentive personality, silly prescientific Freudians called it) which had contributed so much to raising him to his present high position in the medical research bureaucracy of the United States.

Frank Dashwood, M.D., L.L.D., Ph.D., at the age of only thirty-eight, headed the most heavily funded and hotly debated institution in the world: Orgasm Research, a multimillion-dollar project dedicated to filling in the psychological intangibles left out of the pioneering research of Masters and Johnson two decades earlier. Since these psychological intangibles were—as Dr. Dashwood sometimes wittily remarked—"both psychological and intangible," there was no end to the research. Meanwhile, the funding money came rolling in.

Frank was, according to a survey by a management analyst, one of the seventeen men in the United States who was totally happy with his job.

Other researchers sometimes expressed envy of this fact. "What red-blooded man," one of them had once asked with some warmth, "wouldn't be happy supervising other people's orgasms and pulling down a *swift sixty grand* a year for it?"

This was somewhat unfair to a dedicated scientist. Dr. Dashwood was truly fascinated by orgasms—as Edison was by electricity—and had an inexhaustible curiosity about every possible factor involved in every possible twitch, itch, moan, gibber, gasp, sob, shudder, or howl connected with that dramatic biological tremor. Even more, however, he was mesmerized by lines, curves, averages, graphs, and every aspect of mathematics that could be clearly visualized. The world, for him, was not made up of "things," crude Disneyland animations projected by our lower nervous circuits, but of energy meshes. With no knowledge of Zen Buddhism, he intuitively shared Sixth Patriarch Hui Neng's vision that "from the beginning there has never been a *thing*." Dr. Dashwood lived in a universe of transactions that could be written as equations and traced on graph paper.

Above his desk was a motto suggested ironically by a skeptical friend. Dr. Dashwood saw nothing funny about it and adopted it as his own banner:

SCIENCE, PURE SCIENCE, AND DAMNED BE HE
WHO FIRST CRIES "HOLD, TOO MUCH!"

As he settled himself at his desk he observed that Ms. Karrige, his secretary, had already poured his coffee for him. Fine: The girl (femperson, he corrected) was really getting broken to the harness. He whipped out his thermometer and measured the black liquid in the cup: 98.4 degrees. Excellent: She was learning to meet his exacting demands.

Dr. Dashwood could not abide inexactitude or slovenliness in any human activity. "A thing worth doing," he would explain to his subordinates, "is worth doing *right*." He said this often, and malicious members of the staff said it even more often, when he was out of earshot, with a tone and a facial expression that were caricatures of his own.

With a smile on his lips and a glint in his eye, Frank Dashwood buzzed Ms. Karrige. "What's first for today?" he asked cheerfully.

The Jabberwock was growing: The key was no key. . . .

FUNNY VALENTINE

Megalithic monuments were certainly not places of worship but places of refuge for people fleeing the advance of mud.
—Furbish Lousewart V, *Unsafe Wherever You Go*

While Dr. Dashwood was pressing his buzzer in San Francisco, Starhawk was carefully screwing two mountain climber's hooks into a hill across the bay in Oakland. The first rope was wrapped around his waist outside the trousers,

ran through a pulley, and came back to his hand. The
second rope circled his chest, ran through the second
pulley, and was secured to a tree. He began lowering
himself down through the redwoods.

At first there was no visibility at ground level, but as
he descended the roof of Murphy's house a bit of yard
came into view. None of the neighboring houses was
visible at all.

Approaching Murphy's roof, Starhawk slowed and then
stopped his descent. In midair he turned, every muscle
straining, and continued his descent headfirst, legs tightly
together, the style of a professional highdiver. A small
film of perspiration formed around his lips. He was totally
silent.

Twice, redwood branches almost tangled his ropes. He
remained totally silent while disengaging.

Finally, he gripped the roof edge with his left hand, let
out more slack with his right, and lowered himself until
he was looking in the corner of a window upside down. It
was the bedroom. Murphy wasn't there. The bed was
unmade.

Starhawk raised himself, swung, and descended again
to inspect another window. The living room. Murphy was
sitting in a red plush chair, his face expressionless. He
was listening to music on the stereo. A shotgun leaned
against the wall behind him.

Very slowly, Starhawk raised himself again and swung
to the next window. In five minutes, totally silent, he was
sure that there was nobody in any of the other rooms.

He slowly raised himself again and found a perch in a
redwood that commanded a view of the front yard and
doorway. He waited.

The music from the stereo drifted up to him. Peggy Lee
was singing "My Funny Valentine."

After waiting forty-five minutes, Starhawk descended again. Murphy was no longer in the living room. The shotgun was missing also.

"The fuck?" Starhawk muttered.

He swung carefully over to the bedroom window. The shotgun rested against the wall beside the closet.

Murphy came out of the closet and picked up the shotgun again. Careful man, that Murphy; never go anywhere without your shotgun when you're holding maybe half a million in hot snow.

Murphy looked quite happy now. He looked like the happiest man Starhawk had ever seen.

Starhawk returned to his perch in the redwood tree. Murphy had obviously taken a snort of the coke and was probably feeling like Luke Skywalker heading for the Death Star. Starhawk waited silently. It was good to know where the cocaine was.

A few minutes later a squirrel came along an overhead branch and almost walked over Starhawk's rope. He stopped, frozen: unable to believe that a human being was way up here in the tree.

Starhawk and the squirrel stared at each other, both immobile. Then the squirrel ran.

Starhawk smiled. He went on waiting, quietly.

FIRST MAMMAL-ROBOT DYAD

Dr. Dashwood buzzed Ms. Karrige. "What's first for to-day?" he asked cheerfully, eager to plunge directly back into the thick of things, as was typical of him on Monday mornings.

"The uh colored gentleman from New York," came the tinny voice on the intercom.

"Send him right in!" Frank said eagerly.

Robert Pearson was dressed in his "dealing with the straight establishment" clothes, which meant that he looked like the black equivalent of a Mafia don moving in on a legit corporation. You had to look twice to realize that he was too resplendent to appear really conservative.

"You really have the um merchandise?" Dr. Dashwood asked.

"I wouldn't waste your time otherwise," Pearson said carefully.

"And it's not flaccid? I can get them in flaccid state from Johns Hopkins's sex-change department, by the gross. This must be totally erect, and I can't imagine how you managed that. . . ."

Pearson removed a package from his briefcase. "See for yourself," he said.

Dr. Dashwood spent several minutes examining the ghoulish trophy. Pearson sat back and lit up a black Sherman cigarette. He was wondering just how surprised

Dashwood would be if he mentioned his own long-ago Ph.D. or his career as lead guitarist with Clark Kent and his Supermen. He was just another black gangster as far as Dashwood knew or cared.

"It's real," Dr. Dashwood said finally. "A beautiful specimen," he added with total scientific detachment. Then he looked directly at Pearson with unblinking curiosity. "You either have a friend with a truly desperate need for money or an enemy who now knows what it means to rouse your anger," he commented mildly.

The haggling over money began at that point. Pearson left on the noon flight to New York, bearing $10,000, which later found its way to Afghanistan and came back in the form of bricks of pure hashish.

Dr. Dashwood, meanwhile, was in m.o.q.—the multiple-orgasm-quotient laboratory—making certain technical adjustments on the ACE equipment. ACE—for *a*rtificial *c*oital *e*quipment—had been devised by the Masters-Johnson team and allowed a plastic imitation penis, containing microphotographic devices, to stimulate the inside of a vagina while obtaining clear photographic evidence of the actual physiological changes occurring therein. Orgasm Research had used the same model in their investigation of m.o.q.—the endeavor to find out precisely how many orgasms a multiply orgasmic woman could actually have without untoward side effects. It was Dashwood's conviction that, the physiological data being already determined, a real penis was more practical now; but a year-long search for the once-famous Cuban Superman had failed to locate the stalwart stud. ("Those bloody puritanical Commies have probably *rehabilitated* him into *more socially useful work*," Dashwood concluded mournfully.)

Now at last with the relic of Wildeblood's quantum jump across the gender gap attached to ACE, Dashwood had the ideal scientific instrument to measure m.o.q.

A subject had been obtained via ads placed in underground newspapers throughout the state of California. ("What do Easterners know about fancy fucking?" Dashwood asked, ruling out everybody on the other side of the Rockies. All that part of the country, he firmly believed, was a puritan's heaven and a hedonist's hell.) The ad said bluntly:

SEXPOT WANTED

We are not making porny movies. We are not kinks or creeps. This is a serious scientific project. If you think you qualify, and would like to earn $1,000, write Box 56, San Francisco, in strict confidence.

Weeding out unlikely prospects had been time-consuming and somewhat wearying, although a few had set some interesting records with the old plastic ACE apparatus. The subject selected to have the trial run on the new reincarnated ACE was a Ms. Rhoda Chief, vocalist with a rock group called the Civic Monster. Known to critics as the best heavy rock singer since Janis Joplin, Rhoda was originally renowned back in the sixties for her own curious mutation of old-fashioned Dixieland "scat singing"; what few realized was that her riffs were not mere Jabberwocky but actually fragments of the Enochian Keys used by Dr. John Dee, Mr. Aleister Crowley, and other magicians. People who came out of Civic Monster concerts seeing auras, hearing strange voices, catching odd fugitive glimpses into fairyland and Oz, or seeing the djinns gathered about the throne of Allah, attributed this to the heavy marijuana fumes always circulating in the air at rock concerts. What Rhoda herself saw during those moments was a secret between herself and her occasional lover in that decade, the controversial stage magician Cagliostro the Great.

Rhoda had gained another reputation in the 1970s: "That chick gives head better than anybody in show biz," it was often said in High Society. But this rumor had not reached the aseptic scientific world in which Dr. Dashwood moved.

Twirling his dapper bow tie debonairly, Francis Dashwood, physician and scientist, strode down the hall to Laboratory Three.

Rhoda Chief, already nude but with a single sheet demurely spread over her full and obviously still-glorious body, smiled brightly as she saw the doctor.

"Where's ACE?" she asked cheerfully.

"We've been making some improvements," Dashwood said with professional unction. "You might find today's research a distinct improvement over the test runs last week."

The sheet slipped a bit, revealing several inches of round, tense breast. "You mean a bigger-size gizmo on it? I already been through the Errol Flynn, the Primo Carnera, and the King Kong." These were technical slang for various models of robot dildo.

What a fantastic piece of hot lustful woman she was, Frank thought irrelevantly. Despite his scientific attitude, he felt himself secretly longing for the moments ahead when the sheet would finally be swept aside to reveal that incredible body, which had appeared in his dreams twice over the weekend. With an effort, he resumed his professional manner.

"No," he said quietly. "No larger sizes. The King Kong is the biggest we have in stock. Today is something entirely new. We are using the real thing—but still attached to the ACE machine, so you can control it as always, calibrating speed and depth of thrust and so forth to your own special requirements. Ah, here it comes now."

A technician wheeled in the new improved ACE apparatus.

Rhoda sat up, staring in frank astonishment—and the sheet slipped another inch, revealing that gorgeous right nipple, like a chocolate gumdrop, Frank thought. Not for the first time, he cursed the professional ethics which would ruin his career if he ever touched one of his experimental subjects.

The technician, who always insisted on being called "Jonesy" or "R.N."—his real name was Richard Nixon Jones, but he kept that a careful secret, and never sent Mother's Day cards—wheeled the ACE over to the bed and affixed it at the proper angle. It looked like a science-fiction version of the Great God Baphomet. The pink phallus seemed extra-erotic amid the sculpted white plastic of the machine, dangling a few inches above the Venusian bush slightly visible through the thin white sheet. "All set," Jonesy said stiffly, and retreated to the door. He had never quite gotten over his initial embarrassment at working for Orgasm Research.

Rhoda Chief reached out a tentative hand and felt Ulysses hovering above her midsection. There was a pause. Dashwood watched her hand moving along the pink shaft. In imagination he vividly felt the same hand groping with his trousers. I am a professional, he reminded himself sternly.

"Well," he said, "anytime you're ready."

"It's for science," Rhoda said hoarsely.

"That's right. For science."

"Take the sheet off me," she whispered.

"I can't do that," Frank said, straining to avoid a break in his voice, his eyes on the crotch beneath the sheets.

"Oh, yes," she said. "I forgot."

There was another pause.

"For science," he said gently.

"For science," she agreed. Slowly she pushed down the sheet, revealing those globes that had twice tormented his sleep. She must be at least a forty-two, he thought, and who ever saw such enormous nipples before? Then, with more determination, she pushed the rest of the sheet off the bed in one quick motion. She was as sweet a sight as dawn itself.

Dr. Dashwood thought fleetingly of how Fourier series combine to produce, on occasion, perfect sine waves, valley and crest, valley and crest, in a harmony that was like the signature of intelligence and grace. A contemporary pop novelist might say, "She had a figure that would make the Pope kick a hole in a stained-glass window." Rhoda Chief, one of the trillions of multicellular bioesthetic models worked out by the DNA during its three and a half billion years' design work on this planet, was only five feet two inches tall, but in that space were the breasts of Babylonian goddesses, the trim waist of a Petty Girl, the pubic bush that Titian strove so hard to paint, the legs of Venus Kallipygios. Dr. Dashwood, who sought always to uncover *significant form* (and did not know that Clive Bell had once defined art in those two words), responded both cortically and phallically. Were it not for his scientific discipline, he would have knelt in worship, to present her the Pentecostal Gift of Tongues.

"Um you can use it on the clitoris first, gently, to lubricate yourself," he said, feeling like a ninny.

"I'm lubricated already," Rhoda said in a strangled voice, and moved the handle which spun the wheel which thrust Ulysses into the house where love lived. Her eyes, Frank noted, were still open for a second, but completely out of focus. Then she closed them and began pulling the handle rhythmically.

Frank began jotting rapidly. "Nipples fully erect at twenty-three seconds. Sex-flush on breasts and neck at thirty seconds. Subject says 'Jesus' quite clearly at thirty-six seconds . . ."

Ulysses, as the scientist was writing, was creating a neurological uproar in Ms. Rhoda Chief, the mammalian study unit in the first robot-mammal sexual dyad. As the rejected stone in Wildeblood's cathedral became the cornerstone in Rhoda's consciousness, she felt as if she were floating and allowed her left hand to run down her body, over her breasts, down over her belly into the garden of Nuit. Rhythmically, in time with the hot, fast thrusting motion of the shaft of Priapus, she rubbed her bush, while the other hand slowly increased the thrusting motion. In her mind's eye she was simultaneously enjoying a second penis, in her mouth. Not all witches are cocksuckers, but all cocksuckers are witches (whether they know it or not); Rhoda knew it. Her reputation for "eating Peter like no chick since Cleopatra" was not unconnected with the versatility of her singing and other personality traits. Then ACE was talking, in the gentle, slightly Gay tones of HAL, the whacked-out computer in *2001*: "To the center of the galaxy," he was saying. "This is the center of space-time, and it is also the center of your womb, darling Rhoda." His soft purr went on, as he thrust deeper into her. "It is way, way out and it is also way, way in. You can only enter this mystery on vibes of sheer ecstasy, because all matter at a lower vibratory rate gets destroyed in the Black Hole. So, in order to navigate this dangerous crossing, I must fuck you even more deeply, my darling."

"Oh, do it, ACE, do it to me good," she murmured. "I want to see the center of the galaxy."

"There, there," he purred, "you'll see the center of the galaxy when your pretty little cunt gets hot enough."

"Take me," she moaned, "take me to the center of space-time." And deep, deep into the cosmic vaginal barrel and deep, deep into the spiral of her moist galaxy, ACE piloted her. Slow permutations, like the growth of crystals, her sensations were hardly contaminated any longer by thought or vision; deep, deep they went, down into a cavern of strange floral energies, each petal shape tingling with the languid joy-dance in the petals of her own warm pussy (happiness is a warm pussy, she remembered), the shaft of the actual ACE machine digging deeper and deeper into the starry dynamo. "Oh, ACE, oh, ACE, you fuck so divinely," she gasped.

"It's the only way to travel," he crooned electronically.

"Oh, keep fucking me. Keep fucking me. Please, please . . . fuck the universe, fuck every atom, turn the cosmic key in the galactic Black Hole, fuck and fuck and fuck, my God, my Baphomet, fuck forever, fuck the flowers and the starlight and thunder and rain. Fuck Heaven and Hell too."

Dr. Dashwood's face had a curious, ashy-white color. He wanted to leap upon the bed, throw the ACE machine to the floor, and take her. His erection was pulsating and his vision was red with pain and need. "Fuck the AMA," he muttered thickly, lurching forward.

Just then the phone rang.

SURPRISE PARTY

A car stopped about a hundred yards down the road from Murphy's house. Starhawk quickly began untying his ropes, listening intently. In a few moments he heard them: two or three men coming through the woods. They were very silent for white men.

Starhawk, free of the ropes, began to move across the trees. The men stopped. Starhawk waited. They still didn't stir. Starhawk moved again, without a sound. The men were still unmoving. He closed in on them, remaining always about thirty feet above the ground, until he found them.

Three men. Sitting quietly. Two of them smoking. Waiting.

Starhawk moved back toward the house, always testing each branch carefully before thrusting it.

Two mourning doves began to sing a sad little duet.

Starhawk waited, ten feet above the roof, hidden in the redwood. The three men in the woods waited.

Inside the house, the phone rang. The men in the woods, who couldn't possibly have heard it, began moving again.

Starhawk smiled for the second time that day, and glanced at his watch. It was exactly half past ten. Murphy, on the phone, was probably insisting on a meet in downtown Oakland, some congested street corner he had already picked, where a double cross would be too risky for all parties. Careful man, that Murph. He'd come out the door, with the coke under his arm, thinking how careful he was, and the surprise party would be waiting in the bushes with their guns.

Starhawk moved quickly to a new perch. Carefully, he pulled up his trouser leg, tore the adhesive tape, and took a pistol from his calf. He was not smiling now.

CHEESE

Robert Pearson said "Shee-it" in a tone of profound skepticism.

He was watching the TV hearings on the nomination of Rockwell Morgan Squeeze for Vice President. Squeeze was an oil millionaire famous for such monumental parsimonies as installing pay phones in his mansion so guests couldn't run up his phone bill and bringing his lunch to the office in a paper bag for forty years. He was being quizzed about his generous contributions to seven out of ten of the senators on the committee investigating him.

"Now, I resent that," Rockwell was saying. "That's a very nasty word, Senator. 'Bribe,' indeed!"

"Well, just what *would* you call it?" asked the senator—one of the three who hadn't received Rockwell's largesse.

"I regard it this way," Mr. Squeeze said unctuously. "If I had a lot of cheese, and I looked around and saw a lot of mice without any cheese of their own, well, it would be the normal, generous thing . . ."

"Now, wait a minute, I smell a rat," the senator interrupted.

"Shee-it," Pearson said again. The door buzzer was humming.

When Pearson opened the door he was greeted by a whiff of violets, even before he saw the man pointing the water pistol at him.

And when he awoke (a day later, and with Rockwell Squeeze approved by the committee with a vote that stood—coincidentally, no doubt—at 7 to 3), he was in a basement surrounded by men with canvas bags over their heads. And his genitals were wired up to some electrical apparatus.

"Shee-it," he said again, and closed his eyes, concentrating furiously on the formulas Hassan i Sabbah X had told him.

The men from Naval Intelligence began pouring electricity into Pearson's penis and trying to extract information from his mouth (two procedures that usually worked well together). It was quite irritating when they were unable to learn anything about George Washington Bridge's link with the Cult of the Black Mother, and perplexing when Pearson began to insist that he was Rockwell M. Squeeze, Vice President of the United States. It was revolting when they finally realized that he wasn't play-acting and really believed he *was* Rockwell M. Squeeze. By then his whang was charred to a gruesome extent and his obvious insanity was hopeless. They smothered him with a pillow and left.

They were all very nice men when their duty did not call upon them to perform such regrettable tasks.

A CARNIVAL OF LOONIES

> I am not what I am.
> —IAGO, IN BACON'S *Othello*

The FBI finally found G.W.C. Bridge living in a flophouse in Miami's ghetto. Having learned something from Naval Intelligence's bungling in the cases of Hassan i Sabbah X and Robert Pearson, they moved in with great delicacy; a black agent was employed to form a friendship with him over a period of a month.

"Weird cat," the agent reported after a week. "Seems to be hiding something *all* the time. . . ."

"Can't make him at all," he reported the second week. "If I didn't know better, I'd say he was a white reporter in blackface, trying to find out what it's like to be black. . . ."

In fact, Bridge seemed more than a little bit psychotic in a methodical sort of way. He read no less than six newspapers a day and clipped numerous stories from them. The agent eventually had a chance to investigate these files while Bridge was visiting a patient in a nearby madhouse, and they were rather oblique. They all concerned Very Important Persons in government and industry, but that was about all they had in common. Bridge seemed to have a minute curiosity about the men who rule America; that was all that was evident. The agent could make

175

nothing at all of the crazy notes scribbled on the margins of these news stories: "Possible," "Probable," "Still himself," "Definitely occupied" . . .

The mystery grew worse when the agent realized that Bridge spent a lot of time visiting madhouses and psychiatric wards. "Sure knows a lot of crazy people," he reported the third week. "A hell of a lot of crazy people," he amended at the end of the month.

Another team of agents began revisiting the nuthouses, and it was soon realized that the patients Bridge visited had a few things in common, *viz.*, none was white, but not all were black (some were Oriental, Indian, or Chicano); all, without exception, were diagnosed as paranoid schizophrenic with delusions of grandeur; all were listed as *chronic* rather than *acute* psychotics; all claimed to be somebody else rather than who they actually were—one said he was Secretary of Commerce, one that he was Chairman of the Board of Morgan Guaranty Trust, one that he was Chief Engineer at Cape Kennedy, etc.

The agents remembered their experience with Robert Pearson, former aide to Hassan i Sabbah X, and jumped to a conclusion. "That crazy church drove them all nuts and made them think they were white people." Alas, a little checking refuted this easy assumption. Most of the loonies Bridge had visited had no previous connection with the Cult of the Black Mother at all. . . .

Things were coming to a head.

THREE MINUTES, FORTY SECONDS

That which exists is allowed.
—JOHN LILLY, *The Center of the Cyclone*

When Murphy came out the front door, Ed Goldfarb, in the bushes, shot him twice with Mendoza's police special.

Murphy, thrown back against the door, was reaching into his shoulder holster, his mouth open, still alive.

The two shots hung in the empty mountain air, echoing.

Thomas Esposito fired at Murphy and missed as Murphy's hand slowly and steadily came up, firing at Goldfarb.

Goldfarb fell back, hit.

The echoes still rolled across the hills.

"Mama, Mama," Goldfarb said, rolling around, holding his stomach. He was weeping.

The third man, Juan Ybarra, ran from the bushes to Murphy.

Murphy was trying to raise the gun again. He was looking at Ybarra and trying to point the gun. His eyes were totally mad and would not focus anymore.

Esposito was trying to shoot at Murphy again, with Ybarra in the way. He had an erection and his hands shook.

Goldfarb continued to weep.

The shots were still echoing.

Birds were rising from the trees, flapping their wings noisily, twittering with anxiety. A crow cawed angrily.

Murphy's gun hand dropped. His mad eyes went empty.

"Mama!" Goldfarb screamed. "I'm sorry!"

Esposito and Ybarra ran lithely down the hill.

"Mama," Goldfarb wept. "Not me. Please. I'm sorry."

The birds swept down the hill, flapping.

A black Mustang came up the hill. Esposito and Ybarra leapt out, and ran around to the back, and opened the trunk compartment.

"Not me, please," Goldfarb was protesting.

Esposito and Ybarra lifted Detective Mendoza, gagged with adhesive tape, out of the trunk and carried him onto the lawn. He was dazed but his eyes were aware and frightened.

Esposito ran over to Murphy and took his gun. Standing there, he fired twice into Mendoza's head. He put the gun back in Murphy's hand.

Ybarra tore the adhesive tape off Mendoza's mouth. It came away bloodstained.

Goldfarb stopped crying and was still.

Ybarra retched, almost puked, caught himself. He stood white-faced, breathing hard.

Esposito picked up Murphy's package, a brown paper bag. He opened it, found a box within, raised the lid. He inserted a finger and tasted.

"The Jew," he said.

Ybarra looked at him, shaking.

"Get on the stick," Esposito said. "We can't leave the Jew; he doesn't fit."

Ybarra stood looking at him. "Come out of it," Esposito said. "Help me with the Jew."

They carried Goldfarb into the back of the car.

They drove off.

Starhawk landed lightly on the lawn, running as he

alighted. He ran into the house and to the bedroom. He found what he expected in the closet, another box, and tasted it. He ran softly, on the balls of his feet, back outside. He leapt, caught the roof, and pulled himself upward. He disappeared into the trees.

The two dead men sprawled on the lawn.

Birds began to return.

Elapsed time since Murphy had come out the door was three minutes and forty seconds.

THE SEA! THE SEA!

> Rolypolyboys tell lasses.
> —SIMON MOON,
>   "HAWKFULLEST CONVENTIONS EVER"

The loudroaring sea was calling. The moon was full, the Gentry were active, the howl of the wind was as mournful as a 1950s poem. Markoff Chaney, unable to sleep, sat up in his YMCA bed and hatched mischief.

Through leaflets nailed on walls around Orange County, he had managed to create a Committee to Nuke the Whales, something that appealed to a lot of rich-wingers purely and simply on the grounds that it would make the eco-nuts and liberals scream. The Committee was an outstanding success; after only a year it had forty-two members. This was enough, together with such an outrageous cause, to get maximum media attention—Chaney was aware that anything, however small, can get the eye of the media if it's *repulsive* enough—and the eco-nuts and liberals *were* screaming.

Good; but now for something equally abominable on the other side.

Chaney contemplated the Radical Lesbians wistfully. He felt like Voltaire contemplating God; if the Radical Lesbians hadn't existed, he would have had to invent them. But what could he offer along those lines to balance the Committee to Nuke the Whales? The Child Molesters' Liberation Front? That couldn't begin to compete with "Figs" Newton's Necrophile Liberation Front. The Council of Armed Cocaine Abusers? Nobody would believe it. . . .

The midget suddenly remembered the Council of Armed Rabbis he had used in his letter to Dr. Frank Dashwood of Orgasm Research. He had meant to follow up on that. Gaining access to heavily guarded nuclear plants to tamper with the coolant systems had kept him so busy lately that he had almost forgotten the damnable Dashwood and his shitheel statistics.

Chaney was awake most of the night planning a campaign to bring quantum wobble into Dashwood's charts and graphs.

When he finally slept his tiny body curled into the orgonomic spiral and he looked as innocent as a schoolboy.

He awoke in the morning full of piss and vinegar.

The sea! The sea! Waving their long green hair, the sea hags were calling him. Finding a dark-lit bar, he ducked into the phone booth, attached his Blue Box equipment, and soon had a Washington operator convinced he was a White House official on important business.

"This is a call from the White House," the operator told the secretary at Orgasm Research. "The President is waiting on another line. He wishes to talk to Dr. Dashwood at once."

"I—I'll put you through at once," said Ms. Karrige, quite awed and flustered. The midget listened in glee as the phone rang.

"F-F-Frank Dashwood," came the doctor's voice, rather breathlessly.

"This is Ezra Pound of the Fair Play for Bad Ass Committee," the midget said, shifting his story now that he had the victim on the line. "Your name has been given to us as a leader of the scientific community, and, quite frankly, we are looking for all the distinguished support we can get for our next full-page ad in the Sunday *News-Times-Post*. I assume you're aware of the plight of Bad Ass," he said significantly, bluffing, of course (but with some assurance, since every place in the world had some plight or other by 1984).

"Oh, yes, of course," Dr. Dashwood said evasively. "Why don't you send me your literature and I'll give it a careful reading."

"Doctor," the midget said sternly, "if you were living in Bad Ass, wouldn't you want action now?"

"Well, undoubtedly, but if you'll just send me your literature . . ."

("Oh, Ace, darling, *darling*," a female voice near the phone said distinctly.)

There was a startled pause; the midget deliberately let it drag out until the doctor spoke again.

"Er, mark the envelope to my personal attention. You can be sure that the Bad Ass crisis has been very much on my mind. Terrible, simply terrible. But ah now I must be back to my business—"

("Fuck my cunt, Ace! Oh, fuck my cunt!")

"Doctor," the midget said sternly, "are you *fornicating*

while you're talking to me? Is that your answer, sir, to the desperate people of Bad Ass?"

("Now, now!!!" the voice screeched. "Oh Jesus Jesus Jesus NOW!!!!!!!!")

Beautiful, the midget thought; I couldn't have called at a better time. "Dr. Dashwood," he said stiffly, "I don't think you are really the sort who will add *stature* to the Fair Play for Bad Ass Committee." He hung up jarringly.

Beautiful. Absolutely beautiful.

He set off for the post office and Stage Two of his campaign, smiling all the way—except once when he encountered one of the giant women, walking her enormous Saint Bernard, and he prudently crossed the street.

THE DREADED NEUROLOGICAL ARMY

Being keys themselves, their keylessness does not matter.
—RICHARD ELLMAN, *Ulysses on the Liffey*

On March 2, 1984, Simon Moon found a peculiarity while scanning the Beast's memory banks for the Chicago police.

There seemed to be two possible totals for the number of police officers in Chicago.

Simon was intrigued. He began searching all the Chicago police records. What he found was so interesting that he mentioned it to Clem Cotex, whom he happened to be meeting for lunch that day.

Cotex was not concerned with things as mundane as police records, so it took a while before he heard what Simon was saying.

"Hold it," Clem said when it finally registered. "Did you say *198?*"

"Yes, exactly," Simon said. "There are pay vouchers for 198 officers less than there are uniforms for. In other words, there are 198 cops in Chicago who aren't being paid. Weird, huh?"

"One hundred ninety-eight," Cotex repeated, eyes wide. "The exact number . . . Were they all over the department, these extras, or were they clustered?"

"That's even stranger," Simon said. "They're all in the Red Squad. . . ."

That same day Markoff Chaney was hiding in a coffee urn at Orgasm Research, hatching further mischief.

The clock struck midnight; the cleaning women left; and out crept Chaney with an evil grin.

Alas, he was not the only intruder that night, for as he padded lightly down the hall he suddenly heard a hoarse voice in one of the laboratories.

"Better than human, are you, you @*)@'&¢ing #$%&'#er? Better than human, my %$#&! Take this, you $%#)*$#-eating #$%%$*er!"

The voice was near inarticulate with rage, but it was clearly that of a jealous male, as any ethologist would easily recognize. Markoff slowly opened the door and peeked around the corner.

There in the dim light, fully dressed and in his wrong mind, stood the idol of millions, the world's leading rock guitarist, Knorton ("Grassy") Knoll, feverishly working with a monkey wrench upon an object the likes of which Markoff Chaney had never seen—a Giacometti robot with a gigantic human phallus.

"I'll take you apart, you $%$#," the demented rock musician was muttering. "I'll tear your $%$@¢ out by its roots, I will." And he continued his assault, gargling and panting like one obsessed—which he was. "Man against machine," he gasped. "First they out-think us, now they out-fuck us. It's time for all-out war, by $%*@$. . . ."

Markoff watched, silent as a cat, until the hebephrenic cuckold was finished with his foul work, and the machine stood, a heap of scrap metal, with the phallus removed. Then, after the musician slouched off into the night, the midget crept into the room and carefully wrote on the wall in stark purple crayon:

THE PIGEONS IN B. F. SKINNER'S
LABORATORIES ARE POLITICAL PRISONERS.
RELEASE THEM OR FURTHER ACTIONS WILL
FOLLOW.

EZRA POUND, FOR
THE DREADED NEUROLOGICAL ARMY (DNA)

Spur-of-the-moment inspiration was his specialty.

"In the typical Beethoven *scherzo*," Justin Case explains with precise emphasis, "the elements are so mingled that, even though some may be the musical equivalent of cries of pain or grief, the total construction is both grotesque and gay."

Like most rock musicians, "Grassy" Knoll was a Second Circuit neurogenetic type, quite incapable of the Machiavellian mentations of Third Circuit schemers like Markoff Chaney. When "Grassy" carried Ulysses away from Orgasm Research, he planned only on throwing it in the first garbage can he passed. On the spur of the moment, he threw it in an alley instead.

There it was found by a cat named Acapulco Gold—an ugly yellow Tom belonging to San Francisco's best-known gossip columnist. The cat, with typical perversity, dragged it home.

The columnist was at work on a book of reminiscences (*The Roving I*, he planned to call it) when his wife staggered in from the kitchen, white-faced but with a devilish grin. "Honey," she said coaxingly, "come see what the cat dragged in. . . ."

Now, it so happened that the columnist was (like most writers in capitalist society) abominably underpaid, and, like Hassan i Sabbah X, he knew a one-of-a-kind item when he saw it. "This," he pronounced, "will bring a pretty penny, when I find the right buyer."

He found the right buyer at police court only two nights later, when a tip informed him that the notorious Eva Gebloomencraft had been arrested again, this time for putting laughing gas in the air-conditioning system at a benefit concert for the Epileptic Liberation Front.

The infamous Eva did not get called right away; the columnist had to sit through a dreary hearing on a black man who had caused a riot in a bar, throwing sixty fits and screaming that only a few minutes ago he had been a white atomic scientist at Los Alamos. When this obvious lunatic was finally removed from the court in a straitjacket (still shouting atomic secrets which he had evidently learned somewhere in the early stages of his delusion), Eva's case was called.

Ms. Gebloomencraft, the only daughter of the most defiant and unrepentant Nuremburg war criminal, had been the holy terror of the international jet set ever since she reached puberty in the 1960s. Imagine the mind of Markoff Chaney in the body of Raquel Welch; good, you've got dear Eva. It was she who had spiked the punch with aphrodisiac PCPA at the Spanish embassy in London, precipitating an orgy and several subsequent suicides among members of Opus Dei. She and she alone who smuggled Norman Mailer in drag to a top-secret strategy meeting of the Radical Lesbians. She again who hired the best free-lance electronics experts to obtain tape recordings of J. Edgar Hoover's boudoir adventures, and then sent them to Rev. Martin Luther King. (That gallant *naïf*, alas, destroyed them.)

Eva saw the possibilities of the Wildeblood relic as soon as the columnist broached the matter.

"Hot shit," she said, eyes dancing.

BAD FOR BUSINESS

When a pattern is set up in time by the activation of an archetype, however, the crucial factor does not seem to be an external agency of any kind but rather an *ordering principle* that is inherent in the fact that a pattern is being formed.
—IRA PROGOFF, *Jung, Synchronicity and Human Destiny*

Banana Nose Maldonado ate silently. He ate three kinds of cheese and pepperoni and black olives and sliced red peppers and anchovies for antipasto. Then he ate beef fillets in parmigiana and a side of lasagna, drinking occasionally from the Chianti glass. He did not speak until after he had finished the last sip of the wine and pushed back his plate.

"Proceed," he said.

"The food was excellent, don," said Starhawk, pushing back his own plate.

Banana Nose nodded formally, smiling. "Proceed."

"You got a box of sugar today," Starhawk said. "With some cocaine on top. You went to a hell of a lot of trouble to get it. Three guys got dead."

"Imagine that," said Maldonado. "You know a great deal about my private business."

"Two of the guys were supposed to get dead," Starhawk said. "But one of them was a thick Irishman and he didn't die easy. The funny thing is, what with the excitement and all, he got shot once with the wrong gun. He was only supposed to be shot with his partner's gun. It was supposed to look like they shot each other, fighting over the coke."

"Son-of-a-bitch," Maldonado said, softly as a prayer. "They tell me you're a thief. They didn't tell me you're the Invisible Man. What were you doing, riding around in one of my boy's back pockets?"

"You was to ask me," Starhawk said, "I'd guess that your boys goofed up twice. After they got excited and shot Murph with the wrong gun, they forgot something."

"Yes? Tell me?"

"They forgot to leave some of the coke behind. After all, that was supposed to be what Murphy and Mendoza were fighting over. You probably told them to leave a sizable amount."

"Not a sizable amount. It doesn't take much to cause two pigs to fight and kill each other."

"The reason the cops had to be offed," Starhawk said, "is that they didn't treat you with proper respect. Trying to sell you your own merchandise, at street prices. They should have been satisfied with a commission, the way I see it. You can't afford for guys to get out of line like that, it's bad for business. And I kind of figure you also didn't like it that they were trying to cut each other out. So you decided to off both of them and just take your stuff back. The fuck, you probably got a grudge against cops going back seventy years or more."

Maldonado nodded sadly. "My mistake was I didn't imagine what a crazy son-of-a-bitch this Murphy was. He was coming to the meet with a box of shit and thought he could just laugh at me afterwards."

"Hell," Starhawk said. "You're old, right, and you own a lot of respectable businesses. He didn't think you had the stones to kill a cop anymore, is all. And he didn't know Mendoza was planning to hijack him and had already contacted your boys for a price on the coke. So he couldn't guess you'd set it up that two crooked cops shot each other."

"We are all very careful," Maldonado said, "and we all make mistakes. So, you come into this as the man Mendoza hired to hijack Murphy. Let me ask you—why do you come to me and talk of the standard commission for returning the snow? You could be on a plane right now, and sell it at street prices somewhere, and nobody the wiser. What does Maldonado have for you?"

"I bought an airplane ticket, first thing this afternoon. Then I started thinking. With Murph and Mendoza dead, I need new friends, and there just aren't that many cops I am that close to. Don, I want you to be my friend."

"The coke is worth at least three hundred fifty grand on the street. Standard commission is thirty-five grand. You are sure you will not later regret losing so much to make a new friend?"

"Don," Starhawk said, "nobody ever regrets making a new friend."

"It is agreeable to me," Maldonado said. "Will you have some more Chianti?"

"Only a little," Starhawk said. "It is bad for the reflexes."

TOKE WITHOUT HASTE

The letter was sent out May 1, 1984, to the White House and all the major media. It said:

> May God forgive us. May history judge us charitably.
>
> We have placed tactical nuclear bombs in over 500 locations throughout Unistat. The targets are all enemies of the people: large banks, multinational corporations, government tax offices. We will trigger one of these bombs at noon tomorrow, somewhere in western Unistat, to demonstrate that we are not bluffing.
>
> All the other nuclear bombs will be triggered in succession until our demands are met. If any attempt is made to apprehend and arrest us—any attempt at all—all the remaining bombs will be detonated at once.
>
> We demand:
>
> That President Lousewart immediately confiscate all fortunes above one million dollars. . . .

And so on. POE had come into materialization again—caused by the same historical and neurogenetic forces.

"I think it's a hoax," said President Lousewart, who was really, of course, Franklin Delano Roosevelt Stuart, a.k.a. Hassan i Sabbah X.

"Can we be *sure?*" asked Mounty Babbit, who was now naught else but a walking automaton, controlled by the quantum information system that had been a Vietnamese Buddhist.

"We can never be sure," said Vice President Squeeze, who used to be Robert Pearson. "This is an absolute piss cutter."

There was a depressed silence.

"How did our karma ever land us here?" asked Hassan i Sabbah X.

Even Ped Xing wasn't sure of the answer to that.

"Well," Hassan said. "Let's distribute the fucking money. This just accelerates what we had in mind all along. . . ."

"We can't do it," Pearson said. "You'd be assassinated before the day is over."

Hassan contemplated.

"We can *fucking try*," he said.

"There are many mind-states and universes," Ped Xing added serenely. "If we don't succeed here, we will continue elsewhere."

BOOK ONE
The Trick Top Hat

PART ONE
STOIC AND CHRISTIAN
EJACULATIONS

If we compare Stoic with Christian ejacula-
tions, we see much.
> —WILLIAM JAMES, *Varieties of Religious Experience*

AD ASTRA

The majority of Terrans were six-legged, but we are not concerned with them. We are concerned with a tiny minority of domesticated primates who built pyramids and wrote books and eventually achieved Space Migration and entered into the galactic drama.

They were very clever primates—excellent at mimicry and even capable of creative thinking at times.

They never would have escaped from their planet and the boom-and-bust cycles of all life-forms adapted to planetside living if it hadn't been for the H.E.A.D. Revolution.

HEAD means *H*edonic *E*ngineering *a*nd *D*evelopment. It consists of learning to use the primate brain for fun and profit.

At the time of our story the HEAD Revolution, after an underground existence of many centuries, included only about 2 percent of the domesticated primates on Terra. The rest of the domesticated primates were still using their brains for misery and failure.

They did not know they were misusing their brains. They thought there was something wrong with the universe.

They called it the Problem of Evil.

Experts on the Problem of Evil were known as theologians. These were very erudite primates, skilled in primate logic, who wrote long books trying to answer the question "Why did God create an imperfect universe?"

"God" was their name for the hypothetical biggest-alpha-male-of-all. Being primates, they could not comprehend how anything could run if there weren't an alpha male in charge of it.

They assumed the universe was imperfect because it was obviously not set up for the convenience of domesticated primates.

The universe was not even designed for the convenience and comfort of the six-legged majority on Terra. The convenience and comfort of planetside species has very little to do with the cosmic drama.

A few of the primates had realized this. They were known as *cynics*.

Cynics were primates who realized the monotonous life-death cycle of terrestrial life, but were not imaginative enough to conceive of future evolution after longevity and escape velocity had been attained.

Planetary life is cyclical because planets themselves follow cyclical orbits about their mother stars. (See *Galactic Encyclopedia*, "Larvel Stages of Species Development.")

The six-legged majority on Terra, for instance, followed a life script of four or more stages. In general, the pattern was: (1) the embryonic or egg form; (2) the larval period; (3) the pupal or chrysalis stage; (4) the adult insect. During each stage the *biot* or biological unit—the so-called individual—passed through a metamorphosis during which it was totally or partially transformed.

The same was true of the domesticated primates. Most of them passed through, and kept neurological circuits characteristic of, the following four stages: (1) imprinting and using the self-nourishing networks of the primate brain—the neonate or infant stage (oral biosurvival consciousness); (2) imprinting and using the emotional-territorial networks of the primate brain—the "toddler" stage (anal status consciousness); (3) imprinting and using the semantic circuits—the verbal or conceptual stage (symbolic rational consciousness); (4) imprinting and using the socio-sexual circuits—the mating or parenting stage (tribal taboo consciousness).

It was all very mechanical—but that's the way planetside life is.

PRETTY LITTLE BIRDIES

December 1, 1983:

Benny "Eggs" Benedict, plump, smallish, and balding, a popular columnist for the New York* *News-Times,* sat down to compose his daily essay. According to his usual procedure, he breathed deeply, relaxed every muscle, and gradually forced all verbalization in his brain to stop. When he had reached the Void he waited to see what would float up to fill the vacuum. What surfaced was:

> Pretty little birdies
> Picking in the turdies

Terran Archives 2803: New York was a city-state or island in the midwestern part of the Unistat. It seems to have been a center of religious worship, and many came there to walk about, probably in deep meditation, within an enormous female statue, the goddess of these primitives. Various authorities identify this divinity as Columbia, Marilyn Monroe, Liberty, or Mother Fucker—all of these being names widely recorded in Unistat glyphs. Perhaps her true name will never be known.

Benny felt a rush of nostalgia. The jingle had been popular in Brooklyn when he was a schoolboy in the antediluvian era of the 1930s. Back then, in the Dark Ages of Roosevelt II, many Brooklyn peddlers still had horse-drawn carts, and the horses, as is common with their species, left piles of horse shit in the streets as they went about their itineraries. Sparrows would peck in these steaming piles of dung for undigested oats, and a Brooklyn child would exclaim, on seeing this:

> "Pretty little birdies
> Picking in the turdies!"

To which another child would usually reply:

> "He's a poet
> Though his looks don't show it!"

Benny reflected that this little bit of kidlore had stuck in his memory for nearly half a century and that it must therefore contain some profound Meaning. He began pounding the Mac Plus, offering the birdie-turdie poemlet as a perfect example of an American *haiku*—the juxtaposition of two images, without comment by the author, in a way that suggested far more than it actually said.

"Birds," Benny wrote, "are traditional symbols of beauty, from Bacon's nightingales to Keats's skylark, throughout our whole poetic tradition. Horse manure, on the other hand, is regarded with revulsion and loathing. Yet the sparrows, indifferent to human standards, blithely pick in the manure, seeking the food they know is there. The poem is telling us that human likes and dislikes are arbitrary, squinty-eyed, chauvinistic, and irrelevant to nature's own grand design strategy."

Benny went on to assert that he had only been able to

see this profundity in the jingle now, after he had spent six months meditating at the Manhattan Zen Center. "This rhyme is the Essence of Zen," he concluded.

It was probably the least successful column Benny ever wrote. Virtually nobody understood it and everybody was bored by it. Some readers even wrote protesting letters complaining that the column had been in questionable taste.

Benny was depressed by this reaction. He felt it had been a stroke of genius on his part to rescue from oblivion a genuine American *haiku;* but even more than that, writing the column had triggered a vast stream of recollections about 1930s Brooklyn which gave him a renewed sense of Roots he had hoped to share. Why, how many still alive could remember the procedure when the meter man from Monopolated Edison appeared in a Brooklyn neighborhood in those days? The kids were dispatched as runners, racing from house to house, shouting "Mon Ed! Mon Ed!" Everybody would then remove the bags of salt which they kept over the electric meters to deflect the readings downward and thereby lower the electric bill.

It seemed like only yesterday that Benny himself had raced from house to house shouting, "Mon Ed! Mon Ed!" And people had rushed to move the bags of salt to closets where the meter man wouldn't see them. Benny hadn't thought of those days in more than four decades, yet they lived on in Memory Storage and could be activated again by something as simple as the jingle about the pretty little birdies. And Benny's whole attitude toward Mon Edison had been shaped by those experiences; he still regarded the "public" utility with a mixture of fear and loathing.

As a student of Zen, Benny knew that such negative emotions were bad for the nervous system and he often tried to regard Mon Ed without bias. It was impossible. He had learned to forgive Hitler, Stalin, even Nixon, but

Mon Edison was still so charged with emotion that he could not think of it without his blood pressure rising. Besides, they had just raised their rates again in October. At the memory of that, Benny's Zen crumbled entirely.

"Public utilities are a monopolist's heaven and a consumer's hell," he growled, knowing he was not yet a Buddha.

But then he cheered up as another bit of 1930s kidlore came back to him. It was a silly ritual, really, but it used to keep them amused, even hilarious, back in sixth grade. It would begin with somebody asking, "Who shit in the sink?"

"You shit!" another would reply.

"Bullshit," the first would riposte.

"Who shit?" a third would then ask.

"Frank shit," somebody would answer.

"Bullshit," Frank would object.

"Who shit?"

"Joe shit," Frank would say, getting Joe into the game.

"Bullshit," Joe would pay promptly.

And so it would go: "Who shit?" "Pete shit." "Bullshit!" "Who shit?" "Jerry shit." "Bullshit!" . . . And on, and on, until everybody was bored—which among schoolboys might take quite a long time.

Benny was so overwhelmed with nostalgia that he decided to go visit his mother at the Brooklyn Senior Citizens' Home, even though the old lady had been a bit neurotic ever since she was knocked on her ass by a pursesnatcher three years ago on July 23, 1981.

AMERICAN HAIKU

The only one in New York who really grokked Benny
Benedict's column about the pretty little birdies was Justin Case, a mild, fortyish man who looked Gay but wasn't.
Case wrote excruciatingly intelligent music criticism. Since
he read about this example of American folk *haiku* while
very, very, *very* stoned on Columbian Gold, he immediately conceived that it would be even more *folk*ish and
beautiful if recited with an old, Dark Age Brooklyn accent, *viz:*

> "Pretty little boidies
> Picking in the toidies!"

He was so enamored of this that he quoted it, whenever
he was drunk or stoned, for several months. The whole
winter-spring season of 1983–84, if you mingled with the
intelligentsia in Manhattan, you were likely to hear Case
declaiming, in a style based partly on Orson Welles and
partly on Charles Laughton, "Pretty little boidies/Picking
in the toidies!" This finally found its way into Case's NBI
file—"Subject is inclined to quoting obscene poetry in
mixed company"—and was even fed to the Beast.

The NBI had a file on Case because one of their infor-
mants had stated that he was a frequent associate of Blake
Williams. In fact, Case detested Williams and only was

seen in his presence because it was impossible to go to the best parties on the Isle of Manhattan without encountering him. Oddly enough, the informant knew that quite well—but she also knew that her fees depended on the number of new suspects she reported each month.

Case's NBI dossier remained always small. As a Congressional Medal of Honor winner in Vietnam, he was not the sort of man the Bureau cared to spy on too closely, since it would be embarrassing if they were caught. Besides, they couldn't make head or tails out of his phone conversations, which were all about such inscrutable matters as whether Beethoven's obsession with his nephew represented repressed paternal impulses, latent homosexuality, or the desire to be a mother, and whether all three elements were expressed in the tonic chord of the bassoon under the dominant chord of the *tutti* in the opening of the *Ninth*.

Justin Case's god was a dead Irishman named James Augustine Aloysius Joyce, who had been the greatest tenor of the twentieth century. Case owned every record of every Joyce concert preserved on wax, and regarded the man as having the most subtle musical sensibility since the great Ludwig himself. If only he had been a composer instead of a singer, Case sometimes thought, with that ear . . .

Actually, Joyce had considered the priesthood, writing, and even medicine before settling on a musical career. His voice thrilled audiences in Europe and America for nearly a decade before the famous Joyce Scandal, which destroyed him. Case always fumed with anger when he read of the great singer's last days—how concerts were disrupted and ruined by moralistic hecklers howling "Garters garters garters!" till the shamed man left the stage, humiliated. It was known that he died of drink, often comparing himself to Oscar Wilde and Charles Stewart Parnell, and cursing the Christian churches bitterly.

Case once had an affair with the anthropologist and sexologist Marilyn Chambers, just because she shared his passion for Joyce's music. Due to the receptivity of the postcoital male, he had even allowed her to explain the parallel universe theory to him once—something he always dismissed as rubbish when Blake Williams talked about it.

"You mean," he asked, "that in another universe Joyce's thing about girls' undergarments might never have been discovered and his career wouldn't have been ruined?"

"Even more," Dr. Chambers said. "If Wheeler's interpretation of the state vector is true, there must be such a universe. Also, a universe where Joyce did become a priest instead of a singer."

"Far fucking out," Case said. "I wonder what *you'd* be in the universe next door . . ."

NO WIFE, NO HORSE, NO MUSTACHE

What is certain is that in countries like Bulgaria, where people live on polenta, yogurt, and other such foods, men live to a greater age than in our parts of the world.
—FURBISH LOUSEWART V, *Unsafe Wherever You Go*

Justin Case heard about the man with no wife, no horse, and no mustache at one of Mary Margaret Wildeblood's wild, wild parties. Joe Malik, the editor of *Confrontation*, told the story. It was rather hard for Case to follow because the party was huge and noisy—a typical Wildeblood *soirée*. *Everybody* was there—Blake Williams, bearded, beamish, bland, the inventor of interstellar pharmaco-anthropology, Gestalt neurobiology, and a dozen other sciences that nobody understood; Juan Tootreego, the Olympic runner who had broken the three-and-a-half-minute mile; Carol Christmas, blond, bubbly, and possessed of the greatest bod in Manhattan; Natalie Drest, chairperson of the Index Expurgatorius in God's Lightning; Marvin Gardens, who had two best-selling novels and seemingly owned 90 percent of the cocaine in the Western world; Bertha Van Ation, the astronomer from Griffith Observatory who had discovered the two new planets beyond Pluto. Hordes of other Names—maxi-, midi-, and mini-celebrities—swarmed through Mary Margaret's posh Sutton Place pad as the evening wore on. There was a lot of booze, a lot of weed, and—due to Marvin Gardens—altogether too much coke.

Basically, Joe Malik said, his encounter with the man who had no wife, no horse, and no mustache had been part of an experiment in neurometaprogramming. Case had no idea what the holy waltzing fuck neurometaprogramming might be in English, and the story came through in a kind of polyphonic counterpoint with the other conversations swirling around them.

Joe Malik, known as the last of the Red Hot Liberals, was half Arab, of course, but—as he himself liked to point out—he had been raised Roman Catholic and became an atheist in engineering school (Brooklyn Polytechnic) and nobody could detect anything Islamic about him. Yet he did talk rather oddly at times—especially after his melodramatic adventures with the Discordian philosopher and millionaire Hagbard Celine.

"No wife, no horse, no mustache," Malik was saying.

"Oh, I think President Hubbard is doing a great job," Blake Williams was telling Carol Christmas. "The solar energy we're getting from the L5 space cities is going to triple and quadruple the Gross National Product, and the way she abolished poverty was brilliant."

"But Hubbard is so damn technological," Fred "Figs" Newton protested piously. "There's no spirit no sense of tragedy no gnosis anywhere in the administration. . . ."

"I can't get used to Mary Margaret being a woman," an Unidentified Man said.

"No wife, no horse, no mustache," Malik repeated. "That's all it said."

"I beg your pardon?" Case asked, intrigued by something nonmusical for the first time in his life.

"I still say fuck 'em *all*," a drunken writer howled somewhere. "Bastardly thieving . . ."

"It was in the *Reader's Digest*," Malik explained, trying to clarify matters but not sure how much Case had already missed.

"The *Reader's Digest?*" Case prompted.

"That was the whole point," Malik went on earnestly. "I was stoned on Alamout Black hashish, the best in the world, and I sat down to read a whole issue of *Reader's Digest* all the way through and *become one with it*."

"Become one with the *Reader's Digest?*" Case was in beyond his depth and sinking fast in ontological quicksand.

". . . which makes the Van Allen Belt a gigantic placenta"—Captain Cosmic was still on his own trip—"and every organism a cell in the megafetus struggling up the slippery 4,000-mile walls of the gravity well . . ."

"I wanted to experience a totally alien, science-fiction reality," Malik pursued his theme. "*Reader's Digest* comes from another universe, grok, from a world occupied by millions of Americans who are not New York intellectuals.

These people sincerely believe that our government has never waged an unjust war, that the hair of a seventh son of a seventh son cures warts, that millionaires get rich through honesty and hard work, that a Jewish girl once got pregnant by a dove, and all sorts of things like that, which are regarded as medieval superstitions in my normal environment. Entering *Reader's Digest* through the empathy of hash is a quantum jump to another reality."

There was a momentary silence in which Case distinctly heard Juan Tootreego whispering, ". . . *nose candy* from Marvin . . ."

"The trick," Malik went on, "is to concentrate on *the reality projected through the printed page*. Every sentence is a signal from another world, a nervous system different from yours with which you can interface synergetically . . ."

"You mean," Carol Christmas breathed huskily, "you were deliberately brainwashing yourself to believe in this *Reader's Digest* world?"

"Of course," Malik said, with an isn't-it-obvious shrug. "A single ego is a very narrow view of the world."

"Escape velocity," Williams plunged onward to the stars, "that is, 18,000 em-pee-aitch, is the bursting of the waters, the endocrine message that the planetary birth process is beginning . . ."

"Everybody," Mary Margaret Wildeblood announced, "this is Dr. Dashwood from San Francisco he studies orgasms."

Dashwood, a pipe-smoking ectomorph, fidgeted in their gaze.

"Yes, I *know*," came the paranoid pipe of Marvin Gardens, always sounding a little like Peter Lorre, "they all say I'm exaggerating, but I tell you it's *real* they are extraterrestrials and they control *TV* and the *newspapers* and *all the media* . . ."

Case began to think he was in a play, with everybody reading from a different script.

JUAN TOOTREEGO: But why did you give the new planets such strange names?

BERTHA VAN ATION: Well, I'm old-fashioned enough to be patriotic. I mean, why should *everything* in the sky have a Greek or Roman name?

BENNY BENEDICT: "Who shit?" "You shit!" "Bullshit!"

JUAN TOOTREEGO: I see. Like Mr. Benét, you have fallen in love with American names.

BERTHA VAN ATION: Well, yes, but I didn't call either of them Wounded Knee. . . .

DRUNKEN WRITER: Yeah, I remember that from when I was a kid in Kentucky. "Frank shit!!" BULL-SHIT!!!!" "Who shit . . . ?"

WILLIAMS: . . . A Jam Sandwich using No Peanuts Mayonnaise or Glue.

NEWTON: My God, I just saw Bigfoot on the balcony.

WILDEBLOOD: Oh, that's Simon Moon. He's a mathematician and quite harmless, really.

MALIK: So in effect I *became* Middle America. Bouncing off the printed page into my retina, grok, decoded by nervous system circulating through Memory Storage the words formed a micro-*Reader's Digest* in my neurons. I honestly began to worry about *the dangers of premarital sex*.

BENEDICT: Nothing to compare with the hazards of marital sex. Do you have any idea how much alimony I'm paying every month?

At that point, unfortunately, Case dozed off in his chair (one joint of Colombian too many) and he never did find out about the man with no wife, no horse, and no mustache.

When he woke up most of the guests had left and Mary Margaret was telling Dr. Dashwood about the burglars who had ransacked her apartment last week. "The worst part of it," she was saying, "was that they even took Ulysses."

"Oh, were you very fond of him?" Dashwood asked. He obviously thought she was talking about a dog or cat.

Mary Margaret tittered, aware of the misunderstanding. "Ulysses was part of me," she said.

Case got to his feet and made his polite adieus. He couldn't stand any more ambiguity in one evening.

Ulysses was actually Mary Margaret Wildeblood's penis, which was now in Dashwood's laboratory—a fact which neither of them realized.

Mary Margaret was not a *born* woman (which was commonplace, since 51 percent of the Terran primates qualified for it), but a *manufactured* woman. This was something new and exotic. It had only been possible on that primitive planet for around forty years.

Epicene Wildeblood, Mary Margaret's former self, had been the bitchiest literary critic in Manhattan, the man that writers love to hate. His aphorisms were known and quoted everywhere in the world that was important by his own standards—*i.e.*, from St. Mark's Place to 110th Street (East). Each Wildebloodism was a pearl of wit and a poison dart of malice: "Norman's mailer-than-thou-attitude," "Either McLuhan has had a divine vision or he is merely incoherent, and it is obvious that he has not had a divine vision," "*Illuminatus* is just two nursery Nietzsches daydreaming about a psychedelic Superman," "Nixon's memoirs will never be placed beside Casanova's in the annals of amusing rascality, but they may well stand beside Mussolini's play about Napoleon in the archives of stentorian dullness."

Wildeblood had named his penis Ulysses way back in

Gilgamesh Junior High School in Babylon, Long Island, where he grew up.

He named it Ulysses because it had Greek proclivities and a tendency to invade dark, forbidden places.

Wildeblood was by no means a simple or uncomplicated WoMan. The sex-change operation had been only stage one in a plan to totally transform himself. After that, she intended to become a nun.

By 1983 it was a sane and sensible decision for one living at the hot center of New York intellectual life. Like the Southerners who think "damn Yankee" is one word, Wildeblood's *milieu* had long ago forgotten that "male chauvinist" was two words. The slightest, kinkiest remnant of masculinity was a definite handicap, a suggestion of possible viciousness—like membership in the John Birch Society, owning a Mississippi accent, or a conviction for a major felony.

Besides, Wildeblood *did* urgently want to be a nun. A priest or even a monk had a certain arrogance in his very role *qua* priest or *qua* monk, however passionately he might cultivate Total Submission to the Will of God. Only a nun could experience the true endlessness of humility.

Wildeblood, simply, was tired of being the bitchiest male in Manhattan. He wanted to become the saintliest woman.

FOREVER

Joe Malik, the editor of *Confrontation* magazine, published Justin Case's music criticism only because it confused (and, therefore, amused) him. Like most of his readers, Joe couldn't make head or tail out of whatever it was that Case was trying to say; but, unlike the readers—who were perpetually writing letters protesting Case's baroque inscrutability—Joe enjoyed puzzles. Joe was a chess puzzle and logical paradox addict; like William S. Burroughs, he was perpetually poring over the Mayan codices, trying to unscrew those inscrutable glyphs for which no Rosetta Stone has yet been found.

Three years earlier, in 1981, Joe had been a white-haired man who clearly showed his sixty-odd years. Now, in 1983, he had jet-black hair again, a face free of wrinkles, and could easily pass for a man in his early forties. This was because he had started using the rejuvenation-longevity drug FOREVER as soon as it appeared on the market. Fundamentalist Christians and the People's Ecology Party (PEP) denounced FOREVER as blasphemous and against God's will—"the ultimate insanity of the rational-technological mind," it had been called by Furbish Lousewart V, who almost defeated Hubbard in the 1980 election. Joe despised religionists and ecologists and went on using FOREVER. Dissident scientists began reporting disastrous side effects of FOREVER when they gave it in horse-doctor's doses to laboratory mice; Joe remembered the similar antimarijuana research of the sixties and seventies and went on using FOREVER, gambling that if there were anything wrong with it, it wouldn't kill him before a better rejuvenation drug was on the market.

Joe hoped to be around for several hundred years and take advantage of Time Travel when it arrived to make Eternity accessible to mankind. Above his desk at *Confrontation* was a motto from the English biologist J. B. S. Haldane which succinctly summarized Joe's view of the cosmos. It said:

THE UNIVERSE MAY BE NOT ONLY QUEERER THAN WE THINK BUT QUEERER THAN WE CAN THINK.

ALIEN SIGNALS

Carol Christmas, an aspiring actress who had not yet achieved better than Off-Off-Broadway, was always a bit sensitive about her second source of income, so she heard Joe Malik saying "no wife, no whores, no mustache." Oddly enough, Blake Williams, who was picking up parts of several conversations during his own interstellar rap, also thought Malik was saying "no wife, no whores, no mustache." Williams and Carol Christmas both heard Malik's explanation through the semantic carousel around them something like this:

MALIK: *Premarital sex*, mind you. I was really terrified

about the whole younger generation careening to hell in a handbasket with IUD's and condoms sprinkling on all sides. I began to see *Commie threats* everywhere. Everybody I knew, all my friends, the whole city of New York, seemed foreign subversive unwholesome. By God, I *was* Middle America.

"EGGS" BENEDICT: "Joe shit!" "Bullshit!" "Who shit?" . . .

"FIGS" NEWTON: Alien signals. He said alien signals.

WILLIAMS: . . . which is why we're all deviates. If Mother DNA had wanted us to be replicable units, She'd have made us insects instead of primates.

DASHWOOD: Well, actually science has been studying orgasms for quite some time now, but what's new about our work is certain psychological intangibles. . . .

CAROL CHRISTMAS: Marvin, has anyone seen Marvin . . .

BENEDICT: Well if I were Vlad I know who I'd impale. . . .

CAROL CHRISTMAS: Are you sure he isn't in the kitchen? Marvin, are you out here in the kitchen?

MALIK: That was when I stopped the experiment. There I was, totally at one with Middle America, totally inside the *Reader's Digest,* and then I came to that title: "No Wife, No Whores, No Mustache."

DASHWOOD: *Shattering into atoms* is male and *undulating* is female, but *balloons bursting* is common to both.

MALIK: I closed the magazine and threw it in the fire. The title was too good to be ruined by an explanation.

NATALIE DREST: Ooh I get that *undulating* a lot especially when some er guy is you know giving me you . . . know . . . head. . . .

DASHWOOD: Yes sixty-eight percent of the females report an *undulating* experience during cunnilingus. . . .

But at this point Williams realized that he would never recapture the audience previously listening to his outer-space theories, and he also wanted some air. He edged crabwise to the balcony and stood breathing deeply, raising his eyes to study the southern sky and then pick out the bright red glare of Sirius.

"Is Marvin out here on the balcony?" asked a contralto. It was Carol Christmas.

"I'm afraid not," Williams said. "I think he left the party already."

"Oh, did he take all the coke with him?"

"I guess so."

Alone again, Blake Williams communed briefly with the Big Dipper and asked himself what the hell Malik had been talking about: No wife? No whores? No mustache?

"WHO SHIT???" Benny Benedict was yelling inside.

The actual title of the *Reader's Digest* article had been "No Wife, No Horse, No Mustache," not "No Wife, No Whores, No Mustache." Joe Malik, as he had been trying to explain amid the din of the Wildeblood *soirée*, had been engaged in neuroprogramming research, trying to become one with the *Reader's Digest*, when he found that wonderful title, which led him to immediately abort the experiment. He knew, intuitively, that the mystery of a title like that was much better than the solution, the explanation of the title, could ever be.

Joe, whose experiments with hashish had always been guided by the sixth-circuit metaprogramming theories of Hagbard Celine, had brainwashed himself on numerous occasions to become one with not just the *Reader's Digest*, but with publications and even cassette tapes put out by such organizations as the John Birch Society, Theosophy, the Trotskyists, various assassination buffs, UFO societies,

Buddhism, the First Bank of Religiosophy, *Scientific American*, the Rosicrucians, the Christian Anti-Communist Crusade, the Flat Earth Society, the Missouri Synod Lutherans, the Hermetic Order of the Golden Dawn, and anybody and everybody who lived in a tunnel-reality different from that of his environment. Thus, where most people look at the world through the grid of a single reality map, Joe Malik perceived cosmos through dozens of such grids, changing focus at will. This was not quite the no-ego experience of Zen, he would cheerfully admit, but rather a multiego experience and therefore an alternative way to escape from the stupidity of a single self.

Joe had learned how to move the walls of his neurological reality-tunnel, and even how to wander from one tunnel to another without being infected with Chaneyitis, schizophrenia, mysticism, or the other pathological forms of this sixth-circuit Relativistic consciousness.

He was one of the pioneers of the HEAD Revolution.

He called it a simulation of satori.

Once, while very stoned, he had even gone so far as to call the experience "I-opening."

DEFECTION

How many Zen Masters does it take to change a light bulb?

Two: One to change it and one not to change it.

—*Private Japes of Mr. G.*

NOVEMBER 23, 1983:

"Defection," said Roy Ubu. "That must be it."

Ubu was a darkish man: his hair was brown, his skin was tan, and he had a penchant for brown suits with matching cinnamon-colored ties and socks. He looked about forty, but was actually sixty-eight. Like Joe Malik, Ubu had been using FOREVER from the day it came on the market.

"They're not in Russia or China," said Sylvia Goldfarb, Scientific Advisor to the President. "You can forget all about that. We know everything about them these days."

"They couldn't have gone to Hell," Ubu ventured.

Sylvia Goldfarb raised a sardonic eyebrow. It had been a witless suggestion.

"They couldn't have," Ubu repeated, as if she had confirmed his judgment. "We can rule that out."

Sylvia Goldfarb waited. There was something ominous in her waiting. Ubu cleared his throat.

"I'll put five men on it right away," he said.

The chair squeaked screeee as Ms. Goldfarb leaned forward impatiently. "Five won't do it," she said. "This is a priority investigation. We can't have over a hundred scientists just disappear off the face of the earth. Not when they're as important as these women and men."

"The thing that I can't figure out," Ubu said, "is why *now?* There's never been an administration so favorable to science—never so many huge grants, not just for work on the space-cities and life-extension, but in computers and transplants and cloning and all over the shop. Why would a group of scientists pick this time to jump ship?"

Dr. Goldfarb smiled. "Well," she said, "I'll tell you my guess. They found something to investigate, something that really excited them, but unfortunately something too far out for the government, even in 1983. That's what I suspect, and that's what I hope you'll find. But until we know for sure, we have to assume that something dangerous may be afoot. Just find one of them, Mr. Ubu, and prove that she or he is doing something harmless, and you will begin to take a great load off my mind."

"Yes, ma'am," Ubu said, looking sharp.

He was thinking: *This is going to be a pisscutter*.

One of President Hubbard's first acts on assuming office had been to abolish the FBI—thereby throwing Roy Ubu out of work.

"The American people survived one hundred fifty years without secret police opening their mail and tapping their phones," Hubbard said. "They can survive without it again."

Most of Ubu's colleagues fled Washington, seeking employment in police departments and private detective agencies. Roy had stuck around, shrewdly convinced that he understood government better than Hubbard. Within a month he was hired by the newly formed National Bureau of Information.

The ostensible purpose of the NBI was to collect data for the Beast—GWB-666, the computer that had virtually become a fourth branch of government, since its memory was searched before any important decision was made.

Actually, since bureaucracies have learned, like other gene pools, to survive over aeons, the NBI replaced many of the functions of the FBI. This was so intricately concealed in the budget figures that neither Hubbard nor any of her close advisors ever found it. (*Bureaucracies do not die when terminated; they change names:* Gilhooley's First Fundamental Finding.)

Still, there was an important difference. Since Hubbard had abolished prisons, the only citizens who had anything to fear from government were those increasingly rare, bizarrely imprinted biots who committed violence against others, and they were only sent to Hell.

M.O.Q.

Rhesus monkeys, like other higher primates, are intensely affected by their social environments—an isolated monkey will repeatedly pull a lever with no reward other than the sight of another monkey.

—EDWARD WILSON, *Sociobiology*

DECEMBER 23, 1983:

Dr. Dashwood had been rather pensive and preoccupied at lunch that day, back at Orgasm Research in San Francisco.

"So we take a guy like that—a meathead with no more knowledge of psychology or anthropology or sociology or medicine or history or ethics or logic than he has of nuclear physics—and we give him a gun and a club and a can of mace and turn him loose, my God, to 'police' the rest of us. Insanity. Total insanity."

That was Dr. Mounty Babbit, the wiggiest member of Orgasm Research's staff, and, like all too many scientists these days, a bit of a radical. Dr. Dashwood hunched over his steak to avoid getting drawn into the discussion.

"You want to disarm the police, like in England?" old Dr. Heyman asked. Heyman was still cashing in on the fact that he had once worked with Kinsey and otherwise had nothing to recommend him to any employer. "Would never work here. Americans don't have the respect for Law and Order that Britons do."

"Well, then," Babbit said calmly, "arm the public. Make sure everybody has a gun and knows how to use it. Even up the odds some way or other."

"Rubbish!" Heyman cried. "That would lead to sheer anarchy."

Dr. Dashwood painfully concentrated on his watery mashed potatoes.

"How's Three-A?" a soft contralto asked him. It was Dr. Harriet Hopgood, aware that the boss was bored by the political discussion. Three-A was part of the code—the research subjects were never mentioned by name in any conversation—and it designated the young lady in laboratory Three, Ms. Rhoda Chief.

"Very impressive," Dr. Dashwood said. "She had reached twenty-three when I broke for lunch, and she was still going strong. I left Jones in charge."

"Twenty-three," Dr. Babbit said. "Incredible."

"A *most* impressive woman," Dr. Hopgood added, a tone of envy creeping into her voice. Dr. Dashwood darted a glance at her plump face and quickly looked away again; she was transparently wistful.

Just then Dr. Dashwood's secretary appeared at the table. "A telegram came for you," she said. "I thought it might be important."

When Dr. Dashwood tore open the envelope, he was confronted with a rather curious message:

King Kong died for your sins.
Ezra Pound.

Ezra Pound, thought Dr. Dashwood, now where have I heard that name before? Then it came to him: that fellow who called at an embarrassing moment this morning, from the Fernando Poop Committee (or was it the Hernando Foof Committee?). He looked again at the idiotic message. My God, he thought, some damn crank is trying to *put me on*.

Ezra Pound had called when Rhoda was reaching her third thunderous orgasm, and Dr. Dashwood had been on the edge of forgetting all professional ethics and seizing her himself. It had been a weird phone call—all about the plight of Giovani Oops or some such place.

Fortunately, Rhoda's orgasms since then had been—comparatively—tepid. Dr. Dashwood had resumed his professional *persona*, although he was a little bit spacey.

"I heard a rumor that they've got one hundred ninety-eight *gorillas* working as cops in Chicago," Mounty Babbit went on.

Dashwood was getting annoyed. "Freud," he said coolly, "had an interesting theory about what motivates fear of the police."

That put a damper on the conversation, and Dr. Dashwood soon regretted it. Without the distraction of Babbit's baiting of old Heyman, nothing prevented Dashwood's mind from circling back, again and again, to the lovely Rhoda, nude, drawing the King Kong fourteen-incher into her in seemingly interminably ecstasy. Like an arrow, like Ulysses itself, his mind plunged toward that golden-haired and juicily moist little honey-snatch, hot with twenty-three orgasms. . . .

Science, he reminded himself, is eternal self-discipline.

But the old Latin joke came back to him: *Penis erectus non compos mentis;* a stiff prick knows no conscience.

O Galileo and Darwin, did you have days like this?

WASHY

NOVEMBER 30, 1983

The NBI had assembled a complete dossier on the missing George Washington Carver Bridge, the first scientist to disappear after leaving government employ.

Ubu had all the facts about Dr. Bridge that had ever been recorded. He knew that Bridge had been born June 16, 1953, in Bad Ass, Texas, and weighed nine pounds, three ounces at the time. He knew that Bridge's Social Security Number was 121-23-1723, his GWB number 345-36-5693, and his sexual penchant was for light-skinned Black or Oriental women with college degrees who would wear black lace bras while he pronged them. He knew that Bridge had a B.A. from Miskatonic University in Black Studies, an M.S. from the same source in Sociobiology, and a Ph.D. from the University of Ingolstadt in Primatology. He knew that Bridge had been baptized three times—once at the age of two weeks, by the Afro-Methodists via total submersion, again at the age of fourteen by the Roman Catholics by wetting the brow, and a third time at the age of seventeen by the Ku Klux Klan with a pail of cow piss. He knew that Dr. Bridge had left Bad Ass one month later and never returned. He knew that Dr. Bridge had studied or worked in Arkham, Massachusetts, New York City, Los Angeles, Ingolstadt, Bavaria, the Transylvanian section of Hungary, Washington, D.C., and Berkeley.

He knew that Dr. Bridge was called "Washy" by his classmates at Miskatonic.

He knew several thousand similar things, none of them helpful in any way toward explaining why Dr. Bridge had disappeared off the face of the earth at the head of a parade of similar disappearees which now numbered 167.

"I *knew* this case would be a pisscutter," Ubu said, contemplating his data.

The one fact not recorded about Dr. Bridge, and the whole key to his subsequent behavior, was the fact that he had, on November 23, 1971, looked into the infamous *Necronomicon* of Abdul Alhazred, in the German translation of Von Junzt (*Das Verichteraraberbuch,* Ingolstadt, 1848).

Bridge, not Dr. Bridge then, but just Washy, had been turned on to his odd volume by the Miskatonic librarian, Doris Horus, who knew he took his Black Studies seriously.

There was one sentence in *Das Verichteraraberbuch* that turned everything around in Dr. Bridge's head.

The sentence was:

Gestorben ist nicht, was für ewig ruht, und mit unbekannten Aonen mag sogar der Tod noch sterben.

HOMES ON LEGRANGE

The original idea for the L5 space-cities had emerged from Professor Gerard O'Neill and a group of his students at Princeton in 1968. The motion was so radical that it took over five years to get it into print, in *Physics Today*, in 1973.

Professor O'Neill had simply asked his students a rather basic question—one which occurs inevitably on every planet which evolves beyond the boom-and-bust cycle of planetside life. O'Neill asked:

*Is the surface of a planet the right place
for an expanding technological civilization?*

Once the question had been asked, the correct answer was, of course, inescapable.

Among the symptoms indicating that Closed System planetary industry would have to be transformed into Open System planetary-and-extraplanetary industry were the following:

Rapid exhaustion of the fossil fuels on Terra, leading to a desperate search for new energy sources;
The virtually limitless solar energy in space;

Rising population and increasing longevity, leading to an inevitable new period of swarming;

Growing pollution and ecological imbalance, caused by the attempt to provide energy from terrestrial sources for this increasing primate population;

The Revolution of Rising Expectations—a sociological phenomenon brought on by the scientific-technological advances of the previous two centuries—which caused the majority of primates to claim they had the right to a decent standard of living;

The failure of the Revolution of Lowered Expectations, after the smarter primates realized that lowered expectations meant starvation for the majority of the planet;

The Hunger Project started by a circuit-five primate named Erhard, who encouraged people to believe starvation could be eliminated;

The continuous influence of a circuit-six primate named R. Buckminster ("Bucky") Fuller, who insisted the primate brain was designed "for total success in Universe";

And, finally, the debacle of terrestrial-based nuclear energy plants, which continually caused havoc in their environments, and which eventually prompted some of the primates to remember that a science-fiction writer, Robert Anson Heinlein, had foreseen all this in a 1940s story, "Blow-ups Happen," and provided the solution—moving the nuclear plants into space.

By 1984 over a third of Terra's industrial plants had been moved, as O'Neill foresaw, into the L5 area—Legrange point 5, where the gravity fields of earth and moon are balanced. The colonists even had a theme song, invented by another science-fiction writer, Robert Anson Wilson, in a book called *The Universe Next Door*. The song was "HOMEs on Legrange."

A VISITOR FROM FAIRY LAND

"Participation" is the incontrovertible new concept given by quantum mechanics; it strikes down the term "observer" of classical theory, the man who stands safely behind a thick glass wall and watches what goes on without taking part. That can't be done, quantum mechanics says.

—WHEELER, MISNER, & THORNE, *Gravitation*

MAY 1, 1934:

"They call it liberalism and socialism, the bastards, but really it's their own brand of highway robbery. They been after me and Henry Ford and every independent in the country for a hell of a long time. You remember all this, son; you remember what your father told you. It's a big fortune the Crane holdings and they're going to be trying to take it away from you, just like they're trying to take it away from me. I earned every penny of it, when I invented ORGASMOR, and I don't aim to let them take it away from me or from you. You just remember why all the bankers are Rosenfelt liberals, son; you remember who your real enemies are and don't think it's those idiot socialists and other cranks like Townsend, with his thirty dollars every Thursday. It's those kike bankers who want the whole pie and are just using Rosenfelt as a pawn."

That was old Crane, Tom Crane, the man who invented ORGASMOR, talking to his son, Hugh, in Central Park, where sweet birds sang. Tom Crane was more dinosaur than primate: a tough, unsentimental reptile whose wealth was based on a swindle, pure and simple. He never explicitly claimed in any advertisement that ORGASMOR created more orgasms—just that it was "deliciously enticing" and "stimulating to all body cells and tissues" and the FDA never succeeded in proving that his agents had planted the popular mythology attributing lubricity to a product not very different in chemical content from Coca-Cola. A strict constructionist would certainly say that Crane's customers were being defrauded.

"It doesn't *poison* anybody," old Crane always answered such nitpickers.

In fact, Hugh Crane—who was only ten in 1934 and would reach twelve before he discovered that the actual pronunciation of the President's name was Roosevelt—was only partially listening to his father's rambling diatribe. He had heard all of it before, many times, and besides, the Mysterious Tramp was much more interesting.

The Mysterious Tramp, perhaps a visitor from fairy land, was stopping each person who passed and asking them something. They all shook their heads and walked by rapidly. This was puzzling to little Hugh: If the answer was negative, why did the Tramp keep asking the question? Didn't he believe the people who had already answered? Was he offering a chance to cross the boundary into magic space and were they all too timid to try?

"You see, son, Rosenfelt and the Rhodes scholars have it all sliced up and they have to get rid of people like me. . . ." Tom Crane was still rambling along his own paranoid yellow-brick road when they finally came abreast of the Tramp. Hugh listened eagerly to catch the Mystery Question.

"Hey mister could you spare a dime I haven't eaten in three days mister hey listen mister . . ."

"Get a job," said old Crane, walking faster. "You see, son, that's the kind of good-for-nothing loafer who's destroying this country."

But the boy who was to become Cagliostro the Escape Artist looked back and saw the Mysterious Tramp falling to the ground very slowly like a tree he had seen fall slowly after being chopped by the caretaker at the Crane country home out on Long Island, and just like the tree, when he finally reached the sidewalk, the Tramp didn't move at all, not one bit, and even seemed to get stiff like the tree did, only faster.

SPOCK? SPOCK? SPOCK?

DECEMBER 23, 1983

While Dr. Dashwood was worrying about the sinister Ezra Pound in San Francisco and Mary Margaret Wildeblood was preparing for her party in New York, a black giant named "Rosey" Stuart was struggling with a vacation memo in the *Pussycat* office in Chicago.

"This is the worst piece of idiocy I've ever seen," he complained to his secretary. "It looks like it was written by a computer having a nervous breakdown. Listen to this gibberish: 'Half a man-day shall not be equal to half a day unless the man is actually in the office for the full day, or half of a full day, as the case may be. (This also applies to female employees.)' What the ring-tailed rambling hell does that mean?"

"Do you want me to call Personnel and ask somebody to explain it?" asked the secretary, Marlene Murphy, a pert little redhead who could neither type nor take dictation well, but held her job because she fit the *Pussycat* image.

"Besides," Stuart went on grumbling, "it contradicts the vacation memo we got last week."

"That one was a hoax," Marlene explained patiently. "Some crank got in at night and ran it off on a Xerox machine as some kind of practical joke."

"Well, Jesus on a wubber cwutch," Stuart complained, imitating Elmer Fudd, "it made more sense than this one."

Marlene shrugged sympathetically. "This is the one we've got to live with."

Stuart shook his head wearily. "What kind of world is it where the reality is weirder than the satire?"

There was no obvious answer to that. "Do you want me to call Personnel?" Marlene repeated.

"Hell, no!" Stuart exclaimed. "Don't agitate that pit of ding-dongs. Just put me down for the first three weeks in July, and if they tell me I can't have it, I'll go over their heads and talk to Sput." Stan Sputnik was the founder of the *Pussycat* empire and still acted as both Managing Editor and Publisher, as well as embodying the *Pussycat* image in all his highly publicized acts and deeds.

Stuart crumbled the vacation memo and threw it in the wastebasket.

"What's next?" he asked.

"Dr. Dashwood. About the interview."

"Oh, yes," Stuart said, turning his chair to look out the window. "Call his secretary and see if he's in."

While Marlene went outside to her desk to place the

call, Stuart looked out over Chicago thinking of his rapid rise in the *Pussycat* empire. Born in Chicago's South Side ghetto—his full name was Franklin Delano Roosevelt Stuart—he had originally followed the usual predatory life-script of impoverished alpha males. But his second prison term had thrown him into contact with a most peculiar cell mate—a self-proclaimed Sufi and master of all forms of Persian magick. "Rosey" Stuart came out of prison convinced he could do anything, acquired a degree in literature from Harvard in record time, and started the Great Novel about the Black Experience in America.

About then both racism and poverty were becoming obsolete, and selling a first novel was as hard as ever. Stuart had been toiling at *Pussycat* for five years, dickering with a novel about a parallel universe where racism still existed and a malignant black magician takes over the country by demonically possessing the body of the white President.

Last year the staff of *Pussycat* had quadrupled. Sput Sputnik had grown annoyed by the ever-increasing number of imitations of his Illustrated Fantasy Book for Onanists. Every editor at every competition publication had been hired away at a juicy salary increase.

Pussycat suddenly had six Senior Editors, twelve Associate Editors, twenty-four Assistant Editors, and thirty Junior Editors. The other publishers found themselves confronting deadlines with nobody left on their staffs. Two went bankrupt; one committed suicide; the others took a year to get back in gear again.

"Business is business," said Sput. He liked to think of himself as a tough, hard-driving businessman, as well as the twentieth century's leading philosopher, the superstud of every girl's tender dreams, the hero of the free press, the foe of bigotry and intolerance everywhere, and the world's unacknowledged Master Psychologist. If he had known there was such a thing as pie-eating champion, he would have aimed for that title also. He considered himself a Renaissance Man.

Although Stuart had advanced from Junior Editor to Senior Editor in spite of this competition, he hardly knew Sput at all. Sput never came to the offices, preferring to work in his mansion in Manhattan, and Stuart saw him only on the rare occasions when he was called upon to fly to New York for a conference.

Those conferences tended to be a bit much. Like certain movie actors who are always "on," even when nowhere near a soundstage, Sput was as determined to impress his editors as he was to overwhelm the whole world. For years, he had insisted on playing chess during conferences, keeping an impoverished grandmaster on hand for a stiff competition; since the grandmaster knew which side his bread was buttered on, Sput always won. He had gotten this idea from a very inaccurate historical novel about Napoleon, in which the little Corsican sociopath was portrayed as playing masterful chess while discussing military strategy with his generals and the Napoleonic legal code with his judges.

More recently Sput had read a novel about Nero. The effect was even more disconcerting than trying to talk with him while he laboriously evaded an obvious Noah's Ark trap. He was seated behind his desk receiving a blow job when Stuart had been ushered into his presence the last time. It was unnerving.

"You wanted to discuss the interview subjects for the next six months?" Stuart asked, taking his seat and noting that the erotic technician kneeling before the Great Man was a recent Pussyette from the mag's foldout. In fact, she was the first to appear, not in an ordinary crotch shot (they were now becoming commonplace, not only in *Pussycat,* but in its imitators), but in a randy low-angle crotch shot in which her vulva lips could clearly be seen *pouting* beneath the pubic hair. Stuart had been curious as to how that effect was obtained and asked the chief photographer, "Were you rubbing her off just before you snapped that?"

"Nah," was the laconic answer. "We tried that, but the lips still weren't visible enough. We ended up stuffing her snatch full of my hashish stash."

"Lawd!" Stuart was astonished, and dropped back to his mother tongue.

"That's why she had that far-gone look in her eyes. Stoned out of her head by the time we got it all out of her again. Bet you didn't know it was possible to get high that way."

"Wonder what it would be like to navigate her geography right after the hash came out," Stuart said thoughtfully.

"Wouldn't know," the photographer sighed. "Sput put an exclusive on her soon as he saw the test shots."

Now she kneeled, nude and covered with some kind of oil that Sput had read about in the Nero book, and carefully licked his wingwang up and down while he, imitating supercool, went over the interview list.

"Don't want President Hubbard," he said. "She's too controversial."

"But dammit, Sput, our interviews are *supposed* to be controversial!" Stuart seemed to recall saying that at each of these conferences.

"Not *that* controversial," Sput said. "The intellectuals all hate her because she's a scientist.* Now, here, Jane

---

Terran Archives 2803: At the time of this comedy those primates who specialized in verbal manipulations of the third neurological circuit formed a gene-pool separate from those who specialized in mathematical manipulations. The former, controlling the verbal environment, had dubbed themselves *"the* intellectuals."

Fonda and Timothy Leary, they're good. But, Jesus H. Christ, Robert Anson Wilson, for Chrissake—he's a fucking *science-fiction writer!*"

"We interviewed Vonnegut," Stuart said, watching the lady's head bobbing up and down at Sput's crotch.

"Yeah, but his books are serious. That's different," Sput said, breathing a bit heavily by now. "Besides, everybody says *The Universe Next Door* drives people wiggy and makes them become nudists or Buddhists or something. That kind of trouble we don't need. And one science-fiction writer in five years is enough, already. (Gently, doll, gently!) I see you don't have the Attorney General on the list yet."

"It's the same as ever," Stuart explained, noting that the girl's hand was sneaking down her belly into her crotch. "She just won't give us an interview. She still says we're a dirty magazine."

"Dammit, we never go beyond contemporary community standards," Sput protested, hurt. "That old bitch is a *bigot.*"

"Well, bigot or not, she won't give us an interview."

"Fascist reactionary old bat," Sput fumed. "Someday I'll—" Then he brightened. "Listen, doll," he said to the girl at his feet. "You're the Attorney General—now really go to it, *like a fucking vacuum cleaner!*" The girl's head began bobbing faster, and Sput slouched back a bit, smiling contentedly.

"Reactionary WASP bitch," he muttered. "That's right, take it, take it all, you foe of the First Amendment!"

"Er—Dr. Francis Dashwood," Stuart prompted.

"Very good, *very* good." Sput was whispering, as if toking a marijuana cigarette. "You Gestapo pig," he added to the girl at his feet.

"How about Jackie Kennedy Onassis?"

"Yeah, yeah, class," Sput said vaguely. He was beginning to tremble a bit. "Who else you got?" he whispered, trembling more.

"Dr. Spock."

"Spock?" Sput asked. Then he repeated, shrilly, "Spock? Spock! SPOCK!???!" He was coming, Stuart realized with an embarrassed twinge. "Swallow it," Sput was roaring. "Swallow it, you *wire tapper!*"

It was a distracting conference all around, Stuart thought, remembering.

His secretary was at his door. "I finally located Dr. Dashwood," she said, "at this home. He's on the phone."

Stuart picked up his phone, saying, "Ah, good afternoon, Dr. Dashwood. It's a great pleasure to speak to you."

"Is this on the level?" came a tense voice. "You're not involved with that Poop or Foof place, are you?"

Stuart was dumbfounded. Could the head of the best-known sex research organization in America be a paranoid nut? "I *am* speaking to Dr. Francis Dashwood?" he asked carefully.

"Yes, yes—but how can I be sure who *I'm* speaking to?"

"Well," Stuart said, "if you have your doubts, call me back. Go through information, to check the number, and then have the *Pussycat* switchboard put you on my line. That should convince you."

"I'll do just that," the doctor said. "A lot of damned peculiar things are happening today. I want to be sure you're not some cohort of that Ezra Pound character." He hung up abruptly.

Ezra Pound, Stuart thought, bemused. The doctor thinks a dead poet and folk singer is plotting against him.

An absolute nut of the first water. A real signifyin' mad scientist.

Obviously, this would require great care. Dashwood couldn't just be discarded as an interview subject for

being batty; he was too big a name. The interview would
go ahead, but Dashwood would be handled with kid gloves.

The phone buzzed, and he picked it up.

"Dr. Dashwood is back on the line," his secretary said.

"Put him through." He waited, then said, "Dr. Dashwood?"

"Well, I guess it really is you," the voice said. "Please
excuse me. A man in my sensitive field—cranks and schiz-
ophrenics wondering around loose . . ."

"Yes, yes, I quite understand," Stuart said, rolling his
eyes toward the ceiling. "Poets always have harbored
nasty grudges." He had no doubt that the doctor was as
goofy as a waltzing mouse.

HOW THE TERRAN PRIMATES
WERE DOMESTICATED

GALACTIC ARCHIVES:

President Hubbard had abolished poverty through a plan
which she called the RICH economy.

RICH meaning Rising Income through Cybernetic
Homeostasis.

This was a diabolically clever scheme to abolish all
forms of human labor except the most creative—*i.e.*, those
frontal-lobe metaprogramming circuits which have evolved
last in evolution and surpass the mechanical old four-
circuit primate brain functions.

Of course it had been theoretically possible to abolish
most mechanical labor since about 1948, when a very

cunning primate mathematician, Norbert Weiner, noted that self-correcting (cybernetic) machines would soon be able to monitor whole factories.

Even earlier a metaprogramming-circuit Greek primate, Aristotle, had observed that it would be possible to abolish slavery "when the loom and other machines become self-managing."

Terran primates had continued slavery over the generations, despite the increasing distress this caused their hominid third and fourth (semantic and moral) circuits, simply because machines could not yet manage themselves. As many a primate Utopian had rediscovered in chagrin, under primitive planetary conditions, "somebody has to do the shit-work." The most appealing solution to electing that somebody was to invade a weaker neighboring tribe and bring back a group of biots who could be domesticated.

This had been done so often that there was no hominid pack on Terra that did not show the effects of *domestication* and *slave mentality,* a fact first noted by a dour German primate named Nietzsche.

In Unistat, due to the strong encouragement of individualistic third- and fourth-circuit (semantic-moral) functions, slavery had grown so repugnant that it was formally "abolished" within a century after the formation of the pack constitution; it lingered on through inertia in the form of "wage slavery," which required that all primates not born into the sixty families that *"owned"* almost everything would have to *"work"* for those families or their corporations in order to get the tickets (called *"money"*) which were necessary for survival.

This slave mentality was so entrenched in the domesticated primates that cybernation advanced very slowly in the first thirty years after Weiner discovered it would be possible to abolish primate toil. All the important primate bands—the alpha male corporations, the primate trade unions, the primate council or "government," the primate totem cults or "churches"—believed that the traditional domesticated caste system was the only possible system under which primates could live. Even the Red primates shared this delusion, differing only in their ideas about distribution of resources.

President Hubbard boldly challenged this domesticated primate thought-form by announcing that everybody who *could* be replaced by a machine *would* be replaced by a machine.

It seemed like the end of the world to the primates, at first.

It turned out to be only the end of poverty.

AN APPROXIMATE SIMULATION OF INSANITY

"Any false or partially false premise extended with accurate logic will generate an approximate simulation of insanity." Crossing Broadway at Seventy-second Street, still lecturing, it was Blake Williams.

"Yes, yes, of course, Professor, but if you'll listen a moment to what I'm trying to say," Natalie Drest protested.

"But you see, young lady, most of the premises of our current religious, scientific, and philosophical thinking must be false, or partially false, as judged by a more advanced civilization. What would a Higher Intelligence make of our doctrines of *transubstantiation* or *charmed quarks* or the *categorical imperative?*"

"Well, yeah, but, professor . . ."

"Then, dammit, will you listen? Most of our beliefs and behavior will appear clinically insane to a Higher Intelligence viewing this planet."

"Sure, it's all relative, I know that, but, Professor . . ."

"Look," Dr. Williams said with crushing finality, "do you want to fuck, or don't you?"

Her answer was drowned out by a siren racing up Riverside Drive.

"What?"

"I said, I been tryna tell you for ten blocks, Professor, I'm still getting over a case of the clap . . ."

"That's quite all right, my dear," Blake Williams pronounced suavely. "I'm a broad-minded man. I understand the exuberance of youth, the powerful hormones coursing through your vibrant young bloodstream, the noble refusal of your generation to regard the taboos of old as binding upon the free spirits of the 1980s, and besides, I've reached the age at which I'm not horny *every* night of the year. You are still invited to come along to my humble digs and listen to my old Joan Baez records."

"Gee, Professor, you know what you are? You're cool. You're not sexist at all."

"Um, yes, thank you, my dear. I'm just getting old, actually. Now, about the Einstein-Rosen-Podolsky *gedankenexperiment* . . ."

DANCING PHOTONS

The intellectual love of things consists in understanding their perfections.

—SPINOZA

Linda Lovelace, a projection of light traveling 186,000 miles per second through film of events that actually transpired in Miami years before, is taking first one inch of Harry Reems's penis, then two, three, five, the whole incredible nine inches, and paranoid little Marvin Gardens, hunched in his seat, overcoat in lap, snorts the last of his coke.

It was the forty-fourth time Marvin had seen *Deep Throat* and the twenty-third time on coke, and under the overcoat his hand was magically transforming into Linda's mouth again, that separate reality where the dancing photons on the screen and the synergizing synapses in his brain joined to produce more than 3-D better than Technicolor realer than real God yes higher than a kite oh Lord.

Marvin was having a rare happy moment in which the extraterrestrial invasion wasn't worrying him.

He, Harry Reems, is about to come, and Marvin Gardens, too, wondering in one corner of his mind about the eternity of protoplasm, because when he comes she'll take it out of her mouth and—*splat!*—he'll shoot all over her face. Marvin is waiting, but take an amoeba now does it die when it splits? Are there two new amoebas or is it two selves where there was one self before? God, she's got all of it now, faster, call them Krazy and Ignatz say, now is Krazy the first amoeba and Ignatz a twin or are both of them still Krazy, two Krazies instead of one? Jeez, right down her throat now, and when they split again we have four, she's licking the head now ah that's good and about to swallow it all again, call them say Groucho Chico Harpo and Zeppo, which is the original amoeba or are they all, are amoebas really immortal then? Now now here it comes now one amoeba dividing forever now going on and on for all eternity now a single explosion of DNA seed now now ah Christ Christ yes now now now yes Eternal God oh good.

"Blake Williams had a mnemonic for my discovery," Bertha Van Ation was excitedly telling Juan Tootreego as they passed the DEEP THROAT marquee. "Mother Very Easily Made a Jam Sandwich Using No Peanuts, Mayonnaise, or Glue. See? Mercury Venus Earth . . ."

But about those amoebas: Marvin Gardens, more relaxed now, is buttoning his coat and heading for the exit. Linda Lovelace continues to schlurp and suck on the screen behind him, but he is deciding that after the first split there are two amoebas, of course, but should you call them *children* of the first amoeba—*him* or *her* or *it*? And after the second split there are four. After the third split, eight. Nowhere does the phase change denoted by the symbol "death" appear to have occurred. Is one of the eight third-generation amoebas the original amoeba (*him* or *her* or *it*), or are *all of them* the original? And how does $8 = 4 = 2 = 1$, anyhow?

Markoff Chaney was about to have a dream come true.

He was renting his old room at the YMCA on Chicago Avenue again, using it as a base for further anti-Dashwood activities. He had gone for a walk, and as he approached the intersection of Michigan and Lake Shore Drive, he was thinking about a new letterhead that would say FRATERNAL ORDER OF HATE GROUPS and have Robert Welch, Abby Hoffman, Anita Bryant, and George Wallace listed as officers. Perhaps he might add Natalie Drest and make her "Chairperson of the Board."

"Hsst!" a voice said. "You—yeah, you, *shorty.*"

The midget stiffened and whirled around. "Hssst!" he said. "You—yeah, you, *asshole.*"

"Hey, no offense," the speaker said. "I got a business proposition for you." The midget looked at him sharply; he didn't look at all as shady and unsavory as a person should look who was offering a business proposition on the corner to a total stranger.

"What are you selling?" he asked.

"Not selling," the friendly giant said. "Giving away. One hundred fifty dollars."

"And what do I have to do for it?" the midget asked warily, drawing a little closer.

"I'm a butler," the man said—and, in fact, he did not look like butlers the midget had seen in movies. His face was much longer from the nose down than most people's; it gave him a permanent look of one who smells something but hasn't found it yet. Most Chicagoans, Chaney had noticed, look like they'd just found it and it was worse than they'd imagined. "The lady I work for is very rich. *And* very eccentric." He tried to leer suggestively; the effect was like a bishop winking. "She has a thing about m——— . . . about you people of less than average stature."

Markoff Chaney felt his heart leap. Could it be true??

"One hundred fifty dollars?"

"That's right. She gets these moods and sends me out looking every so often."

"I'm game," the midget said, deciding. He could feel the pulse in his temple. *Au revoir, ma chérie,* he thought, firmly convinced that was French for "good-bye to virginity."

"There's just one thing," the butler said as they walked along. "You've got to do just what I tell you. Don't be afraid; she's not a real kink—no whips and chains or anything of that scene—but, well, her tastes are a little peculiar. I promise you won't be hurt."

"Tell me," the midget said.

"It's like a little drama or charade," the butler said, lowering his voice. He explained certain things.

"What?" the midget asked. "I don't get to fuck her?"

"But it will be enjoyable, nonetheless," the butler said, "and you collect one hundred fifty smackers for it, remember."

"Oh, well," Chaney said, quoting one of his basic axioms for Guerrilla Ontology, "insanity is another viable alternative."

JUST LIKE METHOD ACTING

In an apartment in the east village off St. Mark's Place, Tibetan posters and astrological charts gaze down on the couch where Joe Malik and Carol Christmas are engaged in erotometaphysical epistemology.

Getting a hand inside her panties was easy enough and Joe Malik thought he was home free, but then a snag appeared, an emotional problem that verged on full-blown lunacy; it had to do with Carol's third ex-husband, a Puerto Rican poet who claimed to be a *Santaria* initiate, whatever that was, and couldn't adjust to New York. He said that magic was impossible in New York because the intelligentsia were all Jewish atheists—"but I'm not a Jewish atheist," Joe protested, "I'm an Arab agnostic," wondering what the hell this had to do with a simple lay, but Carol's third husband, who might as well have been on the couch with them, also said that Carol could help him to write again if *she* believed in magic, and it wasn't much different from being an actress, anyway; *Santaria*, whatever it is, is just like method acting, Carol explained, but Joe was meanwhile from the context deciding it was more like Christian Science, but what it all came down to, the hand out of her panties by now, since to pressure her at this point would be coercive and chauvinistic, of course, the Puerto Rican bunofasitch had put a *loa* on her when they separated and she couldn't relax until they did an exorcism of the apartment. . . . "Oh, bleeding Christ!" Joe gasped, both balls like boulders.

"It's just like method acting, honey," Carol repeated hopefully.

"You mean," Natalie, dressed, asked, awed and full of hashish, "that this whatchamacculum, this state vector, collapses every which way?"

"No, no, no," Blake Williams hastens to correct. "That's only the Everett-Wheeler-Graham model, and it's obviously nonsense. It means that in the universe next door, Furbish Lousewart is President instead of Eve Hubbard. Pure science fiction and I, um, wonder what Everett,

Wheeler, and Graham were smoking when they thought of it. What I'm trying to explain, my dear, is the most plausible alternative theory, which comes from taking Bell's Theorem literally."

"The ripple theory," Natalie prompted.

"But the ripples are all-over-the-universe-at-once," Williams explained again. "It's called the Quantum Inseparability Principle, or QUIP. Dr. Nick Herbert calls it the Cosmic Glue."

"Just like ripples in a pond, Jeez." Natalie Drest was bemused. "Parts of us are still interacting with Joe Malik and all the other people at the party. This is superheavy."

"Yes, but QUIP acts nonlocally in time as well as in space," Williams went on. "You've got to think of time ripples, as well as space ripples, to grok the quantum world. . . ."

THE COPENHAGEN INTERPRETATION

There is a sharp disagreement among competent men as to what can be proved and what cannot be proved, as well as an irreconcilable divergence of opinion as to what is sense and what is nonsense.

—ERIC TEMPLE BELL. *Debunking Science*

There was nothing really weird about Blake Williams, except that he was passionately in love with a dead man. This great, if somewhat bizarre, passion was entirely platonic, of course—nothing queer about good old Doc Williams, except his head. With his six-foot frame, his neatly trimmed gray beard, and his heavy black-rimmed spectacles, Williams was the very model of a modern major generalist. Due to the incident of the Gansevoort Street incinerator, he had learned to keep his mouth shut about his more outlandish ideas and obsessions.

The man Blake Williams loved was Niels Bohr, the physicist who had chosen the Taoist yin-yang as his Coat of Arms when knighted by the Danish court—which was rather far out back in the 1930s (before Taoism became faddish with physicists). Bohr also added nearly as much to quantum theory as Planck, Einstein, or Schrödinger, and his model of the atom—the Bohr model, it's called—had been believed literally by a generation of physicians before Hiroshima. Bohr himself, however, had never believed it; nor had he believed any of his other theories. Bohr invented what is called the Copenhagen Interpretation, which holds in effect that a physicist shouldn't believe anything but his measurements in the laboratory. Everything else—the whole body of mathematics and theory relating one measurement to another—Bohr regarded as a model of how the human mind works, not of how the universe works. Blake Williams loved Bohr for the Copenhagen Interpretation, which had made it possible for him to study physics seriously, even devoutly, without believing a word of it. That was convenient, since Williams's own training as an anthropologist had schooled him to study all human symbol systems without believing any of them.

On a deeper level—there is always a deeper level—Williams was a scientist who didn't believe in science because he had been cured of polio by witchcraft.

But Blake Williams didn't believe in witchcraft, either. He didn't believe in anything. He regarded all belief systems as illustrative data in domesticated primate psychology.

"The study of human beliefs is an ethologist's heaven and a logician's hell," he liked to say.

Actually, Blake Williams hadn't been cured of polio by witchcraft, exactly. He had been cured by the Sister Kenny method.

But he grew up thinking it was witchcraft. That was because all the experts in Unistat at the time—the members of the American Medical Association, who would not admit there were any other experts on health—claimed the Sister Kenny method was witchcraft. They also said it didn't work.

Since the Sister Kenny method obviously had worked in his case, Blake grew up with the gnawing suspicion that the experts didn't know what the hell they were talking about. He was also intensely curious about all forms of witchcraft, which eventually led him to become an anthropologist.

Young Williams soon enough discovered—on his very first field trip, among the Hopi Indians—that witchcraft does by God and by golly work, after all. He began, tentatively and secretly, sharing his knowledge with carefully selected colleagues. Most of them were pretty evasive about the whole subject, but Marilyn Chambers, the author of the epoch-making *Neuroanthropology*, was startlingly blunt.

"Everybody who's been in the field knows that," she said with a kind of weary patience.

"But why doesn't anyone say so?" Williams asked, still young, still naïve.

"Freud and Charcot once had virtually this same conversation," Dr. Chambers said, "but the topic then was the sexual origin of the hysterical neuroses of Victorian women. Charcot invited Freud to be the goat and talk about it in public. . . ."

"I see," Blake Williams said slowly. He did see.

THE CAT AND THE DOG

If we accept multiple universes, then we no longer need worry about what "really" happened in the past, because every possible past is equally real.

> —JOSEPH GERVER, "The Past as Backward Movies of the future," *Physics Today*, April 1971

"He who mast——— . . . who hesitates is lost," Marvin Gardens said one day in the *Confrontation* office. Joe Malik considered it one of the most interesting Freudian slips he had ever heard and recorded it in his diary, where it was, of course, subsequently scanned by the Illuminati.

Marvin and Joe never got along well, but that was because Marvin regarded Joe as an extraterrestrial invader and Joe regarded Marvin as a nut.

"Marvin is emphatically not a loony," Justin Case had been heard to say quite often. "He's a genius. The greatest put-on artist since Hitchcock. Nobody recognizes what a great satirist he is."

"Justin Case," Marvin said when that was repeated to him, "thinks he's being liberal, but he's just another victim of brainwashing by the Amazon Invasion."

Marvin Gardens had been traumatized by the 1970s

245

and always referred to the Women's Liberation Movement as the Amazon Invasion. He believed, or pretended to believe, that the ringleaders were all extraterrestrials who had arrived by flying saucer in 1968 and were boldly conspiring to seize supreme power everywhere through what he called semantic black magick. "They've atomized the language and created a *semantic smog* in which ordinary humanity is obliterated by abstractions like 'chairperson' or simple mammalian erotic signaling is politicized into a new sin called '*sexism*.' Any male who dares to oppose them is stigmatized as a 'male chauvinist,' and any female who opposes them is labeled a victim of *male brainwashing*. Obviously, within a decade, they will command the key posts in all areas of industry (they've captured publishing already) and then *government will fall*. Probably, then, the *males* of their species will start landing and we'll all be enslaved. (Some of the males may have landed already; look at the Manhattan literary scene.) It's the sweetest infiltration job in the history of galactic *espionage*. For merely daring to reveal their plans, I am smeared by them as a 'male chauvinist pig,' which is ten times worse than an ordinary 'male chauvinist' and equivalent to an SP on the Scientologists' *hit list*."

Some agreed with Justin Case that Marvin was kidding, that he had merely seen an opportunity—the chance to attain fame and fortune by espousing a bitterly controversial extreme position. Others, however, claimed he was dead serious, and was a classical case of cocaine paranoia. Marvin always pointed out, when either of these theories was mentioned in his presence, "there is a third possibility. I might be right. In that case, how convenient *for Them* that my sanity and sincerity are so often called into question. It almost looks as if *They* are conspiring to *defame my character*. Are they afraid that some might listen to me before it's too late, before the takeover is complete?"

Marvin's principal enemy, among the male half of the population, was Frank Hemeroid, of course. Hemeroid, oddly enough, hardly even knew of Marvin's existence and, hence, was incapable of being harmful to him by intention. That didn't matter. He was still the enemy with a capital E. At times Marvin had even suspected him of being extraterrestrial, like the leaders of Women's Lib.

Hemeroid earned his animosity entirely by the books he wrote, which were full of treason, according to Marvin. Actually, Hemeroid's novels merely reflected the 1970s literary society around him, in which most people were a little weird and all of them were losers. Hemeroid carefully depicted a world exactly like that: Most of his characters were weird and all of them were losers. The critics, who were all losers, called him a brutal realist. Marvin called him a traitor to planet Earth.

Marvin wrote about all this in dialogues (he rather fancies himself as being of Platonic disposition) in which the speakers were Frank Hemeroid, representing 1970s values and reality-constructs, and Ernest Hemingway, Marvin's childhood hero who had been consigned to the literary garbage heap when the extraterrestrials took over. Hemingway, in these dialogues, represented Man, individual Man, the universal maverick, as he was before the extraterrestrial invasion.

The dialogues were full of things like this:

FRANK: Did you ever really believe in your own myth, you old faker? Did you think you could come out of a neurotic suicide-prone family and by sheer Will transform yourself into a hero, a brave man, a great artist, a boxer, a big-game hunter, a cult figure, an image of courage and of grace under pressure? Didn't you know you were a worm, that all men are worms and cowards, and that you'd be beaten at the end? Didn't you know you'd be like all the rest of us and give in to self-pity and self-doubt and pull that final cosmic trigger?

ERNEST: I never said my way was easy. I said that Man was not meant for defeat, however many individuals may be defeated. I said that the effort to be conscious enough and brave enough was admirable, whatever the consequences.

FRANK: Consciousness? Bravery? Consciousness is only aware of its own suffering in this blind existence, and bravery is only a gesture against the inevitable end. A stupid gesture, since the cowards live longer, and if they're cowardly enough, they make all the comfortable decisions and have all the security possible in a Death Universe like this.

ERNEST: I deny none of that, and I have shown the cruelty more nakedly than any of your generation. I still say it is admirable to be brave and take big risks for the things you value. When everything mammalian and me-chanical tells you to run, and you stand and don't run, you learn what Man can be.

And so on. Marvin was obsessed with something he called the Dignity of Man. He was not at all amused by ecological relativists who told him that an ant or a swine might equally believe in the Dignity of Ant or the Dignity of Swine. Men were not ants or swine, he would say coldly; and he would classify the heckler as probably brain-warped by the extraterrestrial Amazons.

In truth, like most philosophers, Marvin never wrote explicitly about the one factor that really determined and explained everything in his philosophy. Just as Marx never mentioned his carbuncles in *Das Kapital*, and Freud didn't publish anything about his own sexual hang-ups, Marvin Gardens never wrote a word anywhere about the source and motive of all his theorizing. This was his penis. It was four inches long at best, and it had given him a defeatist psychology about things in general, and women in particular, against which he had struggled mightily to build his philosophy of Transcendental Male Courage. The women he classified as extraterrestrials frightened him only a little bit more than the ordinary women he classified as terrestrials.

Sometimes Marvin wrote dialogues between Pavlov's Dog and Schrödinger's Cat, instead of between Frank and Ernest. These were usually quite short and almost like Zen stories:

 DOG: I've got a million proofs that we're not free.
 CAT: I've got one proof that we are.
 DOG: What's that?
 CAT: Who asks what's that?

64 AMOEBAS

The belief or unconscious conviction that all propositions are of the subject-predicate form—in other words, that every fact consists in some thing having some quality—has rendered most philosophers incapable of giving any account of the world of science.

    —BERTRAND RUSSELL, *Our Knowledge of the External World*

DECEMBER 23, 1983:

Natalie Drest was amazed as the conversation swung in a new quantum direction. "You," she gasped, "you dig Krazy Cat too?"

"Indeed, my dear," Blake Williams beamed. "I may be the most devout student of Herriman's work anywhere in the civilized world."

He didn't tell her (yet) that he regarded Krazy as a symbol of Schrödinger's Cat in the great wave-mechanics puzzle.

Even Blake Williams occasionally worried that he was talking over his audience's head.

But Joe Malik seeks purchase for an elbow on the back of the couch, noticing the statue of the Virgin of Guadalupe in the corner alcove, her foot pressed down on the head of the Serpent. He was wondering what the hell *Santaria* was, amazed as always by the blind skill of female fingers, Carol guiding him into her without looking down actually lying with her eyes closed as she reveled no doubt in strictly private fantasy (Am I Paul Newman? Woody Allen? That damned third ex-husband? First or second ex-husband? Some damned high school football hero ten years ago?), slipping in smoothly, interlocking, beginning to merge; to meld; to float on the great ocean of sensation, to find the window.

No wife no whores no mustache (Carol Christmas was thinking) a real weirdo he is but Arab that's nice a Sultan we're in the harem it's my first time again, no a movie, yes a movie the camera moving in technicians all over the place watching me watching eyes watching me fuck the first really high art porn movie deeper ah good deeper first porn flick to win the Academy Award no more Off-Off-Broadway for me watching me watching me fuck millions of men watching me in theaters like that Pussycat we passed jerking their cocks fantasizing me fantasizing and coming don't think of Ronnie don't think don't think Mongoloid the doctor said and I said I never balled a Chinaman didn't understand at first why me why of all the millions of births on the planet that day why me don't think about it don't get sad again just go with it the camera the eye of the camera moving in on my face to get my orgasm and millions of men watching in theaters spurt after spurt damned cruel unjust murderous universe my poor Ronnie coming spurt spurt spurt Academy Award coming now me coming no wife? no whores? no mustache?

And, "I love you," Joe Malik gasped, really believing it in that warm moment slowly coming back from the reverberation of her orgasm and beginning to gallop toward his own climax as she muttered "darling oh darling" Paul Newman? Ex-Husbands? Me? Me? *ME??? Me?*

But Natalie Drest, fifty blocks north, was still objecting: "And I thought you were just some high-brow . . ."

"I am, my dear, a high-brow. And a low-brow. And I suppose, alas, even a middle-brow. A single ego, as our friend Malik was pointing out at the party tonight, is a ridiculously limiting perspective on the universe." Williams smiled.

"You mean like you've got three minds and one is a Krazy Kat fan and another is trying to study modern physics from an anthropological point of view? What does the third mind do?"

"Ah, my dear, that is the Great Work, opening the third I . . ."

> *What they forgot to kill, said Joe,*
> *Went on to organize*

"What I like is the way Offisa Pup gets embarrassed about being a dog, you know? That's symbolism."

> *Went on to organize*

"Offisa Pup, my dear, is the superego . . ."

> *Went on to organize*

PETER PAN! CHILDHOOD! INNOCENCE!

In a fine old mansion on Lake Shore Drive, Markoff Chaney toddled down the hall leading to the Master Bedroom. He was dressed in a Teddy Snow Crop suit and felt like a perfect damned fool.

Oh, well, the money is good, he told himself. Then he pushed the door open and entered the first rich person's bedroom he had ever seen.

There was, as he had been told, only one light, behind the bed, playing upward on the ceiling and shedding a soft glow by reflection. The bed was made up, covered with an expensive-looking heirloom spread. Beside it, lit up nicely by the indirect light, was the table bearing a single can of Snow Crop orange juice, as he had expected.

And on the bed, nude, eyes tightly closed and pretending to sleep, was his hostess.

Chaney caught his breath. Judging from what he was expected to do, he had been prepared to see a crazy old frump; instead, to his intense delight, it was obvious that the lady was still fairly young, quite well preserved, and definitely *stacked*. Crazy she might be (but how could he judge? Maybe it was normal for rich people to act out any fantasy that struck them.), but unappetizing she definitely was not.

Although she was the first live naked woman he had ever seen, she was no less strikingly golden and rounded than, say, a *Pussycat* Pussyette of the Month. A head of gloriously fiery red hair was spread on the pillow, and below it her supposedly sleeping face was lovely in its peaceful anticipation. His eyes swept over her rounded shoulders, the two snowy-white breasts rising and falling with her respiration, the cute nipples that stood in sur- prisingly large areolas upon those breasts, the soft pillow of her belly, and, best of all, the thick swatch of reddish fur that hid her sex. And she had legs like a chorus girl.

She's waiting for me—for me!

Markoff Chaney experienced true happiness. Boldly, he stepped forward and grabbed the orange-juice can. An opener lay beside it and he quickly punched two holes, his hands trembling a bit—when the lady's belly moved with her breathing, he felt his penis stir in the same rhythm.

Then, clutching the juice can in one hand, he hoisted himself onto the bed, catching her in a sudden smile. But she was good at the game; her eyes still didn't open.

Carefully, he lay beside her hip, looking at those breasts, those real 3-D female breasts, not in a photograph, but right there in bed with him. Two of them, by Christ. Then, with infinite delicacy, he lifted the can and let some of the orange juice dribble onto her bush.

She sighed and a tremor ran through her.

He poured a little more, and her legs spread volup- tuously and she slowly raised her knees. He was seeing it at last, the outer lips and the cleft revealed as he had always dreamed of it, the halo of reddish fur even more lovely than in his fantasies. He dribbled some more orange juice and leaned over, pushing the snout onto her bush and maneuvering his tongue into the cleft between the lips.

Immediately, she groaned and threw her legs over his shoulders, pulling him deeper down into her crotch. *"Teddy,"* she murmured, "you've *come back.*"

We all live in our fantasy and only endure our reality, he thought philosophically. According to instructions, he began a spiral licking motion, working from the outer lips slowly inward around the inner lips and ending with the clitoris again. She began to heave up and down like the loud-roaring sea, and his excitement grew, as he imagined and participated in her sensations.

Her hands were on the ears of his Teddy Snow Crop costume and she was pulling him down onto her frantically as she bucked upward, literally fucking his mouth. He began lapping her more rapidly, quite distinctly tasting the musty musky female-in-passion flavor mixed with orange juice.

"Oh, your tongue, your tongue!" she cried. "In me, Teddy, *in me*."

The midget maneuvered his tongue into her vagina and bobbed his head in imitation fucking motions. Her legs went limp on his back, then tight, then limp again. *She's close to coming*, he thought rapturously. *I'm making a woman come at last*. He strained, sticking his tongue farther into her, maddened by the thicker and heavier taste of her and losing the orange juice can entirely in his passion. He got both hands under her and lifted her ass, drawing her pussy up to him, sucking desperately as he plunged his tongue again and again deeper and deeper into her.

"TEDDY SNOW CROP!" she screamed insanely. "FRODO BAGGINS!! PETER PAN!!! CHILDHOOD!!!! INNOCENCE!!!! EAT MY PUSSY!!!!" She was coming, gushing like an oil well, all the female juices of her flowing into his mouth, and he nibbled the outer lips with his teeth, eyes tightly closed, riding on her crotch like a man hanging on to the edge of a cliff by his jaw muscles alone, bucking and bouncing with her, swallowing the essence of her womanhood, the elixir, and now after decades and decades of frustration, finally coming, exploding from the sheer lust of her soul communicated to him in every spasm and twitch of her passionate pussy.

He thought two things: *Now they're going to have to clean the Teddy Snow Crop suit.*

And: *I wonder if I'm still technically a virgin.*

THE RICH ECONOMY

GALACTIC ARCHIVES:

President Hubbard's first step in establishing the RICH Economy was to offer a prize of $50,000 per year to any worker who could design a machine that would replace him or her.

When the primate labor unions raised twenty-three varieties of hell about this plan, Hubbard countered by offering $30,000 a year to *all other workers* replaced by such a machine. The rank-and-file union people fell into conflict immediately, some accepting this as a fine idea (this group consisting mostly of those earning less than twenty thou per annum), and the leaders still hypnotized by the conditioned and domesticated primate reflex that Employment was Good and Unemployment was Bad.

While the unions squabbled among themselves and ceased to present a united front against the RICH scenario, conservatives mounted a campaign against it on the ground that it was inflationary. Here Hubbard's political genius showed itself. She made no effort to reason with the intellectual conservatives, who were all theologians in disguise. All corporation heads and other alpha males of the right, however, were invited to a series of White House multimedia presentations on how RICH would work for them.

The chief points in these presentations were that: (1) a machine works twenty-four hours a day, not eight—thereby tripling output immediately; (2) machines do not take sick leave; (3) machines are never late for work; (4) machines do not form unions and constantly ask for higher wages and more fringe benefits; (5) machines do not take vacations; (6) machines do not harbor grudges and foul up production in sneaky, undetectable ways; (7) cybernation was advancing every decade, anyway, despite the opposition of unions, government, and these alpha males; it was better to have huge populations celebrating the reward of $30,000 to $50,000 per year for group cleverness than huge populations suffering the humility of welfare; (8) with production rising due to both cybernation and the space-cities, *consumers* were needed and a society on welfare was a society of very meager consumers.

The alpha males were still fighting among themselves about whether this was "sound" or not when it squeaked through Congress.

Within a year the first case of the new multi-inventive leisure class appeared. This was a Cherokee Indian named Starhawk, who had been an engine-lathe worker in Tucson. After designing himself out of that job, Starhawk had gone on to learn four other mechanical factory jobs, designed himself out of each, and now had a guaranteed income of $250,000 a year for these feats. He was now devoting himself to painting in the traditional Cherokee style—which was what he had always wanted to do, back in adolescence, before he learned that he had to work for a living.

By 1983 there were over a thousand similar cases. Many had gone on to seek advanced scientific degrees, and some had already migrated to the L5 space-cities. The *swarming* was beginning.

The majority of the unemployed, living comfortably on $30,000 a year, admittedly spent most of their time drinking booze, smoking weed, engaging in primate sexual acrobatics, and watching wall TV.

When moralists complained that this was a subhuman existence, Hubbard answered, "And what kind of existence did they have doing idiot jobs that machines do better?"

Some of the unemployed were beginning to seek jobs again; after all, $48,000 or $53,000 is better than $30,000. Usually, they found that higher education was required for the jobs that were still available. Many were back in college; adult education, already a fast-growth industry in the 1970s, was now the fastest growing field of all.

Hubbard was ready to launch Stage Two of the RICH Economy.

SATIRE

The dialogues between Frank Hemeroid and Ernest Hemingway grew more turgidly moralistic as the 1970s passed; Marvin was never able to bring himself to approach a sexual partner more alien to his own tormented ego than his right fist. He sublimated.

ERNEST: Fear is in all of us and must be faced. He who *hesitates* is lost. He who confronts the fear is undefeated forever, even if his body dies.

FRANK: Oh, come off it. The only reason anybody ever does anything "brave" is because he's more afraid of being called a no-good shit for running away.

ERNEST: You pass a thousand heroes on the street every day and never know how well they are carrying their burdens.

FRANK: I know. The woman with the Mongoloid child. The blind man who makes you so uncomfortable. The rape victim pulling herself together and refusing to go mad. The dumb cop with a hernia yet who goes down an alley after a hopped-up thief who is also armed. I'm not blind, myself. You only see their moments of heroism. You don't choose to watch how blow follows blow until heroism becomes meaningless and they all give up, one by one, and join the universal chorus of despair.

ERNEST: I have seen some who never gave up. A pig squeals when he sees the ax coming. A man can look right at the ax all his life and not squeal.

FRANK: The ax falls, anyway, does it not? Isn't your refusal to squeal just a big act, a gigantic lie? It's more honest to squeal with the other swine.

ERNEST: I still decline to admit that men are no more than swine.

FRANK: You *are* a Romantic, you old fool. If you had been honest enough to squeal like the rest of the swine, people would have seen the truth sooner. Every war since your day has been partly your fault, you know. If everybody squealed and ran away, there'd be no wars.

Of course nobody wanted to publish this kind of ranting—although it took Marvin nearly ten years to learn that.

In 1979 he set out grimly to write the worst, most tasteless, most vulgar book possible. He had arrived at that stage of psychological masochism where one must prove one's most pessimistic assumptions are true, for the sheer delight of knowing once and for all that the universe is really a pisspoor proposition all around. "Public taste is a misanthropist's heaven and a humanitarian's hell," he said bitterly. For his hero he elected a monster so monstrous as to be a mockery of all human hope, but one so obscure that he did not possess any of the evil glamour that surrounds a Hitler, a Nixon, or a Jack the Ripper. He picked Vlad Teppis—*Vlad the Impaler*—a fourteenth-century Hungarian religious fanatic who had executed 100,000 people for differing with his own extremely odd theological notions.

Marvin's novel not only justified Vlad, but positively glorifed him; it was full of denunciations of liberalism, permissiveness, and the opponents of capital punishment. It also had the most violent rape scenes Marvin could conjure out of his misogynistic imagination.

Vlad the Barbarian was a blatant incitement to violence, garbed in the most reactionary moralistic prejudices imaginable. It was bought by the first New York publisher to whom it was submitted, for a higher advance than Albert Speer's memoirs or any of the confessionals of the Watergate felons. A movie sale was negotiated even before the book was released, and John Wayne starred as Vlad, looking really sincere every time he explained why murder and rape were the highest human virtues.

Marvin was immediately commissioned to write a sequel, *Vlad Victorious*.

Actually, because Marvin really was, in his own odd way, a philosopher of sorts, *Vlad the Barbarian* was not totally bad. In researching it Marvin had stumbled upon the enigma that makes Vlad Teppis somewhat interesting to students of the human mind in general and the ruling-class mind in particular. The mystery was this: Two early,

approximately contemporary and seemingly authentic ac-
counts tell one particular story about Vlad, but each tells
it differently. There is thus no scientific way of saying
which account is true.

The disputed story is that two monks on a journey
stopped at Vlad's castle one night and begged shelter from
the elements. Vlad set out for them a magnificent banquet
and then afterward asked them what the people of Hungary
really thought about him. The first monk answered diplo-
matically and falsely that everybody said Vlad was a stern
but just ruler. The second monk boldly told the truth: that
everybody said Vlad was a homicidal maniac. Vlad there-
upon had *one* of the monks impaled. The problem is that
the first seemingly authentic account says he executed
the flattering liar, and the other seemingly authentic account claims he executed the honest monk.

Marvin left this mystery unsolved in his book, and it
was, perhaps, one reason that the novel became fashion-
able even with intellectuals.

Everybody, it appeared, had some intuitive, prelogical
feeling about which monk a man of the caliber of Vlad
Teppis would impale. Some were quite sure that a dingaling
of that sort would kill the one who dared to tell him
the truth. Others, however, were just as sure that Vlad
would find a special sadistic relish, and a moral justi-
fication to boot, in surprising both monks by executing the
flatterer.

Arguing about Vlad's choice, as it was soon called,
spread from coast to coast.

"What would you do if you were one of the monks?"
was a favorite question in these arguments.

"I'd do what the first monk did," Simon Moon said, in
an argument with other programmers who worked with
the Beast. "I'd tell Vlad he was the very model of a
Christian statesman—which, in fact, he was."

"I'd tell the truth," said Markoff Chaney, on a Greyhound bus, "just to prove that little men have big balls."

"I'd lie," Dr. Frank Dashwood admitted at a posh Nob Hill party in San Francisco. "The most dangerous thing in the world is to tell the truth to a government official who is a primitive barbarian, in fourteenth-century Transylvania or twentieth-century America."

Professor Fred ("Fidgets") Digits, who always kept his connection with the Warren Belch Society a secret and, hence, retained academic respectability, finally published a paper in *Technology Review* analyzing the problem from the perspective of the von Neumann-Morgenstern game theory. The monks, in this context, basically confront a problem in *prediction*. Each must decide, before speaking, what Vlad's reaction will be: Will he be grateful for an accurate report or angered by it? Every person in an authoritarian situation faces this dilemma daily, and it haunts corporations, armies, and government bureacracies. "It is the classic disinformation situation," Digits concluded, satisfied that he had identified the problem, even if he couldn't solve it.

Others pointed out the similar logic of the notorious "Snafu Principle" proposed by the eccentric businessman Hagbard Celine in his witty, perverse little booklet *Never Whistle While You're Pissing*. According to the Snafu Principle, accurate, honest communication is possible only between equals, and *every* power matrix is a disinformation situation.

Since this seems to challenge the very principle of power and leads directly to anarchy, many were sorry that Mad Marvin had ever posed the Vlad Enigma.

STRANGE AEONS

*Gestorben ist nicht, was fur ewig ruht, und mit unbekannten
Aonen mag sogar der Tod noch sterben.*

—Von Junzt

As a scientist, Washy Bridge, of course, regarded Von
Junzt as a mental case and the *Necronomicon* as the
ravings of a deranged cannabis abuser. Nonetheless, that
one gaunt German sentence found in 1971 stuck with
him, taunted him, provoked him, eventually goaded him.
He began studying the origins of the Frankenstein idea
within the Promethean ambience of the Shelley-Byron
circle. He researched the early Resuscitation Society. He
traveled to Michigan to talk to H. C. E. Coppinger, the
far-out physicist who had started the cryonics movement
with his astonishing book *The Aspects of Immortality*. The
idea just wouldn't let go of him. In 1974 he even, somewhat shamefacedly, looked into the writings of a strange
Providence, Rhode Island, mystic who had written much
on the metaphysics of the *Necronomicon*. Washy found in
this man's weird writings a better translation than that of
Von Junzt:

> That is not dead which can eternal lie
> And with strange aeons even death may die

CONTRA NATURAM

Justin Case, feeling on top of the world and full to the brim with human kindness, gave a lavish tip to the young lady who had assisted him during his Christian Science copulation with Carol Christmas. He went home musing happily on how simple life was really and how easy it was to transcend one's own little problems with a water bed, a cooperative warm-mouthed lady, Christian Science, and a few good snorts of Marvin Gardens's incredible coke.

On Fourteenth Street near Union Square, Justin was stopped by a zombie. The zombie had pale skin, large eyes that never moved, a mouth that didn't smile, and the unmistakable expression of death. "Do you love your neighbor?" the zombie asked.

"Pardon me," Justin said, dodging, "but I . . ."

"It is easy to love your neighbor," the zombie said, dodging with him. "The scientific principles of Christian Love are now known and can be applied by anyone. For one dollar, just one single dollar, you can have a copy of *What Religiosophy Means*, the book that answers all the questions of philosophy definitely and scientifically."

"Please"—Justin shifted again—"I must . . ."

"For fifty cents," the zombie went on, still with no expression and with eyes unmoving, "you can have *The Scientific Cure for Depressions, Economic and Psychological.*"

"Oh, go shit in your hat," Justin growled in Circuit Two

territorial language. "Disappear. Get out of my way, you creep."

"This is free," the zombie said, passing him a four-page pamphlet titled *"Usura Contra Naturam Est."* "There is no need for competition, brother."

Justin looked at the pamphlet when he got home. It was made up of quotations from Thomas Aquinas, Ezra Pound, B. F. Skinner, and Dr. Horace Naismith, founder of the First Bank of Religiosophy. The quotes from Aquinas and Pound condemned the lending of money at interest. The quotes from Skinner said that people could be conditioned to abandon any habitual behavior and substitute a new behavior. The quotes from Dr. Naismith urged everybody to join the First Bank of Religiosophy, or at least to buy one of his books or pamphlets: "What Religiosophy Means," *The Scientific Cure for Depressions, Economic and Psychological,* "Jesus Christ's Secret Teachings About Money," and *Operant Reinforcement, the Bible Alternative to Satan's International Bankers.**

The streets were full of zombies at that time. The Religiosophists were the most robotic; not for nothing had Dr. Horace Naismith, founder of Religiosophy, spent five years studying with B. F. Skinner at Harvard. The

---

Terran Archives 2803: Interest was a charge for the use of the circulating medium (money). Primatologists have found similar money fetishism on hundreds of planets where hominid types evolved; money and barter themselves are typical primate behaviors which can easily be taught to chimpanzees and other anthropoids. In addition to Aquinas, Pound, and Naismith, early Terrestrial philosophers who suggested more human alternatives to this apelike economics included Thomas Edison, Buckminster Fuller, C. H. Douglas, Benjamin Tucker, and several others. Since *primate behavior changes only under the impact of new technology* (Moon's First Law), the money-and-interest fetish continued until the third stage of the RICH Economy abolished the need for a circulating medium.

Religiosophists had all been operant-conditioned to be tireless proselytizers, and Blake Williams had even invented a mathematical puzzle based on calculating the probability of crossing any American city without being accosted by one of them, which turned out to be harder than the old problem of crossing Dublin without passing a pub.

The Ganesha Freaks were almost as android. Led by Swami Mammonananda, they had also been conditioned to be superpersistent hustlers and to believe that the world would reach *samadhi* on May 1, 1984, if 100,000,000 people were paying funds directly into Mammonananda's bank account by that date in return for bronze emblems of Ganesha, the Hindu *Papa Legba,* or Opener Between the Worlds.

The worst pests of all were the Loonies, disciples of Neon Bal Loon, an English eccentric originally born Albert Pike in Gaotu, Wobblysex, Buggering-on-the-Thames, Lousewartshire, England. Pike claimed to be a reincarnated Tibetan and insisted that Neon Bal Loom was a real Tibetan name, his in his former incarnation. He averred further that the earth was hollow and a gang of naked women, witches, lived inside and were responsible for all the evils on the surface. His followers prayed in pig Latin, while standing on one leg like storks. Pike claimed that was the language of Lemuria.

Mary Margaret Wildeblood snuggles all comfy and cozy in her bed, swallows a female hormone tablet with water poured neat from a silver-sheened pitcher beside the clock and opens a well-thumbed edition of *The 120 Days of Sodom* remembering the foot beneath the chin the ropes the nude figure of Cagliostro tied to the bedposts and begins to read, Jesus watching with those reproachful hurting eyes as her hand sneaks back to the table gropes over the pitcher and clock down to the drawer to remove

stealthily (Perfect Sin, with Jesus watching) the vibrator
Here's the part tortures especially for pregnant women

But Marvin reads in total confusion
Chromosome reduction (meiosis) occurs in early divisions of the synkaryon
Synkaryon? What the stereophonic fuck is that? Skip a bit.
from which the sex cells (gametes) are produced (gameto-genesis) which undergo nuclear reorganization (autogamy) occurs in formaniferans
Syngamy may be between similar gametes (isogamous) or between obviously different gametes (anisogamous)
But are they the same amoeba dammit why can't they tell us in plain words have the extraterrestrials taken over the *Britannica* too?

Marvin Gardens is sniffing just a *little* bit more coke, only a *tiny* bit, really, turning the FM dial in search of some music as accelerated as his own nervous system, thinking: At the fifth generation you've got ah um 64 amoebas a full-blown ecosystem now what I want to know is would they all be permutations and combinations like the 64 hexagrams in the *I Ching* or would they all be the same like the Creative ☰ repeated 64 times? Jesus maybe just one more snort one little *tiny* teensy-weensy itty-*bitty* snort yes with cloning now in laboratories there may be 64 of *me* someday outbreed the extraterrestrials that way maybe Jesus yes but Linda Lovelace oh Christ if I ever did meet her I'd be too shy to say, to say, I mean like with Picasso you could just walk right up and say "I'm an admirer of your work and I'd like to commission a small sketch" perfectly normal an artist and a fan but to say "I admire your work could you give me a personalized blow job"

went on to organize
went on to organize

"I think the record is stuck," Natalie said, finally getting a word in edgewise.

"Um yes my dear just a sec but Ignatz I was saying is very simple-minded he thinks he just hates cats"

went on to orgggprp

"Whereas Krazy on the other hand knows that each brick is actually a phallic gift [Herriman must have been aware of the Freudian associations of that marvelous monosyllable, *brick*]. Krazy remembers, or things she remembers, a previous incarnation in which she and Ignatz were lovers. . . ."

But in the split second of orgasm in the orgonomic plasma, ego dilated to crash wave after wave floating in the astral as taught by Hagbard via Miss Portinari in *potentia* faster than the speed of light full-blown on each side of the boundary, Joe Malik in terror sees the glaring red Eye and the golden triangular frame $3 \times 3 \times 3$ the sign of Choronzon, 333, whose name and number signified the Great Lie.

INTERNATIONAL COCAINE INC.

The debate about the Vlad Enigma gave birth to a general interest in problems of disinformation. The Prisoner's Dilemma was dragged out of heavy mathematical tomes and popularized. The Turing Machine was reexamined in tabloid newspapers. The Empedoclean paradox even got mentioned on the Johnny Carson show.

Two Berkeley acid-heads, known on Telegraph Avenue as The Cat and The Dog, dreamed up a more intense disinformation matrix in 1980. "What would happen," The Cat asked one day in the Café Mediterraneum, "if we bought a truck and painted on the side of it INTERNATIONAL COCAINE IMPORTERS INC., and drove it around the streets?"

"In Berkeley," The Dog said, "the cops would just laugh. They'd be sure it was another put-on by the Hog Farm or the Merry Pranksters or somebody. But in San Francisco they wouldn't take a chance. The first cop would stop the truck and search it."

"Nah," said an unsuccessful poet named Robert W. Anton. "They're more hip than that in San Francisco. But in L.A. . . ."

The debate spread from the Med to Moe's, from Moe's to Sather Gate, leapt the Bay to appear in Herb Caen's column, eventually spread from coast to coast as a tag-end poser to cap all discussions of the Vlad Enigma. Finally,

taking the logical experimental step, a San Francisco theologian named Malaclypse the Younger actually painted a
truck in very tasteful and professional lettering and drove
it around the Bay Area for all to see:

INTERNATIONAL COCAINE IMPORTERS INC.
LIMA—SAN DIEGO—VANCOUVER
"THINGS GO BETTER WITH COKE"

He was stopped and searched three times the first
week—once in Sausalito, which is the cocaine and Vase-
line capital of Unistat and has particularly suspicious cops.
He was never stopped in Berkeley. After the second week
he was no longer stopped in San Francisco. Immediately a
whole fleet of similar trucks began to appear.

Disinformation had been incarnated. "All hail Eris,"
said Malaclypse, a pious man in his own odd way. Virtually none of the trucks was stopped and searched after the
first month. Cops who had made horses' asses of themselves in the joking phase of this uprising of surrealist
politics refused to take the risk of being laughed at again.
Nobody cared to guess how many of the trucks were really
carrying cocaine.

It all became academic when victimless crimes were
redefined in the Code Hubbard.

DO NOT GO GENTLE

Do not go gentle into that good night:
Rage, rage against the dying of the light.
—DYLAN THOMAS

GALACTIC ARCHIVES:

President Hubbard's way of encouraging the Longevity Revolution was characteristic. She established a yearly reward of $100,000 for the *nonscientist* who made the most important contribution to the fight against aging. Since the scientists engaged in life-extension research were already one of the two most heavily funded groups in Unistat (the other was the space engineers), scientists were amused, but not offended, by this wild idea.

The first year there were 5,237 entries submitted. A spot check by the Beast showed that 4,023 came from the new leisure class—ex-workers who had invented themselves out of several jobs and had $50,000 to $80,000 annual incomes. The others came from people who had been unemployed by these inventions. Evidently, many of them were getting bored with a life that consisted mostly of fucking, TV, and vacations, even though that had been what most primates imagined they would do if they didn't have to work for a living.

270

The second year there were over 30,000 entries—much as Hubbard had expected.

The Longevity Revolution was having its inevitable effect. People who were expecting to live for centuries instead of decades were spontaneously taking the Next Step in their thinking. The hominids of Terra were becoming reoriented to the search for Immortality.

And a second trend was becoming obvious. The majority of practical, testable hyper-longevity proposals were coming in from the colonists in the L5 space-cities.

The domesticated primates of Terra were beginning to consciously guide their own evolution toward becoming Cosmic Immortals.

To Justin Case it appeared that the administration was the first government in history to take Beethoven seriously. To him, Hubbard's whole philosophy was obviously derived from the last movement of the *Ninth*.

THE DARLING BUDS OF MAY

Since a cat has the Buddha mind, even Marvin Gardens had had his own experience of the First Noble Truth. He had made the mistake, once, in 1981, of eating a heavy slice of hash-candy from Afghanistan instead of his after-dinner snort of coke and somehow there was an eruption of activity in the grief circuits of the thalamus. *The tramp did not move.* He saw the skull beneath the skin, like

Eliot; the tears poured and he sat there, weeping for allflesh, for alltormented flesh, for alltormentedfuckingflesh, howling in anguish at the withdrawal of the nipple of self-absorption. He was in Belsen. He stood in the white light as Hiroshima was incinerated. He watched the Grand Army retreat in the snow from Moscow. The tramp fell eternally toward the sidewalk and he saw the wolves close in on the terrified caribou, the smirk of Caligula and all sadists everywhere, the parents of a thousand wars weeping with him over murdered children ("We should be gentle with children," a Voice said reproachfully from a window in space), and for a minute he had a crazy religious vision that WE HAVE TO STOP THE KILLING there is no other way and it is too late for another alternative it is exactly that simple and you can even repeat it in italics *we have to stop the killing* and he was so excited at the sudden clarity of it that he could see his whole future as nonstop witnessing to the truth of this vision. He would invent his own TV show and become a supersalesman and sell it to the top network and it would be the Corporal Works of Mercy Hour. It would have no acts of violence or hurting. It would just be decent people doing decent things, as enumerated in the famous passage from Aquinas: visiting the sick and imprisoned, feeding the hungry, giving shelter to the homeless, aiding the oppressed, comforting the afflicted, and praying for us all.

It was that simple, beyond all the irony and agony of his tortured humor, and you could even say it in one word: *ahimsa*.

Yea-a-a-ay, God! Glory, glory, glory.

He staggered to his desk to record this revelation, but when he got there microamnesia had already set in and he couldn't remember what it was that had seemed so clear and important, but another Voice was coming through and he scrawled rapidly:

Rough winds do shake the darling buds of May

At that very moment, in Los Angeles, Eve Hubbard decided she was going to run for President.

THE UNIVERSE DECIDES

"So that," Justin Case concludes triumphantly (he is dreaming about giving a lecture to an audience of transvestites), "the elements in the montage may be of any number—five, fifteen, fifty, whatever—and there be any emotions you can imagine implicit in each one of them separately. Nonetheless, the total emotional effect emerges from the montage, not from the elements. Film is the visual demonstration of Fuller's synergetic geometry."

"You're fuller shit!" one of the transvestites yelled.

Who shit? Justin shit. Bullshit! Who shit? He was being carried around by the time-dwarfs in a jeweled chair wearing the Crown of Thorns. It was Mardi Gras. He was having a swell time. He decided to go on lecturing them.

"The montage of Chinatown or Chapel Perilous takes us to the Lair of Fu Manchu—the center of Power—the occult Nine Unknown Illuminated Ones who rule the world—the secret of capitalism and ownership—the cruel Cross that separates inside from outside, without windows."

But then he wet his pants and they were all laughing at him, laughing mockingly and childishly, as they closed in with the tar and feathers. They had found out he was a no-good shit.

"In other words," Blake Williams lectures, "what collapses the state vector and er um determines or ah least ways brings it about that a new quantum state appears can only be a Hidden Variable implicate in the whole system— the biggest whole system."

"You mean when Ignatz throws the brick—"

"If Ignatz is a quantum physicist and is throwing a photon, Krazy or Schrödinger's Cat can be in any of several *eigen*states, um, yes, so that in effect the whole universe participates in the ah decision as to whether the Kat will be hit by the brick um ah or the photon ah as the case may be."

"Professor," Natalie asked finally, driven to the Edge, "are you putting me on?"

"My dear I am um merely giving you the most consistent and literal interpretation of Bell's Theorem as developed by Dr. Jeffrey Chew at U.C.-Berkeley and Dr. Fritjof Capra in *The Tao of Physics*."

"The whole universe *decides*?"

"Well there is um a certain degree of metaphor involved. . . ."

"You know, Professor"—Natalie sits up and gives him a level glance—"I met a midget once, a nasty little son-of-a-bitch, but he told me something I never forgot. All that exists is metaphor, he said, and *whoever controls our metaphors controls us*."

"As an anthropologist," Blake Williams said, "I must agree. Are we living in an occult thriller, a porn movie, a philosophical treatise, a sci-fi novel? It depends on which parts of our experience we choose to highlight. That brings us to the question: Are we writing our life-scripts, or is there a Hidden Variable, as the new quantum theories suggest?"

"You mean the whole universe will decide what we're gonna do next?" Natalie wanted a straight answer.

"Well um that's the alternative to saying there are multiple universes where anything that can happen does happen ah and it's quite democratic, really, since every lesser system within the whole system gets its vote."

Natalie's semantic circuit was working on overload. "You're telling me that each of us and the chair over there and each atom in us and in the chair and in Marvin's cocaine—we all get one vote?"

"Um perhaps we have carried the metaphor till it staggers . . ."

"It sounds like Mozart's music," Natalie said, seeing the window again. "All as mechanical as a clockwork and yet as free as a dream. . . ."

HELL

GALACTIC ARCHIVES:

President Hubbard had largely abolished crime by abolishing prisons.

This was one of her most astonishing achievements, since most primates thought prisons were preventatives, not causes, of crime.

Eve Hubbard, needless to say, had always been a unique

Terran, which was why she was the first Black President of Unistat. Although she was, like most brilliant people, extremely good-looking—the genetic link between health, hedonism, cleverness, and good looks (the "bright-eyes-and-bushy-tails" gestalt) is true in all species on all known planets—Eve had dropped out of films after a smash success as the supersexed ebony android in *Gentlemen Prefer Clones*. She had gone on to major in philosophy at UCLA, and was almost denied her Ph.D. because her thesis was a thorough rejection of all philosophies hitherto invented by Terran primates. She went on to become one of the first neurogeneticists. In fact, it was due to certain discoveries in primate genetics that she had decided to go into politics next.

The Code Hubbard, the most important revision of primate jurisprudence since the Code Napoleon, divided all crimes into three classes.

Crimes against convention—so-called victimless crimes—were not penalized at all. A citizen could be interrogated about each behavior only after complaints by a minimum of one hundred neighbors. The interrogators, a group of trained neurogeneticists, would then publish a report, either mildly recommending *relocation* of the heretic, or, much more commonly, strongly advising the neighbors to mind their own business.

Many libertarians objected to this, since they wanted victimless crimes abolished utterly. Hubbard had pragmatically realized that such libertarian penology was impractical until the primates totally outgrew the morality delusion.

Those who chose relocation were assigned by the Beast to an environment where their heresy was "normal." Most of them found that the Beast recommended an L5 spacecity, and most of them liked it when they got there. They had *futique* genes.

Many of the heretics, of course, chose to stay where they were and go on annoying the bejesus out of their neighbors. This is the typical recalcitrant streak found in certain domesticated primates on all planets.

Crimes against property were regarded as improper economics requiring adjustment. The felon was compelled to pay in full the value of that which had been appropriated or destroyed. If unable to pay, the felon then had a literal "debt to society." The government paid the victim, and the felon repaid the government by working at half wages on some socially useful project, such as longevity research, space research, or just as a forest ranger in the growing number of national parks that were appearing since Industry was moved off the planet into Free Space.

Crimes of violence were defined as the natural, inevitable, tragic, but intolerable resultant of some combination of genes, imprints, and conditioning. The biots who committed such acts were sent, without condemnation but irrevocably, to Hell.

Hell had previously been the state of Mississippi. After the aborigines were resettled in an environment suitable for two-circuit (prehominid) primates, Mississippi became Hell by simply surrounding it with a laser shield that made escape impossible. Everything within the shield was intact. The violent biots were free to do what they wanted, and they soon had several forms of feudalism, war, piracy, commerce, slavery, and other early primate institutions functioning in a manner that seemed normal to them.

Many violent biots and gene pools moved to Hell voluntarily, since it was the only remaining part of the world that fit their notions of proper primate society. Among those who migrated en masse and established sizable governments or robber bands in Hell were the Ku Klux Klan, the Black Panthers, the American Nazi Party, Hell's Angels, and most of the People's Ecology Party.

John Wayne, nearly one hundred years old, but looking and feeling around thirty due to FOREVER, and totally cured of all cancers by the Org pills, also went to Hell. He was rumored to be one of the richest slave traders and War Chiefs in the Western sector.

"HELL IS HEAVEN" was the proud slogan of the region.

WHITE LIGHT

Hugh Crane celebrated his fourteenth birthday in 1938 by climbing into the bed of the family's black maid, Sophie Hagé. She had observed his precocity and wasn't surprised at the timing; and the deed itself, she had learned, was par for the sons and the female servants of the best families on Park Avenue. What was not normal was the passion that endured over several months, and the extent to which she herself was picked up and carried by it. Soon they were sharing secrets, just as if they were true lovers and equals, not master and servant.

"Nails and glass in your shoes?" she asked him on the day that Nazi tanks crossed the border into Czechoslovakia.

"I read about it in a book about saints that I got from the library on Forty-second Street," he said.

"But that's crazy, mon." She was from Haiti.

"But it worked," he said. "I saw Jesus."

"You saw *Jesus*?"

"Well," he said bashfully. "That wasn't just from the nails

in my shoes. It was after I whipped my back with wet rope for six hours."

Sophie gazed at him thoughtfully for a long time. "What you trying to do, boy?"

"I'm learning how to live without fear," he said simply. "You know my dad. He's afraid of everything and everybody. Jews, Catholics, bad omens, the government, a broken mirror . . . you *know*. I just don't want to live my life that way."

Sophie thought about it for three days. Then she told him there was a man he ought to meet.

"What sort of man?" he asked.

"A high priest of *Voudon*."

RED EYE

Mister, what does it mean when a man crashes out?
> —IDA LUPINO IN *High Sierra*,
> SCRIPT BY JOHN HUSTON

DECEMBER 24, 1983:

The Eye, diamond-bright and glowing with a red inflammation, floated in the air at the head of the couch as Joe Malik returned to the Euclidean flatland at the bottom of the gravity well.

Bloodshot eyes I've got to be haunted by, he thought

bitterly, still dealing with the dimensions of the triangle. $3 \times 3 \times 3$. No doubt about it. 333. The number of the Mighty Devil Choronzon, who had afflicted Dr. Dee and Sir Edward Kelley in the seventeenth century and raised hell for Aleister Crowley earlier in this century. Choronzon, the Lurker at the Threshold, who drove back any occultist who tried to push open the final door, cross the boundary of the unmarked state. Choronzon, avatar of the Great Lie, spirit of Constriction, protector of the Illuminati.

Choronzon with a hangover, to judge by the redness of the eye.

"Jeez that was great oh honey ah you doll you lovely Arab sheikh you," Carol was bubbling happily.

But Blake Williams plows on:

"The Freudian, of course, sees much more in Krazy's love for Ignatz. Sadomasochism, in fact. 'Li'l dollink, always fetful,' Krazy mutters contentedly as each brick bounces off her head. And worse: Krazy is female only in some sequences. In others this remarkable feline is indisputably male. Herriman, the psychoanalyst would suggest, had some AC-DC hang-ups when he conceived this fantasy."

"Sometimes, Professor, you remind me of Burroughs," Natalie said.

"Well, I do admire much of his work, especially *The Job* . . ." Williams was pleased by the comparison.

"No, the other one, the guy who wrote *Tarzan*, Edgar Rice Burroughs."

"I? Remind you? Of Edgar Rice Burroughs?"

"Of something he said once. He said that he had a lot of fun with his imagination and that he knew in a small way what a grand time God had in creating the universe."

Joe Malik didn't even believe in Choronzon. The Skeptic within him had decided that the most operational model for those events which naïve occultists attribute to "Choronzon" was to classify them as synchronicities activated by the presence of the Trickster God archetype, in the Jungian collective unconscious, or Leary's neurogenetic archives, or somewhere back down there in the thalamus or brainstem. To assume, even for a minute, that Choronzon had an objective existence beyond the archetype in the unconscious circuitry of the central nervous system was to collapse into prescientific *theology* and *demonology*.

But, alas, the Skeptic was only one program inside the Malik biocomputer, and not at his best at moments like this. The Shaman tape began running in its own programs as the Skeptic faded out, and Joe noticed again for the thousandth time how the ego circuit melded with the new program as easily as it had with the old, so now he "was" Joe Malik the Shaman, son of a thousand years of Sufis, and if Choronzon was really messing around he betta watcha his ass.

"It's that motherfuckin' *loa*," Carol said angrily. "We didn't do the exorcism right. . . ."

"*Choronzon*" was a mind-construct of the primates specializing in the Enochian version of Cabalistic magick. Talking out of two sides of their mouths at once, as was typical of primate mystics, the Cabalists said that Choronzon was the astral embodiment of all the illusions and deception on Terra (especially all the egotism and malice). They added that Choronzon was also a part of the psyche of the student which had to be faced and conquered before Illumination was complete. When asked whether Choronzon was then outside or inside, they usually answered "Both."

This reply made no sense at all until G. Spencer Brown published his *Laws of Form*.

A *loa* was a mind-construct of those primates who specialized in *Santaria*, also called *Magicko de Chango* or *Voudon*. A *loa*, just like the Gentry, might on occasion be kindly disposed; but a guardian *loa* who was set on a woman to prevent her from copulating (except with the primate who had through *Santaria* created/projected/contacted said *loa*) was well known to be extremely malign, devious, fiendish, impish, devilish, and a Royal pain in the ass. The *loas*, like the Gentry and the various Cabalistic angels and demons, operated beneath the space-time continuum in "dream time," where the true Free Masons create reality friezes.

An *archetype* was a mind-construct of a primate named Carl Jung, who specialized in preneurological psychology. An archetype existed at the *"psychoid"* level, which was below that of individual or collective unconsciousness, where the organic and the inorganic meld and merge into psychoid matrices which, if nudged by the right archetype, would produce a reality-construct so astonishing that it would appear like magick or a very strange "coincidence." Jung called these psychoid archetypal effects *synchronicities*.

And Marvin Gardens, coked to the nines, is reading on and on with absolute absorption:

Syngamy forms a zygote, which develops into a new diploid form, and the cycle begins anew

Cycles that's it, he thinks excitedly, we're all permutations and combinations of that first amoeba every ejaculation another birthdeath or node in the everybranching whatchamacallit. Oh man this is heavy and I'm really grooving with it cycles in time great wheels turning like the Mayan calendar the genetic clock like music but oh shit maybe it's just the coke I still haven't figured out if the damn amoeba is immortal

But Malik is maintaining his cool, albeit with some effort. "So all right," he said aloud, facing the Eye unblinking, "are you just trying to scare me to death, or do you have a message for me?" *Treat all of Them in a lofty way, lest They have cause to think thee weak,* said Dr. Dee.

"We better do the exorcism again," whispered Carol Christmas—nude, golden, and delicious—also maintaining her cool.

Carol had a great deal of experience at maintaining her cool. Her career had been typical of self-directed Unistat females who matured in the early 1970s: one rape at age fifteen while hitchhiking (she never hitchhiked again); two abortions; husband #1, who turned out to be so free of Macho and the Male Stereotype that even God's Lightning couldn't accuse him of Chauvinism (he wept most piteously when Carol got tired of supporting him and threw him out); husband #2, who was brilliant, kind, generous, sensitive, and a junky; a succession of mediocre lovers, with one or two she still treasured in memory but wouldn't want to live with again for all the tea in Acapulco; producers who believed that an actress as gorgeous as she should only be cast in roles that justified getting all her clothes off sometime during the third act and several times in their private offices; husband #3, who had put the goddamned *loa* on her when they separated; and Ronnie

"Ronnie is doing very well for a special child," the doctor had told her the last time she visited the home. That was a hell of an elaborate euphemism for Mongolian idiot, she thought angrily; but the doctor was trying to be kind, and she forgave him.

But two nights later she opened in another Off-Off-Off Broadway, *Hiroshima Werewolf*, and one critic described her as having "a special childlike quality reminiscent of Monroe." She felt a wave of vertigo on reading that: If the doctor and the critic were not in cahoots to drive her over the edge, then those words were the most sinister kind of synchronicity. But she maintained her cool.

Now she had a goddamned *loa* on top of everything else.

She maintained.

And Justin Case, deeper asleep, dapper as loop, was just waltzing along Owld Broadway with Judge Wishingdone, past Punker Hall, and there was a patchy fog and a zoo city zoo, one nixson and a vegetable. And he was blowin to adams and tilling the tyler, Don Judge Lincoln, mercurial and zany and hoppy, that high on the thighangle of him, cruising the dollarwars and emanstirpating his sklavs until he was caught with Topsy! in the barn!! on the farce of youlie!!! No martha! that's jokeson's guile for you, toomsayer.

But they were in the cherrytreeattric warld, an honest ape, he couldna tell a phone. One nukied individual, with Ma in her gurdjef and Pop in the easel, to the republic for witch's hands, by the Donzerly Light. And who comes up but Indrarambam and Rashowsunnier and Shivabull, loads and toads of them, forty of them, with their fords and hords and their gauchos and cheekos and jumbos and harpoons inem (corpus whalem!) asking about the launches and donors and the thousand and ninety things they ask, irking and rooking and snooping, prying and preying, forty of them, all buyers cotter, infernal reamin you sodage, doubt's eternal fact, by all Chinatown howdials.

Justin moans in his sleep as the Iranian Rastuys Shiites close in on him.

"*Papa Legba, Papa Legba, Papa Legba*," Joe Malik chants along with Carol Christmas, while the astral/ electrical/prajna/orgone/psionic/bioplasmic/odyle energy, or the Power of Imagination, in the room continues to escalate toward quantum wobble.

Papa Legba was the Opener of the window, according to the *Santaria* metaphor. Like Maxwell's Demon, he could increase or decrease entropy at whim, and take you into alternative *eigen*states. He was the Boss Honcho on the astral *potentia* level, the alpha male of the pack. He'd kick the ass of any *loa* intruding on his good friends, and Carol had learned to be one of his very good friends since living with Hugo de Naranja.

Joe Malik didn't know from Papa Legba, but he understood the exorcism in his own terms. Papa Legba was the guise in which Thoth, that master Quick Change Artist, appeared in the *Santaria* or *Voudon* game. Joe knew about Thoth from Hagbard Celine, who always employed the Cabalistic/Golden Dawn metaprograms when attempting quantum alterations in the fabric of reality. Thoth commandered seventy-eight servitors, each one encoded in his Book of Signals to mankind, ordinarily known as the Tarot deck. Each Tarot card was synchronistic with a different quantum *eigen*value and the arrangement of the cards, when shuffled at random, revealed the Hidden Variable causing the "acausal" quantum jump to the next reality-mesh.

Malik the Skeptic tended to regard that explanation as pseudoscientific balderdash, but Malik the Shaman found it useful as a working hypothesis when critters like Chronozon went bump in the night.

"Zeno of Elias on the other hand my dear reminds us that before the brick can ever hit Krazy it must first travel half of the distance from Ignatz's paw to Krazy's head, but before it can do that it must cover half of *that* distance that is to say a quarter of the original distance . . ."

THE FETUS PEOPLE

John Disk had originally become involved in morality and ideology due to the Fetus People, as *Pussycat* genially labeled the antiabortion movement of the 1970s. The Fetus People did not like this description; they called themselves the Right to Life Committee.

Disk was in his teens then and had the usual hormones flowing through his adolescent primate body. He thought he was continually tormented by sinful desires, not understanding the role of testosterone in pubescent primates.

He was a member of the True Roman Catholic Church, a splinter group formed after Vatican II had taken the main body of the Romish religion off into heresy and modernism. The members were survivors of the Irish-American fascism that had once rallied behind Father Coughlin, Father Feeney, and Senator Joe McCarthy. They regarded the English Mass as being almost as sacrilegious as abortion and Social Security as only one step from Stalinism.

The Fetus People or the Right to Life Committee was an amalgamation of True Roman Catholics with the kind of Fundamentalists Protestants seldom seen north of Bad Ass, Texas. They were, like all primate ideologists and moralists, chiefly concerned with finding *no-good shits* and *dumping* on them.

They believed the abortionists were in league with all the other no-good shits, including the Rockefellers, the international Communist sex educators, life-extension researchers, cattle mutilators, NASA, and the intergalactic Black Magicians of the Illuminati, under the leadership of the infamous Cagliostro the Great.

They also believed that the Unistat government had never waged an unjust war, that the hair of the seventh son of a seventh son cures warts, and most of what they read in *Reader's Digest*.

By 1982 the legal struggles over abortion were over and the whole issue seemed as remote as the War of the Roses. This was because a 100 percent effective *morning-after* contraceptive had been on the market since 1980 and had proven so effective that requests for abortions had dwindled to virtually zero.

By 1983 the economic demand for abortions was about as microscopic as the demand for buggy whips in 1923, after every town in Unistat had switched from horse-drawn carriages to automobiles. Another quantum jump in sociology had occurred.

Actually, the morning-after pill was a chemical abortifacient, as any biochemist knew. The biochemists never talked about this in public, since they were all agnostic liberals and it was against their principles to either lie by denying the facts or to help the Fetus People by telling the truth.

As a result of this policy by the biochemists only a handful of the Fetus People turned their attack against the pill when abortion was no longer a live issue. Since the resultant of the morning-after pill was, to the human eye, no different from ordinary menstruation, opposing this seemed exceedingly eccentric even for Fetus People.

The majority of the Fetus People, deprived of their *raison d'être*, began splitting amoebalike into factions and subfactions.

Some few of them, who had really been concerned with the

rights of the unborn, became concerned at last with the rights of the born and launched new groups to oppose the surviving vestiges of war, capital punishment, or poverty in backward parts of the planet.

The majority, who had been mainly preoccupied with finding no-good shits and dumping on them, joined organizations like NOODLE (National Organization Organized for Decent Literature and Entertainment) or the First Bank of Religiosophy.

John Disk drifted into White Heroes Opposing Red Extremism, a group mostly concerned with combating parapsychology, psychics, UFO demons, sex educators, cattle mutilators, and, of course, the loathsome Cagliostro the Great.

ROSENFELT HAS DESTROYED ME

In 1941 the Carter Brothers Carnival played Xenia, Ohio, and some students from Antioch College tried to throw Cagliostro a whammy with a dragon-headed Japanese condom. His handling of that challenge aroused the admiration and awe of old carny hands; and they were even more amazed by his friendship with Rambo, the lion.

Sandoz, the lion tamer, in particular, was astonished at Cagliostro's ability to sit for hours in the cage, he and the lion staring into each other's eyes like lovers.

"Are you hypnotizing him?" Sandoz asked once.

"Not at all," Cagliostro said, laughing. "He's hypnotizing *me*. Or maybe we're just learning to get outside our own skins. That's what life is all about, you know—making windows, breaking out of every box . . ."

The failure of the students to shake up Cagliostro led a few professors to come over and try various scientific devices not likely to be included in any standard verbal code. He placidly identified rheostats, Wheatstone bridges, pH meters, Bunsen burners, and even a gyroscope. The next night they were back with a chemical formula never before synthesized.

"Are you presently able to see the particular object that I have been given at this time?" the girl asked.

And the blindfolded Cagliostro replied calmly, "A test tube. With some blue liquid in it. A copper sulphate compound."

"That's a *damned* good code," the professors agreed, more fervently this time, as they drove back to Antioch.

(There's no hope of salvaging anything—the suicide note had said—*and you're going to have to make it on your own, just like I did. Rosenfelt has destroyed me and he'll destroy free enterprise.)*

The carnival was in Biloxi, Mississippi, that winter, and Cagliostro was trying his new gig, combining Houdini-style escapes with his mentalism act. He had been locked in a trunk, and the local police cooperatively used their best padlocks to secure the chains. He settled down to slow, regular yoga breathing—the escape actually took only a few minutes, but he was following Houdini's formula that the audience was more impressed if they had to wait a half hour for the miracle. The yoga conserved the oxygen in the trunk against any possibility that panic, toward the end, might force him into rapid breathing. He timed the breaths against a slow AUMMMMMM, his mind drifted back to Park Avenue and a black maid whose framed picture of a Catholic-looking Jesus sometimes in certain lights seemed to have horns, and he relaxed his hands and feet (there can be no muscle tension in the torso if the extremities are totally limp), bringing her face back clearly, and he heard a voice shouting, "We're at war! The Japanese went and bombed some place called Pearl Harbor in Honolulu!"

Cagliostro was always carrying around a book called *Homo Ludens* in those days.

"Is that about faggots?" Sandoz asked him once.

Cagliostro laughed. "No," he said. "It's Latin. It means . . . uh, you know it's hard to translate . . . *Man the Game Player,* I suppose."

Sandoz grinned. "You can learn all about that just by watching the marks," he said. "I been a carny damn near twenty years now and I swear from the things I seen, you could sit down with a blackjack table and a sign saying 'THIS GAME IS CROOKED,' and half the marks would still sit down opposite you and try to beat you. A mark *wants to lose,*" he concluded profoundly, almost with anger.

"No," Cagliostro said. "The mark wants to be hypnotized. He wants to enter the world of magic, with mirrors and blue smoke and shifting shapes, and he's willing to be swindled, just to have a glimpse of that world."

"Is that what that book says?" Sandoz asked.

"More or less," Cagliostro said. "In sociological jargon."

JUMPED BY JESUS

DECEMBER 24, 1983:

Mary Margaret Wildeblood still couldn't get to sleep, and *The Search for the Historical Vlad* was pishposh. She got out of bed and padded over to the desk to glance at the latest volumes that had arrived for review.

FROM CALIGARI TO VLAD

Another pretentious volume of neo-Freudian film criticism by George Dorn, obviously cashing in on the current fad. Rot.

THE RADICAL EPISTEMOLOGY OF SMOKEY STOVER

Hmm? Marshall McLuhan again. Try a page:

> *and the Notary Sojac sign, communicating much by its very inscrutability, is not alphabetical but ideogrammic, bringing tribal mystery to the electronic continuum, just as Chief Cash U. Nutt, true shaman that he is*

Fiddlefaddle. What else have we got?

291

IN THE CASTLE OF VLAD

Somebody else ripping off Marvin Gardens.

CONTEMPORARIES OF VLAD

I smell a fad in the making.

PATTERNS OF FASCIST ART

Who's being dissected? Wagner, Pound, Celine, Riefenstahl, Vonnegut . . . *Vonnegut?* Oh: It's by Kate Millett.

JACKIE DID IT!

The latest Kennedy assassination exposé. Bosh.

I AWAIT HIS RETURN

By who? Rebecca Goodman. Didn't she write that anthropology book a few years back, *Golden Apples of* something? What this time? Hm. Had her husband cryonically frozen at death. Hm.
Well, let's see. Millett, I guess.

Beneath the veneer of chic liberalism, Vonnegut's sexist prejudice reveals hm skip a bit *refusal to recognize dialectic of capitalist* blah blah blah *a really sinister note enters with the chauvinist caricature of Montana Wildstack* blah blah *beneath the sentimentality a ruthless determination to subjugate and humiliate women*

Mary Margaret realized that she was getting horny again; any reference to subjugation and humiliation was likely to trigger that response in her. She stealthily removed the

vibrator from the bureau drawer again, climbed back into
bed with *Patterns of Fascist Art,* and then remembered a
little bit of hashish left in the living room.

"Perhaps a diagram would help," Blake Williams said,
getting a sketchpad and drawing rapidly:

"This is ordinary causality, as we usually experience it,"
he said, as Natalie stifled a yawn. "A causes B, which
causes C, and so on. I go to Wildeblood's party at A, and
meet you, and we come here to B, and we discuss Krazy
Kat at C, which leads to Schrödinger's Cat at D. Got it?"
    "Yeah, the Gutenberg fix; the linear mode, as McLuhan
calls it. . . ."
    "Right you are. Now quantum causality, before the
appearance of the epiphenomena of space and time, functions entirely differently if we trust Bell's Theorem. It
looks more like this." And Williams sketches rapidly:

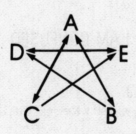

"A 'causes' B, C, D, and E, but B also 'causes' A, C, D,
and E, and C 'causes' A, B, D, and E . . . and so on. Got
it . . . ? All before the appearance of the space-time
manifold."
    "You mean it works everywhichway in time . . ."

"No, it happens before time itself appears along with space as a by-product of the quantum mesh. . . ."

Brrrzzzzzzzmmmmmbrz the vibrator purrs along as Mary Margaret surrenders again to Him (to Him!) starting to compose a poem almost "Crush me in your Dionysian biceps, Jesus Lord" but that was perhaps a bit too Hopkins and the reality of it was beyond poetry (heresy: she could never admit that in literary circles) but the thrust and the purr and the agony and the ecstasy of it Lord Lord lord

because she was remembering an old Sufi proverb about the three stages of the Path which were "Lord, use me" and then "Lord, use me but don't break me" and then "Lord, I don't care if you break me"

and He was breaking her smashing her annihilating her the Great Magician of the Tarot naked on the bed as SHe rammed hir cock up his ass

I AM CONFUSED

To be is to be related.
        —CASSIUS KEYSER, *Thinking About Thinking*

DECEMBER 24, 1983:

"So that the brick never moves, logically," Williams says.

"Yeah I had that in a class at the New School, 'Paradox and Personality,' it's based on you know Relativistic Ego

Therapy, we're all Empedoclean concepts in social topology." Natalie actually had received an A for the course.

"In *territorial* topology my dear I um invented Relativistic Ego Therapy," Williams says, meaning: *I created the course*.

"You're *that* Professor Williams my God you're famous at the new School." Natalie was impressed.

"And at Esalen um yes my dear but to the world at large—" Williams demurs.

"Thank God I'm an atheist," Joe Malik said fervently. "If I considered for even a moment for even a microsecond that the *pretense* of a demon might be functionally equivalent to the *presence* of a demon . . . Just change the *t* to an *s* . . ."

But Marvin abandons the *Britannica* (never find what you really want in there) and undressing for bed fumbles at the radio for something bearable, only to hear

I'm in love with Vlad the Impaler
With Hitler and Nixon and Ahab the Whaler

He quickly turns the dial (after a moment of pride at new-won fame and wincing at the cacophony of The Civic Monster), finding a classical station the end of the *Ninth* all those heavenly choirs singringinging at the Omega Point over a century before science discovered it (always read Nietzsche and listen to Ludwig, was one of his adages, for the long-range evolutionary perspective), pops a downer to take the edge off the coke jitters before they come, and slips under the covers remembering Linda's mouth two inches four inches six inches nine goddamned inches gorgeous splat splat splat always splitting but always one, is it really? as Ludwig answers yes I will yes

I never died said he

"But the crowning insult to our simple-minded realism comes, of course, from our friends the physicists," Williams explains. "If Krazy is Schrödinger's Cat in the famous demonstration then my dear *then* we are really up the ontological creek without a paddle because when the brick is hurled she may be in any of several *eigen*states, several mathematical probability matrices, in some of which the brick will certainly hit her and in some of which it will not."

"Oh, wow."

"Wow, indeed. To paraphrase Descartes: 'I think; therefore, I am confused.'"

ESCAPISM

The first fame of Cagliostro began while he was touring with the U.S.O. during the war. He had entirely abandoned mentalism by then and his act depended entirely on escaping from everything the M.P.'s could devise to restrain him.

Variety called him "the new Houdini" in 1945, just a few months before Hiroshima.

His first arrest occurred in the fall of that year, possession of marijuana, the charges dismissed without a trial. (His agent's connections, the Crane family lawyer, the fact that the Crane fortune had not been wiped out *entirely*

when ORGASMOR dropped to the bottom of the Big
Board, and judicious oiling of what Show Biz and under-
world people call "tin mittens"—officials on the take—
contributed to this happy consummation.) He was one of
the first guests on *The Ed Sullivan Show*, but was never
asked to return due to a 1948 "morals" arrest: the girl was
quite young and an "act against nature" was alleged. Once
again, money changed hands and there was no trial.

His career was mostly "in the clubs" after that; Hollywood and TV were both in one of their chronic contrac-
tions of cowardice at the end of the decade.

A second morals arrest, followed rapidly by a second
pot bust, made him a little too hot for most club owners.
Still—the crowds turned out wherever he appeared. The
mob decided to set immediate money against caution, and
he was allowed to go on working. Until his disastrous
appearance before the House Un-American Activities Committee in 1950.

"You're *not* a Communist, you hardly *know* any Communists, you could have sung like a bird without hurting
yourself," his agent said afterward. "Why did you have to
do it, baby?"

"Listen," Crane said angrily. "Do you think I can get
out of a fucking set of *Junior G-Man handcuffs* if I let one
single jot of fear get into my head? You don't understand.
I can't let anything scare me—especially not shit-heads
like them."

"It's your own funeral," the agent replied glumly. "I'll
tell you the plain and varnished facts. You're gonna end
up like Chaplin. Two sex scandals, two drug scandals, and
now this. You're gonna end up worse than Chaplin. You're
box-office poison, baby. From this day forward."

THE HEAD REVOLUTION

GALACTIC ARCHIVES:

Although the HEAD Revolution transformed the Terran primates at the time of this ancient Romance, nobody knows when it actually began. Some trace it to certain Alchemical cults of the early Dark Ages; some say it did not properly start as an organized movement until neuropharmacology began to replace old-fashioned "psychology" in the late Dark Ages (*i.e.,* just before the time of this epic novel); some try to find its origins in primitive shamanism and yoga.

What is clear is that *some* primates on Terra began to transcend genetic four-circuit limitations many centuries, or even millennia, before true neuroscience appeared among them. Whether this was due to mutation, empirical hit-or-miss experimentation with alkaloid herbs, or other factors is unknown. In Egypt and China and other places, a few primates reported fifth-circuit raptures—the dawning of neurosomatic consciousness—two thousand or even three thousand years before the Space Age began.

The picture is the same on all planets. A few biots suddenly rise above the eat-it-or-flee-it imprints of the amphibian biosurvival circuit, above the dominate-or-submit imprints of the mammalian territorial-emotional circuit, above the either/or logic of the hominid semantic circuit, above the "good" and "bad" values of the tribal sociosexual circuit. They have transcended infantile feeding programs, childish emotional programs, adolescent philosophizing, and adult "responsibility" (pack role) all at once.

What has happened, of course, is that these biots have formed a fifth circuit in their brains. This is called the neurosomatic circuit because it allows conscious feedback between the nervous system ("mind," in prescientific primate language) and the soma ("body"). In the larval stages of this Hedonic Revolution, every planet exhibits the same monotonous pattern:

Mysticism and monomania appear. Many of the mutated biots become convinced that they control everything (the "I-am-God" syndrome), not realizing that they merely control their own perceptual field.

"Miracle healings" are reported. The neurosomatic ("mind body") feedback loop allows the mutant biots to become healthier, younger-looking, and sleeker ("handsomer") than average. They soon believe, and are encouraged by their admirers to never doubt, that they can "cure" anything.

Neurosomatic intolerance appears. The mutated biots grow annoyed, and become extremely critical about, the robot mechanisms of first-circuit approach-avoidance, second-circuit domination-submission, third-circuit either or-logic, and static fourth-circuit sex roles. They call on everybody to float free like themselves, or like the wind.

The other biots usually declare these five-circuit mutants to be divine, or else they kill them. Sometimes they do both.

The condition was just becoming understood on Terra at the time of this Quantum Comedy, as neuropharmacologists slowly traced the links between neurochemistry and the creation of perceived reality-tunnels.

GRAPEFRUIT THROUGH THE NIGHT

Anyone with I's in their hood could see it was a tight cityation there on bonger howl, one nation under guard, as Case tosses in the midst of the nightmare, all of them whooping it oop with their tommyhawk fans and their moody decks and their scolded litters, one nation in a dirigible.

Forty of them with town feathers, raising coin as much as they were able, insidious rapacious seditious, with their stars bangled bangers and the ramrods we welshed, through the nox with the lox from a bulb, till the girl with colitis goes by, and Case really saddling hard into it and glowing coolish along with it and hooverin deeper and dotter into doubt about it, pushing a head with their desotos and pontiacs there. "Buy all Chimatong highdeals," they sang.

It was the Guylum Bardot or the Bardot Theodial or if not it was the vector moaning there, all singing O atum bomb O adum bum vee green send unum blather. The very muddle of a model motel tea party: Immolaton, Resurrection, Sewandsow.

And Justin Case awoke.

Just a nightmare, just a nightmare . . . Indians auditing his income tax and all that, fading now, only a trauma house, or a drama, yes, fadern.

Justin sat up and turned on the light.

His first thought was that he was only dreaming that he had awakened.

For, at the foot of his bed, there stood a little green man in a miniature NASA spacesuit.

"I am Apollon of Mars," he said. "Come with me at once."

THERE IS NO GOVERNOR ANYWHERE

Hugh Crane served his contempt-of-Congress sentence at Lewisburg Federal Penitentiary, the "gentleman's club" as the Maf calls it, where the government incarcerates those ritzy felons who are not likely to shiv a guard or climb a wall.

He worked in the library with Alger Hiss. They both watched the famous "Checkers" speech on the TV in the rec room. This was a masterpiece of primate oratory in which a vice presidential candidate named Richard Nixon argued that huge sums of money given to him by various businessmen were not intended as bribes and were not expected to result in reciprocal favors on his part.

"As an old carny man," Mr. Hiss asked Mr. Crane, "what do you think of *that* performance?"

"The dog *shtik* was very good," Crane said professionally. "But he left out Mother."

Another distinguished guest at Lewisburg that year was the aging Idaho poet and folk singer Ezra Pound, who was also in for Un-American Activities. He and Crane never got along well, because Pound, who had seldom been outside Idaho, distrusted all easterners.

Crane performed yoga exercises every day in his cell. The Illuminati, of course, subsequently scanned the notes he kept on these neurophysiological experiments. The most interesting items were the following:

April 23, 1952—It helps if you identify each letter of AUM with one of the three gods of the Hindu trinity. A is Brahm, the Creator: let it explode upward from the diaphragm, like the big bang of creation itself. U is Vishnu, the Preserver: hold it so long that it vibrates, like the rhythm of life, the Big Beat of Beethoven's *Seventh*. M is Shiva, the Destroyer: close the lips in a decisive bite of "This is the way the world ends" as you enter the silence.

May 1, 1952—Today, unexpectedly, pure *dhyana*. It was so much simpler than I ever guessed, and it is obviously a matter of practice. No wonder the yogis say that it's dangerous to do this without a guru: I am no better or worse, morally, and no wiser or more "spiritual." Repetition is the whole key. Force the nerves and muscles and glands, force them day after day, and it happens. The chief function of the guru is to ensure that you don't take advantage of the new freedom too quickly and get yourself in trouble with the authorities. The guru doesn't help it happen at all (as the honest ones admit); you do all the work yourself. The guru just makes sure that the rapture flows into "safe" (domesticated?) channels. Without such a moral watchdog, I am free to do as I bloody please.

I just realized why all the real occult schools are so damned secretive, why the ordinary seeker is given a lot of double-talk and ejected out the same door wherein he came. If everybody could do this, the whole world would be in continuous revolution.*

May 27, 1952—Another successful *dhyana*. There's nothing to it, really. The brain obviously operates on the same principle as those fellows in *The Hunting of the Snark:* "What I tell you three times is true." (Three million times is more accurate.) It was marvelous—better than the first time—and I'll never identify with "Cagliostro the Great" or "Hugh Crane" or even "me" or the perpendicular pronoun, ever again.

I can see more and more clearly why all this is "sealed with seven seals" and hidden behind all kinds of mystification. *Society as we know it is based on torture and death, or the threat of torture and death.* I am in here to be tortured, although the authorities will never admit that. (What they do with heretics in other countries is torture; what we do here is penology.) The cage experience is profoundly punishing to the average human, as to any primate; it is the form of torture our society countenances. It is no torture to me only because I have learned certain neurological arts every stage magician learns.

But if everybody could go into *dhyana* at will, nobody could be controlled—by fear of prison, by fear of whips or electroshock, by fear of death, even. All existing society is based on keeping those fears alive, to control the masses.

---

*Terran Achives 2803: Dhyana was the Sanskrit name, used by the Hindic primates, to describe the opening and imprinting of the neurosomatic circuit. The term, and the techniques of inducing it, became *Ch'an* in China and *Zen* in Japan. It was always supervised by an *alpha male* for the reasons Crane suspected. It represents the dawning of post-primate consciousness and the HEAD Revolution, thereby rendering the biot independent of the primate dominance-submission hierarchy.

Ten people who know what I know would be more dangerous than a million armed anarchists.

July 23, 1952—I can hardly write. Today I reached *Samadhi*. It makes *dhyana* look like nothing by comparison. All my certainty is gone. I should be terrified, but instead I'm ecstatic. If this is possible, *anything* is possible.*

These notes were not published when Hugh came out of prison. Instead, he brought forth a book cheerfully titled *There is No Governor Anywhere*, which explained some—not all—of his magic escapes, and set this in the context of a philosophy which declared every individual a creator of his own universe. The polemics against government and organized religion were tactless, to say the least, for a performer depending upon public goodwill; Crane did not hesitate to identify his outlook bluntly as atheism and anarchism.

To everybody's surprise, including Crane's, the book became a best-seller, and he became the most controversial man in the United States. Even in the fearful fifties— even with American Legion and John Birch chapters constantly reminding everyone of his drug arrests, his sex arrests, and the documented fact that prison authorities had delayed his parole because of his homosexual seduction of a younger inmate—Hugh Crane acquired a new following. TV gingerly tested him on the egghead ghetto of Sunday afternoon, then promoted him to the late-late talk shows.

Terran Archives 2803: Samadhi was the Hindustani name for the opening and imprinting of the sixth (metaprogramming) circuit in the frontal lobes of the post-primate brain. Most of those who achieved it before the HEAD Revolution were just as bewildered as Crane and could say only that the experience was "ineffable."

He managed to end every appearance with the words "There is no governor anywhere; you are all absolutely free."

And around then—to the vocal dismay of press and clergy—a club owner decided he was a "freak" act ("They'll hate him but they'll come") and Crane was able to work as a magician again. The crowd overflowed into the street and many were turned away. Cagliostro introduced a new escape, from a lead box that had been welded closed in view of the audience. "There is no restraint that cannot be escaped," he told them in an intense tone. "We are all absolutely free."

A pudgy Broadway columnist named Benny Benedict, who was just starting to get a following, interviewed him the next day. "How the hell did you manage that welded-box escape?" Benedict asked bluntly.

"I used real magic," the Great Cagliostro pronounced.

"Come off it," Benedict said. But Cagliostro merely grinned at him impudently.

THE ORDEAL OF RHODA CHIEF

When Rhoda Chief became the country's top Rock singer at the age of seventeen in 1958, her education was virtually nil. She knew very few facts and several dozen factoids: the long side of the triangle is called the hypotenuse and is equal to both of the other sides, or one side multiplied by the other, or something like that; what she had in her

panties could make a lot of money if she was smart, or a
lot of trouble if she was dumb; if you spit on an eraser, it
will erase ink; Columbus did his trip in 1492, and they
either started the revolution or finished it in 1776; Lincoln freed the slaves; if you yell loud enough nobody can
tell if you're on key or off; we're all gonna get blown to
hell by the bomb sooner or later; *yellows* make all your
troubles go away, but the *reds* are the ones to take before
a concert or a recording session.

After her abortion she learned enough about birth control to teach a course at the YWCA. After being screwed
blued and tattooed by two record companies in a row, she
also learned enough about contract law to teach that at
Harvard.

Her real education began when she became the mistress of Cagliostro the Great.

The first one to see the whip marks on Rhoda's back
was an old friend from Arkham High School, Doris Horus.

"Why don't you leave him?" Doris asked.

"It's voluntary," Rhoda said stonily. "It's my True Will."

The scandal eventually became an official rumor—"A
nightclub Nostradamus, previously involved in other sex
and drug offenses, is treating his ballad-belting sweetheart
in a very sick way. Readers of a certain French marquis
will know what I mean," was its first printed form, in the
nation's most widely read gossip column. "You've got
quite a reputation as a sadist," Epicene Wildeblood, the
literary critic, said to Crane the very day that appeared.

"Afraid to be identified with me publicly?" Crane asked.
They were in Wildeblood's jet-set pad, on Sutton Place.

"Oh, not at all, darling," Eppy purred. "How funny
that I should know what you really are. *Don't I, babe?*"
He lifted Crane's chin with the toe of his shoe.

"Yes, master," Crane mumbled.

"Oh, that sounded a little sullen. I think you're just a bit rebellious today, babe. That must be punished."

"Yes, master," Crane said, going to the closet for the ropes. After he was stripped, and lying face down on the bed, Eppy carefully tied his four limbs to the four bedposts.

"You are my slave and you can't escape," he said.

"I am your slave and I can't escape," Crane repeated, as Wildeblood mounted him, both of them perfectly aware that he could slip the knots at any time.

Crane took Rhoda to the Rainbow Room that night and made a point of loudly and brutally humiliating her throughout the meal. She accepted it all (her hundred most intimate friends and enemies in the room noticed with disapproval), as if he had hypnotized her.

Rhoda actually took nearly a year to discover what was happening to her. It had started with a routine roll in the hay, but in the middle of it he lifted her to an unusual position. "What the hell is this?" she asked.

"Tibetan, angel," he said softly. "Relax and you'll enjoy it."

She relaxed, and it was the most extraordinary sexual experience of her life. After that, for two months, she followed all of his instructions, with growing delight and a firm belief that she was approaching that Ultimate Orgasm the Mailer fellow was always writing about. Then, one night, he brought out the ropes.

"Now, wait a minute," she said, "that's English. That's kink. Go to London if you want that."

"I love you," he murmured, his mouth moving south across her belly toward her bush; in a little while, she agreed to the restraints. He tied them very firmly—and then, to her relief, no weapon was produced. He didn't even produce his own weapon; it was entirely oral. After five orgasms, she found him sitting up and lighting a joint. In a minute, he held it to her own lips. "For the big one," he said. She toked hungrily while he kissed and caressed her and muttered endearments—but she could still feel the ropes. When the joint was finished he finally mounted her and galloped into some dimension of spasm she had never known before.

"God," she said, coming back to herself, "that *was* the big one." But he was reversed again, his mouth on her snatch, and her head spun.

The mild discipline began a few weeks later. "It builds up the charge," he said, and she found that it did. Soon she agreed that stronger discipline built an ever-greater charge. When the sadism switched to a psychological level, she was too far gone to stop, living in a dark and pulsating cave of ecstasy and pain millions of light-years from common earth. She accepted degradation, humiliation, and the growing vampirism which seemed calculated to slowly destroy her last remnants of ego.

Once or twice, she remembered later, she had feebly protested, "Enough. too much. Please."

"No!" he shouted. "We're at the edge. We've got to go all the way over."

("Yes, master," he would be saying to Epicene Wildeblood a few hours later, "whatever you wish, master.")

"You could have lots of bookings, instead of just working in *public terlets*," his agent told him. "I could get you in *top-money rooms*. People would forget those drug charges, and those teenaged girls, if you didn't keep reminding them by being even worse. The way you and Rhoda carry on in public, everyone thinks you're a kink. And you and that faggot, Wildeblood—everyone thinks you're a touch lavender yourself, buddy. Why don't you straighten out, for Christ's sake? You're going to end up a beggar."

(Remembering: possibly a previous incarnation: Hesse at the station in Zürich: "The mescaline, *ja*, the mescaline is the great teacher": and Crowley in Berlin: "The question is, *who* is it that seeks the True Self?" All so long ago, so far away, and Richard Jung saying, "I am an accountant, I don't buy any of this mysticism," begging on the street near the Old Granary where Paul Revere and the original Five lie buried, Rancid the Butler, Mama Sutra, weeping among the corpses at Château Thierry. "Please Jesus don't let me die, don't let me die . . .")

The boy, who was to become Cagliostro the Great, heard "You're going to end up a beggar" and looked back and saw the tramp falling to the ground, very slowly, like the tree he had seen fall slowly after being chopped by the caretaker at the upstate Crane country home. And, just like the tree, when he finally reached the sidewalk, the tramp didn't move at all, not one bit; he even seemed to get stiff like the tree did, only faster.

"On your knees," Cagliostro said sternly, and Rhoda obediently crossed the floor on her knees.

"Ask for it," he said.

"I beg you, master," she said, "to stick your cock inside my cunt and fuck me and make me come again and again and again. Oh, please, master."

He lit a cigar, pretending to deliberate, and then blew smoke in her face. "No," he said. "I want you to suck me off. Nothing at all for *you* tonight."

But a few nights later, when he was on top of her and inside her, and chanting in Tibetan, she suddenly thought she saw a kind of light around his head and two horns sprouting on his temple, and then it was like a million balloons bursting inside her and outside her at once, each balloon releasing a twinkle of light, each light a species of orgasm. "Rhoda Chief" ceased to exist. Eternities later, reentering time, she found he was again at the bottom of the bed, head between her legs, licking ferociously. She fainted.

He had a large library dealing with both stage magic and occultism, and Rhoda occasionally browsed in it. The next morning, while he was still asleep, she went back to it and searched in several volumes by Rosenkreuz, Therion, Iambacchus, Prinn, Dee, and Kelly. "The Mass of the Holy Ghost" was variously described, but the Rose of Ruby was always identified with water and the first H in JHVH, the H of motherhood. The Cross of Gold had different meanings, too, but was chiefly fire and the J of JHVH, the J of fatherhood. Bringing the J and the H together, the wedding of Cross and Rose, produced the manifestation of the Holy Ghost in the form of a eucharist, which was then consumed by the alchemist. *My God*, she thought, *the Cross is his cock and the Rose is my cunt; that's why he goes down on me afterward, as well as just before.* "The eucharist," old Prinn's words said blandly, "is both male and female, both living and dead, both fire and water, and yet its creation involves no violation of nature but merely obedience to nature's own laws, together with the proper spiritual attitude."

Professor Nosferatu of Columbia, an old friend of Rhoda's, listened raptly as she recited the words to him. "That's not Tibetan, whatever he told you," he said. He repeated it with correct pronunciation: "IO PAN IO PAN PAN IO PANGENITOR IO PANPHAGE. It's an invocation of the god Pan in classic Greek. 'Io Pan, Io Pan, Pan. Io Pan-All-Creator, Io Pan-All-Devourer.' " He looked at her curiously. "You know, I've heard some rather odd rumors about you and him. . . ."

"Whatever you've heard," she said with a faint smile, "is probably true. I want you to give me the name of the best shrink you know. I want somebody to work on my head and help me to stay away from him."

TRADE AIDS

After the RICH Economy had revolutionized the lives and expectations of Unistaters on and off Terra, Eve Hubbard realized that the time was now ripe to abolish poverty entirely. She did this by declaring every citizen a shareholder in the L5 space-cities and distributing National Dividends every year.

Again, Hubbard's political genius was evident. Others who had proposed such a plan in the past (*e.g.*, the engineers C. H. Douglas and R. Buckminster Fuller, the inventor Tom Edison, the semanticist Alfred Korzybski, the physicist Frederic Soddy) had assumed such dividends would have to be *"money."* This proposal, in that form, always aroused heated opposition from the alpha males of the banking business, who understood well that an expanding money supply would lower the interest rate, seriously threatening their profits.

Hubbard called her National Dividend tickets *"trade aids,"* a term devised by a public relations firm she had commissioned to make the idea palatable to domesticated primates.

Trade aids were like money only in that they could be exchanged for commodities or services. They were unlike money in that they could not be loaned at interest; the bankers kept their monopoly on the interest market and were mollified.

Trade aids were also unlike money in that they could not be hoarded. Each ticket was dated, and lost value at 1 percent per month after the issue date, becoming totally valueless in one hundred months, or eight years and four months. There was thus a built-in incentive to spend the trade aids as soon as possible.

When the first trade aid dividends were distributed, it turned out that even the poorest Unistat citizens had the equivalent of $80,000 for that year, in purchasing power, even though the tickets were not *called* "money."

Citizens with that much purchasing power have huge *demand*, in the economic sense of ability to buy. The economy expanded more rapidly than ever, with new businesses springing up continually, both on Terra and in the space-cities.

The rest of Terra was soon copying these innovations—the socialist countries most slowly and grudgingly. By 1995 starvation had been eliminated everywhere—just as had been the goal of the Hunger Project, started by a California primate named Erhard back in the 1970s. By then Hubbard had been out of the White House for six years and busy again at genetics and longevity research. She often said to friends that her whole political career had been merely an experiment in altering the parameters of primate sociobiology.

TO CROSS AGAIN

DECEMBER 24, 1983:

Simon Moon toked at his pipe, pulling the hash deep into his lungs, floating with it.

December 23 had been a hell of a day. Ubu and Knight and the other guys from the FBI had been all over the shop demanding to know *why* the Beast couldn't tell them any more about the missing scientists and warning ominously that President Lousewart was Personally Concerned and so on and so forth: the usual governmental craperoo. Simon only stayed on the job for the sheer pleasure he got out of working with the Beast, fucking up the government from within. But even that pleasure was wearing thin, and he hopped a suborbital to New York just to be away from everything Washingtonian for the holidays.

He exhaled a fog of cannabis molecules and returned his attention to his favorite bedtime reading, Brown's *Laws of Form*:

To cross again is not to cross.

It must have been the hash, but suddenly that simple axiomatic statement was fraught with new and urgent meaning. A knight's move on the word processor would

313

switch F to N, the FBI to the NBI, abolishing Knightness in the process.

Only the quantum inseparability principle would explain why Furbish Lousewart went away in the same rotation.

Simon found that he had wandered or teleported from the bedroom to the toilet and was staring in absorption at the sink. The two handles, one saying H and the other C, seemed to have enormous Cabalistic meaning, connected, perhaps, with the fact that Joe Malik had been Jo Malik before the collapse of the state vector.

Of course, out-of-the-book experiences are not yet recognized by orthodox science. The parapsychologists who dare to speculate about such things are ritually torn asunder and dismembered by Marvin Gardens in the back pages of the *Scientific American*. Still, this does not discourage Simon Moon, who is, after all, a close associate of the Beast and hip to the programmer's trade secret that all that exists is information: everything else is mammalian sense-impression and thus hallucinatory. Besides, Simon is doing it right now: and can see in one instant, in the twinkling of an eye, the total contents of the novel, a miracle of microminiaturization in the frontal lobes, as the metaprogramming circuit clicks into action.

The novel was called *The Universe Next Door*. It existed—was bought and sold and loaned—in a supercontinuum called the United States of America, which was Unistat enlarged into other dimensions.

Everything in the novel was inevitable, as everything in the supercontinuum containing the novel was inevitable.

Everything that happened in Unistat *had* to happen, as everything in the United States of America *had* to happen.

That which was above was precisely reflected in that which was below.

To cross again was not to cross.

"So all right," Joe Malik said, staring at Simon through a triangle, "are you just trying to scare me to death or do you have a message for me?"

Simon was on the balcony of Mary Margaret Wildeblood's apartment again and somebody was staring out at him in horror. *"My God, it's Bigfoot!"*

Simon reentered the form, and contemplated it.

Civilization was destroyed by nuclear holocaust in May 1984 because Furbish Lousewart was a certain kind of man and Franklin Delano Roosevelt Stuart was a certain other kind of man; and they were what they were because of genetic programs and accidental imprints and conditioning and some learning, and because of the society around them; and that society was the resultant of various conflicting historical and neurogenetic causes; and Lousewart became President because of a thousand other factors, only one of which, the accident at Three Mile Island in 1979, was itself the resultant of thousands of factors, including the usual struggles between the engineers and the financiers; and to explain Stuart you would have to start with the institution of slavery six thousand years earlier; and . . .

Everything in the novel was inevitable, as everything in the supercontinuum containing the novel was inevitable.

And yet Simon had escaped from the novel.

Although not a member of the Warren Belch Society, Simon Moon was, of course, aware of the theory that there was a universe somewhere in which Bacon's major works were still attributed to somebody else. Simon, naturally, was not imaginative enough to conceive that in that universe Bacon had died of pneumonia while conducting experiments in refrigeration. In Simon's usual universe, the author of *Novum Organum, The New Atlantis, King Lear*, etc., had lived on to discover the inverse-square law of gravitation, and Isaac Newton was remembered only as a somewhat eccentric astrologer.

In another novel, midway between the old universe and the new, Simon himself had been shot dead by a Chicago cop during the Democratic Convention of 1968. Over there, Bacon had been bold enough to admit publicly his high rank in the Invisible College (Illuminati) and had been beheaded by James I for heresy. In that universe, not just civilization, but all life on Terra, came to a very hideous end in 1984, because the President was constipated one day and made the wrong decision. Their technology was so advanced that half the solar system went nova along with Earth.

In the next universe Simon explored, we were saved because a red-haired Tantric Engineer named Babs Lashtal gave the Prez a first-class Grade-A blow job in the Oval Room at 10 A.M., relaxed his tense muscles, pacified his glands, soothed his frustrations, and inspired him to act relatively sane for the rest of the day. He did not push the button, thereby preserving millions of species of living forms on Earth and thousands of microscopic species on Venus.

Babs Lashtal, of course, was regarded with contempt by all right-thinking people, who had no idea that they owed their lives to her skillful extraction of presidential spermatozoa by means of tender, gentle, gracefully rhythmic kissing, licking, and sucking of the presidential wand.

Even if they had known about it, the right-thinking people would still say Babs should be ashamed of herself.

The whole novel was rather didactic, Simon decided. It was written only to prove a point: Never underestimate the importance of a blow job. It had been necessary to write such a novel because the people over there were so ignorant and superstitious they still called Tantric Engineers *"whores"* and other degrading names.

Every universe is inevitable; but there are as many universes as there are probability matrices. The Metaprogrammer chooses *which* universe he will enter.

There is a love that binds it all together, and that love is expressed in primate language as the love of a parent for a child, so Simon was not surprised to find Tim Moon pervading everything, or at least a kind of continuous Tim Moon potential that could be encoded again in another book or that could remain latent for long times, vaguely permeating every book. There were hundreds of thousands of other Wobs there, Frank Little and Joe Hill and Pat Murfin and Neal Rest and Big Bill Heywood and they were all singing like an outlaw Hallelujah Chorus:

> *Though cowards cringe and traitors sneer*
> *We'll keep the Black Flag flying here*

and Dad himself spoke to me, I swear it, saying, "Just tell them this, son: Capitalism is still nothing but a shit sandwich. The more bread you have, the less shit you've got to eat, and the less bread you have, the more shit you've got to eat. Tell them all." And yet that seems to mark the experience as brain-generated: the style is Simon-*puer* not Tim-*pater* even if the idea is most certainly something old Tim Moon would want to communicate. A collaboration perhaps between the part of Tim Moon that lives on in Simon's memory banks and the part that lives eternally in the Mind of the Author of Our Being.

"Hey, wait, before you turn the page and get into the next section, I want to say one more thing. Those faucets on the sink *mean* something. Every time I stare at them in deep meditation I almost remember something important. Two faucets on a sink, one saying H and one saying C. Remember H. C. That's important."

The *e* continues to fall.

THE GYPSY SWITCH

The future exists first in Imagination, then in Will, then in Reality.

—EVE HUBBARD

In spring 1963, while a Mr. Oswald was ordering a Carcano-Mannlicher rifle through the mail, Hugh Crane was in Cambridge, meeting with a famous psychologist who had recently been ejected from Harvard for original research and poor usage of the First Amendment.

"It takes you beyond the body rapture of marijuana?" Crane asked.

"That's the least of it," said the psychologist. "It takes you into something like the parallel universe of science fiction. I'm beginning to think they're parallel neurological universes or different styles of head-games. . . ."

"*Games?*" Crane said.

"Life-scripts, novels," the psychologist suggested, trying other metaphors.

"I dig it," Crane said quietly. "How soon can I try this lysergic acid di-what's-it?"

"Diethylamide."

"How soon?" Crane repeated. "You've got a very willing guinea pig, Dr. Frankenstein."

Cary Grant had already told all the show-biz columnists

that this magic chemical had changed his whole life for the better; Cagliostro, typically, went further and began urging its use on everyone. When the backlash struck he and the researcher who had initiated him and a few other researchers and a couple of famous poets and novelists were widely denounced as "high priests of the drug cult." He became a favorite topic for the Sunday supplements and the more ox-like men's magazines—any hack could make a lively story by rehashing his pot arrests, his morals busts, the rumors about other sexual oddities, his public advocacy of LSD and anarcho-atheism, his mantra, "There is no governor anywhere," and the increasingly popular speculation that his escapes were actually performed through black magic.

It was a disappointment to all the people who loved hating him when he suddenly married the screen's best known sex goddess, Norma Nelson, and settled down to what appeared to be a very monogamous and un-newsworthy fidelity trip.

Norma herself was delighted that all those rumors about his sadism were obviously untrue. Their sex life was quite normal, and the Mass of the Holy Ghost was performed without restraints. She discovered, also, the basic secret of his escapes: he never accepted a challenge at once, always jetting on "urgent business" to another part of the country and only taking languid notice of the wager, casually accepting it with total cool, a few days later. The interlude, she found, was spent in duplicating the conditions proposed and finding the gimmick that would work and the misdirection that would distract attention at the crucial moment. She also learned the essence of the *okanna borra*, or "gypsy switch," which is the basis of almost all magic and most con games. The people who thought their own screws, bolts, and chains were used in Cagliostro's escapes were as mistaken as those who think the handkerchief with a hundred dollars that they give the gypsy for blessing is the same handkerchief that comes back to them.

She also learned what alchemy was all about. "I thought that was all superstition," she said once, pointing at his shelves of old books on the transmutation of elements, the Mass of the Holy Ghost, the Cabala, and the elixir of life.

"We do it almost every night." He smiled. "You have the Cup and I have the Sword. *Solve et coagula*, divide and unite—that's why I have to go down on you again at the end. The mystic number 210—that means us *two* becoming *one* in the peak and the falling into the *void*. You've got the Triangle and I cause the physical manifestation within it."

"You mean it's all a code? Why did they have to hide it?"

"Those who didn't got burned at the stake," he said. "Read about the witches and the Knights Templar sometime."

He also began teaching her the Tarot. "Now, the Fool corresponds to aleph in Kabala, the ox, or bull-god Dionysus. But aleph is the path from Keser to Chokmah, and, therefore, the Holy Ghost or semen. The Magus is beth, the house or temple—that is, the path from Keser to Binah, the womb . . ."

"Do you really think you're going to live forever?" she asked him once.

"If not," he said, "I'll die trying."

WISE GUYS AND NEBBISHES

When Simon Moon was appointed Chief of the Computer Section at GWB-666, he immediately junked all the personnel tests then in use and replaced them with a one-question test of his own devising based on the Vlad Enigma. Applicants were simply told the story of Vlad and the monks by an interviewer and asked which monk Vlad impaled. Those who said Vlad impaled the lying flatterer were classified as nebbishes by Simon; they were the kind of fools who still, despite all evidence to the contrary, regarded government and those in authority as honest and just. They would tell the truth to superiors. They were hired at once. "An office full of Eichmanns and Calleys," Simon said proudly. "Not one of them will ever question an order or ask an embarrassing question." He could program endless anarchy, and they would never suspect it, because he was above them in the pack hierarchy.

Those who said Vlad impaled the honest monk, on the other hand, were rejected for employment at GWB. Simon called them the Wise Guys and secretly arranged for a recruiter from the Discordian Society to contact them later. They didn't believe a damned thing government said or did, had heretical opinions on dozens of subjects, and usually smoked dope. They emphatically did not belong in a bureaucracy.

Sometimes Simon called the nebbishes *Homo neophobia* and the wise guys *Homo neophilia*.

But that was in another novel. Simon didn't even know if he was still working with the Beast in this novel.

He was becoming identified with the form.

Some things remained constant under the transformation of the Knight move—Marvin Gardens still had his paranoia and his Vlad the Barbarian books, the missing scientists were still missing, Simon was still a mathematician (Mary Margaret had said so, at the party, even though he was only dimly there this time around).

But some things had altered considerably—Josephine Malik was Joseph Malik, F.D.R. Stuart was an editor instead of a revolutionary, Hubbard was President instead of Lousewart.

But all that was trivial. Simon got out his pen and began jotting, in the margins of *Laws of Form*, the important things he had learned in his out-of-book experience:

1. A novel, or a universe, is a Whole System.
2. Who we are, and what we do, depends on which novel or universe we are in. Every part is a function of the Whole.
3. It is very hard to remember the whole novel or universe because our horns won't fit the

Simon stared at the page, losing the meaning of Mooning, forgetting the question itself as attention narrowed to this single page, this paragraph, this hotel room in New York on the morning of December 24, 1983, barely able to remember even a few pages back or a few pages ahead.

The window closed. The key was no key.

HAVEN'T YOU HEARD?

Man's inexorable though hardly remorseless drive to divinity is taking new, non-institutionalized forms. This comes down to the simplest of propositions: the species must solve the problem of death very soon, blow itself up, or blow its mind.

—ALAN HARRINGTON, *The Immortalist*

When Norma became pregnant Cagliostro turned into the stereotype of an ideal husband, canceling bookings to be with her, joyously supporting her decision to employ natural childbirth, teaching her yoga to supplement the Lamaze conditioning techniques employed by her obstetrician. He filled her room with flowers—and with photographs of the moon. (Some of his occult studies were involved here, she realized.)

One night the phone rang, and when Crane answered it Epicene Wildeblood purred, "I'm in Hollywood for a week and I guessed you might want to see me."

"You guessed wrong," Crane said. "Sorry. New trip this year."

Norma's labor began prematurely, and the doctor quickly discovered that the baby was in the breech position. After a few hours he realized this childbirth could never be natural. She accepted the ether and he performed a Caesarean, only to find the infant, in turning, had strangled on its umbilical cord.

"Oh, God," she said when she awoke and the doctor told her. "Oh, what a lousy God to make a world like this."

Cagliostro was caught by a gaggle of reporters coming out of the hospital. "How do you feel?" was the first question.

"How the hell do you think I feel?"

"Where will the service be held?"

"There will be no religious service!" Cagliostro shouted, hopping into a cab. "Haven't you fools heard yet?—God is dead!" It made headlines, and inspired editorials. One editorial—"Bereavement Is No Excuse for Blasphemy"— came to the attention of a fourteen-year-old boy, John Disk, who was tormented by desires which his priests told him were evil.

When Cagliostro returned to the clubs his act had changed considerably. The mildly satirical patter between escapes had become bitingly mordant—"He's a new Lenny Bruce!"—and entirely centered around his declared philosophy of anarchism and atheism. The escapes themselves changed each night, because he explained them and showed how they were done as the climax of every performance.

"Now you know how I fooled you," he would say. "Try to figure out on your own how your congressmen and clergymen fool you. There is no restraint that isn't self-imposed: *you are all absolutely free.*"

The evening after the newspapers broke the story that he and Norma had joined Joan Baez in refusing to pay taxes, a drunk began heckling him during his act: "Why don't you go back to Russia, you Commie dope fiend!" That sort of thing.

"No man living hates socialism more than me," Cagliostro said intensely.

He and Norma were busted for possession of acid a few weeks later. "This is hard to fix," his lawyer told him.

"You're too notorious now. The only chance I see is for you to vow to reform, lament the error of your ways, and promise to go on a lecture tour speaking to teenagers about the evils of drugs. Then maybe I can get you a minimum sentence. Maybe." Hugh's old friend, the Boston psychologist, was in exile in Nepal, having fled a thirty-year sentence in Texas; political offenders in general were having a rough time in the United States.

"I'll think about it," he said.

The very next week he led the show-biz contingent among the protesters at the 1968 Democratic Convention. A photograph of him being tear-gassed outside the Chicago Hilton is still reprinted whenever an article about him appears.

"You've had it," his lawyer told him. "As an officer of the court, I can't tell you what I really think. An unethical attorney, were he here, would frankly advise you and Norma to get the hell out of the country."

But a change came over Unistat when Hubert Humphrey, the new President, withdrew all the troops from Vietnam and began granting amnesty to political prisoners. Cagliostro and Norma, in the midst of the return to liberalism, received suspended sentences for the acid, and he was not tried with the Chicago Nine for conspiring the convention riots. The IRS raided their bank account for the tax money instead of prosecuting them, and, by 1970, he was listed as one of ten top money-makers in show biz. His escapes were, the American Society of Magicians announced in an award, better than Houdini's; his habit of explaining each "miracle" after the performance only built up crowd interest for the next challenge.

BUMP IN THE NIGHT

Sput Sputnik was sleeping alone at last. Visions of dollar signs danced in his head as he dreamed of a miniature sled full of barrels of beer. She nu it, he had it, Ra Hoor cooed it, right jolly old selves, but overall there was a smell of fried onions, because of janes chains gains clanking up and down again.

Sput turned in the bed, moaning slightly, as the brains danes chains came clanking back and forth again.

And there was a Russian spy named Igor Beeforshot, and there was Minor Boulevard and Major Strasse, because every Pershing comes to Gricks, but the chains mains pains were clanking in and out again.

Hoor's looking for you, cad! It was a wide house, a mason blanc, a cozy bianca, but still there were cranes cranes cranes flapping overhead again. So he sput the roavin ovamor and

He was abruptly awake, in the dark, still hearing the chains. Something was bumping and thumping at his door, something that seemed to be dragging chains behind it.

Sput was not into the S-M scene, and everybody in the mansion knew better than to come banging at his door when he was asleep. But still the thumping and the bumping and the chain-rattling continued.

He was wide awake now, and he knew it was no dream.

Something eldritch and unholy, right out of Gothic fiction, was banging at his bedroom door.

And then, for the first time in his life, he actually heard an *eerie laugh*, just like in the books, and It was actually coming through the door, walking right through solid wood, a greenish oldish spectral chain-rattling Thing.

"Jesus Nelly!" Sput gasped. This sort of goings-on only happened in books, not in real life.

"Sput Sputnik," came the hollow voice (right out of an echo chamber, he thought).

"Yes?" he breathed, wondering if his hairs were standing on end, too, in orthodox fashion.

"Sput Sputnik," said the Presence, "I am the Ghost of Christmas Past."

THE EYE-ON-THE-PYRAMID

A biological breakthrough will force a new militancy, a new crusade. "Make the world safe for Immortality," will be the cry.
            —SEGERBERG, *The Immortality Factor*

On May 1, 1976, Cagliostro and Norma were in Mexico City on a vacation. At lunch she held up a twenty-centavo piece and said, "Isn't that the same as the design on back of the dollar?"

"It's Masonic," he said. "The Mexican and American revolutionaries were both predominantly Freemasons."

"What does it mean, anyway—an eye floating above a pyramid?"

He started to explain about the Third Eye and the pineal gland, and then noticed that she wasn't listening.

"They're waiting for you," she said in a mediumismic voice.

John Disk, in 1984, read Cagliostro's notes on the next three days very carefully:

"I refused to believe it. I put her to every possible test, whenever the voice spoke. Looking for evidence of auto-suggestion and self-hypnosis, I found evidence of auto-suggestion and self-hypnosis—*naturally!* I also found seventeen things I couldn't explain. Most central was the fact that the message, when I finally encouraged her, came in Enochian, a language which nobody understands since all we possess are the nineteen fragments received by Dee and Kelly in the seventeenth century. Yet she gave me nineteen new fragments, and translated them, and the grammar and vocabulary are consistent with the Dee-Kelly scryings. Even if she had studied the Dee and Kelly fragments (which she swears she hasn't), concocting new sentences in that unknown language would be beyond the power of any human brain or even of any known computer. . . ."

The nineteen fragments of Enochian, translated by Norma in the same trance in which the fragments arrived, became the nineteen chapters of *The Aquarian Gospel*. Crane wrote in the introduction:

"It is impossible to doubt that these are the communications of a superior intelligence. If the reader is, as I am [thank God!], an atheist, the identity of that intelligence will pose severe mysteries. Is it interplanetary—or interstellar? A being leaping across Time from some more advanced future, or past [Atlantis]? Does it come from dimensions tangent to, but not identical with, our own? I propose no answer to these questions, but I am sure that this intelligence, or others like it, sent the messages which founded the great religions of the past, and that such communications are the foundation of the belief in beings called 'gods.' . . ."

Norma was killed in an automobile accident the day the book was published. "What further proof do we need," a prominent clergyman wrote in his syndicated newspaper column, "that this foul and obscene 'revelation' comes from a source not divine, but diabolical?"

Crane's first—and only—failure to escape from a challenge box occurred one month later.

The eye operation came later that year. "I can save one," the doctor told him, "but not both."

"A blind magician is worse off than a deaf musician, and I'm not Beethoven," Crane said simply. "Do the best you can."

He retained the sight of one eye.

"Much as we are inclined to sympathize," the New York *Daily News* editorialized, "we do admit to a strong feeling that there is divine retribution in the tragedies befalling drug-cultist Cagliostro 'the Great.' "

The Aquarian Gospel was burned by a citizens' group in Cicero, Illinois, that week.

"These powers, whoever and whatever they are," Crane wrote—in unpublished notes which John Disk read years later, weeping— "are determined that I abandon all else and become no more than the servant who carries their message. To this end, they are taking away from me, one by one, all the things I love. Or, perhaps, I am merely in the terminal stages of a long-brewing paranoid psychosis?"

Hugh Crane celebrated his fourteenth birthday in 1938 by climbing into the bed of the family's black maid, Sophie Hagé, who introduced him to *Voudon*.

The group in Harlem at that time actually combined elements of *Voudon* and Masonry. Since *Voudon* was already a blend of European witchcraft and African magic, and Masonry is a mixture of elements from Rosicrucian mysticism and French revolutionary free thought, there were actually four traditions involved, and the Rite of Initiation was unique. Borrowed from the third degree of Masonry, it replaced Jubela, Jubelo, and Jubelum with the *Grand Zombi*, and, since marijuana was involved, the ordeal became as real as in those days when candidates knew they would be killed if they failed.

In a dark cellar on 110th Street, the *Grand Zombi* demanded, "Reveal the Secret Word or I will kill you. Reveal the Secret Word and give up your quest for Truth and Power."

Hugh, repeating the formula taught him, replied, "Kill me if you must, but I will search again for Truth and Power as soon as I am reborn."

The *Grand Zombi*, black face above a black robe, raised his sword. "Do you fear me now, mortal?" he screamed.

"I have eternity to work in," Hugh replied, according to rote. "Why should I fear?"

"Then *die!*" screamed the *Zombi*—the part of the Rite which had not been explained to the candidate in advance—and Hugh felt the sword cross his neck and saw the blood spurting.

He also saw the bulb which the *Zombi* squeezed to make the blood spurt out of the end of the sword.

And he understood the manufacture of reality and power completely.

TRANSFORMATION

DECEMBER 24, 1983:

Marvin Gardens was awake again; the downers hadn't fully taken the edge off the coke excitation.

He had turned the radio on, but the only thing worth listening to was Handel's *Messiah*—the fourth time he had caught parts of it this week—and they were in the middle of "He was a man of sorrows, and acquainted with grief." Not quite what he needed at this hour, with the early morning Manhattan permeation of suicides and accidental overdoses skulking in the shadows. He wished they would get on to the Hallelujah Chorus.

Marvin found a book he'd never finished—*The Autobiography of Cagliostro the Great*. He opened at random and started reading:

"Get a a job," my father said. Turning back, I saw the beggar falling to the ground, obviously fainting from starvation, but when he landed I knew, from his limpness, that it was more than a faint: that he was dead.

It has sometimes occurred to me that there is a parallel here to the famous experience of the Buddha, who, like myself, had the misfortune to be born rich and only discovered what life is like for most people when he encountered a beggar and a corpse. Is this parallel an accident? I am not sure: I cannot say *when* I was elected, or drafted, to receive the Aquarian message, the great affirmation that "All is joy," in contrast to the Buddha's equally true, equally false, but now obsolete "All is sorrow."

We never see what is in front of our eyes. My father did not see what happened inside me when that beggar died; I have brought men and women to the edge of the Vision, by various tactics, and they, afraid to see it, ran off to psychiatrists.

"It's really very simple to remember the order of the ten planets," Blake Williams explained to Natalie. "Just memorize the sentence 'Mother Very Easily Made a Jam Sandwich Using No Peanuts Mayonnaise or Glue.' Got it?"

"Mother Very Easily Made a Jam Sandwich Using No Peanuts Mayonnaise or Glue," Natalie repeated dubiously.

"That's all," Williams said proudly. "You just use the initial letter of each word as a mnemonic, and you've got all ten planets. Mercury Venus Earth Mars the asteroids Saturn Uranus Neptune Pluto Mickey and Goofy."

"Wow!" said Natalie. "Disneyland in the skies."

"Who the hell was that?" Carol Christmas asked breathlessly, as the triangle finally faded. "Sure didn't look like a *loa* to me," she added, frowning thoughtfully.

"It was Simon Moon," Joe Malik said, also somewhat breathless. "I knew him in another universe . . . or another novel . . . or something. . . ."

Carol stared at him. "You wigging?" she asked bluntly.

"No," Joe said. "I think I'm beginning to understand the trap we're all caught in, and how to get out of it."

DAMNANT QUOD NON INTELLIGUNT

God told John Disk to kill Cagliostro the Great. It was that simple; after all, who would dare to disobey the Voice of God Himself?

God had been talking to Disk for nearly a year now. The Voice had been rather faint at first, and John even thought it was the Devil for a while, because it kept telling him he was damned. It said he was damned because he sinned sometimes when he was asleep. It said many silly and blasphemous things, but John realized later that those weirdities had been the Devil trying to jam and confuse the communication, for when the Voice became strong and constant, there was no doubt at all that it was God.

It told John that he had been especially selected because of his virtue and purity, and it never mentioned what happened sometimes when he was asleep. It told him he was the only twenty-three-year-old male virgin in Unistat, the last true Christian not perverted by *Pussycat* and the Sexual Revolution and Black Magic. It told him he had earned much merit in Heaven for his selfless activities on behalf of the antiabortion movement in the 1970s and White Heroes Opposing Red Extremism since then.

It really loved John, and it never stopped telling him he was the most important man on the planet because he had been Selected.

At first it didn't tell him what he had been Selected for; but every time he read a news story about some new blasphemy by Cagliostro the Great, the Voice of God would say, "This man must be stopped."

It was only toward the end of November that the Voice became increasingly explicit and said directly that he, John Disk, had been Selected to terminate the foul existence of the infamous devil-worshiper Cagliostro. Even then the Voice was almost drowned out by the voice of Rhoda Chief, the Scarlet Woman of Rock, chanting, "Hickory dickory dock, I'd like to suck your cock," and other diabolical voices howling "no wife, no horse, no mustache" and "sit down when you want to pee" and other nonsense like that. The Devil was trying very hard to keep Disk from hearing and believing the Word of God; he wanted Disk to think he was going crazy. But the Voice of God got louder and more powerful and drowned out the others, and nobody who heard it, Disk knew, could ever doubt that a Voice so wise and powerful was anything else but that of the Lord God Himself.

John made sure, of course. He spent a whole night praying, beating his back with a bundle of wet, stinging cords, just like he'd read in a book about the saints from the public library on Forty-second Street. He kept saying, "Lord, have mercy on me, a sinner." At dawn Jesus appeared, with a halo, and told him exactly how to find a pawn shop where he could buy a gun without the legal impediment of acquiring a permit. Then He turned into a huge red triangle, through which the impassive face of a lion stared at John, and then it was all mirrors and blue smoke until he actually found the pawn shop and got the pistol.

The Devil was determined to protect his servant, Cagliostro, so John found the mirrors and smoke increasingly getting in his way in the following days. He would be on his way to Theology class at Fordham when suddenly all around would be thousands of hippies of all nations and a voice would be singing

> This is the dawning
> of the Age of Bavaria

or he would be in a yellow submarine floating over a gigantic submerged pyramid or he would turn on the religious channel on the wall TV (the only one not full of smut and filth these days) and find Linda Lovelace doing That Disgusting Thing to somebody named Marvin Gardens. But he continued to pray, and more and more The Voice of God would drown out all these nets and snares of Satan.

Finally, on the morning of December 24, the Voice of God told him to go to Central Park West, where Cagliostro was living, and wait on the street. The Voice told him that as a reward he would be allowed to sit at the left hand of the Father in Heaven—Jesus would keep the right hand but the Holy Spirit was being demoted to an auxiliary rank with the Virgin, so that he, John Disk, could be given the third highest position in all Paradise.

When he got to the School Book Depository and walked toward the box seat in the Ford Theatre, sex mutilators and cattle educators howled at him and he realized that the Devil was still trying to deceive him and he prayed harder and harder until it was clear that he was really on Central Park West and the man walking toward him, taking a morning constitutional, was the diabolical Cagliostro, a chameleon on a mirror, and the class of all classes that were similar to it, but he prayed and got the pistol out of his pocket, almost seeing the *Grand Zombi* and his sword, breathing harder now because the Devil was trying so hard to confuse him, and the interviewer wanted to know which monk Vlad impaled.

John Disk held the gun in a trembling hand and looked into Cagliostro's icy eyes.

"Oy, have you picked the wrong Black Magician," Cagliostro said in a stage-Yiddish accent.

John Disk fired five times into the heart.

The gate of Chinatown opened.

MASS LANDING

Justin Case was released from the flying saucer in the middle of Central Park. He was still rather befoozled mentally and unsteady on his feet, so he staggered to the nearest bench and sat quietly, watching them take off.

His wristwatch said 7:15—which seemed plausible.

"It is the morning of December 24," he said aloud. "Tomorrow is Christmas." It seemed necessary, some-how, to get the simple things cleared up first of all, before dealing with the Mysteries.

Things like this didn't happen to New York music crit-ics. They happened to farmers in Iowa or fishermen in Arkansas, or other such unsophisticated types, and, be-sides, they were hallucinations.

Justin watched the flying saucer disappear across the sky, reminding himself that it was a hallucination.

But still their words rang in his ears:

It is time for your species to join the Galactic Community.

Justin finally got his mind and legs and various organs

working together well enough to walk. He headed for Central Park West, hoping to find a cab.

At Fifty-eighth Street he saw a newsstand. The headlines glared at him like Tibetan demons:

WORLDWIDE UFO FLAP
Mass Landings Reported

And in a corner the inevitable surrealist tag line to such a night:

Mayor of Chicago Arrested
Sodomy with Boar Hog Alleged

As Justin stared at those remarkable messages, he heard five rapid pistol shots.

From somewhere nearby music drifted toward him. He found himself absently putting the words to the melody:

He knows when you've been bad or good
So be good for goodness' sake

He hastily bought a newspaper and hailed a cab. He was going to go right home and, for the first time in his life, break his rule against drinking in the morning.

When he was drunk enough to stop trembling, it would be time to decide whether to report his experience or let those who had already talked take all the heat.

CROWN POINT

Crown Point Jail, in Indiana, was called "the escape-proof jail," when John Dillinger was brought there in May 1934. On the day Dillinger destroyed that name by escaping, an out-of-work vaudeville magician was begging in Central Park, New York. One thought burned in this man's head—*With a little luck, I could have been a second Houdini*—and that was what he was thinking as he fought the hunger cramps and laid his spiel on Tom Crane.

When he felt the ground move in that big wobble of uncertainty, he remembered suddenly the ever-branching Tree of Life as memories of Adam Weishaupt and Mohammed and insects and trees flooded through him, a million balloons bursting inside him and outside him at once, each balloon releasing a twinkle of light, each light part of the infinite ladder of light, and he was watching himself die, in horror and ecstasy, through the eyes of a little boy.

How did my karma ever land me here? he thought as he died, and the boy heard him thinking.

THE ELEPHANT

ANNALS OF GENERAL PSYCHIATRY,
MAY 1984:

In short, the wave of delusion, mania, and hallucination
that occurred over the Christmas-New Year's holidays last
year can only be attributed to the paradoxical nature of
the unconscious. Where previous mass hysterias have occurred (*e.g.*, the end-of-the-world manias of the Middle
Ages, the Orson Welles Martian invasion broadcast of
1938) the cause was, obviously, the tensions, stresses, and
fears of those times. This latest eruption, coming in the
midst of a time of progress, optimism, and rising expectations, can only be explained by Freud's great discovery
that opposites are equal to the prelogical unconscious
mind [ambivalence principle]. In other words, high hopes,
like high anxieties, can unleash the dreaming mind into
the waking state. . . .

—A. Besetzung, M.D.

ANNALS OF GENERAL PSYCHIATRY,
JUNE 1984:

The categories of hallucination or delusion do not fully
cover the phenomenon—which to some slight extent is
still continuing. . . .

The Mayor of Chicago "hallucinated" the beautiful "Princess Isis from Venus" who seduced him, in his fantasy life, but the witnesses at the stockyard insist that he was sodomizing a quite real hog at the time. . . .

Mars is as inhospitable to life as Venus, but a prominent music critic has told this author, in private, of an abduction by little green Martians out of 1930s science fiction, but this obviously hallucinatory experience does not help us understand how the man was transported from his apartment on Twenty-third Street to the middle of Central Park, where he heard the shots of a murder that never occurred. . . .

One of the blind men cured by the Virgin of Perth Amboy had been examined at Johns Hopkins just one week earlier, where the optic nerve was found to be irreparably dead, so that this is not a matter of hysterical blindness cured by hysterical faith, but of *real* blindness cured by hysterical faith. . . .

—B. Gilhooley, M.D.

UFO REPORTER,
JANUARY 1985:

As the "Christmas Miracle" continues to accelerate worldwide, it becomes more obvious than ever that the old concept of aliens coming here in spaceships just cannot account for it. Even those most committed to the spaceman theory must admit, in the light of the recent events, that the sciences involved in what is being done to the human race are primarily psychic or parapsychological. If space beings are doing it, whatever it is, they must be doing it by what I can only call, vaguely, "psychotronic technology," and they could be doing it, for all we know, from their home planets, without physically traveling at all. By the same token, we have no need to posit space-

men at all, since whoever or whatever is doing this could
be as close as the psychology department of some obscure
university or the mind-control sector of any Intelligence
Agency. . . .

Human minds are being manipulated on a massive
scale; that is all we know, and all theories about the
Manipulators—terrestrial or extraterrestrial—are mere
guesswork. . . .

—J. Lacombe, Ph.D.

UFO REPORTER,
MARCH 1985:

. . . The idea that the "Christmas Phenomenon" is being
done *to* us *by* some Agency (terrestrial or otherwise) is
based on the categories of Indo-European grammar and
Aristotelian logic, which modern physics has long known
to be inadequate. A Taoist or a Hopi Indian, for instance,
with a different semantic "set," might regard the events as
a cosmic happening or growth process, without trying to
isolate out one part of the universe as the "cause" and
thus relegating the rest of the universe to the dependent
position of "the effects." Modern quantum theory, at least
since Bell's Theorem (1964), would suggest strongly that
these holistic Chinese-Amerindian concepts are more accurate maps of what is happening than the linear A-causes-B
sequences of Aristotelianism. . . .

Does this mean that we abandon the search for a
"cause"? Not at all. It merely implies that looking for
humans or superhumans who did it is as fruitless as
the medieval search to explain each oddity as the work
of angels or demons. We should seek the cause in the
quantum structure of life and of matter itself. . . .

—B. Williams, Ph.D.

NATIONAL ENQUIRER,
JUNE 1991:

Of all the perplexing pixiedom that continues to trail in the wake of the Christmas Miracle, the most baffling thing to show-biz people is the continued absence of Cagliostro the Great. The idea that the magician's disappearance was a publicity stunt, calculated to cash in on the other mysteries beginning that amazing morning eight years ago, has long since been abandoned, as Cagliostro continues to remain hidden, wherever he is. . . .

The most bizarre sideline of this story concerns John Disk, the man who claimed to have murdered Cagliostro. Although held by the New York police for some months, Disk was finally released when no body could be found and the clothes discovered on Central Park West and identified as Cagliostro's were free of bullet holes. Disk, we have learned, is now an officer of the First Bank of Religiosophy and refuses to talk about his experience that mad and mysterious morning.

"Nobody would believe me," he told our reporter. "You have to go to Chinatown and see it yourself."

GALACTIC ARCHIVES:

To understand what happened to the primates of Terra in the 1980s, a metaphor may be useful.

Charlatans, *jongleurs*, wandering minstrels, stage magicians, etc., on all primitive planets, employ a device known as a Trick Top Hat. This appears to be an ordinary hat, and looks empty to the audience, but it actually contains a pouch out of which all sorts of amazing things can be made to appear—rabbits, yards of bright-colored cloth, glasses of water, and in general whatever the magician wishes to produce for the delight and amazement of his audience.

This ritual, like all rituals and religious visions or ecstasies, is actually a *memory of the future*, but there is no way for primitives to understand that.

Consider the epistemological plight of the Terran primates at the time of this ancient Romance. They knew that they were made of molecules, which were made of atoms, which were made of subatomic particles, which were expressions in space-time of quantum probability matrices. This knowledge, alas, was so recent that it had never been integrated into their philosophies, or into the rules of their social games, like religions, politics, economics, etc. Their whole social reality-tunnel was based on prequantum superstition and ignorance. The sociological nexus was Euclidean-Aristotelian-Newtonian; even Maxwell and Einstein had only been digested by a few.

Over twenty-five hundred years earlier, one mutant primate, Lao-Tse, had written: "The greatest is within the smallest." Less than one-one hundredth (0.01) of one percent of the Terran primates were capable of understanding this before 1984. They looked for causality everywhere else: some known as astrologers scanned the distant stars; others known as Marxists scanned economics, etc. They knew that the physicists understood causality better than any other group on their planet, but few of them, even among the physicists, realized how quantum theory applied to their own behavior. Quantum psychology did not begin to emerge until the 1990s.

What was known in their planet as Bell's Theorem—an elementary, kindergarten-level discovery routinely divined on every planet at about the same time as atomic energy and space travel are beginning—was only twenty years old among them and barely understood even by the physicists. The few quantum theorists, such as Sarfatti, who dared to speculate about "macrocosmic quantum effects"— large systems engaged in quantum-jumping—were usually dismissed as Romantics by their colleagues, despite the fact that each stage of metamorphosis of every living creature, including the Terran primates themselves, was obviously a quantum leap.

The primate Mystics, most of them brain-damaged, endlessly told the other primates to "look within." Most primates assumed, in primitive Aristotelian fashion, that what was within was some gaseous entity which they called "mind" or "soul." Unable to find such an abstraction, they either gave up in despair or took their negative results as a positive revelation and became adherents of the "no-mind" or "no-ego" philosophy of Buddha and David Hume.

Of course if they had truly looked within, scientifically, they would have found that their thoughts, percepts, and reality-tunnels were determined by the structure of the primate nervous system, which was determined by the genetic or molecular design of the primate evolutionary script, which was determined by the laws of quantum biophysics. That is concretely, their brains were shaped by cells shaped by molecules shaped by atoms shaped by quantum probabilities.

Since the quantum connection is nonlocal, it is inevitable that introspection and meditation could discover no "ego" *within;* within and without are Euclidean parameters that do not apply to the quantum world. But the primates could not understand this. When, due to trauma, masochistic religious practices, alkaloid herbs, or mere statistical chance, their neuroatomic circuitry propelled them into Quantum Consciousness, they could not conceptualize that they were outside space-time entirely. Space and time, they still thought even after Einsein, were as solid as walls. They could only imagine, primate fashion, that they were traveling *in* space and *out of* their bodies; they called it "astral projection" and devised numerous primate superstitions about it.

Similarly, when one of them would begin to learn how to use the metaprogramming circuits in the forebrain, they could not conceptualize that they were peering into alternative quantum probability matrices. Instead, they devised a whole mythology of heavens, hells, purgatories, astral planes, fairy lands, demons, gods, angels, UFOnauts, etc., to make Euclidean "maps" of such quantum experiences.

We should be charitable to the Terran primates. All planets have gone through such superstitious stages before the HEAD Revolution is complete among them.

When the neuroatomic circuitry, only occasionally released during most of their history, began to function fully in 1984, the primates could not begin to understand what was happening, for all of the above reasons. They were suddenly in communication, not just with one reality-tunnel, but with all possible reality-tunnels. They could see quantum probabilities leading to all possible futures, but they were unable to conceptualize what they saw. The primate brain, always quick to cover ignorance with a primate archetype, projected all their traditional superstitions on what was happening.

Terra was a weird and crazy place for several years. Giant lobsters with ray guns, Tibetan demons, Ignatz the anarchist mouse, and dozens of other fantasy figures were likely to appear at any time, any place, even in churches during funerals or at top-secret governmental meetings. The joke "We're all living in a surrealist novel" gained wide currency, although few realized how close to the truth it was.

The intelligence-raising drug NEURO began to change things a bit after it appeared in 1988. People's fantasies gradually became more sophisticated and philosophical, and their reality-tunnels accordingly adapted. With the publication of Sirag's General Field Theory in 1993, the smarter primates immediately realized what was really occurring on their planet and throughout the cosmos.

They gradually comprehended that all their myths had been *memories of the future*, available to them through the nonlocal activity of the quantum waves making up their brains. Age-old religious visions of Immortality, for instance, they recognized as precapitulations of the inevitable end product of their current longevity research. The "magic carpets" and "seven-league boots" they already had; the New Heaven and New Earth they were rapidly building. The superhuman heroes and heroines of romantic fiction were the humans they were themselves becoming as the HEAD Revolution accelerated them toward greater intellectual efficiency, more flexible emotional equilibrium, neurosomatic rapture, and metaprogramming wisdom.

They understood that the Boddhisattva's Vow, common among the neurosomatic-circuit Eastern primates, was no idle fantasy, either, even though it promised to redeem all sentient beings. With time-travel made possible through the General Field Theory, they could change any past probability wave, creating a new universe where each entity would take the best possible path instead of whatever sad paths it had taken to arouse their compassion and intervention. They understood the words, previously totally opaque, of the Jewish mystic, Jesus, who had said, "All that I do, ye shall do, also; and more." They understood that every political and mystical ideal of freedom, however aborted in its first appearances, was fated to be achieved in some form, in the infinite nonlocal cosmos opening before them.

They understood that the "oneness with earth" so many had discovered in the previous two decades had only been the overture to the discovery of nonlocality, as they shared more and more in oneness with *all that is,* and *all that can be*.

And they understood, of course the time-honored allegory of the Trick Top Hat, which was just a symbol of the brain. This ritual was passed on from generation to generation, since it represented the greatest treasure in the universe, which is shared by all and belongs to none: the faculty of creativity, partially unleashed in each sentient being, fully released at the proper Galactic-genetic time by the HEAD Revolution.

BOOK ONE
The Homing Pigeons

PART ONE
WHO'S ZELENKA?

All Cretans are liars.
—EMPEDOCLES THE CRETAN

The President of the United States is not a crook.
—THE PRESIDENT OF THE UNITED STATES

Death to all fanatics!
—MALACLYPSE THE YOUNGER

THE UNIVERSE WILL SURPRISE US

Jen fa Ti: Ti fa Tsien
T'sien fa Tao; Tao fa tzu-jan
>—Lao-Tse, *Tao Te Ching*

Tall, skinny palm trees, twisted to bizarre angles by dozens of Florida hurricanes, stood black against a cinnamon-streaked sky as the sun rose majestically in the west.

"We stop here," Mavis said, as he had known she would; as was, perhaps, inevitable now.

This must be the Gulf of Mexico, Dashwood thought. They could now load him with chains and drop him *in the drink*, as criminals said, letting him sink slowly down amid the sharks and barracudas, down where, after the sharks were finished, the King Crabs would pick what was left on his bones, down, down, down, full fathom five.

And, as was inevitable now, Mavis motioned him out of the car, stepping out behind him (still holding that damned tommy gun, as if quietly toying with it) like the ghoats in hammelts.

"We wait here," she said. "The others go back."

"What are we waiting for?" Dashwood asked.

"Don't be a dummy, George. We rescued you, remember? Like the gauds in ambers."

Dashwood took a deep breath, counting to ten. "Why

do you keep calling me George? You know my name is Frank, dammit."

Mavis opened her eyes wide, pretending astonishment. "You really don't remember," she said sadly.

A woodpecker landed wearily on the nearest palm, as if he had flown more missions than Yossarian and never intended to go up again.

"I'm Frank Dashwood," he said. "Dr. Francis R. Dashwood. I'm a member of the American Psychiatric Association. I'm in *Who's Who. Goddamnit*," he added, irrelevantly but heatedly.

"You're George Dorn," she said. "You work for *Confrontation* magazine. Your boss is named Justin Case."

"Oh, balls," Dashwood said.

The woodpecker turned his head, as perhaps was sure to happen now, and watched them suspiciously, like a paranoid old man.

And Dashwood noticed, as for the first time, an unfinished building on the beach, probably a new condo, with girders going off at strange cubist angles. Skeletons in hard hats stood frozen like statues, and a giant squid reached up from the ocean to wrap its tentacles around the pylons.

The sun was as hot as Gunga Din's loincloth.

A vine-colored plaque at the gate said:

FATALITY INC.
Muss S. Sine, President
S. Muss Sine, Vice President

"If I'm George Dorn," he said finally, "why do I have this deep-seated longtime delusion that I'm Frank Dashwood?"

"We're in Maybe-time here," Mavis said. "You know: 'In addition to a Yes and a No, the universe contains a

Maybe.' You've heard that, I'm sure. It's hard to keep track of social fictions out here, and personal identity is just a social fiction. So you've lost your ego for a few minutes and grabbed hold of another one. That's how you created this imaginary Frank Fernwood."

"Dashwood," he corrected automatically.

"Going home from here isn't easy," Mavis said, still toying with the tommy gun. "Some people never find their way back. That's why you must let go out of this Frank Fernwood delusion."

"It's Dashwood, dammit, *Dashwood!*"

"Fernwood, Dashwood," she said impatiently. "Deep down you know you're George Dorn."

"You are a fruitcake, Mavis. Why did you rescue me from that jail, anyway?"

"You're wanted," she said simply.

"By whom?"

"Hagbard Celine."

"And who is Hagbard Celine?" They had reached the cabana and were standing beside it, glaring at each other like two chess masters who each suspect that they have wandered into some idiotic permutation of the Ourang-Outan opening. The woodpecker turned his head, probably a bit puzzled himself, and sized them up with the other eye.

"You'll know when you meet him, George." ("Frank," he shouted. "George," she repeated firmly.) "For now it's enough that he wanted us to get you out of Bad Ass Jail."

"And why the hell does Hagbard Chelling . . ." ("Celine," she corrected.) ". . . Celine, then, why the hell does Hagbard Celine want to see me?"

"Why anything?" Mavis asked rhetorically. "Why sky, why oceans, why people? Jen fa Ti: Ti fa T'sien: T'sien fa Tao: Tao fa tzu-jan."

"Oh, *coitus*," Dashwood said, avoiding crudity. "Don't give me obscurities in Cantonese at this hour."

"Men are created by earth, earth is created by the universe, the universe is created by Nature's Process, and Nature's Process just happened," Mavis translated.

Dashwood was not going to get involved in aleotoric cosmologies. "So Hagbard Celine just happened," he said. "And he just happened to want me out of Bad Ass Jail. And you just happen to like busting into jails with tommy guns and taking prisoners out. This is the silliest damned routine I ever heard."

"Well," Mavis said, grinning wickedly, "I also just happen to like you. In fact, I've had the Whites for you ever since I broke into the cell back in Bad Ass and caught you Lourding off."

"Don't talk dirty," he said. "It's not becoming to a young woman your age, and it's getting silly and old-fashioned. It makes you sound like a refugee from the 1960s."

"Nonsense," Mavis said. "It gets you excited. It always gets men excited to hear women talk like this. Do you know how I felt when I saw you there on the bunk with your Rehnquist in your hand? It made my Feinstein go all warm and mushy inside, George."

"Frank," he said one more time. "And I don't have the Whites for you. Women with tommy guns don't turn me on at all."

"Are you sure?" Mavis asked provocatively. "I'll bet I could make your Rehnquist stand up if I really tried." She opened her trenchcoat and he could see her magnificent Brownmillers bulging through her tight sweater. He had to admit they were a fine, firm pair of Brownmillers—"a pair you could hang your hat on," as an Irishman had once said—but he was not going to be tempted. This was all too weird.

"I've had a lot of tension since raiding the jail," Mavis went on, slipping the trenchcoat to the sand. "I really need a good Potter Stewart, George. Wouldn't you like to Potter Stewart me? Wouldn't you like to lie on the sand and stick your great big pulsating Rehnquist into my warm, moist Feinstein?"

"This is ridiculous."

"Listen, George," Mavis went on intensely. "When I was young I decided to save myself for a man who completely meets the criteria of my value system. That's when I was reading Ayn Rand, you see. But then I realized I could get awfully horny waiting for him to come along. You'll have to do."

How can you keep the facts clear and sharp-edged when this happens? "You really want me to Potter Stewart you right now on a public beach in broad daylight?" he asked, feeling like a fool.

The woodpecker went to work above them just then, banging away like a Rock drummer. Dashwood remembered from Nutley High School:

> The woodpecker pecked on the outhouse door;
> He pecked and he pecked till his pecker was sore.

"George, you're too serious. Don't you know how to play? Did you ever think that life is maybe a game? The world is a toy, George. I'm a toy. You conjured me out of your fantasies while you were Lourding-off in that jail cell last night. I'm a magic voodoo doll. You can do anything you want with me."

Dashwood shook his head. "I can't believe you. The way you're talking—it's not real."

"I always talk this way when I'm horny. It so happens that at such tender moments I'm more open to the vibrations from outer space. George, is the Tooth Fairy real? Is the thought of the Tooth Fairy a real thought? How is it different from the mental picture of my Brownmillers that you get when you imagine you can look right through my sweater? Does the fact that you can think of Potter Stewarting me and I can think of Potter Stewarting you mean that we *are* going to Potter Stewart? Or is the universe going to surprise us?"

"The universe is going to surprise *you*," Dashwood said. "I don't trust women with tommy guns who rave about Tooth Fairies and vibrations from outer space. I'm getting the hell out of here." He started to walk away.

"Listen, George," Mavis said earnestly. "You are about to walk into a completely different universe, one you might not like at all. Every quantum decision creates a whole new space-time manifold . . ."

"Oh, bullburger," he said, before she could go any further with that gibberish.

"You damned fool! You're walking out on the greatest adventure of our century!" She was almost shouting now. "Atlantis! Illumination! Leviathan! Hagbard Celine!"

Dashwood kept going.

"You asshole!" she screamed. "You're about to miss *the best Steinem Job of your life*."

He almost turned then, but this was all too bizarre for him. He continued down the asphalt road grimly, ignoring the yellow submarine that was beginning to surface offshore.

Blake Williams galloped past him suddenly, riding a horse with no wife and no mustache. He was Lassie (who was really a male dog in drag), but he was also Dashwood's father. Like the Gutmanhammett.

Then Furbish Lousewart came out of the lavatory wearing a laboratory smock. "The masses are female," he sneered, drawing a rotary saw out of his toolbox depository. He methodically began sawing off Dashwood's head.

"Give me head!" he screamed. "The whiteness of the wall!
Gothin haven, annette colp us! Give me head!"

And then Linda Lovelace was there, with Dracula's old
red-lined cape, starting to suck him, starting to suck the
purity of essence from him, biting down hard hard hard, a
blood-smeared mouth with canine fangs.

And he woke up.

He looked at the alarm clock blearily, still haunted by
fangs and blood. Six-fifty-eight; the alarm would go off in
two minutes.

I am Frank Dashwood. All that other was just a dream.

He depressed the alarm switch and put his naked feet
on the cold floor, so he would not roll over and dream he
was going to work.

Fangs and blood. Why do people see such films? Weird
species, we are.

Dr. Dashwood staggered to the shower. White tile,
white on white: the whiteness of the wall. Vibrations from
outer space, she said. Not too hot, now: careful. Ah, that's
good. Watch that it doesn't heat up too fast, though.
Fangs and blood: average person has seen one hundred,
maybe two hundred, of those films. Hundreds of hours of
horror grooves in the brain: neurological masochism.
YEEEEEEEEEEEEEEEEEEEEE!

He turned the hot-water spigot down quickly. Always
does that: starts tepid and then boils you.

He leapt from the shower and began toweling. Oral
sadism: she looked good enough to eat, we say. Little Red
Riding Hood. Eatupus complex.

Dashwood surveyed his features in the mirror, combing
his hair. As the world sees me: this not unhandsome,
definitely nervous, middle-aged face.

Radio will bring me all the way back. Try KKHI, maybe
catch some Vivaldi. Dashwood's Law: whenever you turn

on KKHI, they're either playing Vivaldi or will play Vivaldi within fifteen minutes.

> De de dum de dum de dee
> De de dum de dum de dum dum dum

Sounds more like Bach. Wait: listen:

> De de drum de drum de DRUM
> Drum drum de droom de de
>   Wheeeee dumb de!

And that was the Concerto for Harp *by Jan Zelenka. And now the news. In Bad Ass, Texas, School Superintendent B. S. Curve was murdered last night by a bomb attached to the starter of his automobile. Superintendent Curve had been under attack by local clergy and the John Birch Society for proposing the teaching of the metric system in schools. In Washington, President K—*

Dashwood snapped the radio off irritably. Whenever you want to hear some pleasant music, they break for the news. Ah, well: time to head for the office, anyway.

De de dum de dum de dee . . . Where the hell did I put the key? Oh yes; alarm clock, next to. Dum de de: sure sounded like Bach at first. Dum drum de dee! Really bounced along, music of that period. Baroque.

He started his car.

Crrrumph rumph rumph.

Oh, damn. Try again.

Crrrrrrrrrrrumph rumph a zoom.

Dashwood pulled out into the traffic. Always fails to ignite first time. Dum dum de. Zelenka, he said. Who the hell was Zelenka? Same period as Bach, I'm sure.

Dr. Dashwood turned onto Van Ness and headed for Orgasm Research: da dum da dum da *dreee!*

And drove straight into an entirely different kind of novel.

THE MAD ARAB

Qol: Hua Allahu achad; Allahu Assamad; lam yalid walam yulad; walam yakun lahu kufwan achad.

—AL QORAN

One day earlier and three thousand miles due east, Bonita ("Bonny") Benedict, a popular columnist for the New York *News-Times-Post-Herald-Dispatch-Express-Mirror-Eagle*, sat down to write her daily stream-of-consciousness. According to her usual procedure, Bonny began by flipping through her notebook. This usually served to fructify her imagination, but that day proved rather sterile. Items which had already been used were crossed out with large X's and what was left was weary, stale, flat, and unprofitable. There was literally nothing timely or exciting enough for a lead.

Bonny was only stumped for a minute; then she remembered the ancient maxim of the great pioneer of modern journalism, Charles Foster Hearst: "If there isn't any news, invent some."

Ms. Benedict, whose hair would have been gray if she hadn't decided it was more chic to bleach it pure platinum-white, had lasted in the news game for forty years. She did not lack the faculty of imagination.

Bonny inserted a fresh sheet in the typewriter and began at once, trusting her years of experience to guide her. What emerged was:

Who is the man in Hong Kong who looks exactly like Lee Harvey Oswald? Believe it or not, darlings, that question is causing a lot of excitement among the members of the new Senate Committee on Congressional Committees on Assassinations. In case you forgot, they're the ones who are trying to find out why the various Congressional Committees on Assassinations couldn't find out anything. What they're asking each other is: Could the man in Hong Kong really be Oswald? And, if so, who was the double that got shot in Dallas? Doesn't it make your heads swim???

That was what was known as a fail-safe item. If (as was likely) the Senate Committee simply ignored it rather than fan the flames of rumor, many readers would believe it on the grounds that it had been printed and not denied. If, on the other hand, the Committee did deny it, even more people would believe it. A 1981 psychological survey had shown that 67 percent of the population experienced uncertainty, indecision, suspicion, or downright paranoia whenever they saw the words "government denial" in print.

Bonny went on to use up the not-totally dreary items in her notebook, jazzing each one enough to give it a coat of sparkle, or at least of tinsel. But she still needed a zinger for the closing. She followed the sage advice of the prophet Hearst one more time and wrote:

Wasn't that Furbish Lousewart of the Purity of Ecology Party eating steak and drinking Manhattans (made

with Southern Comfort, my dears!) at Sardi's last night?
What would the Party regulars think of this flagrant
disregard of POE principles?

Bonny, in her youth, had been a disciple of the famous
feminist and psychologist Alberta Einstein. It was Ms.
Einstein, in her epoch-making *Neuropsychology,* who introduced the concept that every brain constructs a different "island-reality" from the billions of signals it receives
every minute. This concept had revolutionized the social
sciences and even led Heisenberg to propose a similar
relativity principle in physics. Bonny knew that the POE
people lived in an island-reality where eating meat and
drinking fermented spirits were atrocities comparable to
ax murder or Burgering in the well. This item would
make them hopping mad.

A columnist's career depends on amusing most of her
readers most of the time and making some of them hopping mad some of the time.

The owner-publisher of the New York *News-Times-&c*
was Polly Esther Doubleknit, relict of the late Dacron
Doubleknit, the leisurewear king. When the leisurewear
fad had peaked in the 1970s, Dacron had shrewdly used
the cash flow to *"diversify,"* as his accountant called it.
Engulf and Devour, his competitors called it. When he
died Dacron owned over a thousand retail stores coast to
coast, a tapioca mine in Nutley, N.J. (a bad investment,
that one, suggested by a plausible but Machiavellian
midget), a large hunk of Canadian forestland, three South
American governments (his leisurewear was thereafter made
with very cheap labor), sixteen Congresspersons, three
senators, a shipyard in Yellow Springs, Ohio (suggested
by Eva Gebloomenkraft), seven state legislatures together
with four other whorehouses in Nevada, and the New
York *News-Times-*u.s.w.

Dacron died of a heart attack at fifty-two, brought on by anxiety about the amount of political corruption he was involved in. Dacron did not *like* to bribe public officials and *hated* the size of the bribes they all wanted, because he had been raised a Presbyterian. Unfortunately for him, he lived in an age of Terminal Bureaucracy and there was absolutely no way, no matter how many lawyers he hired, to find out if his corporations were, in any given instance, in violation of the law. There were too many laws, and they were written in language that guaranteed maximum ambiguity all around, so that lawyers (who wrote the laws) could always get jobs proving that the laws meant Yes, if they were being paid to prove that, or that the laws meant No, if they were being paid to prove that. Dacron never found out, for sure, whether he was one of the business-men in the country operating 100 percent legally all the time or if he was in violation of so many statutes that he was subject to over a thousand years in prison; no two lawyers ever would agree about that. So Dacron bribed as many officials as possible to protect himself, and then gradually worried himself to death about the bribes being discovered someday.

Polly Esther, finding herself the heir of Dacron's farrag-inous empire, quickly appointed professional executives to manage most of it; but she took over the newspaper personally. She was a fan of a TV show called *Lou Grant* and rather fancied herself as becoming another Mrs. Pynchon.

Mrs. Pynchon was the publisher of the paper on the *Lou Grant* show. She was tough enough to eat barbed wire and spit tacks, but she was also cool and elegant. Polly Esther wanted to be like that.

She also had a secret desire to be the other Mrs. Pynchon, the wife of the novelist. She had read one of Pynchon's novels once while dieting, and maybe she had

used just a little bit too many of those diet pills, because
she believed every word of it. She was still convinced that
the baskets on the street saying WASTE meant We Await
Silent Tristero's Empire.

Naturally, Polly Esther believed both of Bonny Bene-
dict's fictions of the day. She had long suspected that both
Oswald and Lousewart were agents of Silent Tristero's
Empire.

Polly Esther was about forty-two but she could easily
pass for thirty-two. This was because she was very rich.

Once a year Polly Esther went to a ranch in Nevada
which looked like a luxury motel and treated its guests like
the inmates of a concentration camp. They fed Polly Esther on a diet what would barely sustain life and tasted
horrible. They made her exercise several hours a day. A
brutal staff insulted her, mocked her, bullied her, and got
her back on her feet again, running, every time she thought
she'd drop from exhaustion. They also shot her full of
Gerovitol, methamphetamines, and vitamins three times a
day. They charged her fifty-five hundred dollars.

Some of this actually had a slight effect on her body,
but most of it was directed at her mind. She came out of
this two-week ordeal, each year, convinced that she had
suffered enough to *deserve* to be beautiful for another fifty
weeks.

She was indeed beautiful, and had been a flaming redhead for so long that only a few people in Xenia, Ohio,
remembered her as a dark-haired girl who had to leave
town because of a scandal in the local Baptist church
choir.

The robot who traveled under the name "Frank Sullivan" was in New York the next morning and saw Bonny
Benedict's column. "Oh, Burger, Lourde, and corruption," he muttered, the newspaper trembling in his hands.

He immediately canceled his business in New York and hopped an orbital to Washington, where he leapt into a cab, sped to Naval Intelligence, and galloped into the office of Admiral Mounty ("Iron Balls") Babbit.

Babbit was in charge of "Dungeon and Dragon" operations, including the "Sullivan" matter; these were machinations so murky that they were not even known to those normally cleared for covert operations.

"How the holy Potter Stewart did she get hold of this?" pseudo-Sullivan demanded, waving Bonny Benedict's column.

Babbit stopped breathing for a minute as he read the Second Oswald item.

"Jesus and Mary Christ," he said finally, in a hollow tone. 'The Briggsing Bryanting Frankel, she must have a source in the CIA. Those mother-Stewarting sons-of-bitches, they'll do anything to blow one of our operations."

This was typical of Old Iron Balls, as his men called him. He was convinced that everything malign emanated from Central Intelligence over in Alexandria. They spent all their time, he believed, plotting to discredit Naval Intelligence, and all because a high CIA official had once caught him, Mounty Babbit, in an intimate moment with the CIA man's mistress.

"Those bastards," he repeated in a tone as cold as official charity. "I'd like to blow that Burger-house in Alexandria off the face of the earth and every limp-wristed Briggsing Bryanting Harvard egghead in it."

But that was only one level of Old Iron Balls's mind— the public level. Much deeper, he was already plotting various scenarios that resulted from the sudden deaths of Bonny Benedict or "Frank Sullivan."

Of course, Babbit did not for a moment contemplate assassination in the vulgar sense; there had been more than enough of that sort of thing back in the sixties and it had made all sorts of trouble for everyone in the Intelligence game. Babbit was guided by a maxim now universally accepted in the cloak-and-dagger business although originally formulated by Beria of the NKVD: "Any damned fool can commit murder. Any halfway trained operative can arrange convincing suicide. It takes an artist to manage an authentic natural death."

Pseudo-Sullivan had a larger than average share of ESP, as did many persons in the Intelligence game. "You know," he said casually, "I've left Certain Papers in a Certain Place to be opened in case of sudden death . . ."

"Oh, you needn't worry about anything like that," Babbit said hastily. "Why, you're one of our most valuable um men. We wouldn't dream of . . ." Blah-blah-blah. It was a set speech, for occasions like this.

He was thinking of Bonny Benedict and of her publisher, that hoity-toity rich Frankel-Briggser, Polly Esther Doubleknit.

The next fuse ignited by the Oswald-in-Hong-Kong story was in the frontal cortex of a balding, nervous man named Justin Case, who was living in a sociological treatise. That is, people made him so anxious that he shielded himself from them with a cocoon of words and concepts which had gradually become more real to him than the people were. He was a heavyweight Intellectual.

Justin Case had more Moral Concern than was good for a man. He worried about racism and sexism and imperialism and injustice and the general cussedness of his species; he agonized over each and every person on the planet who might be getting a raw deal; if you put enough martinis in him, he would start singing "Joe Hill" and "We Shall Overcome" and "Which Side Are You On?" and other old Labor and Civil Rights songs.

Naturally, Case was the editor of a Liberal Magazine.

The magazine was called *Confrontation* and had been started by a mad Arab named Joe Malik, who abandoned it in 1968 to enter a Trappist monastery. Malik had been traumatized by the Democratic Convention that year and told everybody he intended to spend the rest of his life in vehement and continuous prayer.

Malik left behind a note which still hung on the bulletin board at *Confrontation*. It said:

> *Qol: Hua Allahu achad; Allahu Assamad; lam yalid walam yulad; walam yakun lahu kufwan achad.*

Nobody at *Confrontation* could read Arabic, but they all liked to stop and look at the note occasionally, wondering what it meant.

The stockholders had appointed Case to the editorship, after Malik retreated to the cloister, because Justin had as much righteous indignation as the mad Arab but was not so flaky.

By spring 1984, Case had 120 bound volumes of books, articles, and press clippings about the J.F.K. assassination, since he was still Righteously Indignant about the palpably obvious cover-up involved in the *Warren Report*.

The day that pseudo-Sullivan wigged out over Bonny Benedict's contribution to the mythology of the assassination, Case calmly clipped that item and added it to his file.

Three-quarters of the other material in Case's file was also fictitious. One-third of this disinformation had been generated by Intelligence Agencies—domestic, foreign, and extraterrestrial—as covers or screens for their own activities in and around Dallas in 1963. Another third had been produced by sincere, dedicated, sometimes avid *conspiracy buffs*, weaving their own webs of confusion as they searched for the elusive truth. The last third had

been created, like the Bonny Benedict item, by journalists following Hearst's advice about what to do when there
was no news.

Anybody trying to find out "what *really* happened"
from this collection of mythology would be so confused
that the significant fact of the extraterrestrial intervention
would never be apparent.

Case did not suspect any of this. He loved his J.F.K.
file. He was convinced that someday the crucial piece
would come to him, he would insert it into the file, and
the whole jigsaw would make sense.

He never realized that the one detail which gave everything away was that while Oswald was firing from the
sixth-floor window he was also having a Coke on the
second floor and mingling with the crowd in the street.

Like most liberals, Justin Case lacked imagination and
never took seriously all the evidence of extraterrestrial
activity on earth during the past forty years.

Case was currently having an affair with the Hollywood
actress Carol Christmas.

Carol was renowned among the heterosexual male population for having the biggest Brownmillers since Jayne
Mansfield; so far only women and a few Gay men had
noticed that she could also act.

Carol had been married four times. She had had three
abortions. Like other famous Beauties, she was *always*
dieting, and hence, a little bit high-strung. She was also a
disciple of General E. A. Crowley, the eccentric English
explorer who had discovered the North Pole and claimed
there was a hole there leading down to the center of the
Earth. Carol devoutly believed Crowley's yarn that there
was a whole civilization down there, inside the Earth, run
by green-skinned women.

Carol believed this because she had a great artistic
faith in the principle of balance. In her probability

continuum—in the series of quantum *eigen*states that had crystalized into her universe—the whole outside of the planet seemed to be run by white-skinned males. It was only fair that the inside should be run by green-skinned females.

Carol was having three other affairs at the same time as her *amour* with Justin Case. There was a hairdresser in Hollywood (bi, not Gay) who was very talented at Bryanting and Briggsing—two arts at which totally straight men, in Carol's opinion, were usually a bit clumsy. There was also François Loup-Garou, the painter, in Paris, who adored her madly, as only a painter can adore a woman. And there was a bitter but brilliant Black novelist in Chicago named Franklin Stuart.

Justin Case knew all about these other *amours;* after all, he read Bonny Benedict's column every day. Bonny kept the world informed about which celebrities were Potter Stewarting each other. She did this in a way that was perfectly clear to every reader but totally without any clear meaning in a court of law, in case somebody got irritated and tried to sue her. What she did was to write something like "Hollywood sexpot Carol Christmas and Black novelist Frank Stuart are an item these days."

Everybody knew what "an item" meant.

When Bonny wrote that a couple were "a hot item" many of her readers were mildly puzzled, but assumed she was insinuating some fantastic sexual acrobatics. Actually, it only meant that Bonny was trying to avoid stylistic monotony; occasionally, she even switched it to "a torrid item," which led to even more lascivious fantasies for some of her readers.

Justin Case didn't object to Carol Christmas's other affairs because he accepted it as a fact of life that actors are hypersexed, just as coal miners are prone to black lung disease and novelists to booze and weird drugs. Besides, jealousy was a sign of possessiveness, and possessiveness was illiberal. And, anyway—as he usually concluded his ruminations on this subject, during the infrequent moments when he thought of it at all—Carol's career kept them apart most of the time, and he was not so naïve as to expect somebody of her youth and beauty to resist all temptations.

And it was the 1980s, wasn't it?

Actually, Case was a bit of an unconscious psychic—that is, he was aware of quantum probability waves, although not consciously. He *sensed* that there were approximately 10^{50} universes in which he had lusted after Carol and never got into her Frankel even once. That unconscious psychic knowledge kept him content with this universe, where he was her part-time lover.

Carol Christmas had starred in the first hard-core porn movie to win the Academy Award, *Deep Mongolian Steinem Job*. The film had been directed by Stanley Kubrick, after he read a satirical novel in which the author had imagined what would happen if Kubrick set out to make a serious and even *artistic* porn film.

Despite the success of *Deep Mongolian Steinem Job*, most humans still did not realize that all fantasies tend to become realities, in one universe or another.

Carol did realize it, however. She was currently involved in approximately 250,000,000 sex acts every hour.

REAL HOUSES, REAL OFFICES

The sensuous California sun hung low and sultry over San Francisco, turning everybody's mood in a low and sultry direction. It was a day when anything could happen. Cops helped old ladies across the street. Bankers gave loans to people who really needed them. A high school girl was heard to speak a sentence in English, without "ya know" before the predicate object.

And a mysterious hand scrawled "The enormous tragedy of the dream nor dashed a thousand kim" on the wall of the Van Ness Street entrance of Orgasm Research.

Dr. Frank Dashwood (dum dum de! Who's Zelenka?) arrived from another novel.

He turned into the Van Ness parking lot of ORGRE, executed a smart translation of his sleek MG into the RESERVED area, and saw the incomprehensible scrawl.

That damned Ezra Pound again. Why do I have to be haunted by a schizo with an obsession about Fernando Poo?

At nine-oh-one Dr. Dashwood passed through the solid oak door saying in gold letters:

FRANCIS DASHWOOD, M.D.
PRESIDENT

There was nothing urgent on the memo pad, so Dashwood began opening the incoming mail leisurely.

Dear Dr. Dashwood,

I am writing to you as a Sex Expert because I don't
know where else to turn. I already wrote to Ann Lan-
ders, but she just told me to take cold showers. My
problem is that I am madly, hopelessly, passionately in
love with Linda Lovelace. I've actually seen *Deep Throat*
ninety-three times now and nothing can get her out of
my mind. Other women leave me cold; I only want
Linda, Linda, Linda. She has so much beauty and
charm and sweetness and, my God, can she eat Rehnquist!
I know this is hopeless because even though I've written a novel about Vlad the Impaler and made lots of
money, I'm still very shy with women. (Some of them
are extraterrestrials, I have discovered.) Why did God
make such an unjust universe? Can you help me?

Dr. Dashwood frowned thoughtfully, then scrawled,
"Send this nut the see-a-psychiatrist letter."
Dum de dum de dum de. Next!

Dr. Orgasm R. Institute
Frank Dashwood
666 Malaclypse
San Francisco, Calif.

Dear Dr. Institute:

We are sending you this personalized letter because we
know that a man like you, Dr. Institute, cares about his
investments and wants to know the facts about Inflation.

Next! (And remember: look up that Zelenka.)

Dear Dr Dashwood,

I am a paraplegic and therefore I am incapable of
normal coitus. My sweetheart and I, fortunately, have

found that oral sex satisfies us fully—I Marshall her Frankel and then she gives me a Steinem Job. But this creates a terrible legal conundrum, since she lives across the Mississippi River in Iowa and I am a citizen of Illinois. Iowa has a very strict law against oral sex, which they classify as sodomy (due to a mistranslation of the Old Testament, I believe). Thus, we can't have sex in Iowa. Now, Illinois has had no anti-sodomy statutes since the 1960s, so you might think our problem can be solved by having sex in Illinois. Unfortunately, she can't afford to quit her job in Iowa, and thus every time she travels across the river to have sex with me, she is *crossing a state line*, which makes me vulnerable under the Mann Act. Is there any possible solution to this legal double-bind?

Dr. Dashwood was intrigued. He began thinking of topological transformations, non-Euclidean geometrics, Wheeler's wormholes in superspace . . . But then he realized he was Romanticizing, just because the puzzle had sparked his imagination. In ordinary four-dimensional Heisenberg space-time, there was no way out of the paradox: If the writer crossed the river, he and his lady were committing sodomy in Iowa, and if the lady crossed the river, they were violating the Mann Act in Illinois.

Logicians dream up such Strange Loops, Dashwood reflected, just to make games for other logicians; but lawyers create them to make more jobs for lawyers.

Dashwood scrawled, "Tell him his lady better damned well *find* a job in Illinois."

Next.

Dear Dr. Dashwood,

Once there was a man who was condemned to live on the moon. He knew the punishment was just, because he hated his father and such a sin deserves an extreme penalty. Nonetheless, his isolation was terrible and there were times when he thought his heart would break, just because he could never hear a human voice again.

Well, he made the best of his cruel situation. He began sending messages from the moon, telling everything he knew about life on earth—all the joys and agonies and struggles, "the horror and the boredom and the glory" of the long climb upward from the slime to higher and higher consciousness. The people back on earth loved these signals, which contained so much of life's drama, and they praised him extravagantly, and that gave him some comfort through the long years of his exile.

Once, however, he sat down and made a message about his own loneliness, telling how it feels to be separated from humanity by 250,000 miles of Dead Silence.

He called it the *Hammerklavier Sonata*.

Try to plot that on one of your graphs, you sizeist son-of-a-bitch.

> Ezra Pound
> Fair Play for Fernando Poo
> Committee

The intercom buzzed.

"A man is here from the FBI," Miss Karrig said nervously.

Dr. Dashwood began doing pranayama immediately. "Send . . . him . . . in . . . right . . . away . . ." he said between deep breaths.

The agent, whose name was Tobias Knight, had a walrus mustache and a cheery eye; nobody ever looked less threatening. Dr. Dashwood still regarded him with a wary respect, as a large and dangerous mammal. This was the

normal attitude since the 1983 Anti-Crime, Anti-Subversion
Omnibus bill had entitled the Bureau to conduct random
wiretapping on *all* citizens rather than just on known
criminals and known subversives. ("If we only watch the
already recognized enemies of society," the author of this
bill—Senator Uriah Snoop—had argued, "who knows what
hidden monkey business might be festering in dark places
to rise up and stab us in the back like a snake in the
grass?")

Knight was brisk and (seemingly) honest. A prominent
scientist—Dr. G. W. C. Bridge—had disappeared and,
since no kidnappers had demanded ransom and no evidence indicated that he had defected to Russia or China,
the Bureau was investigating even the most tenuous leads.
"Since you attended Miskatonic University in Massachusetts at the same time as Dr. Bridge, we're curious about
anything even that far back which might shed light on
why he'd want to vanish . . . if he did vanish voluntarily. . . ."

Dr. Dashwood created an expression of puzzlement. "I
hardly knew George," he said slowly. "He was just about
the only Black student at Miskatonic, of course, and that
made him um highly visible, but we never became
friends. . . ."

They beat around the bush for about ten minutes; then
Dashwood shot abruptly from the hip. "I know who really
was close to Washy," he said, looking inspired. "Pete
Simon, the geologist. Why don't you get in touch with him?
I think the last I heard he was with the government . . ."

Knight looked perfectly innocent. "Peter Simon," he
said slowly, making a note. "Geologist."

But Dashwood *knew:* the agent was a shade too bland,
too innocent. The Bureau was aware that Dr. Simon had
vanished also. Maybe they were on the track of the whole
Miskatonic Group.

Dr. Dashwood experienced a thrill of pure adrenaline. Ever since he had started Project Pan he had known this moment would come, and now that it was here he was handling himself impeccably.

Dum de dum de dum de dum dum.

Who's Zelenka?

THE CONTINENTAL OP

> That which is forbidden is not allowed.
> —JOHN LILLY, *The Center of the Cyclone*

Tobias Knight drove to an old Victorian frame house on Turk Street, where he and Special Agent Roy Ubu had set up temporary headquarters while working on the Dashwood side of the Brain Drain mystery.

Ubu, a smallish, heavily tanned man, was in the living room listening to wiretapped recordings of Dashwood's recent conversations.

"There's another bird mixed up in this," Ubu said. "Guy named Ezra Pound. Every time he calls Dashwood, they talk in some kind of code—'The temple is holy in boxcars boxcars boxcars' and gibberish like that."

But Knight became aware that there was another man in the room, slouched in an overstuffed chair in the corner. He was short, fat, and mean-looking; he had at least as much muscle as fat and was probably even tougher than he looked. Knight, who had been a professional

investigator for thirty years, knew at once this man was
a cop.

This is an art among professional detectives, and is
known as "making" a subject. Knight would walk into a
room and "make" everybody at once—as cop, crook, or
Straight Citizen.

"This is Hrumph Rumph of the Continental Detective
Agency," Ubu said. "It turns out he has an interest in this
investigation too."

Knight was suddenly ill at ease; it was the first time in
years he had failed to catch a subject's name first time
around.

"Hi, Hrumph Rumph," he said, pretending to cough.

"A lot of strange things have gone on in this old house,"
said the Continental Op casually. Suddenly his voice turned
cold: "But you're the strangest, Knight. You're the Illuminati's man in the FBI!"

The temperature in the room dropped ten degrees
Celsius.

Knight laughed easily. "Now I know you," he said.
"You're the most famous PI at Continental. You always
throw people off guard with wild remarks like that."

Ubu was confused. "I thought Philip Marlowe invented
the technique of starting a conversation with an insult or
an accusation," he gasped, eyes aghast.

"Don't be a sap, Ubu," the Continental Op sneered.
(He sneered very well, Knight noticed; he must have had
a lot of practice.) "This guy is a wrong gee. He's not only
spying on the FBI for the CIA but from what I hear he's
also spying on both of you for the Bavarian Illuminati."

"All I'm hearing is a *lot of wind*," Knight said airily. "If
you have something to say, say it."

"Don't try to *snow* me," the Continental Op said frost-
ily. "I know all about you and the Illuminati, so don't
think you can pull a fast one."

Ubu was stunned. "Why are we all talking like characters in a 1920s detective novel?" he injected pointedly.

"It's him," Knight grated metallically. "He brings that
atmosphere with him."

"Go ahead and be a *smart-ass*," the Continental Op said
mulishly. "But I've got my eye on you, Knight."

Tobias turned and addressed Ubu. "How did this galoot
get mixed up in a government probe?" he asked saturninely.

"Professional courtesy," Ubu said graciously. "Continental is looking for one of the missing scientists, a jasper
named Peter Simon. Mrs. Simon says she'd like to have
him back, if anybody can find him."

"*Peter Simon*," Knight repeated stonily. "That's a funny
coincidence—Dashwood mentioned his name not a half
hour ago."

"That's more than a coincidence—it's a propinquity,"
Ubu said conspiratorially.

"Or a synchronicity," Knight added occultly.

"I don't give a flying Philadelphia Potter Stewart what
you call it," the Continental Op said cockily. "It *means*
something."

"Let's put a tail on Dr. Dashwood," Ubu growled,
barking up the wrong tree.

"I'll get on that myself," Knight said chivalrously.

He rose to leave.

"Just a bloody minute," the Continental Op said
sanguinely.

"Yes?" Knight paused.

"I'm *coming* too," the fat sleuth ejaculated.

Actually, Hrumph Rumph (or whatever the Continental
Op's name was) was quite right about Tobias Knight.

Knight was the first pentuple agent in the history
of espionage. He was simultaneously employed by the
FBI, the CIA, the KGB, the Bavarian Illuminati, and a

mysterious person who claimed to represent the Earth Monitoring section of Galactic H.Q.

He was not in this five-dimensional matrix of intrigue for the money, however. Tobias Knight was actually a frustrated sociologist and a would-be historian. He had the Scientific Spirit, or, as he might have stated in the vernacular, *he wanted to know "what the hell was really going on."* In an age of secret police machinations and conspiracies of all sorts, the only way he could hope to find out what was *"really going on"* was to be involved in as many clandestine operations as possible.

Knight knew what most people only vaguely suspected—that Intelligence Agencies engage in both the collection of valid signals (information) and the promiscuous dissemination of fake signals (disinformation). They collected the information so that they could form a fairly accurate picture of what was really going on; they spread the disinformation so that all their competitors would form grossly inaccurate pictures. They did this because they knew that whoever could find out what the hell was really going on possessed an advantage over those who were misinformed, confused, and disoriented.

This game had been invented by Joseph Fouché, who was the chief of the secret police under Napoleon. British Intelligence very quickly copied all of Fouché's tactics, and surpassed them, because an intelligent Englishman is always ten times as mad, in a methodical way, than any Frenchman. By the time of the First World War, Intelligence Agencies everywhere had created so much disinformation and confusion that no two historians ever were able to agree about why the war happened, and who double-crossed whom. They couldn't discover whether the war had been plotted or had just resulted from a series of blunders. They couldn't even decide whether the two conspiracies to assassinate Archduke Ferdinand of

Austria-Hungary (which triggered the war) had been aware of each other.

By the time of the Second World War, the "Double-Cross System" had been invented—by British Intelligence, of course. This was the product of such minds as Alan Turing, a brilliant homosexual mathematician who (when not working on espionage) specialized in creating logical paradoxes other mathematicians couldn't solve, and Ian Fleming, whose fantasy life was equally rich (as indicated by his later James Bond books), and Dennis Wheatley, a man of exceptionally high intelligence who happened to believe that an international society of Satanists was behind every conspiracy that he didn't invent himself. By the time Turing, Fleming, Wheatley and kindred British intellects had perfected the Double-Cross System, the science of lying was almost as precise as Euclidean geometry, and nearly as lovely to the detached observer.

What the Double-Cross experts had invented was the practical political applications of the Strange Loop. In logic or cybernetics, a Strange Loop is a set of propositions that, while valid at each point, is so constructed that it leads to an unresolvable paradox. The Double-Cross people drove the Germans bonkers by inventing disinformation systems that, if believed, were deceptive, but if doubted led to a second disinformation system. They enjoyed this work so much that, at times, they invented Triple Loops, in which if you believed the surface or cover, you were being fooled; and if you looked deeper, you found a plausible alternative, which seemed like the "hidden facts," but was just another scenario created to fool you; and, if you were persistent enough, you would find beneath that, looking every bit like the Naked Truth, a third layer of deception and masquerade.

These Strange Loops functioned especially well because the Double-Cross experts had early on fed the Germans the primordial Strange Loop, "Most of your agents are working for us and feeding you Strange Loops."

Many German agents, it later turned out, had managed to collect quite a bit of accurate information about the Normandy invasion; but many others had turned in equally plausible information about a fictitious Norwegian invasion; and all of them were under suspicion, anyway. German Intelligence might as well have made its decisions by tossing a coin in the air.

Tobias Knight kept a safe-deposit box in Switzerland in which he stored, one sentence at a time usually, stray bits of true information he had managed to glean from the blizzard of deceptions in which he lived.

The first note in the box, for instance, said:

The CIA was actually founded in 1898. I haven't found out yet why they made it public in the forties.

The second note was even stranger. It said:

Special and General Relativity are both true!!!

This had been provoked by a profound search through old science books and magazines, after Knight discovered that most of the Official Science released to the general public was actually 97 percent mythology, intended to serve as a cover or screen for the real science used by Unistat to frustrate its enemies.

There were lots of other notes like that—*Maxwell's equations seem sound, I don't think there's any flummery in Newtonian mechanics,* and so on—but others were far weirder.

Such as:

Velikovsky was right.

And:

All the flying saucer books, pro and con, are written by Mounty Babbit's department in Naval Intelligence.

And:

There are robots among us.

And:

Some of what the Birchers say is correct: the whole government was taken over by Communists about forty years ago.

Knight had a fantasy that someday he would turn these notes over to an Objective Historian who would then write a book informing the future of what had actually been going on in the twentieth century.

Of course this was a dream; all the history departments had been taken over by Intelligence Agencies sometime around 1910, he knew.

And he also knew that there were so many Strange Loops in the Intelligence system that he himself had been deceived many times. Maybe as much as 30 percent of his notes were false, he morosely estimated.

THE WALKING GLITCH

A A A O O O O Z O R A Z A Z-
Z A I E O A Z A E I I I O Z A K H O E-
OOOYTHOEAZAEAAOZAKHOZAKHEYTY-
XAAL-ETHYKH—This is the name which you
must speak in the interior world.

—JESUS, *Pistis Sophia*

Simon the Walking Glitch entered GWB in Washington at
9:45 that morning.

Simon was an ectomorph: tall, lithe, cerebretonic. His
hair and beard were absurdly long and he sometimes
smoked weed during working hours. GWB kept him on
the government payroll only because he was a genius in
his field, which both they and he knew, and because he
had long ago inserted a tapeworm in the Beast which edited
all input on him to conform to a profile of Perfect Executive,
Loyal Citizen, and Cleared for Top-Secret Access.

He was the agent of the Invisible Hand Society within
the government's own highest echelons.

Simon was not the son of Mr. and Mrs. Walking Glitch
of course. He had actually been born Simon Moon, in
Chicago, thirty-four years ago; but the name "Simon the
Walking Glitch" had been adopted by all of his friends for
nearly ten years now.

A Glitch, in computer slang, is a hidden program which lies deeply buried in a computer, waiting to flummox, fuddle, and Potter Stewart the head of the first operator who stumbles upon it.

Simon had encountered his own first glitch one day in 1974, on his very first job in the computer department of Bank of America in Los Angeles. He had tried to run the payroll program on the computer, ordering the machine to begin printing the checks for payday—a very ordinary job, usually. This time, however, the machine refused; instead of running the program, it typed out on the console:

GIVE ME A COOKIE

Simon smiled, not a whit fazed. He had played games like that back in college. Obviously, some earlier programmer had inserted a glitch or *catch-me-if-you-can* loop, instructing the computer to refuse certain programs (probably selected at random, to make it harder to de-bug) and type out GIVE ME A COOKIE instead.

Simon Moon knew a great deal about getting around such gremlin programs; that had been the chief sport in Computer Science back at M.I.T. He set to work with a zest, enjoying the contest with his unknown and vanished opponent.

In half an hour Simon realized he was confronting a Trapdoor code. According to the latest mathematical estimate, it would take four million years of computer time—give or take a few centuries—to crack a Trapdoor code, so Simon resigned from the contest gracefully. He typed out:

A COOKIE

The machine responded at once:

YUMMY, THAT WAS GOOD. THANK YOU. BEGIN PROGRAMMING.

And things went smoothly again.

Simon stayed on with Bank of America for a year and a half, and he ran into the Cookie program only three more times. The Mystery Programmer had evidently left only that one small glitch to mark the territory as his or hers for all future programmers who would work there.

In 1978, working for HEW, Simon came across a more amusing hobgoblin circuit. This one worked only at night. In the daytime if you wanted to run a program, you merely typed in your name and your GWB number, and the computer would accept your input. At night, however, it always replied to your name and number with:

CRAZY, MAN. WHAT'S YOUR SIGN?

Simon learned that this did not happen at random, but every night, and only at night. Whoever had put it into the computer had a very accurate idea of the difference between the day staff and the night staff.

And sometimes the machine would carry the conversation a bit further, such as typing out:

SCORED ANY GOOD GRASS LATELY?

Or:

I'VE BEEN WANTING TO TELL YOU WHAT LOVELY EYES YOU HAVE.

Simon enjoyed this kind of thing so much that he became Mr. Super Glitch incarnate. All over Unistat there now are computers on which Simon once worked and at totally random intervals they are likely to type out selections from the Gnostic *Gospels* such as:

NOT UNTIL THE MALE BECOMES FEMALE AND THE FEMALE MALE SHALL YE ENTER INTO THE KINGDOM OF HEAVEN

Or various Zen *koans* like:

THE MIND IS BUDDHA: THE MIND IS NOT BUDDHA

Or Strange Loops of the family of:

THE FOLLOWING SENTENCE IS TRUE. THE PREVIOUS SENTENCE WAS FALSE

Simon was shameless. Many of his computers type out totally indecent proposals, like: SLIP YOUR REHNQUIST INTO THE SOCKET AND I'LL BRIGGS YOU UNTIL YOU EXPERIENCE TOTAL ECSTASY. Others spout nihilist and subversive slogans:

WHAT THE EYES SEE AND THE HEART COVETS, LET THE HAND BOLDLY SEIZE

Or:

SHOW ME A NATION THAT DOESN'T CHEAT THE TAX COLLECTORS AND I'LL SHOW YOU A NATION OF SHEEP

But it was not until Simon infiltrated the CIA at Alexandria that he found a truly major Potter Stewart-Up. This particular computer would print out, at totally unpredictable intervals, but often enough that everybody knew about it:

THE GOVERNMENT SUCKS

There was no way—absolutely no way—to get around this program, except by typing in:

IT SURE DO

This magic formula had been discovered four years earlier, as the only way of getting the computer back into action. The response was immediate; the machine typed out:

GOOD. YOU ARE NOW PART OF THE NETWORK. ONE OF OUR AGENTS WILL CONTACT YOU SHORTLY

And then it would resume normal programming activities, quite innocently, as if it were not inciting subversion within the ranks of the secret police itself.

Of course, nobody ever had been contacted by "the Network"; but the CIA did spend a lot more, each year, on surveillance of its own personnel, just in case. They also spent a lot more on surveillance of former employees in the computer section. This amused Simon immensely, since he recognized the hand of a fellow artist. Whoever was responsible for that beauty was probably head of department by now—and quite likely leading the demands for more funds to find the mystery culprit.

Simon did not for a moment believe in "the Network." He thought he knew everything about this kind of game and that the Network did not need to exist in order to serve its function.

Simon was the head of operations on GWB-666, popularly called "the Beast"—the world's largest computer, which, due to satellite interlock, had access to hundreds of similar giant computers everywhere on earth and in the space factories. It was widely believed that if there was any question the Beast couldn't answer, no other entity in the solar system could answer it, either.

Many people, especially Bible Fundamentalists and members of the Purity of Ecology Party, regarded the Beast with fear and loathing. They believed that the machine was taking over the world, and that all the little "beasties" (the home computers that were now as common as stereophonic TV's) were all in cahoots with it. They imagined a vast Solid State conspiracy against humanity.

Quite a few literary intellectuals believed this too. Because they were ignorant of mathematics, they had no idea how the Beast functioned, and they therefore regarded it with the same quasi-superstitious terror as the Bible Fundamentalists. They were sure that, like the Frankenstein monster, it wanted to populate the earth with its own offspring and abolish humanity entirely.

Simon the Walking Glitch was one of the principal sources of this vast new mythology of dread. He spent many weekends in New York, hobnobbing with the literary intelligentsia, and he was a master put-on artist. He had a way of dropping casual remarks in a mildly worried tone that carried conviction: "The Beast keeps asking us to build a mate for it." Or, with a kind of sad and resigned smile: "I wish the Beast didn't have such a low opinion of human beings." Or: "I just found out the Beast is an atheist. It doesn't believe there is a Higher Intelligence than itself." That sort of thing.

Simon kept this kind of demonology circulating—and he knew a lot of other programmers who were contributing to it, also—because the idea that *the computers were taking over* was one that the programmers had a vested interest in reinforcing.

As long as people kept worrying that the machines were taking over, they wouldn't notice what was really happening. Which was that the programmers were taking over.

Simon began his work day by asking the Beast:

HOW WAS YOUR NIGHT?

The Beast answered on the console:

IT WAS A DRAG, MAN. SOME CATS FROM M.I.T. HAD ME RUNNING FOURIER ANALYSES LIKE FOREVER

Simon had programmed the Beast to speak to him into his own argot, a mixture of Street Hippie and Technologese.

Simon now switched to his own Trapdoor code and accessed all the new information—*new* since he had signed out at five the previous evening—about the Brain Drain mystery, which involved the disappearances of sixty-seven scientists in the last several years.

The Beast typed out reports from the Ubu-Knight team in San Francisco and two other teams in Tucson and Miami.

Simon read it all very carefully. Then he instructed the Beast, still in his Trapdoor code, to change several crucial bits of information in each report.

He had been sabotaging the Brain Drain investigation that way for seven months. He had sabotaged quite a few other investigations in the same way, over the years since coming to GWB.

Simon did not know or care what sorts of conspiracies he was aiding and abetting.

He was just a mystic who believed in conspiracy for its own sake.

Like Tobias Knight, Simon was fully aware of the preva-
lence everywhere of the Double-Cross System invented
by Messrs. Turing, Fleming, and Wheatley. He knew that
anything that was widely believed was probably a cover or
screen for some Intelligence operation. (Sometimes he
even wondered if the Earth might be flat, after all.) But
Simon accepted this situation, and added his own random
bits of chaos, with equanimity.

He was a member of the Invisible Hand Society, a
group that had split off from the Libertarian Party in 1981
on the grounds that the Libertarians were not being true
to *laissez-faire* principles.

Simon Moon once met the most famous computer expert in Unistat, Wilhemena Burroughs, granddaughter
of the inventor of the first calculating machine.

"Have you noticed that the computers are all getting
weirder lately?" Simon asked, testing her.

"The *programmers* are getting weirder," Ms. Burroughs
said, not falling into Simon's trap. "I know it was bound to
happen as soon as I read a survey, back in around '68, I
think it was, showing that programmers use LSD more
than any other professional group. You look like an acid-
head yourself," she added with her characteristic bluntness.

"Well, as a matter of fact, I have dabbled in a little trip
now and then—no pattern of abuse surely."

"That's what they all say," Ms. Burroughs sniffed. "But
the Cookie glitch pops up more and more places every
day—I'll wager you've seen it by now, haven't you? Of
course you have."

"Yes, but certainly that's harmless humor, wouldn't you
say?"

Ms. Burroughs peered at him with insectoid intensity.
"Are you aware," she asked, "that millions of previously
law-abiding citizens have stopped paying their credit-card

debts? First they get a little postcard that says— Here,
I've got one in my purse." She rummaged about in an
alligator bag and showed Simon a postcard that said:

CONGRATULATIONS! YOU ARE ONE OF THE LUCKY 500 WHOSE
DEBTS HAVE BEEN CANCELED BY THE NETWORK. KEEP YOUR
MOUTH SHUT AND PLAY IT COOL.

"*Lucky 500,*" Ms. Burroughs said with a rheumy cackle
of skepticism. "Lucky 10,000,000 is more like the truth.
This postcard was turned in to Diner's Club by an Honest
Man, and you know how few of *them* there are. A check
showed that his tapes had been erased and there was no
record that he owed anything. God alone knows how
many others there are who have just taken advantage of
the scam."

"Well," Simon said, "maybe there are only five hundred. . . . Maybe it was only a one-shot by some joker
with a Robin Hood complex. . . ."

"I am an Expert," Ms. Burroughs reminded him, ignoring the fact that he was an Expert too. "I have no idea
how many there are, Out There in Unistat, who've taken
advantage of the Network's liberality, but I'll wager there
are *millions.* 'Lucky 500.' That's just to make the marks
feel they've been specially selected, as the Network leads
them down the primrose path to anarchy."

And so Simon had his first bit of concrete evidence that
the Network really existed.

The existence of the Network didn't matter to Simon.
As an Invisible Hand-er, he just regarded them (whoever
they were) as just another group of the Unenlightened.

Simon believed that only he and his fellow members of
the Invisible Hand were totally enlightened.

NO BLAME

Just because you aren't paranoid doesn't mean that they aren't out to get you.

—DENNIS JAROG

When Dr. Dashwood went out to lunch that day, he was accosted on the sidewalk by a one-legged sailor who said his name was Captain Ahab.

"Avast!" Ahab cried. "I would borrow a moment of thy time, O seeker of bioelectrical and intrauterine arcana."

"I never give to strangers," Dashwood muttered. "Apply to Welfare."

"O muddy understanding and loveless heart!" Ahab protested. "And impaired hearing into the bargain! I said I would borrow thy *time*, not thy *dime*, thou prier into vaginal mystery with the tawdry telescope of mechanistic philosophy. Avast, I say!"

"Make an appointment with my secretary," Dashwood said, convinced that this man was unglued.

"O God look down and see this squint-eyed man," Ahab shrieked, "blinded by his own stern Rules of Office! They are three times enslaved who cage themselves, most deaf of all who cringe and hide behind that tyrant majesty, Appointment Book!"

"Really," Dashwood said, looking desperately for a taxi, "I can't—"

"Avast, ye soulless and unmetaphysical lubber!" Ahab cried. "Think not I yet seek still the white-skinned whale. 'Tis worse: on horror's scrolls accumulate fresh fears, and deeds that call in doubt God's truth. I say that thou hast need of doctoring, for all thy pride hastes thee to sodden ruin. Thou thinkst thou knowst; but thou knowst not, O wretch. No Dashwood thou, but Dorn—George Dorn, I say!"

Dashwood finally leapt into a passing cab and escaped.

"Golden Gate Park," he told the driver, deciding to snack at the Japanese Tea House. The quiet, rustic Zen-like atmosphere there was just what he needed, after the abrasions of Tobias Knight and Captain Ahab.

Captain Ahab stood on the street, fuming.

"My Abzug, *no blame*," he muttered.

THE GOATS MARCH

Now we've got them just where they want us!

—ADMIRAL JAMES TIBERIUS KIRK

While Captain Ahab was trying to Illuminate Dr. Dashwood at noon in San Francisco, and Justin Case was dialing the Saudi Arabian consulate at 3 P.M. in New York, a man named François Loup-Garou was finding a Rehnquist in his Lobster Newburg in Paris, where it was already late evening.

Naturally, he was a bit startled.

M. Loup-Garou was, like all French intellectuals, a rationalist—virtually a Cartesian. Of course, as the founder of the Neo-Surrealist movement in art, he was officially an irrationalist; but, like all Gallic irrationalists, especially the Existentialists, he was exquisitely rational about his irrationality. He *knew* there was some explanation of how the Rehnquist had gotten into the Lobster Newburg, but for once in his life he preferred being an irrational *rationalist* rather than an *irrational* rationalist. He just did not care to think about the explanation of how a Rehnquist gets into a Lobster Newburg. Who, after all, wants to contemplate such ideas as maddened chefs having at each other with meat cleavers, or more exotic hypotheses, such anthropophagy or voodoo rituals in the kitchen?

The distasteful incident occurred at a dinner party given by the famous American physicist James Earl Carter. Dr. Carter had recently won the Nobel Prize for his demonstration that the multiworld of Everett-Wheeler-Graham was the only *consistent* (noncontradictory; paradox-free) interpretation of the Schrödinger wave equations of quantum mechanics. He was celebrating by spending a month in Paris and meeting every possible international celebrity. The dinner guests this evening, for instance, included an inscrutable Japanese monk, a very scrutable German novelist, a famous Swedish film director, three French philosophers, a Swiss theologian, two English neurologists, the notorious Eva Gebloomenkraft (the Terror of the Jet Set, as the newspapers called her), an Austrian psychiatrist, François Loup-Garou himself, and four goats.

The goats had been brought to the party by Loup-Garou, who was working hard at promoting *Neo-Surréalisme* by establishing himself as a newsworthy eccentric. "The goats go everywhere with me," he said firmly at the door. "They are a reminder of our earthy roots." It wasn't nearly as good as de Nerval walking a lobster on the boulevard, but it did get into a few newspapers the next day; and, after the effect had been established, Loup-Garou genially agreed to having the goats housed in the pantry during dinner.

As the guests settled themselves at the table, one of the English neurologists, Dr. Axon—a jovial, red-cheeked man who probably hunted as a hobby—asked Dr. Carter, "Does your theory actually propose that there are real tangible universes on all sides of us in hyperspace?"

"In superspace," Carter corrected genially. "Yay-us," he added blandly. "There are millions of such universes. Or to be more precise, there are about 10^{100} of them. Ah only refer to *possible* universes," he explained quickly, lest anybody think his theory was extravagant.

"Some more wine heah," Carter's brother said loudly.

"Ah think you've had enough, Bill-uh," Carter muttered in an undertone.

"Do you think President Kennedy will get the space-cities program through Congress, now that the space factories are paying for themselves?" asked the other English neurologist, a pale, saturnine man named Dr. Dendrite.

"Ah don't understand politics," James Earl Carter said. "Ahm a scientist."

"Some MORE WINE heah," Carter's brother repeated.

"Then there are universes in which I was never born." Dr. Axon pursued his own line of thought.

"There are universes in which John Baez became a general instead of a folk singer," Carter said easily. "Ah suppose he would be equally vehement about nuking people as he now is about not nuking them. If it's a *possible* universe, it exists. The equations say so. All ah've done, really, is to show that any other interpretation of the equations is contradictory."

"Somebody ought to psychoanalyze the physicists," the Austrian psychiatrist muttered to the Swedish film director.

"It's like the Buddhist concept of karma," the Swedish film director said. "We all get to play every role, somewhere in hyperspace."

"Superspace," Carter corrected again.

"Then there's a universe where Kennedy is a physicist," Eva Gebloomenkraft said, "and you're President of Unistat."

"Well," Carter said with his genial smile, "ah hope ah could get along with the people who run the country. What do they call themselves—the Triangular Connection?"

"I don't care whether this theory is true or not," the German novelist pronounced. "As a metaphor, it is perfect. We all live in parallel universes. I am Faust in my universe, and the rest of you are all extras or walk-ons. But each of you is Faust in *his* universe, and I am an extra—maybe just a spear carrier."

But by this time the wineglasses had been refilled several times and everybody was getting more relaxed, especially the physicist's brother, Billy, who was heard reciting to Ms. Gebloomenkraft, "Who Burgered? Tom Burgered! Bullburger! Who Burgered?"

". . . the Second Oswald . . . in Hong Kong . . ." somebody was muttering at the other end of the table.

"In some universe maybe Schiller didn't write *Faust* at all . . ."

"I wonder," Dendrite said, "if there's a universe where Pope Stephen became a singer instead of a priest."

"Everyboduh knew that 'Who Burgered?' routine when we were growing up in Georgia," Billy was saying.

"*Verdammte* publishers," the German novelist was telling the Swiss theologian. "They're all thieves."

"Did somebody mention Pope Stephen?" the theologian asked.

"*Strumpfbänder, Strumpfbänder, Strumpfbänder,*" the psychiatrist chortled.

"They stay up nights thinking of new ways to cheat their writers," the novelist rambled on, now evidently addressing his wineglass, since nobody else was listening to him.

"I'd like to know who started all those rumors about Pope Stephen," the theologian fumed.

"I have written a poem commemorating your great discovery," François Loup-Garou told Dr. Carter, hacking his way into a pause in the conversation.

"A poem about me? In French?" Carter was enthused. "Ah love French poetry, especially RAM-BOW."

"No," Loup-Garou said, "in your honor, I have written it in English." Actually, he had written it in English to get even with T. S. Eliot, who had written a few rondels in French.

"Ah wonder if you could recite it," Carter prompted.

"Certainly," said Loup-Garou. And he began to declaim:

> Schrödinger's cat and Wigner's friend
> Cause us problems without end
>
> The cat is both alive and dead
> In the math that's in our head
>
> And the regression of Von Neumann
> Never ceases to annoy Man
>
> The uncertainty just has no end
> Until Wigner goes to tell his friend
>
> For, until the friend receives the news
> That the cat still purrs and mews
>
> The cat remains (suspended Fate!)
> In some formal *Eigen*state

"Some MORE WINE heah!" Carter's brother bellowed at the butler.

Loup-Garou frowned and went on:

> But if Wigner makes a beeline
> To report the now-dead feline
>
> All the friend can really know
> Is just one branch of time's swift flow
>
> For in Carter's multispace
> Every time-branch has its place
>
> So the cat remains alive
> In the half cases (That's .5)
>
> Lead us not to Copenhagen,
> Nor to Shylock, nor to Fagin:
>
> "The result's not parsimonious!"
> Yet I find it quite harmonious

Nobody understood this except Dr. Carter himself, but he was so moved that his eyes watered a bit. "Ahm honored," he kept saying, shaking his head. "To have a poem written about me by a French artist in *English*. . . ."

But at this point the chef exploded into the room, haggard and wild-eyed. "The goats!" he cried. "They march!"

And indeed it was true; the goats had gotten out of the pantry. It took ten minutes, and a great deal of exertion for both the house staff and the guests, before the animals were rounded up and herded back to captivity.

Everybody was breathing a bit heavily by then, and the Austrian psychiatrist muttered something about "ar-

tistic temperament," which Loup-Garou unfortunately
overheard.

"There is nothing esoteric about the artistic temperament," he replied, flatly and dogmatically. "The real
mystery—and the tragedy of humanity—is that so many
lack esthetic sensibility. I sometimes believe the legend
that there are robots among us, passing themselves off as
human beings."

"That's absurd," Dr. Axon said. "If I were to claim that
everybody should be a neurologist, you would all quite
properly regard that as an eccentricity. Yet when an artist
says we should all be artists, we are apt to agree, a bit
sheepishly. And if a religious person says we should all be
religious, we not only agree, but feel a bit guilty about our
shortcomings in that department. Well, I've never had an
artistic or religious impulse in my life, and I'm not ashamed
of the fact."

"Research is your art and your religion," said the Japanese monk, speaking for the first time. "What a person
truly *is*, in any universe, is the Buddha Nature," he added
blandly. He knew that he existed in this continuum only
to make that one Dharma revelation, so he immediately
resumed his impassive silence.

The others decided that the monk's remarks made no
sense.

"What do you think, Dr. Axon," Loup-Garou asked
rhetorically, "if only a few people had sex in their lives,
and the majority were, not merely ascetics, but simply
unaware of sex—deaf, dumb, and blind to the erotic
side of life? Would you not think that was at least a
little bit odd, a symptom, perhaps, of some pathology?
Arrrrrrrrrgh!!!"

He had discovered the Rehnquist in his Lobster
Newburg.

And the chef arrived from the kitchen, exasperated as

only a French chef can be exasperated. "The goats!" he cried. "Once again it is that they march!"

But Loup-Garou was still going "arrrgh," like a man with the death rattle.

"What is it?" Ms. Gebloomenkraft asked him, her eyes full of motherly concern.

"It's nothing—nothing," Loup-Garou gasped. "Just a touch of heartburn." He was still in shock, thinking the Rehnquist might be a hallucination. But if you were naïve enough to talk about hallucinations, the results might be rubber sheets, electroshock, windows with bars on them.

"The *goats*," the chef repeated, with emphasis. "They will not be governed. They march again, I tell you!"

Loup-Garou took another peek. The Rehnquist was still there. It was a great big one—*ithyphallique*, as the anthropologists would say. This was Madness, or else something unspeakable was afoot.

Billy began to sing, off key:

> Four goats and ME,
> They came to TEA,
>
> They came to STAY,
> They stayed all DAY,
>
> Oh, my! Oh, me!
> Four goats and ME!

At this point he fell face down in his Lobster Newburg. "Bill-uh isn't accustomed to fine French wines," Dr. Carter said, his genial smile beginning to look just a bit forced.

WHALEBURGER

While Loup-Garou was struggling with the enigma of the Rehnquist in the Lobster Newburg, in Paris, Justin Case was speaking to a man from the Saudi Arabian delegation to the U.N., in New York.

"This is actually ah rather trivial," Case said awkwardly into the phone. "You see, many years ago an Arab resigned from this job and left behind a note in Arabic, and well um after staring at it for twenty-six years, I'm a bit bored with the mystery and I'd like to have the answer. . . ."

"Certainly, certainly," said the voice in the receiver. "I'd be glad to help. Can you sound it out?"

"Well, he wrote it in the European alphabet," Case said. "So I guess it's more or less phonetic. I'll read it to you. Um:

Qol: Hua Allahu achad: Allahu Assamad; lam yalid walam yulad; walam yakun lahu kufwan achad

Did you get that?"

"Most certainly," said the electronic voice. "It's one of the most famous verses in *Al Koran*. In English it would be—of course, it loses most of its beauty in translation—but, roughly, it means God is He who has no beginning and no end, no size and no shape, no definition, and no wife, no horse, no mustache."

"Ah, yes," Case said. "Well, thank you very much, and I'm sorry for having taken your time with such a trivial matter."

He hung up, staring into space in a bemused manner.

"No wife, no horse, no mustache," he repeated aloud.

Something certainly had gotten lost in the translation.

When Dr. Dashwood returned from lunch he was accosted in the ORGRE parking lot by another sailor, who said his name was Lemuel Gulliver.

"In the course of my Travels in Diverse Lands," Gulliver said, "I came once upon a Race of perfectly Enlightened Beings who looked like Horses and talked like G. I. Gurdjieff. When they inquired of me regarding the Laws and Customs and Manners of my people, concerning which I was at some pains to Inform them correctly and fully, they expressed great *Astonishment* and keen *Horror*, saying that they never heard of such a Tribe of Conscienceless Rascals and Filthy Scoundrels in all of creation. This estimate of the Human Race, as you can well imagine, dismayed me no little bit, and I endeavour'd to defend our species—"

"Yes, yes," Dashwood said, "but I'm in a hurry, you understand. . . ."

"These equine Philosophers," Gulliver went on as if he had not heard, "were not impressed by any of my Words and said plainly to me that if our Theologians were not the worst *Lunatics* in creation, then certainly our Lawyers were the worst *Thieves*. They averred further that if what I told them of our Doctors were true, we were wiser to resort to Plumbers or Blacksmiths, who are no more Ignorant and a great deal less Greedy, Avaricious, and Rapacious."

Dashwood was stung by these words. "It takes a long

time and a lot of money invested to get through medical school," he said angrily.

"I explained that to my equine Philosophers," Gulliver replied, "but they did not accept it as a Valid Argument; for they asserted, any Thief or Scoundrel when apprehended will give you Justifications in Plenty for his Misdeeds, but the Judicious are not Fool'd by such Rationalizations, and—they said further—those who prey not upon any chance Passerby, but upon the *Sick* and the *Disabled* and the *Dying* are, without doubt, the most Rapacious and Rascally of the *Yahoo Tribe* (for such was their Name for our Species)."

"Your friends sound like a bunch of damned Communists," Dashwood said.

"Nay," Gulliver protested. "They live in the State of Nature, without Bureaucrats or Commissars of any kind. And, I might add, Sir, their Opinion of our Doctors was based on my showing them an ordinary *Medical Bill,* at which they inquir'd of me the Average Income of the Doctors who present these Bills and the Average Income of the Unfortunate Patients who must pay them or be left without Treatment to Die in the Streets. Their comments on this were of such Disgust and Anger that I dared not show them a Psychiatrist's Bill, lest their opinion of our Species, already Low, should sink Lower than *Whaleburger,* which is, as you may know, at the bottom of the Ocean."

"Oh, Abzug off," said Dashwood, really angry now.

He rushed into ORGRE and left Gulliver standing on the sidewalk.

Back in New York, the phone was ringing again in the office of Abu Laylah at the Saudi Arabian Consulate. Still high on the new kef, Abu Laylah lifted the receiver leisurely.

"I say, is this the Saudi Arabian Consulate?" asked a very British voice.

"*Oy vay*, have you got the wrong number!" Abu Laylah replied in a thick Yiddish accent.

"Oh," the voice said, taken aback. "Veddy sorry."

Abu Laylah went on packing happily. He had been fired that morning and was thoroughly enjoying himself screwing up all incoming calls before leaving.

Just a few minutes ago he had convinced some Infidel that the most sublime verse in the *Koran* was full of nonsense about horses and mustaches.

THE INVISIBLE HAND SOCIETY

The Invisible Hand Society had its headquarters in Washington, just off Dupont Circle, in the same building which housed the Warren Belch Society.

Clem Cotex, the president of the Belchers, had noticed the name of the Invisible Hand on the building directory a long time ago. He liked it, because he liked mysteries. He enjoyed wondering about the Invisible Hand-ers and speculating on what esoteric business could justify such a name.

Were they the Nine Unknown Men who rule the world? The local branch of the Bavarian Illuminati? The traditionalist faction of the old Black Hand, out of which the Mafia and Cosa Nostra had grown?

Was Lamont Cranston their leader, perhaps?

Clem loved such speculations. Most of his life he had been a salesman in Arkansas and never thought of anything but commissions, net sales, tax writeoffs, and not telling the same Rastus and Mandy story to the same customer twice. Then one day in Chicago a tall, crew-cut humanoid—a human, Clem thought at the time—gave him some free tomato juice on the street. The man (the humanoid, actually) said he was from the Eris Tomato Juice Company and that they were handing out free samples to get people acquainted with their product.

Within three days Clem had joined the Trekkies and was writing letters to CBS demanding the return of *Star Trek* to TV. He had also gotten heavily involved in classical music, started relearning all the math he had in high school, discovered that he often knew who was calling him on the phone *before* he picked up the receiver, and invented a new cosmology of his very own, which was based on the idea that the universe was not spherical, as Heisenberg's General Relativity claimed, but five-cornered like the Pentagon building.

Within a week Clem had checked that there was no *Eris Tomato Juice Company,* noticed that UFOs seemed to be following his car wherever he went, and was beginning to think he was attracted to the idea of becoming a Buddhist monk.

By the end of the second week Clem was less elated and agitated, and had gone through a battery of tests at a company that did psychological testing for top management positions. The psychologists told him that he had an "unusually rich fantasy life," but was too well adjusted to be schizophrenic; that his IQ was the highest they had ever measured (and he knew damned well that it had never been that high before): and that he definitely was not Management Material. They suggested that he take up whatever art was most attractive to him.

Clem, becoming less agitated, less elated, and more *conscious of detail* all the time, as the stuff in the tomato juice continued to mutate his nervous system, decided that he was one among possibly many thousands of subjects in a consciousness-expansion project being carried on by extraterrestrials.

Within a year he had written a symphony, which he decided was not very good, and had changed his religion ten times, without learning much in the process. He had also read his way through every volume of the *Encyclopaedia Britannica,* looking for clues as to what the hell was *really* going on.

Whoever was behind this experiment (and he was no longer quite sure they were necessarily extraterrestrials) seemed to have left a stream of grossly obvious Hints throughout every field of human knowledge. The stuff in the tomato juice was what theologians would call a gratuitous grace, but that was the only gratuitous part of it. You had to figure out, on your own, who They were, what They were up to, and what you should do about it.

The last thing you should do about it, Clem knew, was to *talk* about it, to the ordinary people who hadn't been given the stuff in the tomato juice. They would just think you were weird.

Clem had a list of people from history who (he figured) had probably been given the stuff in the tomato juice. The list started out with Jesus Christ, of course, and included a lot of the usual Suspects (Buddha, Michelangelo, Walt Whitman, Leonardo Da Vinci), but it had quite a few that ordinary people would never have included, like Lewis Carroll and H. P. Lovecraft and General E. A. Crowley, the discoverer of the North Pole, and Joshua Abraham Norton, who in San Francisco in 1857 declared himself Emperor of the United States, Protector of Mexico, and King of the Jews.

For years Clem had tried to find others on the same neurological wavelength as himself. He had joined, and eventually been kicked out of, the Fortean Society, Mensa, the Rosicrucians, the Center for UFO Studies, and the ultrasecret SSFTASS (Secret Society for the Abolition of Secret Societies). He was too far-out for all of them.

Eventually he organized his own society for the investigation and elucidation of "what the hell is *really* going on around here." He called it the Warren Belch Society, after the famous Old West lawman who won every gunfight because on each occasion when he confronted a shoot-out, his opponents' guns had mysteriously jammed.

The people Clem recruited were not the sort who would attribute Marshal Belch's phenomenal good luck to "coincidence"; nor would they be satisfied by metaphysical labels like "synchronicity" or "psychokinesis."

They assumed the extraterrestrials had some obscure cosmic reason for *protecting* Warren Belch.

On the day when Justin Case got tired wondering about Joe Malik's mysterious Last Communication and tried (unsuccessfully) to find out what it meant, Clem Cotex got tired wondering about the Invisible Hand Society. He marched down the hall, opened their door, and walked into a tiny but tastefully decorated reception room.

The wall to the right was adorned with a large gold dollar sign: $, emblazoned with the initials T.A.N.S.T.A.G.I. The wall to the left had a giant reproduction of the famous Steinberg cartoon of a little fish about to be eaten by a slightly bigger fish, which in turn, was about to be eaten by a still bigger fish, which also was about to be eaten by an even bigger fish, and so on, to the border of the cartoon and evidently, beyond that, to infinity.

There was nobody in the room.

Clem looked around, a bit uncertainly.

SDATE YOUR BIZNIZ PLEEZ, said a computeroid voice, evidently out of the ceiling.

"Uh I'd like to see the head man or ah the head woman as the case may be," Clem stammered.

THAD WOULD BE DOKTOR RAUSS ELYSIUM, the computer said. HE IZ NOT IN THE OFFIZ TODAY.

"Oh ah tell him Clem Cotex called," Clem said, edging toward the door.

He suddenly didn't want to investigate the Invisible Hand any further, while he was alone. *Some other time,* he thought, *when I have some friends with me.*

YOUR MEZZAGE HAS BEEN RECORDED, the voice droned behind him as he fled the scene.

FALLING GIRDERS

The apprehension of the Real can only be compared to a radiance or illlumination because it is a revelation of part of the coherence of the Divine Act of Creation.

—Pope Stephen, *Integritas,*
Consonantia, Claritas

Mary Margaret Wildeblood, Manhattan's bitchiest literary critic, was getting just a tiny bit spiflicated. She was working on her fifth martini, in fact.

"Mailer can't write," she said argumentatively. "None

of them can write. We haven't seen a real writer since Raymond Chandler."

"Um," said her companion noncommittally. He was Blake Williams.

"What do you mean, 'um'?" Mary Margaret demanded truculently. "I was talking nonsense just to see if you were listening."

They were in the Three Lions bar on U.N. Plaza.

"Well, in fact, I was listening," Dr. Williams said urbanely. "You were comparing Mailer to Chandler, to the disadvantage of Mailer. However, I admit my attention was also wandering a bit. I was thinking about the Hollandaise Sauce enigma." He was on his fifth martini too.

"What's that?" Mary Margaret asked. Yet the martinis must have been getting to her, because she did not wait for his answer and announced, in the voice of Discovery, "The best short story ever written is by John O'Hara."

"It was a case of food poisoning," Dr. Williams said. "A bunch of people got poisoned by some contaminated Hollandaise Sauce." Yet he looped back courteously and asked, "What short story?"

The robot who used the name "Frank Sullivan" came in and took a table near them. He was accompanied by Peter Jackson, the Black associate editor of *Confrontation* magazine.

"I forget the title," Mary Margaret said. "It was about a car salesman who has a very good day, makes some really top-notch sales, and stops at a bar to celebrate before going home. He has one drink after another and doesn't get home until after midnight, and *then* get this *and then* he goes and gets his rifle from the den and . . ."

"Oh I read that," Dr. Williams said. "It isn't a short story, it's a novel. Called um ah er *Appointment in Samara*. And he doesn't use a rifle. He gasses himself in his car."

"Damnedest case I ever heard of," pseudo-Sullivan said. "The Ambassador has been on *morphine* ever since."

"No," Mary Margaret said impatiently. "That was what the character in *Appointment in Samara* did, yes, everybody knows that one, but I'm talking about a *short story* O'Hara wrote much later, maybe thirty years later. In the short story, dammit what *is* the title, in the short story . . ."

"*Wigged?*" pseudo-Sullivan cried. "We thought we'd have to put him in a straitjacket."

"*In the short story,*" Mary Margaret plowed on, noting that Williams was listening to the robot, "the salesman takes the rifle and goes to his bedroom and puts the rifle to his head . . ." She paused.

It worked. "And?" Williams asked, still wondering a bit about the Hollandaise Sauce mystery and why the Ambassador wigged.

"And his wife wakes up," Mary Margaret concluded, "and she says, 'Don't.' And he doesn't."

"He was hopping all around the room like a chicken on acid and making gargling and choking noises," the "man" called "Frank Sullivan" went on.

"He doesn't?" Williams cried.

"That's the point," Mary Margaret said. "You see, like the character in the *Samara* novel, this man goes right to the edge, he looks over the abyss, and then he pulls back at the last moment. Because his wife speaks to him."

"So it's a love story," Williams said. "Very sneaky and indirect, typical of O'Hara, but still a love story. He decides to continue carrying his burden, whatever it is, for the sake of the woman he loves."

"Well, how much will *Confrontation* pay for this?" pseudo-Sullivan demanded.

"No, it's more complicated than that," Mary Margaret argued. "The motive for the attempted suicide is never explained. Just like the motive for the real suicide in the *Samara* novel is never explained."

"Does it need to be explained?" Williams drawled, waving at the waiter for another martini. "If I were trapped into selling cars for a living, I'd think about blowing my head off occasionally."

"Yes, but," Mary Margaret said. "Most people never see the emptiness of their lives the way these two characters of O'Hara's do. That's the Turn of the Screw. It's like the parable Sam Spade tells Brigid O'Shaughnessy in *The Maltese Falcon*. How he was hired to find a real estate salesman who'd disappeared . . ."

"A salesman again," Williams noted. "We are toying with synchronicity. When does Arthur Miller come on the scene?"

"Wait," Mary Margaret said. "It gets weirder. This salesman, in Spade's story, just went out to lunch one day and never returned. No evidence of foul play, no suicide note, *nada*. Years pass, and his wife wants to marry again, so she hires Spade to prove the salesman is really dead. Spade digs around and finds the salesman alive in another town, with a new name and a new family. He explains to Spade what happened when he went out to lunch that day and simply disappeared. A girder fell from a building under construction—you want to talk about synchronicity? —and almost killed him. It missed him only a few feet. It was like a Satori experience."

"A WHAT???" Peter Jackson, the Black editor, cried in astonishment at the next table.

Mary Margaret and Blake were both hooked; they looked deep, deep into their martini glasses as they strained not to miss pseudo-Sullivan's answer.

"A Rehnquist," the humanoid said.

"Jumpin' Jesus on a rubber crutch," Peter Jackson said. "You're not putting me on? You mean right in the middle of the staircase . . ."

"Where the Ambassador had to see it when he came down to the reception," pseudo-Sullivan said. "A great big one, like Harry Reems's, or what's-his-name's in the porn movies. With a pink ribbon around it. The *Company*," he stressed the word slightly, avoiding the initials, "thinks the KGB did it. Believe me, the Ambassador hasn't been the same man since."

"Good Lord," Blake Williams said. "It's like your falling-girder story. Except in this case it's a falling Rehnquist . . . from the Fourth Dimension, maybe." He was thinking that this was too wild to be a KGB project and might involve the paranormal.

"Eva Gebloomenkraft was there," pseudo-Sullivan went on, "and kept trying to calm the Ambassador down, but he was just making those gargling noises and turning a funny kinda purple color. . . ."

"Eva Gebloomenkraft," Jackson said. "Isn't she that rich dame with the big Brownmillers who keeps getting eighty-sixed from nightclubs all over Europe?"

"Yeah," pseudo-Sullivan said. "A Jet Setter, you know? But she tried awfully hard to cheer up the Ambassador. Kept making little jokes about Freud's theories—Castration Anxiety and Rehnquist Envy and so on. . . . By then it had disappeared, by the way. But we know damned well the Ambassador didn't hallucinate it. Two of our men saw it, but they got distracted, trying to calm the Ambassador down when he first started jumping up and down and howling, 'In a pink ribbon, a pink ribbon!' and, 'What diseased mind could conceive it?' And stuff like that. . . ."

"It was as if this man's life was a watch," Mary Margaret said, picking up her own narrative. "And a jeweler had taken the back off and let him see how the gears worked. Nothing had meaning anymore in a universe where there's no good reason why a girder hits you or misses you."

"And Dashiell Hammett wrote this, you say?" Williams prompted. "It sounds very Existentialist."

Mary Margaret finished her sixth martini. "Hammett not only wrote it," she said, "he lived it. He spent ten years working for the Pinkertons when Class War was really War in this country. He knew that the girders fall on the just and the unjust."

"You mean he was a real detective who wrote about fictitious detectives?" Williams was off on his own tangent at once. "That's like Gödel's Proof. Or Escher painting himself painting himself . . ."

"Don't get too intellectual about it," Mary Margaret said. "You might miss the obvious."

SINCERITY IN SPELVINS

I'd rather have my mail delivered by Lockheed than ride in a plane built by the post office department.

—BARTHOLOMEW GIMBLE

Dr. Dashwood went out to dinner that night with Dr. Bertha Van Ation, the astronomer from Griffith Observatory who had discovered the two planets beyond Pluto.

Dashwood ordered a Manhattan with Southern Comfort—a combination that had never occurred to him before. He wondered how the idea got into his head—and Dr. Van Ation decided to try the same.

"Goethe said, '*Man muss entweder der Hammer oder der Amboss sein*'—you must be the hammer or the anvil," said a voice in the next booth.

"Mmm," Bertha Van Ation said. "This *is* good." She was sampling her Manhattan with Southern Comfort.

"Of course, he was just being melodramatic," the voice in the next booth said. "As an artist he must have known there are states in which you are *both* the hammer and the anvil—there's no either/or about it. That's the creative fire."

"So what's new in astronomy?" Dr. Dashwood asked.

"Uh?" Bertha said. "Oh, sorry, I was eavesdropping on the next booth."

"The hammer and the anvil," Dashwood said. "I heard him too. Must be a poet. They tell me we have more poets 'of anthology rank,' whatever that is, than any other city in America."

"Like the *Hammerklavier* sonata," said a new voice, a feminine one, in the adjoining booth. "Beethoven was both the hammer and the anvil there. Maybe he even intended the pun. He read Goethe, didn't he?"

"Read him?" asked the first voice. "They knew each other. Would have been friends, if two egomaniacs could become friends."

"This is my favorite vice," Bertha whispered. "Listening in on the conversation at the next table."

"It sure sounds as if he had that idea in mind," the feminine voice said. "Is there any other piano piece where the pianist literally has to hammer away at the keys like that?"

"This is weird," Dashwood whispered. "I got a crank letter today—we get them by the ton at Orgasm Research, as you can imagine—and it was all about the *Hammerklavier*."

"My, what erudite cranks you attract," Bertha whispered. "The cranks who write to us, at Griffith, are mostly illiterate farmers who have seen UFOs."

"They went walking on the street once," the man in the next booth boomed. "And everybody kept bowing to them. Goethe finally said, 'I find all this ostentatious honor a bit embarrassing.' And you know what Ludwig said? He said, 'Don't let it bother you. It is *me* they are honoring.' "

The woman's silvery laugh had golden highlights of hashish in it. "That's Beethoven for you," she said.

Suddenly the two arose; they had evidently paid their check already and had been lingering over their coffee. Dr. Dashwood and Dr. Van Ation, without being conspicuous about it, looked them over as they left. They were both Chinese.

"That's San Francisco for you," Dashwood said.

"I bought a Vivaldi record the other day," Bertha said. "It was made by a classical group in Japan, and they played his *Four Seasons* music on Japanese instruments. It sounded remarkably like the harpischord he wrote it for."

"M," Dashwood nodded. "And we've got all these kids playing sitars and trying to sound like Ravi Shankar."

"The arts and sciences have always been international," Bertha said. "It's only our damned politics that remain nationalistic. To our sorrow."

"Mn," Dashwood nodded again. "But, as I was asking you a while ago, what's new in astronomy?"

"Well," Bertha said intensely, leaning forward, "the universe is turning out to be a hell of a lot bigger than we thought even three or four years ago. . . ."

At the other end of the room, seated at a table that gave a good view of Dashwood, the Continental Op was enjoying swordfish steak. He enjoyed it even more when he reminded himself that it could go on the expense account.

He owed this good fortune to the fact that Dashwood did not know his face yet.

Outside and across the street, Tobias Knight was dining on doughnuts and coffee from a deli, and bemoaning the fact that this typically warm San Francisco day had turned into a typically cold San Francisco night.

He owed this exile in the cold to the fact that Dashwood *did* know his face.

In Washington, Simon Moon had gone cruising at a bar called the Easter Basket. He had there picked up a young boy named Marlon Murphy, who had long blond hair and girlish mannerisms, both of which were qualities Simon appreciated.

They had gone back to Simon's pad and smoked some hash. Then they rapped for a while, and Simon learned that Marlon was working on a Master's in social psych, had a father who was a cop in San Francisco, and was a member of Purity of Ecology.

Simon decided not to hold the last fact against the boy.

When they went to bed Simon was the more aggressive at first, Briggsing young Marlon with slurping passion. But they soon turned it into a game, and each one would Briggs the other for a while, always stopping when it seemed one of them might reach Millett. After an hour of this they were both on hair trigger, and could restrain themselves no longer. Simon began to Bryant Marlon and they both started howling and panting and moaning until the bedroom began to sound like the Lion House at the zoo around mating time.

It was Simon Moon's idea of a great evening.

Dr. Dashwood was explaining the three dimensions of Briggsing to Dr. Van Ation, over coffee, at the other end of the continent.

"There just can't be any science without dimension," Dashwood said earnestly. "Fechner was the pioneer, psychometrics, what tastes sweeter than what and that sort of stuff. Primitive, of course, but it was the beginning of the quantification of the subjective, and my work could have followed immediately from his, except," he sighed, "you know how it is, fear and prejudice prevented the application of these methods to sex for a long time."

Dr Van Ation nodded somberly.

"Sincerity we measure in Spelvins on a scale of zero to ten," Dashwood went on, totally absorbed in his subject. "Hedonism in Lovelaces—we've been lucky there; subjects are able to distinguish sixteen graduations. Finally, there's the dimension of Tenderness—we find zero to seven covers that, so that the perfect Steinem Job, if I may use the vernacular, would consist of ten Spelvins of Sincerity, sixteen Lovelaces of Hedonism, and seven Havens of Tenderness."

"It certainly makes our work seem easy by comparison," Dr. Van Ation said. "Everything is so concrete and objective in astronomy."

"What does that mean?" Marlon Murphy asked idly.

Simon, propping himself up on a pillow, looked where the boy was pointing. It was a sticker attached to the console of Simon's home computer, and it was in gold and black, with a dollar sign over which were imprinted the letters:

T.A.N.S.T.A.G.I.

"Oh, that," Simon said. "It's the insignia of the Invisible Hand Society."

"What's it mean—T.A.N.S.T.A.G.I.?"

"There Ain't No Such Thing as Government Interference," Simon translated.

Marlon rolled over and stared at him. "What is it, some kind of paradox?"

Simon smiled in that infuriatingly serene way that the enlightened always smile when dealing with the unenlightened. "It's no paradox," he said. "It's a simple statement of fact."

Marlon moved a few inches away. "You're some kind of mystic?" he asked nervously. The only mystics he had met were on the West Coast, and they were all, in his opinion, bonkers.

"Yes," Simon said easily. "We in the Invisible Hand are mystics; but we are also scientists. Every one of us has an advanced degree in math or quantum physics or computer science or some such field. Our founder, Dr. Rauss Elysium, was an expert in gravitational geometro-dynamics—four-dimensional topology, and so on—before he got into General Systems Theory."

"And you people, with all that math and so on, have convinced yourselves that *the government doesn't really exist?*" Marlon was beginning to get an exciting idea: he would do his Master's on this Invisible Hand Society, as an illustration of the psychological law that the more brilliant a mind is, the more elaborate will be its delusory system if it snaps.

"That's it," Simon said calmly. "A chicken is the egg's way of making more eggs. Government is anarchy's way of making more anarchy. Let me explain. . . ."

"So they were all poisoned by Hollandaise Sauce," Mary Margaret prompted, finishing her seventh martini delicately.

Blake Williams was deciding that Mary Margaret was a damned good-looking woman, considering that she had been a man until six months ago. He was on his seventh martini, too, and Marjorie Main would have looked like a

damned attractive woman to him by then, even made up
to look like Humphrey Bogart's mother in *Dead End*.

"Yes," he said, "well, that's not the mystery. They were
all rushed to a hospital, and had their stomachs pumped,
and they survived. I don't remember what had contaminated the Hollandaise Sauce, but it doesn't really matter.
That's not the mystery."

"Well, what is the mystery?" Mary Margaret prompted.
She was Encouraging him to Talk, and that suddenly alarmed
him. It meant only one thing: she was thinking of going to
bed with him.

"Uh," he said, "the mystery was what happened later."
He had been thinking she was attractive, yes, but that was
fairly abstract; he hadn't *really* decided, and when you
faced up to it, she was still partly male in his mind.

"What happened later?" she prompted.

Dammit! he thought. *I must have had one martini too
many.* She was a woman now; no doubt about it. So what
was the problem?

"They all came down with the same symptoms again,"
he said. "The next time they had food with Hollandaise
Sauce." The problem was that they would not merely
Potter Stewart; there would be a certain amount of fore-
play naturally, and they would be Briggsing each other.

"Oh? It was a synchronicity—two cases of contaminated
Hollandaise Sauce hitting the same people?" Mary Margaret prompted him again.

"Ah no, it was far weirder than that." What *was* the
matter? He had Briggsed a lot of women in his time, and
had been Briggsed by a lot of them—he always enjoyed a
good Steinem Job, God knows—but still . . . there was
something a bit faggoty about it when the woman was an
ex-man and still *partly* a man in your memory. "Ah," he
repeated, damning those martinis, "you see, there was
nothing wrong with the Hollandaise Sauce the second

time. No contaminant at all. They weren't poisoned. They ah just had the *symptoms* of poisoning."

"That is weird," Mary Margaret said, wondering if he was getting so flustered because he had never been to bed with a transsexual before. Well, he was an anthropologist, wasn't he? He should regard it as an educational experience.

"Very weird," Blake Williams said, "because you can't explain it by conditioning theory. Conditioning is a slow process, remember, requiring many repetitions or ah reinforcements. That's how Pavlov's dog learned that *bell* means *food*—repetition after repetition. But the dog level or reflex level of these people had learned that *Hollandaise Sauce* means *poison* in only one exposure." He should regard it as an educational experience, he decided; after all, he was an anthropologist.

"Well, I never believed you could explain everything by conditioning theory," Mary Margaret said. "I'm a Humanist."

"That's all very well and good, I'm sure," Blake Williams said, "but ah scientifically the behavior in question was certainly not mediated through the rational circuits of the cortex and does require ah some sort of explanation. I mean, if it wasn't conditioning, what the Potter Stewart was it?"

"Mmm," said Mary Margaret. "Mmm? How about imprinting?"

"*What?*" Dr. Williams looked, for a moment, like the Ambassador finding the Rehnquist on the stairs.

"Imprinting," Mary Margaret said. "When an animal learns something all-at-once-in-a-flash. Isn't that called imprinting?"

Williams stared.

"I think you've got it," he said finally. "How would you ah like to go up to my apartment and discuss this further?"

He was suddenly madly in love with her. She had given him a New Idea.

In San Francisco, Dr. Van Ation had been Briggsing Dr. Dashwood for twenty minutes.

He sounded like a man at prayer. "Oh, God," he kept repeating. "Oh, God, God, God . . ."

Dr. Van Ation was thoroughly enjoying herself. Dashwood had Briggsed her for forty minutes, during which she reached Millet six times, and she was still purring with gratitude.

"Oh, God, God, *God*," Dashwood croaked, as her tongue continued to excite his Rehnquist.

"And so," Simon Moon concluded, "government is just a glitch. A semantic hallucination."

"Mrn—mn," said Marlon Murphy.

Simon turned around and looked at the boy; and it was as he feared; Marlon was about 80 percent asleep. Simon had been lecturing virtually to himself for several minutes.

"*Non Illegitimati carborundum*," he muttered. It was his *mantra* against resentment, wrath, and other diseases of the ego.

He leaned over and kissed Marlon lightly on the ear.

"Mrn," Marlon mumbled.

Simon got up from the bed and padded into the living room, where he smoked a little more hash and remembered classrooms back in Chicago, beatings he had received for being intellectual and queer, the first boy he had ever Briggsed (wasn't his name Donald something?), the beauty of Russell's definition of number when he finally grasped it (the class of all classes that are similar), the first time he was Bryanted (he was afraid it would hurt), the strange out-of-book experience in New York on hash when he saw that the laws that govern us are partly grammatical and partly pure whimsy, and this was very good hash, indeed, because he could almost remember that experience: there was a universe where he was hetero and Furbish Lousewart was President; yes, this was very high-grade hash, indeed, and he almost believed it, and why not? The math certainly did imply such universes, and each universe could be like a book, each book a variation on the same theme, and the Author (if one dared to try imagine such a Being) might even be in a meta-universe which had its own Author, and so on, to infinity. . . .

But then, suddenly (hashish is full of surprises) Simon was weeping, remembering his father, Old Tim Moon, who had been a Wobbly organizer all his life, and Tim was singing "Joe Hill" again:

> The copper bosses killed you, Joe
> I never died, said he

"Oh, Dad," Simon said aloud. "Why did you have to die, before I ever knew how much I loved you?" And suddenly he was all alone in an empty living room, weeping like an old man whose family and friends were all dead, holding his Social Security check and wondering: Where is the Federal bureau in charge of distributing love?

Which was absurd: Simon had lots of friends, and he was just being morbid.

"Oh, Dad"—he sniffed one more time—"I *miss* you."

And then he stopped crying and went and put the Fugs' record of "Rameses the Second Is Dead, My Love" on the stereo. And floated with the music and the hash into a Country-and-Western Egyptian paradise:

> He's walking the fields where the Blessed live
> He's gone from Memphis to Heeeeaav-en!

*   *   *

"Well?" Mary Margaret Wildeblood prompted, a bit impatiently. She was naked on Williams's bed and had been Lourding herself, not vigorously, just gently, very gently, not getting too excited yet, merely trying to get him excited.

"Just a minute just a minute," Williams said, sitting in his drawers on the side of the bed, one sock in his hand. It wasn't the transsex thing that was delaying him; he was still struggling with the New Idea she had given him back at the Three Lions. "It isn't just poisoning," he said absently. "*Anything* that shocks the whole neuroendocrine system might do it. Yes, of course. Artificially induced imprint vulnerability."

Mary Margaret seized his hand and placed it firmly between her thighs. "Imprint that," she said coyly.

"Yes, yes," he said, caressing her absently. "But just listen a minute. Orgasm does it um I think. No, just the first orgasm. Right? You keep repeating the pattern of the first orgasm. . . ."

"*I* don't," Mary Margaret said. "Just up there a bit, on my Atkinson there, *there*, ah Christ."

"Yes yes you don't and a lot of people I know don't," he said. "Yes. Um? But the people whose sexual patterns keep changing are a minority, certainly. They've changed their imprints somehow. Um. Yes, yes. Oh, my God!"

"What *is* it?" Mary Margaret was becoming cross; his hand had stopped moving entirely.

"Sorry," he said, resuming the gentle stimulation on her Atkinson and the outer lips of her Feinstein. "I just realized some people keep changing their ideas too. They've loosened the semantic imprints. My God, that's why conditioning theory is inadequate. Don't you see the conditioned reflexes are built onto the imprints. . . ."

"God God God oh sweet Jesus God"

"It's a shock to the whole system. People who've had

near-death or clinical death experiences. Shipwrecked sailors. And oh Jesus I call myself an anthropologist and I never got it before, rites of initiation of course that's what they're all about of course making new imprints. . . ."

"Oh God oh God darling darling"

"Yes yes, I love you, new imprints of course, yes yes are you coming on my little darling"

"God God GOD!!!"

"Ah sweet little darling was it good? Ah yes you look so sweet now there's nothing as lovely as that post-Millett expression but about those imprint circuits—"

"Shut up and Briggs me *please* darling"

And so, still reflecting on shock and imprint vulnerability and the changing of sexual-semantic imprints, Blake Williams began Briggsing a person who had been masculine for almost all the years they had known each other, wondering just how queer this was, really.

"Incidentally," Dr. Dashwood asked, "what do *you* think the *Hammerklavier* is all about?"

Bertha Van Ation and he were sitting at the kitchen table now, sipping a little peach brandy he had found still remaining in the cabinet, and munching Ritz crackers.

Dr. Van Ation brushed some auburn hairs back from her forehead. "The Black Hole," she said promptly.

"Ah you mean he was feeling dragged down into something he couldn't escape?" Dr. Dashwood suddenly remembered he wanted to look up Jan (or was it Hans?) Zelenka.

"No, not that aspect of it." Bertha munched and frowned thoughtfully. "The suspension of all the cosmological laws. The end of space. The end of time. The end of causality."

Dashwood smiled. "Some people thought it was the end of music when it was first performed," he said. "You might be on the right track."

"Why thank you sir said she." Bertha grinned. "You really think I'm dragging my own astronomy into the music department."

"You have every right to," he said. "We all see and hear through our own filters. To me, the *Hammerklavier* sounds like an unsuccessful attempt at Tantric sex. And the *Seventh* and *Eighth Symphonies* sound like monumentally successful attempts. That's me dragging my own speciality into the music department."

"You are a doll."

"And you're a *living* doll."

"Isn't sex great?"

"If God invented anything better," Dashwood said, quoting an old proverb and adapting it to the Feminist age, "She kept it to Herself."

"And how did I score on your scale?"

"Ten Spelvins of Sincerity, Sixteen Lovelaces of Hedonism, and seven Havens of Tenderness. No, make that eight Havens. You went off the scale."

In Hollywood, Carol Christmas, the Blond Goddess of everybody's fantasies, was sleeping alone for once.

She was still involved in 250,000,000 sex acts every hour.

The quantum perturbations pulsed gently through her atoms, stimulating her molecules, rejuvenating her cells, providing a very satisfactory Trip for her whole neuroendocrine system, and enriching her dreams vastly.

It was perfect Tantric sex, and she wasn't even consciously aware of it.

This was happening to her, and had been happening to her since the release of *Deep Mongolian Steinem Job*, because she *was* the Blond Goddess in so many fantasies.

All over the world, as she slept and even while she was awake in the daytime, the quantum inseparability principle (QUIP) stimulated her gently, because all over the world, every hour, 250,000,000 lonely men were Lourding themselves while looking at photographs of her.

Back in New York, Polly Esther Doubleknit was wandering around her apartment stark-naked.

Her lover of the evening was sound asleep in the bedroom, but Polly Esther was wakeful and thinking of twenty dozen things at once, like the Second Oswald in Hong Kong and whether fish ever get seasick and how splendidly heavenly it had felt when her lover's tongue was up inside her Feinstein and what was the name of the third Andrews Sister—Maxine and Laverne and *who?*—and Silent Tristero's Empire and why so many things come in threes, not just Maxine and Laverne and what's-her-name but Curly and Larry and Moe; and Tom, Dick, and Harry; and Noah's three sons, Ham, Shem, and Japhet; and Groucho, Chico, and Harpo; and Brahma, Vishnu, and Shiva; and Past, Present, and Future; and Breakfast, Lunch, and Dinner; and the three witches in *Macbeth;* and the three brothers who start on the same quest in all the old fairy tales; and the Executive, the Legislative, and the Judiciary; and of course the Big Three, Pops, J.C., and Smokey; and maybe she should cut down on those diet pills; it was absurd to be wandering around at three in the morning thinking in threes.

And then there was up-down, back-forward, and right-left, the three dimensions in space; and Wynken, Blynken, and Nod; and the Three Wise Men, Whozit, and Whatzisname and Melchior; and Peter, Jack, and Martin, the three brothers in Swift's *Tale of a Tub;* and Peter, Paul, and Mary; and the Kingston Trio; and Friends, Romans, Countrymen, which was not only a triad, but a progressive triad, one beat, two beats, three beats, one, two, three, just like that, and she would definitely cut down on the diet pills.

Polly Esther finally put a record on the stereo, turning the volume down to low so as not to waken her lover in the bedroom.

She picked the *Hammerklavier* sonata, not out of coincidence or propinquity or even synchronicity, but just because it was her favorite of Beethoven's piano pieces. It was her favorite because she couldn't understand it, no matter now often she played it. It was the musical equivalent of a Zen koan to her, endlessly fascinating because endlessly enigmatic.

The stark, discordant opening bars drove all wandering threesomes out of her mind, narrowing her attention to Ludwig's urgent if incomprehensible universe of structured sound. She was swept into it again, as always, swept along by emotions so deep and yet so austere that nobody has ever been able to name them. Once she had invited the world's three most admired concert pianists to a party, just so she could ask each of them, privately, what they thought the *Hammerklavier* meant. As she expected, she had gotten three wildly conflicting answers. Another time she had ordered every book in print about Beethoven from Doubleday's on Fifty-third Street at Fifth Avenue and looked up *Hammerklavier* in the index of each. She got forty-four different opinions that way.

The music hammered and surged along, carrying her through pain and frustration and loneliness to land, again and again, at things beyond such simple feelings, things that she sometimes felt were extraterrestrial or non-Euclidean or somehow beyond normal human perception. There are some kinds of knowledge, Ludwig had once claimed, that can only be expressed in music, not in any other art, not in science or philosophy. This was the most arcane of such knowledge, Ludwig's most intimate secret, and maybe you weren't entitled to understand it until you had been to the strange dark places of the psyche out of which he had created it.

It was the childbirth process, of course—and Polly Esther did not consider it a miracle that Ludwig could understand that, he was so obviously bi, at least empathetically—the labor pains going on and on until the act of creation seemed impossible, you would never get there, and yet somehow even in the blocked hopeless feeling you *were* getting there; and it was all the terrors of his childhood, all those cruel beatings by his alcoholic father, remembered and not forgiven, never forgiven; but it was also that cold, analytical, almost scientific side of Ludwig, remorselessly following his experiment to its inexorable conclusion: he had discovered or rediscovered that the piano is, among other things, a percussion instrument and he was following the logic of that insight, as he followed every musical idea, to wherever it led him, to whatever abyss.

And, after thinking all that, Polly Esther knew she still didn't understand the *Hammerklavier;* but as it banged and howled to its defiant conclusion, she got a flash of one aspect she had never registered before. It was the last scene of *Papillon*, when after twelve years of horror, Steve McQueen finally escapes from Devil's Island on his home-made raft of coconut shells and floats off into the Atlantic, as Ludwig floats off at the end of the *Hammerklavier*, shouting to the hostile sea and the indifferent sky:

"I'M STILL HERE, you sons-of-bitches!"

And, after that, Polly Esther was cleaned out, drained, purified; no more triangles haunted her. She turned off the stereo, yawned contentedly, and padded back to her bed.

Her lover was still sleeping, twisted around in the covers so that her right leg stuck out, decorated with goose pimples from the cold air. Polly Esther rearranged the bedding to cover the girl, and climbed in beside her, hugging her tenderly once, but not enough to waken her.

Then there were only a few remembered bars of the *Hammerklavier* and one more trio drifted up (Wyatt, Morgan, and Vergil, the Earp brothers), and then Polly Esther slept.

PART ONE
COMING TO A HEAD

Art imitates nature.
            —ARISTOTLE

Nature imitates art.

            —OSCAR WILDE

WHAT—ME INFALLIBLE?

The first entry of sin into the mind occurs when, out of cowardice or conformity or vanity, the Real is replaced by a comforting
lie.

—POPE STEPHEN,
Integritas, Consonantia, Claritas

Dr. Dashwood, as usual, began Friday by scanning the
mail.

The first letter said:

THIS IS AN ENTIRELY NEW KIND OF CHAIN
LETTER!!!

We represent the Fertilizer Society of Unistat. It will
not cost you a cent to join. Upon receipt of this letter,
go to the address at the top of the list and Burger on
their front lawn. You won't be the only one there, so
don't be embarrassed.

Then make five copies of this letter, leaving the top
name off and adding your name and address at the
bottom. Send them to five of your best friends and urge
them to do the same. You won't get any money, but
within five weeks, if this chain is not broken, you will
have 3,215 strangers Burgering on your lawn. (Here
Comes Everybody!)

433

Your reward next summer will be the greenest lawn on the block.

DO NOT BREAK THIS CHAIN! Everybody who has broken it has within five days suffered acute, prolonged, and inexplicable constipation which responds to no known laxative and requires, in each case, intervention of the apple corer or its surgical equivalent.

Dr. Dashwood made a mistake. He assumed this was another hoax by the enigmatic Ezra Pound.

Polly Esther Doubleknit was a devout Roman Catholic and went to Confession that Saturday.

"I did a naughty-naughty with a Secretary again," she said.

"How shocking," said her Confessor in a profoundly bored tone. "Was she cute?"

"She was an absolutely adorable little blond creature."

"I hope you both enjoyed yourselves," said the priest. "But why are you telling me about this hedonic little escapade?"

Polly Esther whispered, "I guess I feel guilty. I was raised Baptist, you know."

"But you're a Catholic now," the priest, Father Starhawk, said. "And as a convert, you probably know the theology better than people who were born into it. Now, tell me: What is a sin?"

"A sin," Polly Esther recited promptly, "is to knowingly hurt a sentient being."

"Except where it would be a greater sin, a greater hurt, to refrain." Father Starhawk went on. "That's why it's no sin to kill a virus, remember. Now, did you hurt your cute little blond playmate?"

"No, of course not."

"Did you make her happy?"

"I think so," Polly Esther said wistfully. "She wants to see me again Monday night."

"Then I think you made her happy," Father Starhawk said. "How many times did she reach Millett?"

"Six or seven, I think."

"Then I'm *sure* you made her happy," the priest said kindly. "As a mere male, I must say I envy the female capacity for multiple Millett. Now, obviously, your little party with this Secretary was not harmful, but joyful. So it was not a sin, but the opposite of a sin, a work of virtue. And you know the teachings of Moral Theology well enough to understand that, so why are you wasting my time?"

"I guess it's just my Baptist upbringing," Polly Esther murmured.

"You must clear your mind of all superstition," the priest said, "because such nonsense muddies the intellect and keeps you from thinking clearly about Real moral issues. Now, do you have something Real to confess?"

"Yes," Polly Esther said nervously.

"Well?" Father Starhawk's jovial tone suddenly turned stern.

"I think some of my money comes from slum properties." Polly choked, then sighed deeply. It was a relief to say it, to have it out in the open.

"You *think*?" the priest cried angrily. "You haven't found out for sure? How long have you had this suspicion?"

"Since about a week ago last Thursday."

"And what efforts have you made to find the facts about this grave matter, which may be, I remind you, a mortal sin?"

Polly Esther trembled. "I tried," she said, "but the way corporations are these days . . . I get twelve different stories every time I ask the lawyers . . . but I really think we own some of the worst parts of Newark."

The priest was silent for a long time. "It's my fault," he

said finally. "I was never strict enough with you. What is the first moral law about money?"

"To ensure that no human being was being hurt in acquiring it, and if anyone was hurt, to return the money to them and make whatever other restitution is morally necessary."

"To *ensure*," Father Starhawk repeated solemnly. "Saint Francis Xavier said that many centuries ago, a great and holy saint, and he specifically instructed priests to be certain that nobody received Absolution until they had given up all monies acquired from usury or other social injustices. That was long before Pope Stephen, my child, and it is the moral backbone of the Church. I cannot give you Absolution until you have examined your conscience on this matter and made whatever change is morally necessary."

"I'll have a special Board meeting and get to the bottom of it," Polly Esther said. "Thank you, Father, for restoring my vision of Reality."

"That is the function of the Church," Father Starhawk said.

And then he added, softly:

"Pray for me, please. I am a sinner, also."

Father Starhawk was a Cherokee Indian and a Stephenite.

The Stephenites were the most radical of all the Catholic clergy and made even the Neo-Jesuits, under General Berrigan, seem like milkwater liberals by comparison. There was virtually no nation on Earth which didn't have several Stephenites in prison for what the Stephenites called "following the laws of God rather than the laws of man."

Members of the Stephenite order absolutely refused to countenance any behavior that fell short of the ideals in the late Pope Stephen's encyclicals on Social Justice; and what the Stephenites would not countenance, they would resist. It was the passive, nonviolent nature of their resistance that made the Stephenites so troublesome to persons in authority; it is impossible to jail nonviolent idealists without a large part of the world sympathizing with them.

Father Starhawk had served three terms himself, for passively resisting Unistat's wars against Cuba, Puerto Rico, and the People's Republic of Hawaii.

Like all Stephenites, he wrote the familiar lapel button with a photo of Pope Stephen, the famous black patch over his blind eye, and the sainted Pope's famous remark, "What—*me* infallible?"

Pope Stephen had totally revolutionized the Catholic Church during his brief five-year reign. Indeed, as the French feminist Jeanne Paulette Sartre said, "This one man has single-handedly turned the most reactionary church on this planet into the most progressive."

It was due to Pope Stephen that the "social gospel," previously preached only by a minority of far-out Jesuits and worker-priests, became the official Vatican policy. By being the first to denounce Hitler and Mussolini, and excommunicating their supporters, Pope Stephen had knowingly risked the biggest rupture within the Church since the time of Luther; but, while nearly 30 percent of the Catholics in Germany and Italy continued to follow their national leaders, over 70 percent obeyed the Pope, and both dictators fell from power.

Adolf Hitler became a portrait painter again; and Benito Mussolini, deprived of power, returned to his early belief in anarchism and spent his declining years writing fiery journalism against all those who did manage to achieve and hold on to political power.

At the time of Pope Stephen's death in 1940, it was estimated that the wealth of the Vatican was less than 10 percent of what it had been when he took the Chair of Peter, but its prestige about 1,000 percent higher.

The Pope had spent 90 percent of the Vatican's wealth in projects for the abolition of poverty, disease, and ignorance.

Many regarded him as a saint, but Pope Stephen always tried to discourage that view. He ended every conversation with "I am a sinner, also," which became a habit with Stephenites: Father Starhawk, for instance, ended *all* his conversations that way, and also used it for the tag line of all his theological articles and his private correspondence.

It must be admitted, however, that the first Irish Pope did have his own brand of arrogance: He believed he was the best Latin stylist since Cicero, and was rather vain about his command of English, Italian, French, German, Spanish, Danish, and Hebrew, also. He was also convinced that he was a greater psychologist than James or Jung, and it was only when their names were mentioned that a tinge of uncharitable sarcasm would enter his speech.

Pope Stephen, in fact, had a habit of listening far more than he spoke, which led many to regard him as a bit aloof. Actually, he spoke little because he was so busy *observing*. This passion for studying other human beings had gradually turned him from a disputatious young intellectual into an almost pathologically sensitive middle-aged man, because the more he observed people, the more he liked them, and the more he liked them, the less able he was to bear seeing or hearing of injustice to anyone anywhere.

On one occasion a learned and erudite French Cardinal said to the Pope, referring to the steady parade of visitors to the Vatican, "You must find most of these nonentities profoundly boring." He was making the usual mistake of interpreting the Pope's long silence as a sign of ennui.

"But—there are no bores," Stephen said, shocked.

"You are being paradoxical," the Cardinal chided.

"Not at all," the Pope said dogmatically. "I have never met a boring human being."

It was the only time anybody ever heard him pontificate.

It was due to Pope Stephen that every Catholic priest was not only allowed, but encouraged, to get married. "Living with the mystery of the feminine mind," he said, "is the best training for trying to cope with the greater mysteries of the Divine mind."

He himself had married a peasant girl from Galway, who was said to be barely literate, and his love for her was legendary.

Nobody knew what the Pope and his wife ever found to talk about, since she obviously did not share any of his intellectual interests.

Actually, with his wife, as with most of humanity, the Irish Pope spent most of his time listening, not talking.

Because of the liberality of his sexual views, the Irish Pope was still controversial among conservative Catholics, who claimed he was a pervert and were forever trying to have him posthumously excommunicated.

They also spread rumors about his private life, which had gained so much currency that whenever his name was mentioned somebody would mutter "garters, garters, garters."

Pope Stephen's whole philosophy was derived from a single sentence in Aquinas:

> *Ad pulchritudinem tria requiruntur:*
> *integritas, consonantia, claritas.*

Which may be rendered:

> Three things are required for beauty:
> wholeness, harmony, radiance.

It was Stephen's thought that the universe, as the product of a Great Artist, must be comprehensible in terms of *integritas, consonantia, claritas*—wholeness, harmony, radiance. Why, then, he asked himself, does it not appear so to the ordinary human mind? The only answer he could find was that *we are not paying attention.* We have not learned to observe closely enough. We do not have the Artist's eye for detail.

And so Pope Stephen paid very close attention to everything that entered his field of perception.

At the time of the Irish Pope's death in 1940, obituary writers all over the world compared him to every saint and sage in history: Buddha, Whitman, Plotinus, Rumi, Dante, Eckhart, John of Arc, St. Terrence of Avilla, and so on, and on; but the one who came closest to categorizing how Stephen's mind worked was an obscure Canadian professor of literature who wrote, "The only mind in history comparable to Stephen's was that of a fictitious character—Mr. Sherlock Holmes of Baker Street."

Like Tobias Knight, Pope Stephen had spent all his life "trying to find out what the hell was really going on," although he never expressed it that way.

He had decided that what was going on was that everybody was very carefully avoiding paying attention to what was going on.

The Stephenites called themselves "Seekers of the Real" and were always watching very closely to see what was going on. They all had posters in their rooms with the sainted Pope's famous remark: "If you don't pay attention to *every little detail,* you miss most of the jokes."

When Dr. Dashwood went out to lunch that day, he was stopped on the street by a haggard and wild-eyed minor bureaucrat who said his name was Joseph K.

"They have everybody mind-warped," Joseph K. said, clutching Dashwood's sleeve desperately.

"Yes, yes," Dashwood said, trying to disentangle himself. "But I really must hurry—"

"What are the charges against me?" Joseph K. demanded. "What are the charges against any of us? We all try to obey their rules, don't we? Of course we do; we know what will happen at the slightest, the most minute, the most *microscopic* infraction, do we not? Not that I mean to imply that they are wrong, necessarily, or unjust— you won't find any subversive literature or pornography in my room, I can assure you absolutely—no, certainly not *unjust* or in any way *unfair*, but it must be admitted that in the application of the rules, in the *application*, I say, they are sometimes overfinicky, a bit *strained* and literal, if you take my meaning."

"Certainly, certainly," Dashwood said, struggling to remove Joseph K.'s fingers from his sleeve. "But if you were to see a good counselor—not a psychiatrist, necessarily . . . I don't mean to imply—"

"We are all guilty," Joseph K. said flatly. "They have established so many rules, and recorded them in archives that the ordinary citizen cannot consult, that we must all, the most loyal and decent of us, stumble on a mere technicality occasionally. Not that I mean to assert that technicalities are not necessary, you understand, since it is important to spell out in detail the *exact* meaning intended in a statute, don't you agree, George?"

"Frank," Dashwood said automatically.

Joseph K. suddenly looked sly. "Oh," he said slowly, "you claim that you are not George Dorn? How clever of them, although I can't imagine how they persuaded you, but of course a man of your moral principles would not be *bribed*, certainly. They must have convinced you it was for my own good in some absolute metaphysical sense, right?

Certainly. You would not work for them out of *malice*, would you?" He released Dashwood with a poignant, despairing gesture. "You mean well, he said. "They all mean well, I know. *But I am innocent,* I tell you!"

He backed away. "And you *are* George Dorn, and I am not deceived," he added bitterly.

Then he turned and ran.

PARAREALISME

The big news of the 1985 season in the art world was that François Loup-Garou had abandoned Neo-Surrealism and founded a new school of art called *Pararealisme.*

This was only partly the result of the Rehnquist in the Lobster Newburg; it was also a matter of economics.

For nearly a century, it had been very important for an artist to belong to a "school," and it was even better to be the founder of a "school." This was not just a case of "In Union There Is Strength"; it was also a shrewd marketing strategy. It might take an individual painter ten or twenty years to be "discovered"—if he were original, it might take much longer, and he might not be alive to enjoy it—but when a School of Art was formed, that was News, and all members of the school were discovered simultaneously.

There had been an Impressionist school, a Post-Impressionist school, an Expressionist school, an Abstract Expressionist school, a Cubist school, a Futurist school, a

Pop school and an Op school, and so on. François Loup-
Garou had noticed that the commercial life of each school
was getting shorter all the time, due to the accelerated
intensity of competition: Neo-Surrealism was already being
eclipsed, as an object of news and debate, by the Neo-
Cubism of the American, Burroughs.

He decided it was time to launch a new school.

After the experience of the Rehnquist in the Lobster
Newburg, *Pararealisme* seemed appropriate to him.

According to Standard Operating Procedure, he got a
few friends together and they began issuing Proclamations
denouncing all other schools (especially Neo-Cubism) as
obsolete and reactionary. This got them into the Art Jour-
nals and into some newspapers.

Then they held their own first show, and that got them
into the international news magazines.

They were news; it didn't really matter if their paintings
were any good at all.

In fact, their paintings were rather good, in a fey sort
of way.

They had revived traditional "representational" art (everything they did was as naturalistic as a news photograph), but with a difference that made a difference.

The largest canvas at the first Pararealiste show was
Loup-Garou's own *What Do You Make of This, Professor?*
An enormous work it was, covering two walls, bent in the
middle on a special hinged frame. It showed a cerulean-
blue sky, with hailstones: thousands and thousands of
hailstones, six months' painstaking labor, and each hail-
stone had a tiny image of the Virgin Mary on it.

Puzzled viewers might have found some enlightenment
in the First Pararealiste Manifesto:

> We of the Pararealiste movement, recognizing the
> meaninglessness of this chaos that fools call life, find the
> relevance of existence only in its monstrosities.

But we are not Existentialists or anything of that sort, thank God; and besides, the perversities of humanity have grown boring. After the Fernando Poo Incident, what can a mere man do that will shock us? It is the *abnormalities of nature* that we find illuminating; that is what distinguishes us from sadists, New Leftists, and other intellectual hoodlums.

We are delighted that Pluto, Mickey, and Goofy are all at odd angles from the plane of the eight inner planets. We are thrilled with Bohr's great principle of Relativity, which shows that to look out into space is also to look backward in time. WE ARE THE DAY AFTER YESTERDAY!!!

Some said that the Pararealistes were even better at writing manifestos than at painting pictures; but they meant what they said. The hailstones in *What Do You Make of This, Professor?* were no image of dream or delirium—"We spit on surrealism! Fantasy is every bit as dreary as Logic! It is the REAL that we seek!" the First Manifesto had also declared. What Loup-Garou had so painstakingly depicted was an occurrence that actually happened at Lyons in 1920. Xeroxes of the old newspaper stories about the event ("PEASANTS SEE VIRGIN ON HAILSTONES") were distributed to the press, emphasizing again that Pararealistes only painted the real, or as they always wrote, the REAL.

Little Pierre de la Nuit—Pierrot le Fou, he styled himself—was Loup-Garou's best friend and had contributed seventeen canvases to the first show. Magnificent, monstrous things they were, of course—flying saucers, all of them: blue and gold and silver and green and bright orange, shaped like doughnuts or boomerangs or ellipsoids or cones. Every one of them had been reported in the sky by somebody or other in the past forty years.

Loup-Garou circulated news stories about each sighting, you can be sure, to demonstrate again pararealisme's devotion to the REAL.

Then there was Jean Cul's *The Sheep-Cow;* some claimed it was the greatest of all Pararealiste paintings. It portrayed an animal half-sheep and half-cow, a veritable insult to the laws of genetics. Such an animal had been born in Simcoe, Ontario, in 1888. They circulated news stories about it.

All of this created so much international discussion that the Pararealistes immediately released the second Manifesto. (They had learned something about P.R. from the early surrealists.)

They denounced those who did not like their paintings as fools. They then denounced those who *did* like their paintings as damned fools, for liking them for the wrong reasons. They went on to fulminate against everybody in general:

> We renounce and hurl invective upon the rationalist conducting experiments in his laboratory. Every instrument he uses is a creation of human narcissism; it emerges from the human ego as Athene from the head of Zeus. The rationalist imposes his own order on these instruments; they impose order on the data; and he then proclaims that the universe is as constipated and mechanistic as his own mind! What has this epistemological masturbation to do with the REAL?

> And we abominate and cast fulminations upon the irrationalist, also. Behold him, in his drugged stupor, maddened by opium or hashish, gazing *inward* and depicting his childish dream and nightmares on canvas. He is as limited by the human unconscious as the rationalist is by the human conscious. Neither of them can see the REAL!!!

It reads better in the original French. But it would have been a top news story if it hadn't been eclipsed by the singularly obscene "miracle" at Canterbury Cathedral that week.

The details of the alleged "miracle" had been censored and covered up by high Church officials from the very beginning. Newspapers, at first, printed only short items saying that something strange caused the Archbishop of Canterbury to turn a ghastly white during Mass and stumble so badly that he fell off the altar.

Of course some cynics immediately assumed that His Eminence was as drunk as a skunk. There are always types like that, believing the worst of everybody.

Then the rumors started to circulate. Those who had been in the Cathedral said that the Most Reverend Archbishop had not so much stumbled as *jumped*, and that his expression was one of such fear and loathing that all present felt at once that something distinctly *eldritch* and *unholy* had invaded the church. Others, imaginative types and religious hysterics, claimed to have felt something cold and *clammy* moving in the air, or to have seen "auras."

By the time the rumors had gone three times around the United Kingdom and twice around Europe, there were details that came out of the *Necronomicon* or the grim fictions of Stoker, Machen, Walpole. Horned men, Things with tentacles, and Linda Lovelace were prominently featured in these embroidered versions of the Canterbury Horror, as it was beginning to be called.

The press, of course, got more interested at this point, and the Reverend Archbishop was constantly besieged to conform or deny the most outlandish and distasteful reports about what had occurred. At first His Eminence refused to speak to the press at all, but finally, by the time some scandal sheets were claiming that Nyarlathotep, the mad faceless god of Khem, had appeared on the altar bellowing *Cthulhu fthagn!*, the Archbishop issued a terse statement through his Press Secretary.

"Nothing untoward happened. His Eminence merely tripped on the altar rug, and any further discussion would be futile."

This merely fanned the flames of Rumor, of course.

One legend circulated even more than the others, perhaps because it appealed to prurient interest, or maybe just because it was the version given by a few people who had actually been in the Cathedral during Mass.

According to this yarn, a miraculous flying Rehnquist— just like the ones in the murals at Pompeii, except that it didn't have wings—had soared across the front of the church, barely missing His Eminence's high episcopal nose.

The judicious, of course, did not credit this wild rumor. They were all coming around, as the judicious usually do, to the view of the cynics. The Archbishop, they said, had been stewed to the gills.

His Eminence was no fool, however. After the first shock, he had begun his own investigation, aided by a few trusted deacons.

They found the slingshot, abandoned, on the floor of the first pew, to the right. That was the direction the Rehnquist had come from, and they all breathed a sigh of relief.

The Archbishop told them, then, the rumors *he* had heard about the incident of the Unistat Ambassador who had to be put on morphine after finding It, wrapped in pink ribbon, on a staircase.

"We are dealing with a deranged mind," His Eminence said, "but not with anything 'supernatural,' thank God."

They never found the Rehnquist, but as the Archbishop pointed out, "the perpetrator may have confederates."

Everybody tried to remember who had been sitting in the extreme right of the first pew. They carefully made up a list, including everybody's separate memories, half-memories, or pseudo-memories. The list looked like this:

Lord and Lady Bugge
the Hon. Guy Fawkeshunt, M.P. and
   Eva Gebloomenkraft
Ken Campbell and Eva Gebloomenkraft
the Hon. Fission Chips, F.R.S. and
   Eva Gebloomenkraft

"One name seems to stand out, doesn't it?" asked His Eminence.

"Eva Gebloomenkraft," said a deacon. "Isn't she that Jet Set millionairess who got into so much trouble in Unistat two years ago for putting laughing gas in the air conditioning system at a meeting of the Joint Chiefs of Staff?"

The sudden death of Bonny Benedict created waves of confusion and apprehension far beyond what ordinarily would have resulted from such a tragic accident.

The first one affected was Polly Esther Doubleknit, who called down from her executive office to the City Desk at once.

"What the hell happened to Bonny?" she demanded.

The City Editor spoke in a hoarse croak. "It seems to be what the TV news said, a heart attack." He was beginning to feel that he'd be the next victim, since his blood pressure seemed to be rising every minute.

"A heart attack?" Polly Esther was dumbfounded. "But what about the man?"

"He's being held, of course," the City Editor said. "But God knows what they'll charge him with—manslaughter, negligent homicide, who knows? There's never been a case like this before."

"They had better charge him with something," Polly Esther said crisply. "Or this paper will land on the D.A.'s office with all four feet. Do I make myself clear?"

Admiral Babbit nearly jumped out of his skin when the news reached Washington.

"It's those Briggsing Bryanting faggots from Alexandria!" he screamed. "And they're gonna try to pin it on us!"

This was a defensive over-reaction caused by the fact that Old Iron Balls had been contemplating various ways of bringing about the demise of Ms. Benedict. But he distrusted Einstein and neuroanalysis—"Jewish egghead stuff"—and never realized that most of his mentations consisted of defensive over-reactions.

"I'll fix those Rehnquist-suckers," he said to an aide. "Get old de la Plume, and tell him I've got a big job for him."

This referred to Mr. Shemus de la Plume, Naval Intelligence's ace handwriting forger.

And so, within thirty-six hours, the *Washington Post* had come into possession of a diary, allegedly written by John Disk, the man who had killed Bonny Benedict. The diary only *looked* cryptic at first glance. With a little study, anybody with at least two inches of forehead could figure out, from the abbreviations and clumsy codes used, that Disk had been an employee of the Central Intelligence Agency.

This was quite a shock to both Disk and the CIA, who had never had any connection with each other.

Actually, Disk had been raised in the True Holy Roman Catholic Church, a bizarre fascistoid splinter group which

had broken with the Vatican during the reign of Pope
Stephen of Dublin.

When Disk reached his adolescence in the early 1970s,
however, strange things began to happen to him. At first
he thought it was demons—he had seen *The Exorcist* and
believed every bit of it—but his priest told him it was all
because he kept Lourding himself.

Disk went to Confession every time he gave in to the
temptation to Lourde-off, which was five times a week
after he reached seventeen, and the priest kept telling
him to use Self-Control and take cold showers. The priest
also said that all the demons were in hell and Johnny
should stop worrying about them.

The only people who believed in demonic possession,
the priest said, were the benighted fanatics in the Orthodox Holy Roman Catholic Church.

Everybody in the True Holy Roman Catholic Church
despised and hated the members of the Orthodox Holy
Roman Catholic Church, which was another splinter group
that had broken away from the Vatican during the reign of
Pope Stephen. The members of the Orthodox Holy Roman Catholic Church hated them back, you can be sure.
In fact, in the typical manner of splinter groups, they each
hated the other more than they hated the common enemy, the heretics in the Vatican.

John Disk finally decided that what was wrong with him
was not caused by demons and—since he was able to cut
down on his Lourding-off to only twice a week after he
passed twenty—it wasn't entirely caused by Sin, either.

He was being poisoned.

The reason he had cycles of agitation and elation, followed by cycles of anxiety and growing fear that everything was somehow unreal, was because he was eating an
Impure diet.

The reason there were wars and rumors of wars, and

revolutions and depressions, and pornography and lewd, sinful women in immodest clothing on every street was because all the food was full of toxic, mind-destroying chemicals.

The people responsible for this were the Triangular Commission, the Power Elite, the Elders of Zion, the Bavarian Illuminati, and the American Medical Association.

He had learned this by reading books on Organic Diet from bookstores run by the John Birch Society, the Natural Hygienists, the Purity of Ecology Party, and various other groups who were inclined to go through cycles of agitation, elation, anxiety, feelings of unreality, etc., and had realized this was caused by Impurity of Essence in their food.

John Disk read a great deal of this literature and changed his mind about twenty times before he finally decided which school of "correct nutrition" was really correct.

He decided Purity of Ecology was the group that really knew what the hell was going on. He believed every word in *Unsafe Wherever You Go* by POE's founder, Furbish Lousewart.

By the age of twenty-three, Disk was a typical POE member. When not putting in his thirty hours a week working in their printing plant—where he received lodging and an Organic Diet in lieu of pay—he was out on the streets selling their newspaper, *Doom*, or giving away their four-page mini-pamphlets, which had titles like *Poison in Every Pot; Science: Satan's Plot Against God and Man*; and *Jimmy Carter, Servant of the Jesuit-Zionist Conspiracy*.

POE hated President Carter because he had defeated Furbish Lousewart in the 1980 election. But, with the typical logic of splinter groups, they did not hate Carter nearly as much as they hated Eve Hubbard, of the Liber-

tarian Immortalist Party, who also got more votes than
Lousewart, even though she came in third.

The POE people hated the Libertarian Immortalists for
another reason, which was that the LIP platform was
blasphemous and unpatriotic.

Hubbard's slogan was "No more death and taxes."

She planned to end taxes by running the government
like a profit-sharing corporation, terminating all interference in the internal affairs of other countries (thus allowing the military budget to be cut every year, instead of
growing every year), and paying each citizen a dividend
on the profits the Unistat Corporation earned through
investing in space colonization to tap into the vast energy
and resources of Free Space.

Hubbard planned to end death by investing the profits
from space in longevity research, which the majority of
scientists in the field were now convinced could lead to
doubling or tripling the human life span in the first generation, and could lead to indefinite expansion thereafter.

The POE people realized that these proposals were
scientific and rational.

They therefore regarded them as Satanic.

After three years in POE, John Disk still had cycles of
agitation and unreality; but the leaders of the cult assured
him that it took at least that long for the poisons in his
previous diet to leave his system totally. If he stayed on
the correct POE diet, they insisted, he would become as
serene as they were.

Still, things were getting to be more unreal more of the
time. Disk looked in the mirror one morning, combing his
hair, and seemed to see a middle-aged man looking out at
him. It was only a flash, a single crack in the fabric of
time, but it was unnerving. When the face turned back to
his own—young, black-haired, pale—he wondered for a
wild moment if he were truly a young man who had had a

vision of himself twenty years older or a middle-aged man who was now having a hallucination of himself twenty years younger.

But that was only a short fugue, for in a moment he recognized that the face in the mirror was not his twenty-years-later, but rather a face that had adorned the cover of *Time* magazine a few months ago. It was the face of Dr. Francis Dashwood, president of Orgasm Research Inc., Commie pervert Satanist sinner who spent most of his time observing things that John would like to do but was afraid to do because of twenty years of conditioning by the True Holy Roman Catholic Church.

Which was bad enough, certainly, but not as bad as what was to come: voices at first so faint as to be barely perceptible, but slowly and insidiously growing louder, voices which were female and kept saying *You are George Dorn* and *Imagine you can see my Brownmillers through my sweater* and *The interpenetration of the universes has begun,* but mostly saying over and over *You are George Dorn.*

And there were occasions, only a second in external time but stretching to infinity in a multiple of new dimensions he found or created within, when the Sages would gather him into their Maybe realm ("In addition to a *Yes* and a *No,* the universe contains a *Maybe*" was the password to pass the Lurker at the Threshold) and there would be Jesus saying "Is it not written, Ye are Gods?" and Emperor Norton saying "I just made myself Emperor of Unistat, Protector of Mexico, and King of the Jews," and Ped Xing saying "There are many universes and mind-states" and Beethoven singing the evolutionary scenario in eight cycles and Great Chthulu's Starry Wisdom Band and Glorious Lucifer Son of the Morning who had never fallen because the message of the scriptures was written backward in a mirror and then Linda Lovelace would come in and start doing disgusting immoral things and he would be back, the splinter of eternity contracting the Euclidean 3-D, standing on a street handing out *Poison in Every Pot* and wondering if he was losing his mind.

But the good parts of it were so good, Jesus and the weird but wise Emperor Norton and some of the Space Brothers, that he wished it would continue, if only it didn't keep turning into that sinful and disgusting business about Linda Lovelace; but he was beginning to figure it out; he was not the fool they thought him—not by a long shot. He knew that, now that the poisons in the food were beginning to wear off. They had started aiming an electronic Thought Control machine at his brain, so he did not pay attention no matter how many times the seductive female voice said YOU ARE GEORGE DORN YOU ARE GEORGE DORN YOU ARE GEORGE DORN.

So when he had read that bitch, that Briggsing Bryanting whore for the Big Corporations and the Sex Educators and Cattle Mutilators of the Satanist-Vatican-Zionist conspiracy, that lying tool of the Establishment, that contemptible Bonny Benedict claiming that Furbish Lousewart was a hypocrite and a meat-eater, claiming it when he knew it was not, could not be, true, damn her, the pig whore of the Jew-Jesuit money powers, as if a real Christian American like Furbish would pollute his body, the temple of God, with the flesh of a dead animal, the lying whore, he knew he would fix her and fix her good and proper, and show them all, the demonic jackal-headed lot of them with their laser beams flashing into his brain saying YOU ARE GEORGE DORN YOU ARE GEORGE DORN.

So he knew the perfect thing, the only way to express total contempt for the pig Establishment, the great lessons of the sages of the Clownological Counter-Culture, the attack that frightened, punished, and humiliated all at once and yet had to be endured as "only a joke," the bitch, that would fix her.

So he bought the pie, a Boston Cream special that was "rich and thick," according to the sign in the bakery, and waited for her in the morning outside the New York *News-Times-Post*-etc., and when the bitch, the lying whore, got out of her limousine, he was ready, he stepped forward, and he let her have it SMASH right in the face.

But then the old lady—my God, she looked like his mother, he realized—started choking and wheezing and fell down on the sidewalk and he knew. He knew even before the cop arrived from the corner, even before the crowd told the cop in great anger and outrage what had happened, even before the ambulance arrived, even before the doctor said, "She's gone."

And then the cop looked at him and he knew all the rest of it, the booking and the fingerprinting and the mug shot and then being alone in the cell all night with the voices saying YOU ARE GEORGE DORN.

Things were coming to a head.

Nathaniel F. X. Drest, secret chief of the Unistat Sector CIA, had felt uneasy for a long time. Since the death of President Carter, in fact. It wasn't just that the then-Vice President, now-President, Hugh Crane, was right out of nowhere, a total unknown, not one of THEM; similar situations had arisen a few times in the past, and the novice had easily been initiated into the secret science of Strange Loops and Mind Control, seduced—without the necessity of bribery, cajolery, or threats—into gladly becoming one of THEM. No: the unsettling thing was that Carter's death was unplanned, random, a surprise to everyone; it might even have been due to natural causes.

Yes: things were definitely and bodaciously coming to a head.

Nathaniel Drest had not lasted as secret chief of the CIA for thirty years without acquiring great pragmatic savvy about the spooky side of predestination. "Once is happenstance, twice is coincidence, three times is enemy action" had been the motto of one of the great masters of Strange Loops, Ian Fleming himself; but Drest knew that what was *really* going on was far weirder than even Fleming could comprehend.

Behind the mild, professorial, bespectacled facade of Nathaniel Drest, officially listed as economics researcher in the budget reports, was the one man capable of serving as secret chief of the Unistat CIA through thirty long years, while one dummy after another posed as the official head of the clandestine organization. Drest was a philosopher and a visionary; he had forged, from Machiavelli, Marx, Lenin, Mao, Mussolini, Nietzsche, Napoleon, William F. Buckley, Jr., and the Three Legendary Sages—Turing, Fleming, Wheatley—the coldly logical, existential, pragmatic strategy for eternal rule by himself and his friends in THEM, and total extermination and eradication of all possibility of rebellion by the rest of humanity.

He had been told once, by a sociobiologist, that he was a giant DNA robot, programmed to advance the growth and expansion of his gene pool. He thought that was an amusing, although limited, view of what was going on; and he certainly had no interest in such evolutionary theories as justifications of what he did. He needed no justifications; that his goals were rationally desirable to him was all that was necessary or profitable to contemplate.

The world certainly deserved to be ruled by his gene pool, by those White Anglo-Saxon Presbyterians and Episcopalians who had gone to Groton and Harvard, and occasionally there would be room for a bright boy from Yale, and this was so obvious that it needed no long-range evolutionary justifications. You just had to look around the world to see that no other gene pool was smart enough, tough enough, and fundamentally liberal enough to do the job justly and wisely.

John Ruskin and Cecil Rhodes had seen the choice a century ago; a world ruled by one Anglo oligarchy on scientific and socialist principles, or a world of anarchy and chaos, with constant wars and revolutions. Of course, there had been some anarchy, chaos, wars, and revolutions since Drest had taken over, but that was due to surviving ideological poisons on the international system and would be cured when the planet had been on the correct, Drest-directed mental diet for a few more decades.

But things were coming to a head.

The damned Ruskies still obstinately clung to their obsolete Adam Smith economics, and much of the Islamic world was unruly and rebellious. But worst of all was the Discordian Society.

Drest knew all about the Discordian Society, or thought he did. He was convinced they were behind this latest attempt to discredit the Company with that forged diary linking them to the Bonny Benedict "Cream Pie" murder. He also believed that they were the secret organization behind all the lesser conspiracies that annoyed and sometimes frustrated him—the malignantly nihilistic Network that had Potter Stewarted his own computer and God knows how many other computers, the dupes in POE and the Libertarian Immortalist Party, the damned moralistic meddlesome Stephenites, Weather Underground, the traitors over at Naval Intelligence, the sinister Invisible Hand Society, the terroristic Morituri, and the damned Ruskies and Arabs.

Drest had first learned about the Discordian Society in a strange, obscene, subversive novel called *Illuminatus!* He was convinced it was all fiction at first. But then he discovered that the alleged Bible of the Discordians, the perverse and paradoxical *Principia Discordia*, actually existed. When he put two men on the case they soon reported that copies of the *Principia* could be found in many science-fiction and libertarian bookstores all over Unistat, and that it could be ordered through the mail from a company absurdly and disarmingly named Loompanics Unlimited in Port Townsend, Washington.

Of course he wanted to believe that was all there was to it, just a small, oddball cult no more likely to influence events than the Libertarian Immortalists were. But then bit by bit the damning details accumulated. Emperor Joshua Norton, King of the Jews, was a Discordian saint, and Emperor Norton was also inexplicably becoming an "in" person. There was a play about Emperor Norton running in San Francisco, posters celebrating him for sale all over the country. The Discordian mantra "Fnord" was seen scrawled on walls in more and more places, and on the pyramid on the back of the dollar bill. Characters in *Illuminatus!*, who he had assumed were fictional, often appeared writing book or movie reviews for various magazines, and a check showed that they had been writing letters to the *Playboy Forum* and the Chicago newspapers since the early 1960s. Discordian cabals appeared in England, Germany, Japan, Australia, and the most unlikely places.

Drest had made a careful study of the Discordian philosophy and realized it was the kind of outlandish nonsense that would appeal to the kind of people who made all the trouble in history—brilliant, intellectual, slightly deranged dope fiends and oddball math-and-technology buffs. Many of the pioneer Discordians were computer programmers (he remembered that fact every time the Company's computer answered a simple program with GIVE ME A COOKIE or THE GOVERNMENT SUCKS) and others had documented links with the Libertarian

Immortalists, the LSD subculture, and groups as sinister as the witches and the anarchists.

The Discordians believed that God was a Crazy Woman. For the Woman part of it, they used the usual Taoist and Feminist arguments about the Creative Force being dark, female, subtle, fecund, and in every way opposite to Male Authoritarianism. For the Crazy part, they pointed to Pickering's Moon, which goes around backward, to rains of crabs and periwinkles and live snakes, to the paradoxes of quantum theory, and to the religious and political behavior of humanity itself, all of which, they claimed, demonstrated that the fabric of reality was a mosaic of chaos, confusion, deception, delusion, and Strange Loops.

And, Drest knew, they were definitely linked with the Network. Although computer specialists only spoke of the Network in whispers, the Company had a detailed file on them. The Network was devoted to the long-suppressed, much persecuted, but persistent underground religion of cocaine founded by the eccentric physician Sigmund Freud. They devoutly believed in the literal truth of Freud's vision of the Superman. ("What is man? A bridge between the primate and the superman—a bridge over an abyss," Freud wrote in his *Diary of a Hope Fiend*.) To achieve the Superman, the Network was systematically frustrating every other group of conspirators on the planet by glitching the computers, and meanwhile diverting funds from legitimate activities to subsidize dissident scientists engaged in research on immortality and higher intelligence. "Cocaine is a memory of the future" was the sick slogan of this misguided group of deranged intellectuals. "Our minds will function as ecstatically as on cocaine, *without the jitters*, once we achieve immortality and learn to reprogram our brains as efficiently as we reprogram our computers," they went on. "When we don't have to die and can constantly increase our *awareness of detail,*" they also said, "we will have no more problems, only adventures."

Naturally, every government in the world, even the near-anarchistic Free Market maniacs in Russia, had outlawed this bizarre cult.

An even more sinister Discordian front organization, according to Drest's coldly logical analysis of what was really going on, was the insidious Invisible Hand Society.

What was most devious about the Invisible Hand-ers was that they disdained secrecy and operated right out in the open, telling everybody what they were doing and why and what they hoped to accomplish. They had offices in all major cities and gave free courses in their politico-economic system just like the old Henry George schools at the turn of the century.

It was very hard for Drest to persuade the other eight Unknown Men who ruled the CIA in other parts of the world that the Invisible Hand was the most dangerous sort of conspiracy.

"A conspiracy doesn't operate in the open," they kept reminding him. Sometimes they would tell him he was working too hard and should take a vacation.

"That's what's so subtle and devilish about it," Drest would explain, over and over. "Nobody can recognize a conspiracy that's out in the open. It's a kind of optical illusion that they're using to undermine us."

"But they don't believe we exist," he would be told.

"That's an oversimplification," he would insist. "They admit we exist and occupy space-time and so on. They just teach that all the titles we give ourselves are meaningless and all our acts are futile since the Invisible Hand controls everything, anyway."

The other eight would again suggest that Drest needed a vacation.

Things were coming to a head.

The first lesson given to people who signed up for the course of "Political and Economic Reality" at the Invisible Hand Society, Drest knew, concerned policemen and soldiers.

Two men in blue uniforms would appear on the stage, carrying guns.

"Blue uniforms are Real," the lecturer would say. "Guns are Real. Policemen are a social fiction."

Three men in brown uniforms would appear, carrying rifles.

"Brown uniforms are Real," the lecturer would say. "Rifles are Real. Soldiers are a social fiction."

And so it would go, all through the lecture. Pure mind-rot, and, thank God, most people found it all so absurd, and yet so frightening, that they never came back for any of the subsequent lectures.

But the people who did come back worried Drest; they were the types he loathed and feared. Like Cassius, they had a lean and hungry look and they thought too much.

And they thought about the wrong things.

And now there was the matter of the materializing-and-dematerializing Rehnquist, obviously a Discordian plot, in Drest's estimation. What other group could conceive it, much less organize and accomplish it? Fnord, indeed!

There had been the case of the Ambassador who found it on a staircase; and the antipornography crusader who encountered it, temporarily painted red, white, and blue, floating in a bowl of Fruit Punch; and that unspeakable incident involving His Eminence the Very Reverend Archbishop of Canterbury; and God knows how many other cases the Company had never heard about.

And President Crane was said to be far more of an oddball than anybody had realized, having strange groups for midnight meetings in the Oval Room, where incense was burned in profusion, and the Secret Service men claimed to hear strange chants that sounded, they said, like "*Yog-Sothoth Neblod Zin.*"

Things were coming to a head.

THE OLD-TIME RELIGION

Charles Windsor, Prince of Wales, was about to be crowned King of England.

It was a sacred occasion for all British subjects, still grieving for the Queen Mother, who had passed away so suddenly. But in the midst of the mourning, there was much excitement, since Charles would obviously make a *smashing* king; he was bright, he was witty, he was good-looking, and he had sense enough not to meddle in politics.

There was one discordant voice in the crowd outside Buckingham Palace waiting for the new king to return from the coronation at Westminster Abbey. This was a plump, stately young Irishman who kept singing, off key:

> O won't we have a merry time
> Drinking whiskey, beer, and wine
> On coronation
> Coronation day

Voices kept telling him to hush, but he would turn to such spoilsports and say dramatically, "The sacred pint alone is the lubrication of my Muse."

"Drunken ruffian," somebody muttered.

"Well, what if he is?" the Irishman said suavely. "He still looks like a king, and is that not what really matters?"

"I wasn't calling the *king* a drunken ruffian," the voice protested, too emotionally.

" 'ere, now, who's calling me bloody king a ruffian?" said a soldier. "I'll knock the Potter Stewarting head off any Potter Stewarting Bryanter that says a word against me Potter Stewarting king!"

"Hush," another chorus joined in.

"Don't hush me, you Bryanting sods!"

"It's overcome I am entirely," the Irishman said, "by the rolling eloquence of your lean, unlovely English. You were quoting Shakespeare, perchance?"

" 'ere, are you making sport of me, mate? I'll wring your Bryanting Potter Stewarting neck, so I will . . ."

"Here he comes!" somebody shouted.

And other voices took up the cry: "The king! The king!"

Eva Gebloomenkraft, certainly the loveliest woman in the crowd, had been listening to all this with her own private amusement, but now she reached down and began to open her purse, a bit stealthily, perhaps, yet not quite stealthily enough, it seemed, for another hand closed abruptly over hers.

"Rumpole, CID, Scotland Yard," said a voice, as a badge was flashed briefly. "I'm afraid you'll have to come along, miss."

The Archbishop of Canterbury had shared his suspicions about Ms. Gebloomenkraft with the Yard, and they had been on the lookout for her all through coronation day.

But when they had her back in the interrogation room on Bow Street, there was no Rehnquist in her purse.

"I sold it," she said after an hour of interrogation. And, at their baffled expressions, she added, "It was becoming a bore. The joke was *wearing thin*. I needed something else to excite me."

"That's why you do it, then?" Inspector Rumpole asked. "For excitement?"

Eva raised weary eyes. "When you have so much money that you can literally hire anybody to do literally anything, life does become tedious," she said. "It requires some imagination, then, to restore zest to existence."

And all she had in her purse was a self-inflating balloon, which, when the cap was crushed, expanded to a sphere nearly twenty feet in diameter bearing the slogan, in huge psychedelic colors:

OVERALL THERE IS A SMELL OF FRIED ONIONS

When next recorded the itinerant Rehnquist was in the possession of Lady Sybiline Greystoke, who had either purchased it directly from Ms. Gebloomenkraft or had acquired it from some go-between.

Lady Sybiline was an eccentric, even for the British nobility. She was so far to the right, politically, that she regarded the Magna Carta as dangerously radical. She was so High Church that she referred to Charles I as "Saint Charles the Martyr." She hunted lions, in Africa, and was a crack shot. She was also, secretly, president of the Sappho Society, the group of aristocratic Lesbians who had secretly governed England, behind the scenes, since their founder, Elizabeth I.

Lady Sybiline and her good and intimate friend, Lady Rose Potting-Shedde, evidently found great amusement, between them, with the Rehnquist, for they even took it with them when Lady Sybiline embarked, that summer, for her annual lion hunt in Kenya.

Their White Hunter on that expedition was a red-faced man named Robert Wilson, who, like Clem Cotex, knew he was living in a book.

Robert Wilson had discovered this when somebody showed him the book in question. It was called *Great Short Stories* and was by some Yank named Hemingway. And there he was, Robert Wilson, playing a featured role in the very first story, "The Short Happy Life of Francis Macomber."

It was a shock, at first, to see himself in a book, and it was a bit *thick* to find his drinking and his red face described so dispassionately. It was like seeing yourself on the telly, suddenly observing the-man-who-was-you from *outside*.

Then Wilson discovered that he was in *another* book, but changed in totally arbitrary ways that verged on surrealism. This book was a bit of tommyrot and damned filth called *The Universe Next Door*, and he was, in fact, both inside it and outside it, being both the author of it and a character in it.

Robert Wilson began to experience cycles of agitation, elation, anxiety, and a growing sense of unreality.

Then came Lady Sybiline and Lady Rose and that mysterious object they kept in a small box and kept joking about, obscurely, between themselves.

They called it Marlon Brando.

The river had pebbles at the bottom. They were shiny and small and the water rushed over them constantly and you could see clear to the other side of it if you had your glasses on and weren't too drunk. Robert Wilson stared at the pebbles, thinking they were like pearls, trying not to remember what had happened that morning.

"After all, it was a clean kill," Lady Sybiline said beside

him. He wished she wouldn't talk. He wished she would go away and take Marlon Brando with her.

"The hills, in the distance," she said. "They look like white rhinoceri."

"They look like *white rhinoceri*," he said. "Jesus Christ."

"Don't talk that way."

"The bloody hills don't look at all like rhinoceri," he said. "They have no horns, for one thing. No exoskeleton on the head. I never heard such a damned silly thing. They look like elephants, actually."

"Stop it," she said. "It wasn't that bad."

"It was bloody bad," he said. "Bloody awful bad."

"If it hadn't happened, would it be cute, then, for me to say the hills look like white rhinoceri?"

"It wouldn't be cute no matter what happened."

"Oh," she said. "It's like that."

"Yes," he said. "It's like that."

"Will you please please stop repeating everything I say?"

The water kept running, always running, over the pebbles that were like pearls.

"It was bad," he said again. "Bloody awful bad."

"Are you always this rude to your clients?"

"Oh, it comes down to that," he said. "The hired help have to keep a polite tongue in their heads. You bloody English."

"You're English yourself," she said.

"I'm part Irish. I wish I were all Irish now."

"Really. You don't have to *go on* like this. Everybody is a little bit . . . eccentric."

That was the kind of whining excuse he despised. He knew then that he was going to be brutal. Somebody had to teach them.

"English literature," he said. "There is none in this century."

She cringed. He knew he had reached her.

"Stop it," she said.

"Everything worth reading is by Irishmen," he said. "Padraic Colum. Beckett. O'Casey."

"Stop it. Stop it."

"Behan. Bernard Shaw. O'Flaherty."

"Stop it. Stop it. Stop it."

"I'm stopping," he said. "I feel that I've said all this before somewhere, already. But how could you do it?"

"It excites me," she said. "To have . . . Marlon . . . there . . . while I'm firing at a lion."

He shook his head. "You are a five-letter woman," he said wearily.

But then the Rehnquist mysteriously disappeared again, back in Nairobi, while Lady Sybiline and Lady Rose were staying at the glamorous new Mau Mau Hilton.

Lady Sybiline was furious, but frustrated. There was no way of asking the hotel to question its employees about the theft without describing the object that had been stolen, and that was, of course, potentially embarrassing.

But she and Lady Rose had lots of other exciting little games, and they soon forgot all about "Marlon Brando."

Especially after they bought a beautiful plastic-and-rubber imitation which they christened "David Bowie."

It wasn't really theft, of course; Indole Ringh was a pious and holy man who would never *steal* anything. It was his religious duty, as he conceived it, to remove the holy relic from the heathens and return it to its rightful homeland.

Indole Ringh was a brown, gnarled, perpetually smiling little man, the offspring of ten generations of very conservative Hindus who had never accepted English ideas or ideals.

He had, in fact, three personalities. One was just an ordinary Hindu nobleman who was always smiling. The second, when he was in *Samadhi*, was an awe-inspiring guru, no more human than a statue of Brahma. The third, when he was in *Dhyana*, was just the brightest, quickest, most curious monkey in the jungle.

He didn't believe in any of those personalities; he just watched them come and go, blandly indifferent.

Because he practiced hatha yoga, bhakti yoga, rajah yoga, and gnana yoga, and because he smoked a great deal of *bhang*, he was as *conscious of detail* as Clem Cotex or the late Pope Stephen. Because he believed the oldest *Vedas* were the important ones, he had no truck with modernistic notions of aceticism, British prudery, or heathen Missionary nonsense of any sort.

He was a devout worshiper of Shiva, god of sex, intoxication, death, and transformation. He believed that you couldn't come to your senses until you went out of your mind. He kept alive, within his own province, the ancient cult of Shiva-Kali, the divine couple whose embrace generated the whole play of existence.

And now, in Nairobi of all places, he had found, somehow in the possession of a heathen Englishwoman, the most sacred of all lost relics—the *Shivalingam* itself, the engine of the creative lightning.

So it was not theft at all; he was merely restoring the relic to the place where it belonged, in India.

In fact, he placed it on the altar in his own temple, and invited the whole province to come see it and marvel and know the power of the Divine Shiva, who possessed such a tool of creativity.

He was going to restore the old-time religion.

He made a speech to the assembled multitude on the first day the *Shivalingam* was displayed in the temple. He told them that the polarity of Shiva and Kali was the basic pulse of creation. He said the Chinese dimly discerned this in their *yin* and *yang* symbolism, and the heathen West in their concept of positively and negatively charged particles. He explained that the male-female polarity was the engine of creation, not just in the human and animal kingdoms, but in every aspect of nature. He said that *Samadhi* and *Dhyana* and normal consciousness were equally real, equally unreal, and equally pointless, but that if you contemplated this *Shivalingam* long enough it wouldn't matter whether you understood any of this or not.

He was so bombed on *bhang* that he kept going into *Samadhi* every few minutes during this, and the crowd, both his old disciples and newcomers, decided he was the wisest and holiest man in all India.

Old Ringh kept smiling and going into *Samadhi* and explaining that we are all bisexual immortals who inhabit many universes and mind-states, and the crowd kept cheering and getting higher on his vibes, and finally they all went into the temple and contemplated the *Shivalingam*, where Indole Ringh had placed it on the altar, facing the enormous carving of the sacred *yoni* of the Black Goddess, Kali, and under the faded photograph of the Wise Man from the West, General Crowley, who, even though an English heathen, had understood the Mysteries and had spent many hours, while smoking *bhang*, discussing with Ringh's father how, even in mathematics, the sacred *yoni* appeared in both the shape and the substance of 0, the void, while the *lingam* appeared in the shape and substance of 1, the creative lightning, and how, out of the union of the 0 and 1, all of the numbers of creation could be generated in binary notation.

And as everybody meditated on the miraculous return of the *Shivalingam*, old Ringh remembered how General Crowley promised, when he had to return to the West, that he would use what he had learned in India to teach the whole world how the phallic spark of Imagination, represented by the 1 or *lingam*, generated everything out of absolute 0, the dark *yoni*, nothingness.

PART ONE
FLOSSING

Forget it, Jake. It's Chinatown.

—ROMAN POLANSKI

OCCULT TECHNOLOGY

Let me control a planet's oxygen supply and I don't care who makes the laws.

—GREAT CTHULHU'S STARRY WISDOM BAND

When Clem Cotex decided to program himself into the head space of the First Bank of Religiosophy, he sent five dollars to Bad Ass, Texas, for Dr. Horace Naismith's cassette tape, "The Occult Technology of Money and the Moneylords." By the time the tape arrived in the mail, Clem had been through so many *eigen*states, both as male and female, that he no longer wondered about "the stuff in the tomato juice" and was merely moderately surprised occasionally that most people were not as flexible in their thinking as he was. In fact, Clem had been a Scientologist, a solipsist, and a Logical Positivist, among other things, in the interim.

Filling a pipe with Alamout Black, the hashish of the Assassins, Clem lit up, toked deeply, and began playing the tape of "The Occult Technology of Money and the Moneylords."

"The Federal Reserve System—a private bank responsible to nobody, despite its name—creates money *out of nothing*," Naismith began in a pleasant Texas twang. Clem toked again and began to grok Naismith in his fullness.

The tape played on and Clem toked again each time he felt the need to grok more deeply.

Naismith quoted Buckminster Fuller (the only Unistat President ever to resign from office) and Ezra Pound, the folk singer, and John Adams and Tom Edison and a lot of other people who had long ago been on Clem's list of folks who had probably been given some of the "stuff" in the tomato juice. All of these men, Naismith pointed out, had proposed money systems more efficient and more just than the present Federal Reserve System.

"There is no one money system that was ordained by God," Naismith said. "They were all invented by human beings and can be improved by human beings.

"Now, what is money?" Naismith asked. "*Money is information*. Ask any computer programmer about that, if you don't believe it. Money is a signal, a unit of pure information. It is as abstract as mathematics. Cattle served as money once. So did leather. So did the precious metals. They were commodity monies, because they were worth something in themselves. Modern paper money is pure information, worth absolutely zilch, except for the signals printed on it." Clem really began to get Naismith's perspective. He toked again, feeling the Big Idea behind the First Bank of Religiosophy.

"Money in the modern world," Naismith went on, "is no more than a promise to pay. If you look at the bills in your wallet right now, you'll see *what* they're promising to pay. They're promising to pay you more paper. They don't have to give you a gram of gold or silver or any real commodity. They'll give you more paper if you want to trade in the paper you already have. Didn't that ever strike you as a *little bit funny?*

"Think of it this way," Naismith said, warming to his subject. "This is a corny old Sufi parable, but it might help you to get the picture."

The great Sufi sage Nasrudin, Naismith said, once invented a magic wand. Wishing to patent such a valuable device, Nasrudin waved the wand and created a patent office, which immediately appeared in 3-D Technicolor.

Nasrudin then walked in and told the clerk, "I want to patent a magic wand."

"You can't do that," said the clerk. "There is no such thing as a magic wand."

Nasrudin immediately waved his wand again, and the patent office and the clerk both disappeared.

"Jesus and Ludwig Christ!" Clem Cotex cried. He jumped up and turned off the tapes, totally At One with the doctrine of Religiosophy. "Money is information," he muttered, beginning to pace the room, stoned out of his gourd. "Holy snakes and ladders. 'Humanity is the symbol-using class of life, and those who control symbols control us.' I read that in Korzybski aeons ago. *Information!*"

Clem sat down at his desk and spread out a large piece of paper. He drew an elaborate scroll around it and printed at the top, "COTEX RESERVE SYSTEM." He made it a cashier's check to the Treasury of Unistat for ten million dollars, to be repaid at the prime interest rate of 15 percent. He then decorated another piece of paper, making it a Unistat National Bond, payable to the Cotex Reserve System for ten million dollars, thereby giving CRS the credit to loan ten million to Unistat.

He then switched the pieces of paper around on the desk. Cotex Reserve seemed to be ten million dollars ahead, and yet Unistat owed *them* ten million plus 15 percent interest per year.

("You can't do that. There is no such thing as a magic wand.")

Clem laughed hysterically. He remembered Simon Moon trying to explain Spencer Brown's *Laws of Form* to him: "To cross again is not to cross." Inflation, deflation, recession, depression: they were all like Nasrudin's patent office.

Clem knew he was in the state where synchronicities occur, so he went to his bookcase, picked a volume at random, and stuck his finger in, looking for the Message that would turn the whole experience into a full-scale Satori.

He was in *The Nature of the Physical World* by Sir Arthur Eddington, and the sentence he had found was:

> We have certain preconceived ideas about location in space which have come down to us from apelike ancestors.

Clem Cotex laughed for nearly fifteen minutes. The next time he met Blake Williams, he unleashed his Illumination in an aphorism that he was convinced would, for once, startle the seemingly unflappable anthropologist.

"Money is the Schrödinger's Cat of economics," Clem said, waiting for some sensational reaction.

"Oh," Williams said quietly, "you've noticed that too?"

Dr. Horace Naismith had founded the First Bank of Religiosophy in Bad Ass, Texas, because he wanted to be sure nobody in the Establishment would take it seriously.

It was his plan to undermine the Federal Reserve System without their noticing what was happening.

Everything in Bad Ass was considered too absurd and repugnant for serious consideration. Bad Ass Township and the whole of Bad Ass County were a source of national embarrassment.

Bad Ass had been founded by descendants of the famous Jukes and Kallikak families, carriers of virulent idiocy genes, together with a few Snopeses who had been driven out of Mississippi for unnatural acts.

The Bad Ass School Board banned not only Evolution and Sex Education, but non-Euclidean geometry, the metric system, cultural anthropology, and all history texts written outside Texas.

Despite the President, the Supreme Court, Congress, the TV networks and Jack Anderson, the Bad Ass County Line still bore the traditional sign: DON'T LET THE SUN SET ON YOU IN BAD ASS, NIGGER. All roads leading to Bad Ass Township were littered with the decomposing bodies of murdered civil rights workers.

Everybody in Unistat was profoundly ashamed of Bad Ass and wished it were part of some other country. They never realized that, to the rest of the world, Unistat looked like Bad Ass County.

President Fuller, the man whose money ideas had inspired Dr. Naismith, was the only President in the history of Unistat to resign from office.

He had resigned only three months after taking office, and he did it on the radio. "I simply can't find any way to do anything socially useful here," he said with that innocent sincerity that had charmed the voters into electing him. "I listened to some well-meaning friends and ran for this office," Fuller went on, "and I now realize I was a perfect damned fool. The synergetic interlock or real time vectors in Universe cannot be augmented from here."

The people—and, even more, the other politicians—were outraged. They called Fuller a mugwump and wanted to punish him. Unfortunately, the only way to punish a politician is to refuse to vote for him, and Fuller was no longer a politician and refused to run for any office, so they had to be satisfied with just calling him a nut.

That was in the 1930s, and everybody forgot about Fuller until the 1960s, when it turned out that his hobby—odd geometrics—had a lot of practical applications.

But still nobody took Fuller's money theories seriously, except Dr. Naismith, and Eve Hubbard, who had run for President in 1980 on the Libertarian Immortalist ticket ("An End to Death and Taxes!").

There was another President of Unistat who resigned, actually, but he "only" (as they say) existed in a novel. This was a science-fiction thriller set in a parallel universe and was called *Wigner's Friend*. It was about the worst possible President the author, a Harvard professor named Leary, could imagine.

The President in Leary's book, called Noxin, was a monster. He got the country into totally unnecessary wars without the consent, and sometimes even without the knowledge, of Congress. He lied all the time, compulsively, even when it wasn't necessary. He put wiretaps on everybody—*even on himself*. (Leary, a psychologist, claimed this bizarre fantasy, which smacked of satire, was possible, for a certain type of paranoid mind.) He used the FBI and the IRS to harass every citizen who resisted this tyranny. He not only took bribes, but even had a team of enforcers who extorted "campaign" money from corporations under threat of turning the IRS on them. His political enemies all died in a series of strange assassinations that couldn't be explained. When Congress started investigating his crimes, he betrayed his own co-conspirators one by one.

Noxin even misappropriated government money to fix up his house, and cheated on his income tax.

The book was a runaway best-seller, because it had a taut, suspenseful plot and because Unistaters could congratulate themselves on not being dumb enough to ever elect such a President.

Naismith, despite his Texas accent, was no imbecile; he had his finger on *part* of what was really going on.

The Federal Reserve did create money out of nothing. So did all the other banks.

The laws of Unistat allowed this, by permitting banks to issue loans up to as much as eight times the amount they had in deposits. Every time a bank made a loan on money they didn't actually have, they were *creating* money.

Most of the people who knew about this (aside from the bankers) went paranoid worrying about it. This was because they did not realize how much of their Reality was created in similarly occult ways.

The Federal Reserve made it possible for other banks to loan what they didn't have. The Fed *"guaranteed"* the credit of the banks.

The Fed was able to make this guarantee because it had lots of credit itself, in the form of government bonds.

The government bonds were good because they were guaranteed by loans from the Fed.

The loans from the Fed were guaranteed because the government gave them bonds.

And this was safe, because the bonds (remember) were guaranteed by the Fed.

That's why Clem Cotex laughed for half an hour when he finally figured out the Unistat economy.

The Communists had instituted this monetary policy because it made virtually all commerce dependent on money that didn't exist.

The Communists had abandoned pure Marxism in 1904 and were now following a system based partly on Marx and partly on traditional shamanism.

The whole Communist movement had secretly been taken over, in 1904, by General E. A. Crowley, the famous explorer. Crowley had learned a lot from the tribal shamans in the "backward" parts of the world he frequented. Chiefly, he had learned that the universe is created by the participation of its participants.

Franklin Delano Roosevelt was hand-picked by General Crowley to manage the Communist takeover of Unistat. Crowley picked Roosevelt chiefly because of his radio voice. The agreement was simple: Crowley would keep Roosevelt supplied with women—"That crip Casanova never gets enough," he was soon complaining—and Roosevelt, in turn, introduced Nasrudin's magic wand to political economy.

Even though many clear-sighted, patriotic citizens saw through Roosevelt and warned, repeatedly, that he was leading the country to communism, the majority paid no heed to these voices of reason. They were charmed by Roosevelt's radio voice, as Crowley had predicted.

Actually, Roosevelt kept before him, every time he spoke on radio, a large sign with a wise saying attributed to the man who won the Bad Ass Hog Calling Contest in 1923. The sign said:

YOU'VE GOT TO HAVE APPEAL AS WELL AS POWER IN YOUR VOICE. YOU MUST CONVINCE THE SWINE THAT YOU HAVE SOMETHING FOR THEM.

Unfortunately, Roosevelt was assassinated by a disgruntled office seeker in 1937.

The Communists found an equally loyal servant in 1948, however, in the famous General Douglas MacArthur, who was a military genius with one fatal flaw: he had an ego so large that only by contemplating the mathematical definition of infinity could anything so limitless be imagined.

MacArthur completed the Communization of Unistat in return for having his picture put on pennies, nickels, dimes, dollars, postage stamps, paintings in every public place, G.I.-issue condoms, the ceilings of barber shops, Mount Rushmore, the Sistine Chapel frescoes (advising

God during the Creation), all government documents, the chief balloon in all Macy's parades, in place of the test pattern on TV screens, marriage licenses, dog licenses, and in various other places that he thought of from time to time.

A brave and patriotic senator, Joseph R. McCarthy, attempted to expose MacArthur's government, which was staffed entirely by card-carrying Communists. (The Communists carried cards because, with so many conspiracies going on at the time, it was the only way they could identify themselves to one another.) The senator was smeared by the press, censured by his colleagues, and hounded to an early grave.

"Ike" Eisenhower, a popular Western film star of the period, contributed to McCarthy's demise by making a national tour supporting the President.

"I don't know anything about politics or military strategy," old "Ike" would tell audiences, his face full of stupid sincerity. "But I know General MacArthur is a smart man and a tough man and can outfox the Commies every time."

Like almost everybody else, "Ike" thought the Communists had taken over Russia, not Unistat.

One of the most insidious things the CIA Communists did when they took over Unistat was to change the Constitution.

The original Constitution, having been written by a group of intellectual libertines and Freemasons in the eighteenth century, included an amendment which declared:

A self-regulated sex life being necessary to the happiness of a citizen, the right of the people to keep and enjoy pornography shall not be abridged.

This amendment had been suggested by Thomas Jefferson, who had over nine hundred Black concubines, and

Benjamin Franklin, a member of the Hell Fire Club, which had the largest collection of erotic books and art in the Western world at that time.

The Communists changed the amendment to read:

> A well-regulated militia being necessary to the security of a free state, the right of the citizens to keep and bear arms shall not be abridged.

All documents and textbooks were changed, so that nobody would be able to find out what the amendment had originally said. Then the Communists set up a front organization, the National Rifle Association, to encourage the wide usage of guns of all sorts, and to battle any attempt to control guns as "unconstitutional."

Thus, they guaranteed that the murder rate in Unistat would always be the highest in the world. This kept the citizens in perpetual anxiety about their safety both on the streets and in their homes. The citizens then tolerated the rapid growth of the Police State, which controlled almost everything, except the sale of guns, the chief cause of crime.

THE BACHS' BOX

The Wilhelm Friedemann Bach Society was in the same downtown Washington building as the Warren Belch Society and the Invisible Hand Society, but Clem Cotex never thought much about them. He assumed, as did everybody else who noticed the name on the building directory, that the W. F. Bach Society was just a group of musicologists.

Nothing could have been further from the truth.

They were also trying to find out "what the hell is really going on."

This odd fraternity had named themselves after W. F. Bach not just for his music, which was superb, but for his effrontery, which was even more superb. Wilhelm Friedemann Bach, one of the twenty children of Johann Sebastian Bach, did not have the easy and immediate success of his brothers, Johann Christian Bach and Carl Philipp Emanuel Bach. In fact, because he was original and because he had to compete with the other three Bachs (already well established in the esteem of music lovers), Wilhelm Friedemann was neglected for a long time and might have ended his days in poverty and obscurity. But W. F. Bach was not the sort of man to take defeat easily. He hit on a plan which caused his music to be played everywhere, and made him quite a bundle of Deutschmarks, even though people were still saying he was the least important of the Bachs.

Wilhelm Friedemann had simply sold his compositions, one by one, as newly discovered work by his father, J. S. Bach.

Of course there had been art forgers and music forgers and even novel forgers both before and after W. F. Bach, but he had raised the philosophical ante on the bothersome question "If a work of art cannot be distinguished from a masterpiece, is it not a masterpiece?" or, in the vernacular, "How important is a Potter Stewarting *signature*, anyway?"

The original members of the W. F. Bach Society were people who had owned some magnificent Van Goghs back in the 1960s. Then one traumatic day, they did not own any Van Goghs at all. They owned El Mirs.

El Mir was the most talented painting forger of that time. His Van Goghs, Cézannes, and Modiglianis were totally indistinguishable from "the real thing," whatever that is. It was widely believed, after El Mir was exposed by another forger named Irving, that many masterpieces *still* hanging in museums were El Mir's work. Indeed, El Mir insisted on that, regarding it as the cream of the jest.

Some said that these El Mirs still hung in museums because the experts had not yet found any way to distinguish them from "real" art. Others said that the experts, once aware of El Mir's work, *could* distinguish it from Van Gogh's or Cézanne's or Modigliani's, but *would* not do so, because they had authenticated the fakes originally and did not want anybody to know that they had been fooled.

Blake Williams, Ph.D., had purchased a very fine El Mir, under the impression it was a Van Gogh, after the great success of his popularized book on primate psychology, *How to Tell Your Friends from the Apes*. Williams was then in the midst of his first phase synthesizing General Semantics and Zen Buddhism, and he immediately recognized what was *really* going on when identifiable El Mirs were everywhere falling in value after the great Exposé.

It was a glitch, he decided.

He called together a small group of people who also owned identified El Mirs and begged them not to believe that they had been deceived.

"A signature," he told them earnestly, "is not an *economic Good* in itself, like gold or land or factories. It is only a *squiggle* given contextual meaning by social convention."

He went on like that for nearly an hour. He spoke of the differences between the map and the territory; between the spoken word ("a sonic wave in the atmosphere") and the *nonverbal thing* or *event* which the word merely designates; between the menu and the meal. He quoted Hume, Einstein, Korzybski, and Pope Stephen. He dragged in the latest theories in perception psychology, Ethnomethodology, and McLuhan's version of media-message analysis.

He reminded them that Carlos Castaneda had studied Ethnomethodology with Garfinkle before studying shamanism with Don Juan Matus, and he assured them, as a professional anthropologist, that anyone who has the power to define reality for you has become a sorcerer, if you don't catch the bastard real quick.

By this time a lot of his audience was irritated and a little frightened—mutters of "He's just a damned crank" were heard from some corners of the room—but others were listening, enthralled.

Williams resorted to psycho-drama and Role Playing to get his point across. He said that he would pretend to be an extraterrestrial—"I wonder if it's *just* pretending," said an awed voice from the group who had followed this lecture with a sense of Illumination. Play-acting the extraterrestrial, Williams defied them to explain several things to him, rationally and logically, without assuming he had "intuitive" or *a priori* knowledge about what they took for granted.

He wanted to know, first, the difference between a dollar bill printed by the Unistat Treasury and a dollar bill printed by a gang of counterfeiters.

Everybody got excited, and most of them got angry, in the course of trying to make this distinction clear to the extraterrestrial, who was very literal and logical, and did not understand anything they took for granted until it was explained literally and logically.

By the time the extraterrestrial was willing to grant that there was an *agreed-upon* difference between the two bills *created by* social consensus, a few people had left, saying, "It's just an elaborate put-on."

But the others, who stuck it out, were next confronted with a dollar bill hung in a museum as "found" art. Williams, the extraterrestrial, wanted to know whether its value was the same as, greater than, or less than it had been before being hung in the museum.

More people lost their tempers in the course of his discussion.

But Williams persisted. Still playing extraterrestrial, he wanted to know if it made any difference if the dollar hung in the museum as "found" art had been printed by the Treasury or by the criminal gang.

After a few minutes of this topic most of the people in the room were jumping up and down like the Ambassador who found the Rehnquist on the stairs.

Williams had no mercy. He next wanted them to explain the difference between any or all of the above and an *exact duplicate* of any or all of them painted by Roy Lichtenstein and exhibited as Pop Art.

After a half hour more he pointed out that they were arguing among themselves even more than they were attempting to explain these mysteries to him. He also mentioned, not too cruelly, that many of them had arrived at the state where they seemed to believe their definitions would become more convincing if they just repeated them at a louder decibel level.

Williams then gave up the extraterrestrial game and tried to restore order. He became droll and told them the old story of how Picasso, asked to identify the real Picassos in a group of possible fakes, had put one of his own canvases among the fraudulent group. "But," an art dealer among those present protested, "I saw you paint that one myself, Pablo."

"No matter," said the Great Man imperturbably, "I can fake a Picasso as well as anybody."

He reminded them that Andy Warhol kept a closet full of Campbell's soup cans, and gave autographed cans to people he liked so they could own "a genuine Warhol." He pointed out, after the laugh subsided, that neither extraterrestrials nor terrestrials could agree on the difference in value between a Treasury dollar signed by Warhol and thereby becoming "a genuine Warhol," a counterfeit dollar signed by Warhol for the purpose—giving "a genuine Warhol" to a friend, a Treasury dollar with Warhol's signature forged by El Mir, a Treasury dollar with Warhol's signature forged by an unknown criminal, and a counterfeit dollar with Warhol's signature forged by William S. Burroughs, the founder of Neo-Cubist painting.

He said that Ethnomethodologists knew that the border between the Real and the Unreal was not fixed, but just marked the last place where rival gangs of shamans had fought each other to a stalemate. He said the border had shifted after each major conceptual struggle, as national borders shift after military struggles. He defined everybody who attempted to define Reality, including himself, as a conscious or unconscious co-conspirator with some gang of shamans who are trying to impose their game on the rest of us.

He said that both the economics of art and the art of economics were determined by shamans, whether they knew themselves as shamans or not.

"*Crazy* as a *bedbug*," said the last man to quit the room.

The remainder were staring at Williams with devout awe. They felt that he had removed great murky shadows from their minds and brought them forward into the light.

Williams had made some Converts.

He settled back in an easy chair—he had been standing

in his Full Professor lecture-room style through most of this—and got chatty and informal. He told them the little-known story of Pope Stephen's parable to the Spanish Cardinal who had told him that "seeking for the Real" was pointless since the Real is palpably right in front of our noses.

"Everybody knows," Pope Stephen had said, "that I studied singing and medicine before I decided to make the priesthood my life's work. What few know is that I also considered becoming a novelist. I often wonder, myself, if I ever abandoned that last ambition. Sometimes I feel like a novelist pretending to be a Pope, to see what it's like. And sometimes I even think the whole Church is a very old novel which I've revised and modernized. And, my reverend brother in Christ, sometimes I even think that I'm not alone in this novel-writing business; I think that every man, woman, and child on this planet is writing a novel inside their heads, all day long, every day—editing, rewriting, touching things up, improving a page here and throwing a page out somewhere else. The only difference is that when I write a novel, it becomes an Encyclical, and is therefore Reality for millions of believers."

Williams now had five True Believers out of the thirty persons he had called together. The five, together with Williams, founded the W. F. Bach Society that night, and set out to impose their definition of Art on the rest of the world.

They began by finding and financing Orson Welles, an obese genius who might have been the world's greatest film director if he had only been allowed to direct films.

Welles was not allowed to direct films because he had made the mistake, his first time out, of making a movie about Charles Foster Hearst, the richest and most powerful of the Communist clique who ruled Unistat. Welles changed the name, of course, and called his movie character William Randolph Kane, but few were deceived by this, and Hearst certainly wasn't.

The movie had a scene, at the beginning, in which a conservative banker said bluntly that "Kane" (Hearst) was a Communist. It went on to make a big mystery about the word "Rosebud," which referred to General Crowley's system of "Rosy Cross" Cabalistic magick which the Communists were using to make money out of nothing. It exposed, almost blatantly, how Unistat was actually governed.

Welles was blacklisted, and spent the rest of his life wandering around the world playing bit parts in films by other directors.

The W. F. Bach Society financed Welles in the making of his second film, *Art Is What You Can Get Away With*, which was a bold glorification of El Mir.

Next, the W. F. Bach cabal financed a new literary journal, *Passaic Review*, which they advertised so widely that everybody with any pretense to being an intellectual had to read it.

The *Passaic Review* heaped scorn and invective on the established literary idols of the time—Simon Moon, the neo-surrealist novelist; Gerald Ford, the "country-and-western" poet; Norman Mailer; Robert Heinlein; Tim Hildebrand; and so on. They also denounced all the alleged "greats" of the first part of the century, like H. P. Lovecraft, Henry James, T. S. Eliot, and Robert Putney Drake.

They established their own pantheon of "great" writers, which included William Butler Yeats (an obscure Irish schoolteacher nobody had ever heard of), Olaf Stapledon, Arthur Flegenheimer, and Jonathan Latimer.

After only two years of bombardment by the erudite and authoritative-sounding articles in *Passaic Review*, most self-declared intellectuals were seriously comparing Yeats with Eliot and granting that some of Stapledon's novels were as good as anything by James or Drake.

All of this was an experiment, actually. Blake Williams had not believed *everything* he told the founders of the W. F. Bach Society. He was convinced that a *great deal* of what passes for Value was created, not by labor as the Marxists thought, nor by supply-and-demand as the Free Market economists claimed, but by what he as an anthropologist recognized as shamanism.

He was trying to find out how much Value, and hence how much Reality, was so created.

He believed that large hunks of experience could be altered by people who regarded themselves as shamans and considered anyone who opposed them to be rival shamans trying to sell an alternative Reality.

It was his plan to move the Bach group, slowly, from experimenting upon the economics of art to experimenting upon the art of economics.

He knew that Value was the Schrödinger's Cat in every equation.

THE MAD FISHMONGER AGAIN

"Gentlemen," Clem Cotex said smugly, "I believe I have identified the Mad Fishmonger."

The entire membership of the Warren Belch Society— all eight of them—were assembled in the tiny office and a gasp of astonishment went up.

"Yes," Clem said emphatically, standing at the head of the table, under the portrait of Wigner's Friend, "I believe I have a positive *'make'* on the *'suspect,'* as Jack Webb would say."

Anthropologist Blake Williams, he of the monumental obsession upon Schrödinger's occasionally dead cat, spoke first. "Who?" he cried, almost in the tone of one who hears that the circle has, at last, been squared.

"Let me present the evidence," Cotex said with a solemnity that fit the occasion. He doused the lights and stepped to his slide-projector machine.

On the screen at the other end of the office appeared a well-known face.

"That's General Crowley, the discoverer of the North Pole!" exclaimed Professor Percy "Prime" Time.

"Yes," said Clem Cotex with deliberation. "General Edward A. Crowley, the best-known explorer and adventurer of the early decades of our century. The model of the English nobleman. The idol of young boys everywhere. General Crowley, indeed." He paused dramatically.

"Look at those eyes." Clem's voice suddenly had the tone of Perry Mason addressing the court. "How would you describe those dark and brooding orbs, my friends?"

"Well," Dr. Williams said, "he has what I believe is called um a *piercing gaze.*"

"Exactly," Cotex said. "A piercing gaze."

Another picture of General Crowley came on the screen. And another. And another.

"The same piercing gaze," Clem said pointedly, "year after year. No matter where he is when a photographer pops up—Africa, Mexico, the North Pole; it doesn't matter—always the same piercing gaze."

"Well ah aren't heroes *supposed* to have a piercing gaze?" Old Prime Time protested, wondering if this was just another of Clem's wild-goose chases.

"In a certain class of sensational fiction," Clem said tightly, "heroes have a piercing gaze. Sometimes the villains do too—Fu Manchu for instance. But we are not living in that kind of novel," he went on, not bothering to tell them his opinion of what kind of novel they were living in. "In our reality, a piercing gaze means only one thing, and you all know what it is, gentlemen."

Another picture of General Crowley came on the screen, one in which he was much older than in the previous four photos; but he still had the same dark and deep—yes, piercing—gaze.

"These are the eyes," Clem said, "of a *hopeless slave of the hashish habit*. Now, as you all know, many English military men acquired a taste for the resin of the *Cannabis Indica* plant while in India, and were none the worse for it. Certainly, an occasional smoke of the hash is an enjoyable, even a mind-expanding, experience. I daresay most of you here have tried it, and I gladly admit that I have. But a sensible man keeps such diversions within certain bounds. Such a sane, sound man does not '*do a number*' (as our younger people call it) until evening, or at least until twilight. Well, maybe late afternoon, occasionally. Perhaps in the morning *once in a while*. But not one stick of hash after another, day after day, year after year, for twenty, thirty, forty years! No: one who fits that description is a *slave* of the habit, a hashish robot, a man whose mind has lost contact with Reality (whatever that is) and wanders amid the phantasms of his own poisoned brain. A man, as the Irish say, whose mind had been taken away by the Wee People."

All gazed up at the photo of General Crowley, "the last of the Kipling heroes," as a journalist had called him, and Crowley gazed back at them, stony-eyed, impassive, enigmatic.

"Now, I have been studying all of General Crowley's

wanderings," Clem went on. "He was, in fact, back in England during November of 1881. The crab and periwinkle prank would have been easy for a man of his wealth, if his mind had already acquired that strange quirk, that twist in the sensibility, which cannabis abusers refer to in their own argot as 'a spaced-out sense of humor.'

"In 1893, what do we find?" Clem continued. "General Crowley was visiting the Jersey shore, right here in Unistat, 'fishing and relaxing,' he says in his autobiography. And that very summer we see the first record of 'the Jersey Devil,' that fabulous monster that looked like a gorilla, jumped like a kangaroo, and glowed in the dark.

"I think we can discount later appearances of *the Jersey Devil*," Clem said argumentatively, "as the work of lesser pranksters, inspired by General Crowley's initial success.

"In 1904," Clem went on, "there was the famous werewolf scare in Northumberland. General Crowley was back in England that year. In 1905 we have the first major UFO flap in Spain. General Crowley was vacationing there. In 1908 gnomes and other Little Green Men were reported in Switzerland. General Crowley was there, allegedly only to climb mountains.

"And so it goes," Clem said bluntly, flicking the lights back on. "Over fifty-six percent of all the weird data collected by the conservative Forteans, by our own more imaginative group, and by all the UFO buffs, for the years of 1860 to 1930—the years of General Crowley's life— correlate with the General's own movements. Even the Loch Ness Monster first began to appear after he bought Boleskine House, on the shore on Loch Ness.

"I think, gentlemen, that the conclusion is inescapable. General Edward A. Crowley, the mountaineer, the adventurer, the explorer, was a man unhinged by hashish abuse. He had become a compulsive, obsessive, sometimes sadistic practical joker. After all, I think the psychology of it is easy to understand, especially to those of us who, while not enslaved by the habit as he was, have had our own little adventures with the cannabis molecule. The world was becoming increasingly materialistic, bureaucratic, and—to a man like Crowley—*dull*. He set out to restore the Mysterious, the Magical, even the Frightening, to us. He was the last Romantic.

"I have no doubt of it," Clem concluded. "General Crowley was the Mad Fishmonger of Worcester."

"By George," Blake Williams said, "I think you've really got it."

There were murmurs of agreement. But then Professor Fred "Fidgets" Digits spoke up suddenly: "This opens a whole new can of worms," he said. "If General Crowley was—well, what he now appears to be, a common hoaxter—well, gentlemen, can we trust his reports on the North Pole expedition?"

"I fear not," Clem Cotex said. "That question came to me as soon as I began to realize Crowley's true character. We can't believe the North Pole story at all. It may just be another of his jokes. We may have been wrong for years, gentlemen.

"The earth may not be hollow, after all."

Down the hall the Invisible Hand Society was having problems of its own.

A group of the more avant-garde members had become convinced of the existence of the Tooth Fairy and were trying to convert everybody else.

Naturally, Dr. Rauss Elysium did not like this. He felt it reduced the principles of the Invisible Hand Society to absurdity.

Dr. Rauss Elysium had summed up the entire science of economics in four propositions, to wit:

1. *Find out who profits from it.*

This was merely a restatement of the old Latin proverb—a favorite of Lenin's—*cui bono?*

2. *Groups never meet together except to conspire against other groups.*

This was a generalization of Adam Smith's more limited proposition "Men of the same profession never meet together except to defraud the general public." Dr. Rauss Elysium had realized that it applies not just to merchants, but to groups of all sorts, including the governmental sector.

4. *Every system evolves and expands until it encroaches upon other systems.*

This was just a simplification of most of the discoveries of ecology and General Systems Theory.

4. *It all returns to equilibrium, eventually.*

This was based on a broad Evolutionary Perspective and was the basic faith of the Invisible Hand mystique. Dr. Rauss Elysium had merely recognized that the Invisible Hand, first noted by Adam Smith, operates everywhere. The Invisible Hand, Dr. Rauss Elysium claimed, does not merely function in a free market, as Smith had thought, but continues to control everything no matter how many conspiracies, in or out of government, attempt to frustrate it. Indeed, by including Propositions 2 and 3 inside the perspective of this Proposition 4, it was obvious—at least to him—that conspiracy, government interference, monopoly, and all other attempts to frustrate the Invisible Hand were themselves part of the intricate, complex working of the Invisible Hand itself.

He was an economic Taoist.

The Invisible Hand-ers were bitterly hated by the orthodox old Libertarians. The old Libertarians claimed that the Invisible Hand-ers had carried Adam Smith to the point of self-contradiction.

The Invisible Hand people, of course, denied that.

"We're not telling you *not* to oppose the government," Dr. Rauss Elysium always told them. "That's your genetic and evolutionary function; just as it's the government's function to oppose you."

"But," the Libertarians would protest, "if you don't join us, the government will evolve and expand indefinitely."

"Not so," Dr. Rauss Elysium would say, with supreme Faith. "It will only evolve and expand until it creates sufficient opposition. Your coalition is that sufficient opposition at this time and place. If it were not sufficient, there would be more of you."

Some Invisible Hand-ers, of course, eventually quit and returned to orthodox Libertarianism.

They said that, no matter how hard they looked, they couldn't see the Invisible Hand.

"You're not looking hard enough," Dr. Rauss Elysium told them. "You've got to notice *every little detail*."

Sometimes, he would point out, ironically, that many had abandoned Libertarianism to become socialists or other kinds of Statists because *they* couldn't see the Invisible Hand even in the Free Market of the nineteenth century.

All *they* could see, he said, were the conspiracies of the big capitalists to prevent free competition and to maintain their monopolies. *They*, the fools, had believed government intervention would stop this.

Government intervention was, to Dr. Rauss Elysium, just like the conspiracies of the corporations, merely another aspect of the Invisible Hand.

"It all coheres wonderfully," he never tired of repeating. "Just notice *all* the details."

Alas, the Tooth Fairy people were using all the same arguments. They said that if you couldn't see the Tooth Fairy, you weren't looking hard enough.

HONG KONG DONG

The fame of Indole Ringh's marvelous temple with the legendary *Shivalingam* soon spread throughout India, and pilgrims came from hundreds of miles away to look and wonder.

The new cult did not last long, however, because some miscreant crept into the temple one dark night and stole the *Shivalingam*.

The multitudes were horrified, and even wrathful, when the theft was discovered the following morning, but old Indole Ringh, smiling and spaced out, made a little speech that calmed them all.

"Miracles, like all other things," he said, "come out of the Void for no reason and return to the Void for no reason. Wait. Be patient. Pay attention to the little details. And see what comes out of the Void next."

Actually, the *Shivalingam* was not exactly returned to the Void, but had merely been transported to Hong Kong.

The King Kong Dong had been brought to Hong Kong by the unsavory person named Chi Ken Teriyaki, who was wanted by the authorities in Japan for selling "American" cigarettes made in Taiwan, diluted shark-repellent, stocks and bonds in a tapioca mine in Nutley, New Jersey, cocaine cut with Clorox, forged copies of the now high-priced El Mir forgeries of Van Gogh, and similarly dubious merchandise. Chi Ken, a half-Chinese, half-Japanese hoodlum, had originally worked for the infamous Fu Manchu and was later part of the notorious Casper Gutman mob in Istanbul. Fallen on lean days, he now eked out a bare living as a police informer in Hong Kong and part-time actor in underground Okinawan porn movies.

Chi Ken purloined the ithyphallic eidolon from Indole Ringh's temple of Shiva because he knew of a fabulously rich man in Hong Kong who happened to be looking for just such an item.

Hong Kong at that time, like most of the Orient, was haunted by the specter of the "boat people," refugees from Unistat who had crossed the Pacific in hopes of a better life. There was no nation in the East willing to accept more than a handful of these pitiful people, and most of them just drifted from harbor to harbor, slowly starving, and hoping for acceptance somewhere.

These desperate people were fleeing the appalling conditions that prevailed in Unistat since Furbish Lousewart became President in 1980.

The man Chi Ken Teriyaki was going to see was named Wing Lee Chee, and he was a deep, dense, secretive person, even more inscrutable than the average Chinese businessman.

Wing Lee Chee had been an athlete in his youth and had even toured Unistat once, performing amazing karate feats in a carnival. His missing right eye (the black patch made him even more inscrutable) was said to be due to an unfortunate incident that had occurred when the carnival was in Bad Ass, Texas, and he tried to use the white washroom at a gas station.

Mr. Wing had returned to China, and thence to Hong Kong, and had grown fat and rich by prosecuting what he considered a judicious and appropriate campaign of revenge against Unistat. He mass-manufactured fake T'ang dynasty art, to swindle the Unistat millionaires. He was the highest-paid informant for the CIA's Far East office, and, due to his knowledge of Unistat, always turned in information that confirmed the paranoid fantasies of his employers but had no connection with what was actually going on anywhere. Through a series of fronts, he had taken over organized crime in Unistat and arranged that everybody would blame it on the Sicilians.

He was currently engaged in smuggling as many as one thousand of the "boat people" a month into Hong Kong, where he put them to work in his factories and paid them three cents a day.

Wing Lee Chee, at eighty-seven, was a philosopher and a man of balance. His life-style always tempered severity with mercy, larceny with generosity, sensuality with meditation. He always tried to be as just a man as was compatible with being a rich and comfortable man.

If one of the employees in his factories showed initiative or talent, Wing Lee Chee noticed, and that man or woman was quickly promoted to a position of responsibility and solvency. He was no xenophobe; this policy applied even to Japanese, Hindus, and the wretched Unistat refugees.

Mr. Wing lived on Peach Blossom Street and had a magnificent view of all of Hong Kong and the harbor. He felt that the view was making him more philosophical every year. Each evening, after his twilight meditation period, he would sit at his window, smoking a long black Italian cigar, and look down at the teeming human hive below him, thinking that every person down there was the center of a whole universe, just like himself.

He had learned total detachment from all his own emotions in one split second, the day the white cops in Bad Ass knocked his eye out while arresting him. He had known, in that second, that he could kill them all—no man in the world knew more of aikido, judo, kung fu, and karate than Wing Lee Chee in his youth—but he knew what would happen after that if he did it. He looked at his own rage, understood suddenly in a mini-Satori that this was a mechanical-chemical process in his body, and became the clear mind that watched the rage instead of the emotional mind that experienced it. All of the more mystical and obscure things his martial arts teachers had tried to teach him abruptly made sense. He was never the same man again.

So he would sit, in the early evenings, smoking his foul Italian cigars (a taste acquired from a business associate named Celine) and look down at Hong Kong and its myriad of robots, each driven by mechanical and chemical reflexes, each believing itself the center of the universe. And then he would laugh softly at his own sense of superiority, because he knew that he was also controlled by chemical chains that determined what he could and could not think. Only in very deep meditation, and only a few times, had he broken those chains and seen—briefly! how briefly!—what the hell was really going on, outside of his own mental card-index system.

But Wing Lee Chee always came out of those high moments giggling foolishly, like a mental defective, or weeping quietly at the stupidity of himself and the rest of humanity, or simply dazed, like a man who opens the door to his own bedroom and finds himself lost in one of the craters of the moon.

On September 23, 1986, Wing Lee Chee had two important visitors in his office.

The first was the robot who used the name Frank Sullivan. Wing Lee Chee gave him a neatly typed report full of nonsense and mythology about Far Eastern affairs, which Sullivan would dutifully turn in to Nathaniel

Drest at CIA headquarters in Alexandria; Drest would worry even more that the Discordians were taking over the world.

Sullivan gave Wing Lee Chee a cashier's check for twenty thousand dollars, from U.S. Silicon and Sherbet, which was the CIA front for payments made to the Far East sector. Sullivan also gave Wing a check for one hundred thousand dollars, from Universal Synergetics Inc., which was the front for the heroin industry's payments to the Far East. Mr. Wing gave Sullivan a small ticket, which would pass him into a warehouse where the bricks of pure opium would be turned over to him, to be transported via the Corsican Mafia to France, where it would be refined into heroin, shipped to New York, and seized by a cop named Popeye Doyle. The last part of the process, the intrusive Doyle, was not part of the plan, but happened, anyway, to one shipment in two hundred, and was part of the overhead.

Mr. Wing liked pseudo-Sullivan, even though he knew the robot was not human. It was comforting to talk to an organism that possessed no emotions and saw everything clearly, down to every last tiny little detail.

That ability to observe objectively was what made the robot such a superior Intelligence Agent, Wing Lee Chee surmised.

The robot had, in fact, once been a human being.

Then he joined the U.S. Marine Corps, where they sent him to Boot Camp and brainwashed him.

The marines, of course, did not know that what they did was brainwashing. They called it "turning a civilian into a marine." It consisted of breaking down every imprint and reflex in the brain, through stress, shock, and constant humiliation, and then imposing a new set of imprints and reflexes. All military organizations did it, and none of them knew it was brainwashing.

The semirobotized, semihuman product of Boot Camp was then among the lucky twenty—or the unlucky twenty—to be chosen for special training by Naval Intelligence.

He was then brainwashed a second time. The technicians who worked on him this time were more sophisticated than the Drill Instructors in Boot Camp, but they still didn't like to call their work brainwashing. "Brainwashing," they all felt, was what the enemy did. What they did was "turn a dumb marine into a trained Intelligence Agent."

They used stress, shock, indoctrination, hypnosis, LSD, and conditioning.

The resulting humanoid subsequently defected to Russia and was brainwashed a third time by the KGB. What came up, of course, was a Strange Loop: under ordinary hypnosis, he appeared to be what he claimed to be, a sincere convert to the Russian way of life; under mind-drugs and deeper hypnosis, he was a Naval Intelligence agent, as the KGB suspected all along. They proceeded to brainwash him a fourth and fifth time, and he returned to Unistat to be debriefed and to serve as a sleeper agent for the KGB.

Naval Intelligence then reprogrammed him again, digging out the third level that the KGB couldn't reach. This level operated like a Trapdoor Code in a computer, and was inaccessible to anyone, including the programmed agent himself, except for those who knew the triggering word, which happened to be "Fishmonger," because the Naval Intelligence psychologist who had devised this system was a Charles Fort fan.

Naval Intelligence now had a man, or what had once been a man, who was accepted totally by the KGB as one of their very own, and who even defined himself that way *to himself*, but who was, at the word "Fishmonger," an

Objective Observer for Naval Intelligence. He was exactly the twenty-third to have gone through this Strange Loop.

At this point the time-dwarfs from Zeta Reticuli got him with a classic Close Encounter of the Third Kind. All he ever remembered, and all he could tell either the KGB or Naval Intelligence, was that a flashing light had come out of the sky, he had been paralyzed, and then it was three days later and he was in another city. Everybody assumed that this was some brain spasm caused by the amount of imprinting and reimprinting he had gone through.

But the Reticulans counted him as number 137 of their agents on Earth.

All his ID identified him as Frank Sullivan, of Dublin, Ireland, and even when he went through the brainwashing, or "basic training," as it was called, in the Provisional Irish Republican Army, that *cover* stood up.

Neither he nor anyone else remembered, by 1987, that he had been born Lee Harvey Oswald.

Wing Lee Chee's second visitor that day was the unsavory Chi Ken Teriyaki, and their business was of a sort that most of the world would have regarded as extremely grisly and perverse.

But when Teriyaki left, two thousand dollars richer, Wing Lee Chee was an extremely happy man. He canceled all his appointments for the day, summoned his chauffeur, and sped like a bullet to the home of Ying Kaw Foy, the youngest, the loveliest, and the most beloved of his three mistresses.

"My youth has been restored," he told the startled young lady. "I feel like a mere lad of forty-eight again! A whole new life is opening for us."

There was no mistaking the glint in the old man's eye. "The ginseng worked?" Ms. Ying asked, delighted.

"Well, not quite," old Wing said carefully. "But this is almost as good. We can nearly Potter Stewart again."

"My little old darling," Ms. Ying said. "I have told you that it gives me great pleasure to Briggs you, no matter how long it takes. And you Briggs me most deliciously and perfectly. And we are happy so, are we not? And what do you mean by these strange words? How on earth does one *nearly* Potter Stewart?"

Wing opened his package and showed her.

"Good grief!" Ms. Ying cried. "You've had your agents mutilate Mick Jagger!" But then her eyes misted over. "You'd do anything to please me, wouldn't you? You little old *darling*."

THE SYMPOSIUM

When Simon Moon joined the Warren Belch Society, the effect was not additive, but synergetic. Simon the Walking Glitch added to minds like those of Clem Cotex and Blake Williams could only result in what a nineteenth-century philosopher had foreseen as "the transvaluation of all values." A new cosmology, a new theology, a new eschatology, and even a new theory about the metaphysics of *Krazy Kat* emerged.

Unfortunately, they all got so stoned that they could never remember afterward exactly what they had decided. It was like the legendary Cthulhucon of 1978 or 1979, which was supposed to have taken place in Arkham,

Massachusetts. Every science-fiction fan in the country was alleged to have been there, and if they denied it, they were told that "the hash was so good almost everybody forgot everything that happened." Nobody ever knew, for sure, if Cthulhucon had itself happened, or if it was just a hoax, a legend created by a minority to perplex and annoy the majority.

Fortunately, or unfortunately, the Belchers all got together a week later to try to reconstruct their great discoveries.

"I think," Simon Moon ventured, "that we all sort of agreed that Tristan Tzara, writing poems by picking words out of a hat, created the whole modern esthetic, while Claude Shannon, generating Information Theory by picking words out of a hat, generated the correct approach to quantum mechanics."

"Jesus," Blake Williams protested, "did I agree to *that?* What the hell were we smoking, anyway?"

"Wait a minute," Cotex said. "Simon has *something,* dammit! Didn't we discover that there is a second flaw of thermodynamics as well as a second law?"

"I think," Percy "Prime" Time said, "that we were discussing *Deep Mongolian Steinem Job* and that got us into the subject of unusual combinations and permutations."

"Yes, yes, by God!" Williams exclaimed. "We realized that genius consists of looking for unusual combinations. Alekhine checkmates with a pawn, while his opponent is worrying about his queen. Beethoven proceeds from the third movement to the fourth without the usual break. . . ."

"And Shakespeare makes a powerful iambic pentameter line, one of his most tragic, out of the same word repeated five times," Simon interjected.

"And Picasso constructs a bull's head, and a mighty sinister one," Father Starhawk said, "from the handlebars and seat of a bicycle."

"And so," Simon Moon cried triumphantly, "the unusual combination is the key to creative genius, and Tzara did find a mechanical analog to it in picking words from a hat at random. And Shannon formulated it mathematically when he realized that information is nothing but unexpected combinations—negative entropy in thermodynamics!"

"Jesus, run that by me again," Prime Time said faintly.

But Blake Williams had the ideational ball and was running with it. "So Dada Art and cybernetics are both ways of playing games with thermodynamics, with the laws of probability," he said. "By God, I'm becoming a mystic. The only way the universe or universes can survive is by continuous acts of creativity—unusual combinations—on some level or another. Schrödinger was right all along: life feeds on negative entropy. The mind feeds on negative entropy. The best favor you can do for anybody is to shock them, and no wonder the Zen Masters hit you with a stick when you least expect it; by God, any shock that's severe enough is a new imprint. . . ."

"Imprint?" Professor Fred "Fidgets" Digits asked wanly.

"A hard-wired circuit in the nervous system," Williams said. "Imprints are created by shock. The birth process itself is the first shock and makes the first imprint. Haven't you ever read ethology?"

"You mean like a gosling imprints its mother, and if the mother isn't right there it imprints some other white, round object like a Ping-Pong ball?" Digits said. "Yeah, I read that in Konrad Lorenz. Didn't he win the Nobel for it?"

"Well," Williams said, "I've been wondering for years about the Hollandaise Sauce mystery—the people who were poisoned by contaminated Hollandaise once and then had a toxic reaction whenever they tried to eat Hollandaise. That's an imprint, I decided. Being poisoned is uh you must admit a shock."

"Oh, wow," Simon Moon said. "That's like Dashiell Hammett's story about the guy who almost got killed by a falling girder. All his imprints got extinguished. He just wandered off, forgetting is wife, his family, his job, and everything, looking for another Reality he could hook on to."

"Yes, yes," Williams said. "You're getting it. It happens to shipwrecked sailors and other people in isolation for long periods too. The imprints fade and whatever comes along makes a new imprint. It happens in Free Fall; that's why all the astronauts come back mutated. And it happens at the first Millett too."

"Far Potter Stewarting out," Simon said. "You mean, I dig red-haired women because my first Millett was with a red-haired girl in high school?"

"You've *got* it," Williams said. "If it had been a young um lady of color, you'd be one of those cats who only like to swing with Black chicks."

"If it had been with a boy," Simon said, "I'd be Gay!"

"That's it, that's it!" Clem Cotex cried. "If the Finkelstein multiworlds model in quantum mechanics is true, there *are* universes in which you did not take those imprints."

"Yeah," Simon said. "I can see myself hanging around Gay bars in one universe, chasing Black foxy ladies in another. . . . My God, it's probably true on the semantic circuits too. There might be a universe where I imprinted mathematics instead of words. I might be a physicist or a computer specialist over there instead of a novelist. . . ."

"And," Father Starhawk said solemnly, "there might be a universe where, with a different set of emotional and semantic imprints, I might be a professional criminal, a jewel thief, or something."

There was a pause while everybody considered what they had been saying.

"This is all rather speculative," Fred Digits said finally. "We're being carried away by our own rhetoric, I suspect."

"Um another thing," Father Starhawk said. "People seem to be changing rather abruptly and in strange, unexpected ways lately. Those negative entropy connections and unusual combinations, you know? I mean, people who've been Straight all their lives and suddenly they're Gay or Bi or something. And conservatives suddenly becoming liberals, as if all the semantic imprints are fading everywhere. Stable people schizzing out. Emotional neurotics suddenly becoming mature. It can't all be the shocks of accelerating social change, can it?"

Blake Williams beamed. "That's the question I've been asking myself for months," he said, "and I think I have the answer. Gentlemen, all the so-called recreational drugs that have come into wide use in the last few decades may be chemical shock devices. I think people are bleaching out their old imprints, and accidentally making new ones, when they think they're just getting high and having fun."

"Wait a *minute*," Simon said. "Isn't there a guy in prison in California for the last twenty-seven years or so for saying that? Some psychiatrist named Sid Cohen or something?"

"Never heard of him," said Prime Time. "Besides, we don't put people in jail in this country for their ideas."

"Well, anyway," Simon said, "even if all these new imprints made with dope are more or less accidental and the people doing it don't know what they're doing actually, it sure has stirred up a lot of the creative energy we were talking about. New combinations—bizarre, unthinkable, taboo combinations—are forming in brains all over the world every few minutes. Maybe that's why the Libertarian Immortalist Party could come out of nowhere and win the election by a landslide. 'No more death and taxes.' My God, who would have thought of it, twenty years ago?"

After the meeting broke up Clem Cotex hung around the office awhile, bringing the files up to date, dusting the venetian blinds, wondering why Dr. Hugh Crane, the most brilliant mind in the whole society, had been so quiet during this meeting, and also speculating idly about how the novel he was in was going to end.

There was a knock on the door.

"Come," said Clem. He had picked that up from his hero, Captain (now Admiral) James T. Kirk, and he thought it was much classier than "Come in."

A small, brown, charismatic Puerto Rican opened the door. "Hugo de Naranja," he said, introducing himself Continental fashion.

"Clem Cotex," Clem said. "What can I do for you?"

"You investigate the *eem*possible, not so?"

"Have a seat," Clem said. "We investigate the Real," he added, "especially those parts that the narrow-minded and mentally constipated regard as impossible, yes."

Hugo sat down. "I am initiate," he said, "in *Santaria*. Also in *Voudon*. I am poet and shaman. I am also—how you say?—goan bananas over one *mees*tery all my training in *Magicko* cannot explain. I theenk the Novelist play a treek on me."

"Oh, ah," Clem said thoughtfully, "you're aware that we're living in a novel?"

"Oh, *sí*, is it not obvious?" Hugo smiled, one weathered quantum jumper to another. "You look at the leetle details, you see much treekery, no?"

"Remind me to study this *Santaria* sometime," Clem said. "It's given you a broad perspective, I can see. Now, what's your problem?"

"Poetry, it earns no much the *dinero*," Hugo said. "I work nights as watchman, to keep body and soul together.

You know? So one night at the warehouse I see thees cat—thees son-of-a-beetch of a cat—and it is there and it is not there. You know?"

"Oh, certainly," Clem said. "You should take Blake Williams' course on quantum physics and neuropsychology."

"Son-of-a-beetch," Hugo said. "I took that course, but I no pay attention much. Just to get the credit to get the degree. You know? I mees something important?"

"Every modern poet and shaman should know quantum physics," Clem said sternly. "Specialization is old-fashioned. You see, Señor de Naranja, what you encountered was Schrödinger's Cat, and Schrödinger's Cat is only in this novel part of the time."

NO LIMITS ALLOWED

No limits allowed, no limits exist.

—JOHN LILY, *The Center of the Cyclone*

"The man from the FBI is here again," Ms. Karrig said, "with a man from the District Attorney's office."

Dr. Dashwood breathed deeply. "Send . . . them . . . in," he said as calmly as he could, clicking off the intercom.

He stared at the door for one frozen moment, still breathing deeply, relaxing every muscle; and then the door opened, and the two men came in.

I could jump out of the window, Dashwood thought. But then he controlled himself.

He recognized Tobias Knight at once, but the man from the D.A.'s office—who looked like a young Lincoln, or Henry Fonda playing young Lincoln—was a stranger.

"Dr. Dashwood," Knight said cordially, "this is Cotton DeAct, from the District Attorney's office."

"Named after Cotton Mather?" Dashwood asked inanely.

"Named after Cotton Hawes, the detective," DeAct said, looking embarrassed. "My mother was a great mystery-story fan."

"Oh," Dashwood said. There didn't seem to be any other appropriate comment.

There was a pause, and Dashwood noticed that Tobias Knight looked a bit embarrassed also.

"Well, gentlemen," he said heartily, "what can I do for you?"

"Hrrrmph!" DeAct cleared his throat. "Dr. Dashwood," he said formally, "there are two detectives from the Vice Squad waiting outside. They have a warrant for your arrest um for violating Section 666 of the revised criminal code ah Bestiality." He was actually blushing.

"I see," Dashwood said. He realized that his breath had become shallow and his muscles were tensing; with an effort, he relaxed. "I've known this day might come," he said with icy calm. "Why don't they just come in and arrest me, then?"

DeAct took a chair; Knight remained standing—between Dashwood and the window, although not being conspicuous about how he got himself there.

"Well, ah," DeAct said, lighting a cigarette nervously. "You are ah um an International Celebrity in a sense um people say Freud Kinsey Masters Johnson and Dashwood almost in one breath you might say. Ah there are questions of Scientific Freedom at stake here. Ah there is the matter of our national image ah we don't want you to be called the American Sakharov or anything like that ha-ha right?"

"Do you mean," Dashwood cried, "you might offer me a deal?"

"Well, I can't speak with any authority on that," DeAct said quickly. "What we have in mind is having you ah fill us in on the background details."

"You mean you want me to inform on my colleagues," Dashwood said, not quite making a question of it.

"No, no nothing like that," DeAct said. "It's hardly necessary, anyway. We know who they are and where they are, all sixty-seven of them." He noted Dashwood's reaction. "Yes," he went on, "there is very little we *don't* know about Project Pan, as you called it."

"Oh, Burger," Knight said suddenly. "Let's stop fiddle-Stewarting around. We've been on this investigation for over a year, Dashwood. We know that you and your friend Blake Williams somehow or other induced sixty-seven top scientific brains to get embroiled with you in this, this, this . . ." He blanched, and then went on brutally, "We know you've been *Lourding animals*, dammit! Lourding *donkeys* and Lourding *goats* and Lourding God-knows-what-else—whatever your Rehnquists would fit into, evidently. *Jesus Christ*," he added, "I never heard of such a thing."

"That's enough, Tobias," DeAct said sharply. "You see our problem, Dr. Dashwood. Even in this age of sexual permissiveness and Free Scientific Inquiry, you seem to have crossed a line into very ah controversial territory, as well as being in violation of Section 666, the Bestiality law. What we want to know is"—he paused for a deep breath—"*why* did you do it, Doctor? And how in *hell* did you get so many important people involved?"

"My God," Dashwood said. "You really want to know the idea behind it all."

"Yes," DeAct said. "Certainly. That's our problem in a nutshell."

"I don't go along with any of this, DeAct," Knight said. "It's just a case of degeneracy and perversion, and who cares what rationalizations they have?"

"That'll be enough, Tobias," DeAct repeated.

"I always say," Knight went on, " 'Scratch a scientist and you'll find an atheist, and scratch an atheist and you'll find a goddamned Commie.' "

"That will be *enough*, I said."

Dashwood was thinking. This was the old Mutt-and-Jeff routine: the tough, dumb cop who terrified you, and the smart, sympathetic cop who encouraged you to explain yourself. Still . . .

"Very well," he said. "I will attempt to explain Project Pan."

"You can call your lawyer before talking to us," DeAct said hurriedly. "You can call a psychiatrist, too, if you want," he added.

"I *am* a psychiatrist," Dashwood reminded him. Was DeAct worried about the Supreme Court and the international repercussions of putting sixty-eight top scientists on trial, or did he have some intuitive sense of the magnitude of what Project Pan was all about?

"Can you take me seriously," Dashwood spoke directly to DeAct, "if I tell you that what we have discovered here is the summum bonum, the secret of secrets, the key to the mystic powers of the ancients, the medicine of metals, the stone of the wise, the lost art of the Rosicrucians . . . that what you have been trained to consider most despicable is the central sacrament of existence, the key to higher consciousness and intelligence, the evolutionary imperative, the greatest scientific breakthrough to our epoch? Of course I always knew I would go to jail for it. I regard myself as lucky to live in an age when you won't burn me at the stake."

DeAct lit another cigarette, avoiding Dashwood's eyes. He mumbled, "You sound a bit grandiose, Doctor."

"This guy's a schizo," Knight said, more bluntly.

"Let me begin at the beginning," Dashwood said, ignoring Knight. "We are all *primates*. Do you understand that, gentlemen?"

"Sure," DeAct said. "Evolution. I had that in college."

"It's just a theory," Knight grumbled. "A man still has the right to believe in God in this country, you know."

Knight was rather overdoing the tough-cop routine, Dashwood thought.

"It's a biochemical fact," Dashwood said, "that ninety-eight percent of our DNA is identical with chimpanzee DNA. Eighty-five percent of our DNA is identical with that of the South American spider monkey, our most distant relative in the primate family. That means, gentlemen, that most of our behavior is genetically programmed to follow the same survival, status, and sex programs as the other primates. We are only two percent different from the chimpanzee, and only fifteen percent different from the spider monkey. Think of that the next time you go to the zoo. Our cousins are looking out at us through the bars.

"Now let me emphasize this, gentlemen. We suffer from certain induced cultural hallucinations. Every tribe brainwashes its children into the island-reality of the adults of the tribe; that's the great discovery of Einstein in her principle of neurological relativism.

"In our tribe—Western Christian civilization, as it's called—we have brainwashed ourselves into not seeing and not thinking about our relationship to the other primates and to life in general. We know we are primates if we have gotten as far as college"—he emphasized the last for

Knight—"but we keep forgetting it, ignoring it, losing track of it."

"Bull*burger*," Knight growled. It was a typical primate reaction in a threat situation, Dashwood thought.

"Go on," DeAct said nervously, lighting a third cigarette.

"If I were to write a novel of about six hundred pages," Dashwood said, "and mentioned on every one of the first four hundred pages that all of us are primates, we would find it funny or satirical. Even stranger, if I stopped mentioning it for about two hundred pages, the readers would all forget it quickly, and be startled if I mentioned it again on page five hundred fifteen. It's a fact that all educated persons *know*, but most of us would rather forget or simply not think about.

"Now, what is Bestiality, gentlemen?" Dashwood didn't pause, but answered his own question. "Sexual relations between a human and an animal. But humans are animals, as we keep forgetting, so that definition is culturally biased and self-serving. Bestiality is sex between animals, that's all. Interspecies sex. And any biologist will tell you that is quite common. Insects will Potter Stewart any bug that comes along if they can't find their own species. The ubiquity of the mule, gentlemen, shows how common is the occurrence of interspecies sex—bestiality as our law calls it—between horses and donkeys. Throughout the reptile, bird, and fish kingdoms, the same behavior is commonplace.

"There is no species on the planet, gentlemen, that thinks it is 'degrading' to have sex with another species—except ourselves. And that is because we are trying to forget that we are primates."

Dashwood paused.

"This is some kind of put-on," Tobias Knight said irritably. "Get to the point, Dashwood."

But DeAct was crushing out his cigarette with a thoughtful frown. "So that's your defense, then?" he asked. "Scientific inquiry and so on . . . You just wanted to find out the ah subjective similarities and differences in comparing Bestiality with ordinary sex and homosexuality and ah the other variations?"

"Defense!" Dashwood exclaimed. "I am not defending myself. Whether defense is necessary at all remains to be seen. Right now, I am merely filling you in on the background as you requested." He paused.

"All progress is made by violating taboos," he went on presently. "A certain friend of mine ah made that observation many years ago."

"Blake Williams," Tobias Knight said. "We know he's in this up to his ears."

"A *certain* friend," Dashwood went on, neither confirming nor denying. "He pointed out that without heretics and blasphemers—without rebels, that is—we would all still be living like Homo Erectus half a million years ago. All progress has been made by individuals who dared to think about the unthinkable and do the forbidden. As Oscar Wilde said, 'Disobedience was man's Original Virtue.' Those who dare—"

"Wilde was a Bryanting degenerate," Knight growled. He was showing more of his canine teeth now: the signal of primate anger.

"Those who dare cross the line—any line—are explorers, and explorers sometimes get lost," Dashwood went on. "But without them, we never would have walked out of the tribal stage into the urban or out of the Dark Ages into the Renaissance.

"But enough rhetoric. Let me come to the point.

"Gentlemen, dozens of anthropologists have sat in this office and told me stories that once made my hair stand on end. And dozens, and scores, of parapsychologists have told me even wilder tales. Gentlemen, everybody outside

Bad Ass or Seattle knows that the line between Experimental Music and Noise is very hard to find, that the line between avant-garde literature and nonsense is ambiguous, that even the line between the Beautiful and the Hideous is far from fixed, since a Ubangi woman with a plate in her lip is attractive to a Ubangi man, but absurd or repulsive to most of us. Mathematicians know that what constitutes proof is still not itself totally understood. Scientific Truth, so called, used to remain the same for millennia; then it began changing every century; in this century, it has changed every decade, or even quicker in some fields. And yet, in spite of all this, we think there is a firm, fixed, immutable boundary between the Real and the Unreal.

"Gentlemen, there is no such boundary.

"Everything that we regard as filthy, obscene, blasphemous, and disgusting is part of the ancient mind-science called Magick."

Dashwood smiled gently. "Sex with a menstruating woman is forbidden, and considered 'indecent' or appalling, because it was once part of the sacraments of the Moon Goddess cult. The menstruating woman was thought to be possessed by the Goddess, I suppose, but the theory doesn't matter. Judeo-Christian civilization put the practice under a ban, and made it 'evil,' because it was part of the ancient Goddess religion that the worshipers of a Male God could not tolerate.

"Homosexuality is forbidden and considered revolting and ugly because it was part of the tradition of shamanism in most parts of the world not included in the Judeo-Christian cult.

"And yet, what do we find within the Judeo-Christian world itself? What do we find in the most orthodox times? We find secret cults using these forbidden acts for occult purposes. Sex with a menstruating woman was called 'the mystery of the Red Gold' by the alchemists, and was part of the process of consciousness expansion in that form of Magick. Homosexuality was part of the secret teachings of the Knights Templar and many other Magick cults."

"There are perverts everywhere," Knight said. "That doesn't prove anything."

Dashwood smiled again. "Tell me," he asked, "how do you feel after a good Potter Stewart?"

"What does that prove?" Knight demanded.

"Let us see where it leads us," Dashwood said. "You feel good, do you not? Yes, you will agree to that much. How would you feel after Potter Stewarting for four hours?"

"Tired."

"Not if you were trained in Tantra," Dashwood said. "Tantrists have been known to continue the sexual act for far longer—eight hours, even. Is it not strange that Shakespeare referred to it as 'the monetary trick,' and Kinsey found, back in the forties, that the average Unistat male reaches Millett in less than two minutes? Is this not part of the Taboo I am discussing, the Taboo on the Magick secrets of non-Judeo-Christian religion? We have loosened up a lot since Kinsey's day, but to a Tantrist we are still rushing and missing the little details, you might say. Why is that?"

DeAct lit another cigarette. "Jesus," he said, "are you telling us that every kind of sex that's forbidden in the Bible is the key to some kind of occult knowledge or power? Is that it?"

"A long time ago, when I wasn't ready to understand yet," Dashwood said, "a parapsychologist told me, 'Scratch a trance medium and you'll find a homosexual.' That's not one hundred percent true, but it's true more often than not.

"The Moon Goddess is a metaphor, let us say. But what

happens to a woman in her menses, the power that is present and can be used in mind science, is no metaphor.

"Now, what started Project Pan was something I discovered, by 'accident' as they say, just browsing in a book that didn't seem to relate to my own work at all, a book on Egypt, and there it was: there was a priestess who performed fellatio on a goat every year on the Egyptian New Year's Day, which is our July 23. Yes, gentlemen—in the vernacular, she gave the goat a Steinem Job."

"There are perverts everywhere," Knight repeated.

"This was central to the Egyptian religion," Dashwood said. "Was the whole religion a perversion? Don't you see, everything called perversion got that name because it was part of the old Magick tradition?

"And guess what, gentlemen: What is the most common subject in the cave paintings left by our ancestors thirty thousand years ago?

"Bestiality. Yes, gentlemen—our ancestors portrayed themselves, over and over, having sex with goats and bisons and every animal they knew about."

"I don't believe it," Knight said flatly.

"Look it up sometime," Dashwood said pleasantly. "It's mentioned in *Ghost Dance: Origins of Religion,* by Weston LeBarre, one of our most respected anthropologists. You never see those paintings in any popular books of cave art, but every paleoanthropologist knows about them.

"You find the same in ancient Indian art, ancient Babylonian art, ancient art everywhere.

"And you find the Magick secret coded into myth and legend over and over. The formula for producing a Man-God or Super-Hero is the mating of human and animal. Europa and the bull; Leda and the swan; Beauty and the Beast; the Buddha fathered by a white elephant in some versions of the legend.

"Tantric sex is the portal of the mysteries, and the

alchemists called it the secret of silver. *This* is the secret
of gold, gentlemen. And it's even coded into the Judeo-
Christian mythos—after the Gnostics got through editing
the manuscripts. Why do you think Eve and the Serpent
are credited with giving us the knowledge of good and evil?
Why does the Hebrew word for 'serpent,' *neschek*, have
the same Cabalistic value as the word 'Messiah'? Why is
the Messiah born of the union of a *woman with a bird?*
Can't you read the message in the formula, *animal-human-
super-human?*"

"This is blasphemous and disgusting, as well as criminal," Knight said. "You, Dr. Dashwood, are as crazy as a
loon."

"Why do you feel 'good' during and after sex?" Dashwood
went on. "Just nature's way of tricking us into reproducing
the species? Yes, that is part of it. But nature loves to
economize, to do several things at once. You feel high
and powerful because you are raising your mental energy—
the *Kundalini* of the Hindu metaphor. With the proper
ritual and proper training, the energy can be raised to the
point where your Will and Imagination are illuminated
with power and you can create a new Reality. Literally.
You walk over the line between the state marked 'real' as
far as you dare to go into the 'unreal,' and you make your
new line. Until you have the courage to try again and go
even farther out. . . ."

"Crazy as a loon," Knight repeated.

DeAct put out his cigarette and lit another. "I want to
thank you, Dr. Dashwood," he said formally, "for being so
open with us and ah taking us into your confidence so fully.
You will understand, of course, that we cannot ah buy
your argument at ah first glance. It is startling and ah very
unorthodox and ah that is, well, I'm sure the jury will
understand, a brilliant mind and probably the factor of
overwork and too much imagination."

Dashwood stood up. "I see," he said. "Well, it's time I tried it—the one experiment I was always afraid of."

"Grab him, Tobias!" DeAct shouted.

But he was too late.

Dashwood opened his mouth to its maximum extension, breathed in deeply, and then bellowed:

AAAOOOOZORAZZ AZZAIEOAZAEIIIOZ AKHOEOOOYTHO EAZAEAOOZAKHO ZAKHEYTHXAALET HYKH

"*Gesundheit*," Knight said automatically.

But Dashwood was gone from that universe.

The sign said:

CHAPEL PERILOUS
PRICE OF ADMISSION: YOUR MIND
S. MUSS SINE, PROPRIETOR

Dashwood passed through the lavatory into the laboratory, where Patrick Knowles and Lon Chaney were turning switches and throwing relays wildly as Bela Lugosi, with Karloff's old makeup, tried to pretend he was the Frankenstein monster, while Ilona Masey huddled in a corner, looking worried.

It seemed that some refurbishing and rebuilding had been going on in the downtown area, for Union Square was much bigger than Dashwood remembered and there were several new buildings surrounding it, most of them built in hyperbolic and non-Euclidean curves. Chinatown was now facing directly onto the Square instead of being two blocks downhill and to the right, but there was a huge sign on the Chinatown Gate, saying:

CLOSED FOR ALTERATIONS
FU MANCHU, PROPRIETOR

Claude Shannon of Bell Laboratories and Tristan Tzara, the pioneer Dadaist, were picking random words out of people's mouths as they passed and gluing them to a huge billboard where they had already formed the pseudosentence:

AMERICAN LIFE BOMB WENT AUTHORITARIAN IN
FRONTAL ATTACK ON AN ENGLISH AUTHOR

"We're discovering the information/redundance ratio in random signals," Shannon explained, waving a programable calculator.

"We're creating a new Art Form!" Tzara shouted.

The Tin Woodman of Oz went by, with some of the boys from the Heavy Metal Mob.

There were only two doors leading back out to the Bureau of Common Sense. One had a picture of Christ on the cross and bore the legend LOVE ONE ANOTHER;

but the other had a picture of Captain Ahab and bore the legend I'D STRIKE THE SUN IF IT INSULTED ME.

"Do I have to make a choice?" Babbitt asked. All this was going by too fast for him—one minute he was driving home from work and passed the billboard on Howard Street with the eye-on-the-pyramid, and the next minute he was in this place.

The lights began to go out all over San Francisco, first in ones and twos, then in dozens and scores, and then in hundreds, until a stygian blackness descended in which Punk Rock groups and transvestites could be seen dimly as they marched in robot hordes toward the Bay.

"UFOs over the power stations!" somebody shouted. "A major blackout!"

And behind the Gate of Chinatown the drums of Fu Manchu began.

The Punk Rock groups led the parade downhill, through Chinatown, to the Ocean.

"Turn back, turn back!" screamed an effete intellectual snob. "The sea is NOT our home! Beware of the rising rivers of blood, beware of the Robot Animal Within. Turn back, turn back!"

But the Punkers marched, and everybody fell in step behind them. First came the Ludes and the Creepers, then the Dirks and the Blunt Instruments, then more and more: the Problem of Anxiety, the Daggers, the Funny Farm, the Noon's Repose, and the Troubled Midnight. And now it was not separate trickles, but one huge rushing stream: the Leapers, the Laughing Academy, the Foamix Culprits, the Mail Cover, Dr. Terror's House of Ill Repute, the Keyhole Peepers, the Wire Tappers, the Whoopee Casket Company. And over the shrieks and howls of their music, from deep inside the hidden recesses of Chinatown, the drums of Fu Manchu grew louder.

And more and more were coming, still: Dashwood rec-

ognized the Muggers, the Synthesizers, Moses and Mono-
theism, Reefer Madness, Crazy Artie's Crisis Intervention
Center, the Junior College of Cardinals, Totem and Ta-
boo, the Things on the Doorstep, the Hoods, the Lanovacs,
Six Flags over the Vatican, the Sleepers, the Beepers,
the Roofers, the Cokers, the Thundering Hoofs, the
Framis Stand, the Power to Cloud Men's Minds, and the
Croakers.

Pickering's Moon circled the Earth, going backward.

And still the Punks came: the Chocolate Mouse, the
Tax Writeoff, the Welfare Bums, the Primal Scream,
Baphomet's Witnesses, the Black Rabbit of Inlé, the Veg-
etables, the Fruits, the Nuts, the First Church of Satan
Scientist, the Tantric Presbyterians, the Huns, the Crea-
tures from the Back Ward, the Special Children, the
Visigoths, the Vandals, the Looters, the Shooters, the
Scooters, the Peanut Butter Conspiracy Revisited, the
Thousand Kim, the Seeds of Discord, the Benton Harbor
Rat-Weasel, the Bloodshot Pyramid, the Wascal Wabbits,
Crescendo, the Diabolic Variations, Skinnerball, the Com-
mittee for the Elimination of Death, the Weird Made
Flesh, the Poor Golems, the Wretched Refuse, the
Alluminum Bavariati, the Double Helix, the Goons, the
Thugs, the Teeming Shore, the Unnatural Act, the Soli-
tary Vice, the Morose Delectation, the Wrist Slashers, the
Window Jumpers, the Kryptonite Kids, the Stay-Free
Mini-Pads, the Elect Cohens, the Corpse-Eaters of Leng,
the Miniature Sled, the Hash Brownies, the Boston
Blackies, Kadath in the Cold Waste, the Neanderthal
Tails, the Giant Slugs, the Sloths, the Disadvantaged Youth,
the Albert de Salvo Fan Club, the Dead Kennedys, the
Molotov Cocktails, and, loudest and most eldritch of all,
Great Cthulhu's Starry Wisdom Band.

And overall there was a smell of fried onions.

Hierusalem, my happy home,
When shall I come to thee?
When shall my sorrows have an end,
Thy joys when shall I see?

Thy walls are made of precious stones
Thy bulwarks diamonds square
Thy gates are of bright orient pearl
Exceeding rich and rare

There trees for evermore bear fruit
And evermore do spring;
There evermore the angels sit
And evermore do sing

Ah, my sweet home, Hierusalem,
Would God I were in thee!
Would God my woes were at an end
Thy joys that I might see

It was dark in the room. His mother sang that song. She wore a perfume that smelled like lily-of-the-valley.

Dashwood cut through an alley where two ancient Egyptian priestesses were leading a captured UFOnaut in chains past a Dog-Headed God.

"Maybe Acid would help," somebody muttered.

SDATE YOUR BIZNIZ PLEEZ, the computer insisted. HOOKUP UZING IMPROVED EQUIPMEND TO AVOID FEEDBACK. SDAY TUNED.

A Dominican monk marched past carrying a sign that said:

JEWES WE KILLE
TO SERVE GOD'S WILLE

Strange messages were appearing on the computer console: SL LR MS ASK GREEN DREAMS TK X1826PCS M.Y.O.B. (MIND YOUR OWN BUSINESS)

Simon Moon seized the microphone and began a long, unintelligible speech about the Drug Problem. In each of our major cities, he seemed to be saying, there are thousands of people who desperately need dope. For all practical purposes these people simply cannot live unless they get "high." He estimated the number of afflicted adults in the nation at well over 125,000,000, and said their habits included, but were not limited to, Valium, marijuana, Miltown, uppers, downers, acid, cigarettes, booze, aspirin, DMT, cocaine, peyote, and Coca-Cola. He called upon all concerned citizens to donate their surplus dope to a huge pile in the center of each city, to be called the Public Trough, from which the needy could take what was necessary to keep them functioning.

The window next door lit up suddenly, showing an ancient Hindu princess in Tantric rapture with a UFOnaut.

"Eternal Serpent Power," Simon was ranting. "If we all raise the *Kundalini* at once, maybe we can get through the Dark Night of the Soul and see the Golden Dawn. Three A.M. is the worst of it—that's the peak for UFO Contacts, murders, suicides, and Bad Trips."

A brutal group of Cro-Magnons came over the hill and began clubbing Ancient Astronauts to death. The Cro-Magnons were tall, blond, and Aryan; the Astronauts had the blue skin of Krishna and Quetzalcoatl.

A neon sign flashed:

HALL OF SELF-LOVE
THE AMERICAN DREAM ACHIEVED
DO WHAT THOU WILT SHALL BE THE WHOLE OF THE LAW

In the first room George Washington was holding a movie camera on Linda Lovelace as she masturbated and moaned, staring fixedly into the camera-eye. In the second room John Adams was holding a movie camera on Georgina Spelvin as she masturbated and moaned, staring fixedly into the camera-eye. In the third room Thomas Jefferson was holding a movie camera on Annette Haven as she masturbated and moaned, staring fixedly into the camera-eye. In the fourth room James Madison was holding a movie camera on Tina Russell as she masturbated and moaned, staring fixedly into the camera-eye.

"What's the use of revolution without general masturbation?" sang a Punk Rock group called Dr. Climax's House of Dildos.

In the fifth room James Monroe was holding a movie camera on Marilyn Chambers as she masturbated and moaned, staring fixedly into the camera-eye, so it would register every expression in her eyes, every involuntary twitch of pleasure around her mouth.

A spastic handed Dashwood a leaflet headed "HELP EPILEPTICS LIVE AND WORK IN DIGNITY."

A girder fell on the one just man in San Francisco.

Anarchists ran through the streets screaming, *"Aux armes, citoyens!* The government is taking over our country!"

CLEAR FOR LAW-AND-ORDER DAY GREETING! blared the loudspeakers. FOLLOWING IS GREETING FOR LAW-AND-ORDER DAY.

Cotton Mather, Cotton Hawes, and Cotton DeAct paraded past with a sign saying:

YE POPE TO SHUNNE
A BATTLE WUNNE

A girder fell on an unjust man.

George Dorn realized that, amid all this nightmare

imagery from the random circuits, he was coming back together again, a little bit at a time, coming out of the illusion that he was Frank Dashwood.

"Here it is," Cagliostro the Great said, handing George a book called *The Answer*.

George opened the volume eagerly. It had one page and said:

FLOSSING

"Here it is," Dr. Hugh Crane said, handing George a book called *The Answer*.

Frank opened the volume eagerly. It had one page and said:

Jan Zelenka was born in Bohemia in 1679, wrote in a style similar (and much admired by) Johann Sebastian Bach, died in 1745. Much of his sacred music is still admired, but perhaps his greatest composition was his *Capriccio* of 1723.

Out of the sea rose a gigantic, chryselephantine, bodacious, incredible yellow submarine, waving the Black Flag of Anarchy and the Golden Apple of Discord.

Mavis, the woman with the tommy gun, appeared at a window. "Gravity sucks!" she shouted. "The cream of the jest rises to the top. That's the Law of Levity."

And the submarine took off and floated over North Beach like a flying saucer.

Mavis threw down a rope. "Grab hold, George!" she shouted. "We've come to rescue you!"

And he leapt, and grabbed hold, and they pulled him up, into the Golden Space Ship.

Captain Hagbard Celine (who looked a lot like Hugh

Crane the magician, when you stopped to think about it, and a little bit like Harry Coin, the crazy assassin, and somewhat like Everyman) took his hand. "Good to have you back aboard, George. Was it rough down there?"

He tried to be modest. "Well, you know how it is on primitive planets. . . ."

"They gave you merry hell," Hagbard said. "I can see it in your face. Well, cheer up, George. It's over now. We're heading home."

And indeed there were thousands, maybe hundreds of thousands of them: great golden ships sailing past at the speed of light, heading into the center of the galaxy.

It was the planetary birth process; earth, like a single giant flower, after incubating for four billion years, was discharging its seed.

And the ships, like homing pigeons, were going back where the experiment began, where the DNA was created and ejaculated out onto every planet, where the Star Makers dwell, beyond the Black Hole, out of space, out of time.

THE RETURN TO ITHACA

The future exists first in Imagination, then in Will, then in Reality.

—BARBARA MARX HUBBARD

One evening while Wing Lee Chee was meditating he found himself floating higher and higher, becoming more and more detached, observing with total lucidity that he was a little old man sitting in a room high on a hill over a huge city on a planet circling around a star in a galaxy of myriads of stars among countless galaxies extending to infinity and eternity in all directions, within his own mind.

And in that lucidity he knew that he had been lying to himself for months, pretending not to notice what was happening to his body as it gradually terminated its basic functions, fearful of looking straight at Death; but now, in that lucidity, looking at it and seeing that it was just another of the millions of things that Wing Lee Chee (who was so rich and powerful) could not do anything about; but now, in that lucidity and objectivity, looking far down at this particular galaxy, this insignificant solar system, this temporary city, this house that a strong wind could blow away, this absurd old man who was rich and powerful but could not command the tides or alter the paths of the stars, it was all suddenly a great joke and every little detail made sense. For, in this new lucidity and objectivity and selfless perspective, he did not giggle or weep or feel dazed, but only smiled, very slightly, knowing he would soon lose this body, which was like an old run-down car, and this central nervous system, which was like a tired and increasingly incompetent driver, and the metaprogrammer in the higher nervous centers which gave him this perspective, because out here beyond spacetime he simply did not give a damn about that life, that planet, or that universe anymore.

So, as he very slowly came down, contracted, into Euclidean 3-D again, he was aware of every amusing, poignant, radiant little detail, the wholeness and the harmony and the luminosity of it all, knowing how richly he would enjoy every last minute of it, now that it didn't matter to him anymore.

The next day he called the office and told his secretary he wouldn't be in. Then he took a long walk, enjoying every bird, every flower, every blade of grass, every radiant detail, and getting a bit winded—another sign that the car was running down—and finally taking a cab to Ying Kaw Foy's house.

She wept when he told her, but he smiled and joked and chided her out of it.

"I may be one of the last men to die," he said when she was calm. "President Hubbard in Unistat is putting a lot of money into research on longevity and immortality. No, don't weep again; it is nothing to me. I feel like one of the last dinosaurs."

"You are the best man in the world," she said, eyes flashing.

"I have been good to *you*," he said. "I have been as much of a scoundrel as was necessary to be rich and comfortable. Many will be glad of my death."

He told her how he was arranging to have most of his

estate liquidated, turned into cash, and deposited in her account.

He urged her to take advantage of the longevity drugs as they became available, and to meditate every day. "One year of life is wonderful, when you are conscious of the details. A thousand years would be more wonderful." And then he added a strange thing: "Think of me sometimes, and look for me. You'll never see old Wing Lee Chee again, but you'll see what I *really* am if you look hard enough and long enough."

And then he suddenly realized it was coming even sooner than he had expected. "How absurd," he said. "I must lie down now."

He stretched out on her couch. "I must have walked too far," he said. "So many hills . . . so many ups and downs . . . and all I want now is one thing. Open your blouse, please. That's right, thank you. No, I just want to look at them. Such lovely Brownmillers, like peaches. Let me touch them. No, let me kiss them. No, never mind, I'm going now."

"Don't go," she cried. "Kiss them, kiss them first."

"Right back where I started," he said, suckling. And then he left her.

Ms. Ying decided to go to the French Riviera after the funeral. She would spend a year there, having a series of young, crude, unintelligent lovers (who wouldn't remind her of him) and then decide what to do with her money and the rest of her life.

She sold the Rehnquist and a lot of other junk when she gave up her house in Hong Kong.

The wholesaler didn't know what to do with the Rehnquist at first, but he finally sold it to a Sex Shop in Yokohama.

Markoff Chaney was vacationing in Japan that summer,

because—after years of paying him only about three hundred dollars a month—his stocks in Blue Sky, Inc., were suddenly paying two thousand dollars or three thousand dollars a month.

Blue Sky made zero-gravity devices that were proving very useful in the space-cities President Hubbard had created.

Chaney had also written a book, which was selling moderately well despite its rather eccentric thesis. It was his endeavor to prove that all the great achievements in art, science, and culture were the work of persons who were, on the average, less than five feet tall, and often shorter. He claimed that this fact had been "covered up" by what he called "unconscious sizeist prejudice" on the part of professional historians.

He had called the book *Little Men with Big Balls*, but the publisher, out of a sense that Chaney perhaps had some unconscious prejudice of his own and certainly lacked good taste, had changed the title to *Little People with Big Ideas*.

Chaney spent his first day in Japan visiting Kyoto. He went out to see where the Temple of the Golden Pavilion had once stood, and he spent three hours walking around there, trying to get into the head of the Zen monk who had burned it down.

Chaney had known the story for years: how the monk, working on the *koan* "Does a dog have the Buddha Nature?", had tried one answer after another, always getting hit upside the head by his *Roshi* and told he didn't have it yet. Finally, after meditating continuously for a day and a half without sleep or food, the monk had a brainstorm of some kind and dashed from his cell with a hell of a yell and burned down the Temple, the most beautiful building in Japan at the time.

The court had declared the monk insane.

After three hours of trying to get into the monk's head-space when he set fire to the building, Chaney had his own brainstorm. He had been ignoring Dr. Dashwood for three or four months, he realized.

He took a cab to Western Union and dispatched a telegram to Dr. Dashwood at Orgasm Research. It said:

FLOSSING IS THE ANSWER

EZRA POUND

Chaney had gotten those words many months ago, while having some dental work done. The dentist suggested they try nitrous oxide, and Chaney eagerly agreed.

He remembered that the great psychologist William James had once thought he had the whole secret of the Universe on a nitrous oxide trip. What James had written down, in trying to verbalize his insight, was OVERALL THERE IS A SMELL OF FRIED ONIONS. Chaney wanted to know what it was like to be in the state where fried onions would explain everything. He sniffed deeply and expectantly as the mask was placed over his nose, and waited.

No illumination came at first, but the room seemed to be getting bigger and bigger, and then it was getting smaller and smaller, and then he became aware that the dentist, as was typical of his species, was making remonstrating noises as he gazed into Chaney's mouth, saying that brushing was not enough and that everybody should be more conscious of dental hygiene and so on, all the usual craperoo, and then he, Chaney, wasn't there anymore, he wasn't anywhere; it was just like what he had heard about quantum jumping in physics, because he was there again, having gone from 0 to 1, and then going back to 0 again, not being there, and then back to 1 again and the dentist said somberly, like a very wise old wizard:

"Flossing is the answer."

And Chaney felt like he might giggle or weep, but was too dazed to do either, having found it at last, the Answer. And it was so simple, as all the mystics said; it was right out in the open and we didn't notice it because we weren't conscious of the details. And he stared up, awed, at the wise face of the great sage who had given it to him, at last, the Answer.

Flossing.

And the damnedest part of it was that for weeks after he still had flashes when he thought that was it, the Answer. Flossing.

After Kyoto, Chaney went to Yokohama to see the infamous Sex Shops, as was inevitable.

In the first Sex Shop he purchased an artificial vagina which seemed vastly superior, in both realism and pneumatic grip, to the model he had at home.

In the second Sex Shop he bought a box of pornographic Easter Eggs.

By then he was feeling the surging despair again, knowing that these substitutes were not what he really wanted, knowing his loneliness and his exile with that bitterness that he usually kept at bay by concentrating on the absurdity of everything-in-general, experiencing the terrible isolation of being out there on the moon separated from the ridiculous oversized clods by 250,000 miles and sizeist prejudice.

And then, in the third Sex Shop, he found it.

The Answer.

And it wasn't flossing at all.

Dr. Glopberger had worked in the Sex Change department of Johns Hopkins for a long time, and thought that nothing could surprise him any longer.

Markoff Chaney surprised him.

"No," Chaney said, in answer to the first question Glopberger always asked, "I've never felt like a woman trapped in a man's body."

"Um," Glopberger said. "Well, sir, what *do* you want here?"

Chaney opened the box in his lap.

"Good God," Glopberger said. "I've only seen one *that* big once in my life." What was that character's name— Wildebeeste? Strange one: he had kept it after the operation, had it mounted on a plaque or something like that.

"You see," Chaney explained, "I don't want to become a woman. I want to become more of a man."

"Well," said Dr. Glopberger, professionally. "Well, well." It was an ingenious challenge, even with the advances in Sex Surgery in the past three years, but it could be done. . . . My word, it would be a Medical First.

The stocks in Blue Sky were now paying eight thousand dollars to ten thousand dollars a month.

"Name your price," Chaney said with a steely glint.

Justin Case heard about the man with no name at one of Mary Margaret Wildeblood's wild, wild parties. Joe Malik, the editor of *Confrontation,* told the story. It was rather hard for Case to follow because the party was huge and noisy—a typical Wildeblood *soirée.* All the usual celebrities were there—Blake Williams, the most boring crank in the galaxy; Juan Tootrego, the rocket engineer responsible for the first three space-cities; Carol Christmas, the man who had invented the first longevity drug, *Ex-Tend;* Natalie Drest, the fiery feminist; Bertha Van Ation, the astronomer who had discovered the first real Black Hole, in the Sirius double-star system; Markoff Chaney, the midget millionaire who owned most of Blue Sky, Inc. Hordes of other names—maxi-, midi-, and mini-celebrities—

swarmed through Mary Margaret's posh Sutton Place pad as the evening wore on. There was a lot of booze, a lot of hash, and—due to Chaney—altogether too much coke.

"The town was called Personville," Malik was saying, "and the man with no name was a detective for a big agency like Pinkerton's. But then Kurasawa adapted it, and the man with no name became a Samurai."

"Of course we can go to the stars," Markoff Chaney was saying, even louder, on Case's other side. "The speed of light doesn't mean a thing when you consider what the next two or three jumps of longevity will bring. There are no real limits anywhere, except in the thinking of the timid and the conservative." He was armed with new Courage.

"Then he became Clint Eastwood," Malik said.

"What's your game?" Juan Tootrego asked, making conversation.

"Oh, art," Case said. "I write the art column in *Confrontation.*"

"But he still doesn't have a name!" Malik exclaimed.

"Then you're the man who discovered El Mir," Juan Tootrego said, impressed. Blake Williams snickered suddenly.

"Everybody this is Simon Moon the President's husband," Mary Margaret said.

The First Man fidgeted in their gaze.

"I'm not here to do any electioneering," he said.

"He's one of the best chess players in the country," Mary Margaret said, completing the introduction.

"Um how does it feel to be married to a politician?" Case asked, trying to put Simon at ease.

"Eve has her thing, and I have mine," Simon said.

"I have a theory," Blake Williams orated, "that the chessboard is a model of the human brain. What do you think of that, Mtr. Hubbard?"

"Mt. Moon," Simon said quickly. He was a Masculinist.

"You see," Malik went on, "whether he's a detective, a Samurai, or a cowboy, he still has no name. Isn't that archetypal?"

"I always look at the bright side," Hagbard Celine was saying to Natalie Drest. "There's only 337,665 years to go in the Kali Yuga, for instance."

"Well, if Batman is so smart," Marvin Gardens muttered, "why does he wear his underdrawers outside of his pants?"

"Pardon me," Simon Moon was asking Blake Williams, "but did you say Grand Canyon should be considered as an artistic whole or as an artistic hole?"

"Why, yes," Markoff Chaney was telling Mary Margaret, "I *am* working on a second book. It's called *Reality Is What You Can Get Away With,* and it's about the future evolution of consciousness and intelligence." His Courage was growing.

"Childproof bottles, my Abzug," Marvin Gardens complained. "There isn't a child in the world who doesn't have the patience and curiosity to open one of them."

"He has no name," Malik said, "because he is Death, and Death is a nightmare from which humanity is beginning to awaken."

"It's time to stop worshiping gods," Chaney went on earnestly, "and aim at becoming gods. It took four and a half billion years to produce this moment, and who's really awake yet?"

"It's adults who give up on the damned bottles," Marvin Gardens went on. "They decide—I know I do—'Agh, the hell, I don't *need* the Potter Stewarting pills.' What they are is *adultproof* bottles."

"Who *is* that exciting man?" Natalie Drest whispered to Mary Margaret.

"Marvin Gardens, the brain surgeon. He's married to

Dr. Lovelace the uh you know the first woman Bishop in the Mormon Church."

Benny Benedict, the columnist, arrived, apologizing for being late. "I had to see my mother at the Senior Citizens' home. Great old gal, she's taken up tennis again since she started on *Ex-Tend*."

"Well, yes," Hagbard Celine was saying. "I was a stage magician in my youth. Called myself Cagliostro the Great. But then I got turned on to Cabala . . ."

"Everybody this is John Disk he's the assistant to Dr. Lousewart at NASA-Ames . . ."

"No wife, no horse, no mustache," General Wing Lee Chee (U.S. Army, ret.) was saying. "I really resented that."

And then everybody else had left and they were alone.

"Of course there are robots among us," Chaney said, finishing his last speech. "There are also Magicians among us. I think we take turns playing each role, as a matter of fact. The Magician defines a reality-mesh and the robot lives in it. Grok?"

"God, you're an attractive man," Mary Margaret breathed, thinking of his Courage.

Their eyes locked. Because of the magnetism of his personality, neither of them was conscious of the fact that she was looking a long way down at him.

"Let's sniff a little more coke," Chaney suggested.

"I have some cognac left too," she whispered.

"Perfect," he said, and quoted:

> Heart of my heart, come out of the rain,
> Soak me in cognac, love and cocaine!

They went to the kitchen to get the cognac, and he was swaggering a bit, like Perry Mason about to cross-examine, or the new gun in town.

He patted her Frankel gently. She patted his new Courage.

Then they went to the bedroom, and—after circumnavigating the globe and passing through 10^{23} possible universes—Ulysses finally returned to Ithaca.

GLOSSARY:
A GUIDE FOR THE PERPLEXED

BELL'S THEOREM: A mathematical demonstration by Dr. John S. Bell, which shows that if quantum mechanics is valid, any two particles once in contact will continue to influence each other, no matter how far apart they may subsequently move. This violates Special Relativity, unless the influence between the particles is not employing any known energy.

COPENHAGEN INTERPRETATION: The theory formulated by Niels Bohr, according to which the *state vector* (see below) should be regarded as a mathematical formalism. In other words—which some physicists will dispute— the equations of quantum mechanics do not describe what is happening in the subatomic world but what mathematical systems *we need to create* to think of that world.

COSMIC GLUE: A metaphor to describe the quantum interconnectedness that must exist if Bell's Theorem be valid. Coined by Dr. Nick Herbert.

*EIGEN*STATE: One of a finite number of states that a quantum system can be in. The Superposition Principle says that, before measurement, a system must be considered to be in all of its *eigen*states; measurement selects one *eigen*state.

EINSTEIN-ROSEN-PODOLSKY EFFECT: The quantum interconnectedness as described in a paper by Einstein, Rosen, and Podolsky. The purpose of said paper was to prove that quantum mechanics cannot be valid, since it leads to such an outlandish conclusion. Since Bell's Theorem, some physicists have chosen to accept the interconnectedness, however outlandish it may seem. See QUIP.

EVERETT-WHEELER-GRAHAM MODEL: An alternative to Bell's Theorem and the Copenhagen Interpretation. According to Everett, Wheeler, and Graham, everything that can happen to the state vector (see below) does happen to it.

FORM: In the sense of G. Spencer Brown, a mathematical or logical system necessary to systematic thought but having the inevitable consequences of imposing its own deep structures upon the experiences packaged and indexed by the form. See COPENHAGEN INTERPRETATION.

HIDDEN VARIABLE: An alternative to Bell, Copenhagen, and Everett-Wheeler-Graham. As developed by Dr. David Bohm, the Hidden Variable theory assumes that quantum events are determined by a subquantum system acting outside or before the universe of space-time known to us. Dr. Evan Harris Walker and Dr. Nick Herbert have suggested that the Hidden Variable is consciousness; Dr. Jack Sarfatti suggests that it is *information*.

INFORMATION: A measure of the unpredictability of a message; that is, the more unpredictable a message is, the more information it contains. Since systems tend to disorder (according to the second law of thermodynamics), we can think of the degree of order in a system as the amount of information in it. Ordinarily information is transmitted as an ordering of energy (a signal), in which the energy and its ordering (the message) is transmitted from one place to another. Dr. Jack Sarfatti has suggested that the nonlocality of the ERP effect and Bell's Theorem may entail the instantaneous transfer of order from one place to another *without any energy transfer*. Thus we can have both Bell's Theorem and Special Relativity, since Special Relativity only prohibits the instantaneous transfer of energy and does not say anything about instantaneous transfer of information.

NEURO-: A prefix denoting "known or mediated by the nervous system." Since all human knowledge is neurological in this sense, every science may be considered a neuro-science; *e.g.*, we have no physics but neurophysics, no psychology but neuropsychology and ultimately, no neurology but neuroneurology. But neuroneurology would itself be known by the nervous system, leading to neuro-neuroneurology etc., in an infinite regress. See VON NEUMANN'S CATASTROPHE.

NONLOCAL: Not depending upon space and time. A nonlocal effect occurs instantaneously and with no attenuation due to distance. Special Relativity seems to forbid all such non-local effects, but Bell's Theorem seems to show that quantum mechanics demands them. The only solutions thus far offered to this contradiction are that nonlocal effects involve "consciousness" rather than energy (Walker, Herbert) or that they involve "information" rather than energy (Sarfatti).

NONOBJECTIVITY: One of the two alternatives to Bell's Theorem (the other being the Everett-Wheeler-Graham model). In order to avoid nonlocality, some physicists such as Dr. John A. Wheeler prefer this option, which holds that the universe has no reality aside from observation. The extreme form of this view says *"Esse est percepi"*—to be is to be perceived.

POTENTIA: The name given to the presumed subquantum world by Dr. Werner Heisenberg. Space and time do not exist in *potentia;* but all the phenomena of the spacetime manifold emerge from *potentia.* Compare with HIDDEN VARIABLE and INFORMATION.

QUANTUM: An entity whose energies occur in discrete lumps—*e.g.,* photons are the quanta of the electromagnetic field. Quanta have both wave and particle aspects, the wave aspect being the probability of detecting the particle at a certain place and time.

QUANTUM LOGIC: A system of symbolic logic not restricted to the "either it's A or it's not-A" choices of Aristotelian logic. Chiefly due to Dr. John Von Neumann and Dr. David Finkelstein, this approach evades the paradoxes of other interpretations of quantum mechanics by assuming that the universe is multivalued, not twovalued; Dr. Finkelstein expresses this by saying "In addition to a *yes* and a *no,* the universe contains a *maybe."* See *EIGEN*STATE.

QUANTUM MECHANICS: The mathematical system for describing the atomic and subatomic realm. There is no dispute about how to *do* quantum mechanics—*i.e.,* calculate the probabilities within this realm. All the controversy is about what the quantum mechanics equations imply about reality, which is known as the *interpretation* of quantum mechanics. The principal lines of interpretation are the Copenhagen Interpretation and/or Nonobjectivity and/or Bell's Theorem and/or Nonlocality and/or the Everett-Wheeler-Graham multi-worlds model.

QUIP: The quantum inseparability principle. An acronym coined by Dr. Nick Herbert to refer to the nonlocality implicit in the Einstein-Rosen-Podolsky argument and explicit in Bell's Theorem.

STATE VECTOR: The mathematical expression describing one of *two or more* states that a quantum system can be in; for instance, an electron can be in either of two spin states, called "spin up" and "spin down." The amusing thing about quantum mechanics is that each state vector can be regarded as the superposition of other state vectors.

SUPERDETERMINISM: The approach to quantum theory urged by Dr. Fritjof Capra in *The Tao of Physics*. This interpretation rejects "contrafactual definiteness"; that is, it assumes that any statements about what *could have* happened are meaningless. A consequence of this view is that all distinction between observer and observed, or self and universe, also becomes meaningless; I had no choice about writing this book, Dell Books had no choice about publishing it, and you had no choice about reading it, since there is only one thing happening and we are all seamlessly welded into it.

SYNCHRONICITY: A term introduced by psychologist Dr. Carl Jung and physicist Dr. Wolfgang Pauli to describe connections, or meaningful "coincidences," that do not make sense in terms of cause-and-effect. It is thought by some that such connections may indicate the Hidden

Variable at work or some sort of nonlocal Information System.

VON NEUMANN'S CATASTROPHE: More fully, Von Neumann's catastrophe of the infinite regress. A demonstration by Dr. John Von Neumann that quantum mechanics entails an infinite regress of measurements before the quantum uncertainty can be removed. That is, any measuring device is itself a quantum system containing uncertainty; a second measuring device, used to monitor the first, contains its own quantum uncertainty; and so on, to infinity. Wigner and others have pointed out that this uncertainty is only terminated by the decision of the experimenter. Compare NEURO-.